BELVEDOR AND THE KING'S CURSE

THE BELVEDOR SAGA | VOL 2

BELVEDOR AND THE KING'S

CURSE

ASHLEIGH BELLO

Lies cut like glass.
Be careful when they shatter.

Other publications by Ashleigh Bello in the Olleb-Yelfra Universe:
Belvedor and the Four Corners
Belvedor and the Desert of Secrets
Belvedor and the Trail of Fire
Belvedor and the Golden Rule
A Myrmaid's Kiss

For more information, visit: www.ashleighbello.com

CONTENTS

CITY OF THE FOUR CORNERS
THE JAR OF STONE
UNDOR
Agrarian's District
Healer's District
Vanishing Tunnels
Creator's District
Warrior's District
Tombs
Draminet
NICORA FOREST
BLACK SAND DESERT
BELGRADIA
Fate's Pool
KAMPAULO
MORIAMO
HIGH CITY OF SAINDORA
SEA OF SAINDORA
Empress Isle
NW
N
NE
W
E
SW
S
SE
OLLEB YELFRA
LIZARD INK

BLANCOREN MOUNTAINS
NORTH LUOSE
SOUTH LUOSE
ZAMBIENTH
The Greenhouse
LANZATARÉ
Island of Idris
IMPENETRABLE FOREST
The Treehouse
Starr Caverns
GUANAMARA

"In a world built upon a foundation of lies
and over the bodies of children,
we're all slaves to something,
cursed by our king."

–Master Talis Churry, Healer's District

PART ONE

LIAM BLACK

"WHERE'S ARA?" SAID LIAM, sitting up in the bed. Pale walls stung his eyes, and his throat cracked as his words tumbled out. He recognized this place as Solomon Bell's private well room; he'd visited Arianna here plenty. Looking around, he found her acquaintance seated on the far side of the room. He remembered him by the name of Master Talis Churry.

"You've been asleep for nearly four days. She's gone now and hopefully far from this place," replied Talis. He leaned back in his chair, sipping at a cup of steaming tea that filled the room with a heady aroma. One whiff made Liam dizzy.

"Gone?" he asked, twisting his body toward the door. "Ah—"

There was a pinch at his side. Something felt different… off. He rolled down the sheet that covered him and noticed a newly formed scar on his skin, still tender to the touch. So strange, it looked like a coat of silver paint had been seared into his flesh. With a poke at the long, rigid line of healed skin and another wince at the lingering sting from the attack wound that had caused it, everything came rushing back to him in a jumble of memories.

Arianna's hand in his, a moment of pure relief finding her still alive at the start of the Warrior's District Free Falls Festivals. Grinda Risso with her axe raised above his head.

Preparing to die.

And clear as day, he could still hear the reverberating clang of weapons smashing together, Arianna leaping to his rescue and taking a stand against Grinda. Then came the cheers from the crowd, ones that quickly morphed into screams as his battle for freedom and the Free Falls took an unlikely turn.

Arrows flew through the air, the icy snow tore at his skin, and bodies piled on the ground all around him as he and Arianna ran for their lives across the Square. It was blurry, but he also remembered fighting Sir Dean Westing before Solomon Bell had come to his aid to finish him off. Then, out of nowhere, all he felt was pain. He was again staring into Grinda's storm-dark eyes, ones forever burned into his memories.

Liam was grateful at least that his mind hadn't quite stored the moment when the blade of her axe had met his side. He couldn't *really* remember the agony, just that it had been agonizing. Instead, a sudden and dense blackness had consumed his vision until he'd felt nothing at all.

"She's really gone?" Liam traced the scar with his thumb as fragments of the chaotic night returned in sharp pieces. He would've died had his battle wound not been somehow healed, the severe damage from the injury undone by an incredible and unimaginable force.

Then the black had lifted and he'd found Arianna by his side, begging him to join her and her friend as they fled.

"They ran away," said Talis with a distant gaze, his focus remaining on the little window in the well room. "Escaped to safety. I'm sure of it."

"Right..." said Liam, bowing his head in shame. "I remember now." He closed his eyes a moment to try to imagine a different past, a better goodbye to Arianna Belvedor, his dearest of friends. He wanted to forget, to go back to sleep and pretend it hadn't happened that way at all—he hadn't meant what he'd said. He'd just wanted her to go... to be safe. And everything had been so confusing in the moment.

Of course he loved her too. Whether as just a friend or as something else, whatever it even meant in this world, Arianna was, in fact, one of the *only* people he loved.

He shook his head, pulling his fingers through his tangled hair to attempt to think. "And what of my friend Noah and Master Bell?" he asked, afraid of the answers. "They were with me when..."

When my world flipped upside down.

Talis pursed his lips. "Noah is fine," he replied, his voice wavering on the last word.

He got to his feet, walking over to the bed before Liam could utter another question.

"I kept you here in an induced sleep so you'd be at your strongest. To give you the best chance," Talis explained. "Now that you're awake, you must go back and report to your master trainer." He set his empty teacup to the side. "I would've loved to let you sleep here forever in bliss, but you can't earn your freedom with your eyes closed, son. You have only one opportunity left—"

Talis looked him over, and every line and shadow on his tired face told Liam worse news was coming. He cleared his throat.

"King Devlindor is also departing the district today. It would be unwise if you missed his Farewell Ceremony."

Liam's mouth fell open.

King Devlindor... in the Jar?

"But—"

Talis held up his hand. "The disorder from the first day of

festivals has shadowed any rebelling you may have participated in, and things are unfortunately back to the way they have always been and always will be. The King has made sure of that. You are *still* a slave of the Four Corners."

His words came hollow and empty. *Lies.*

Everything was different now.

"I've done all that I can to help you heal and survive," added Talis. "But I'm sorry… I can't help you through this. No one can. Your future is in your hands now. Just as it was before."

Liam didn't know what to say. When would it all end? The suffering was so continuous in the Warrior's District that this tortured existence seemed normal. But now he knew the truth— he'd seen how people fought back that night, and he remembered how he was healed in the most impossible of ways; at present, he had no words to even begin to describe it. Everything was so distorted in his mind's eye, but he was *certain* he didn't want to die not knowing the full story.

"Please, sir, I can't fight again," said Liam, clutching the sides of the bed. "I can't stay here now after all that happened… I want to join Arianna. Can't you show me the way—"

"No." Talis' expression stayed cold, a deep hopelessness glazing over his eyes as he considered him. "No one will ever escape from here again." He stroked the back of his own wrinkled hand, but there was nothing to hide the shaking. "If you want your freedom, you'll have to earn it tonight in the final day of the Free Falls Festivals to prove your worth, just like everyone else. If you don't fight, you will die."

Liam balled his hands into fists and let his gaze rest on his lap, taking a few deep breaths to try to calm his spiraling emotions. "You and Master Bell helped Arianna and her friend to get out," he stammered, unable to stomach the idea of dueling in the Free Falls for a second time. He turned his gaze back on Talis. "What's changed while I've been sleeping?"

Talis turned away from him, hands clasped behind his back

as his attention again found the window.

"Everything," he replied. "Solomon is no longer with us, and I can do no more for you now that the King has… changed things."

Liam's heart began thrashing against his chest, desperate to be free of its cage. So much had occurred in the last few days that he didn't understand, and so many questions and emotions stirred in his mind. Alas, without freedom or citizenship, it mattered little—one truth that was always crystal clear in the Jar.

"At least give me something," said Liam with a defeated sigh. "What happened that night? Don't send me back out there blind. Everything is not as it was, and I need to know what happened after Arianna left."

Talis turned back to face him, sharp, blue eyes boring into his own as he stepped closer to the bed.

"Return to your trainer and keep your memories to yourself," he snapped. "They'll do you no good until the mountains are behind you. And maybe not even then."

"Yes, Master Churry," said Liam with a gulp, accepting what had to be done. He averted his eyes. "And I'm sorry for your loss… for the loss of Master Bell. He was always kind to us."

Liam felt a shaking hand grip his shoulder.

"Good luck to you, Liam. I wish only for your victory," said Talis, firmly.

A faint spark raced through his body when Talis released his grip—it wasn't natural. But it felt good. The haziness from before fell away as he was reenergized somehow.

Liam looked up to Talis again and held his gaze, knowing that these indescribable things swirling in his memories were not the things of dreams.

"And should you earn your freedom, take these words to heart for what lies ahead." Talis leaned in to whisper in his ear. "In a world built upon a foundation of lies and over the bodies of children, we're all slaves to something, cursed by our king."

He stood back to study him for a moment, so many unsaid things passing between them.

"Never forget that in all that you aspire to do, and then maybe you'll survive the Olleb's injustice."

Liam stared in shock—an open statement from an elder besmirching King Devlindor.

"Thank you," was all he could move himself to say.

I'll never forget any of this.

"I must go now," said Talis. "There's much to be done. Find your master. Tell him you'll fight, and fight well."

He exited the well room and left Liam Black to his thoughts.

LIAM PUT ON HIS BRAVEST FACE, burying his fears as if it were any other day in the districts. And as usual, it was all just for show. Getting to his feet, he found fresh clothes and his cloak folded neatly on a chair near the bed. The silver thread of his identity shone brightly.

Ninety-One.

He pulled them on, hiding the magnificent scar at his side. They felt like chains.

Leaving the well room behind, he found himself in Arianna's training quarters and immediately felt the weight of her absence. It was hard to even fathom, but he hoped with all his soul that she was still alive—free.

She deserves her freedom… after what she did for me.

He crossed the sparring room and stopped in front of a mirror. A large crack had spread from the top to the bottom of its frame, and he wondered how it might've gotten there. He imagined Arianna taking her frustrations during training out on the glass and smiled.

Then he took in his reflection, shocked to see how normal he appeared, when on the inside he felt so twisted.

There was not a scratch or bruise on him to even hint that he'd participated in a rebellion or to indicate he'd recently fought the battle of a lifetime, save for the now hidden scar. And although his tormented thoughts made his heart throb and stomach churn, his muscles didn't even produce the slightest ache to suggest he'd ever been bedridden at all; he was simply Liam Black, slave of the Warrior's District and minus one very good friend.

After pulling in a deep breath and squaring his shoulders, he turned away from the mirror and grabbed a broadsword from a barrel of weapons. Resolving first to search for Noah, he pushed open the door to the outside.

A garish light washed into the room, blinding him momentarily. When he could finally see properly, he wished for anything but sight. The door swung closed with a click, and there was no going back, no returning to the past.

Bodies stretched out before him—some still alive and squirming as death came to claim them, and others most certainly dead. It was like nothing he'd ever seen before in the Dueling Arena. And it was early still, too early for anyone to be training yet.

He recognized all of their faces, every single one. The scraps from the latest Free Falls event.

One more festival to go, Talis had said.

Just one more.

If he wanted to be free and find out the truth, he would need to participate in this massacre of a game. Win or die, there was only one way to leave this prison.

Arianna had been the exception, not the rule.

He stepped over the bodies of his fallen peers, a bloody mess; it sickened him to his core that the district regulators hadn't even taken the time to put some of these people out of their misery. One young man, a friendly dueling partner he'd had many times over the years, gushed blood from his mouth and strange-colored wounds at his side.

What have they done to you?

He stretched his hand toward Liam, unable to speak, unable to move from the spot where they'd left him for dead, tears streaking his dirtied face.

"*Please,*" Liam heard him sputter.

That was enough to harden him against the tough task ahead. Something had to be done.

Liam tightened his grasp around the hilt of his sword and drove it through the heart of his peer, as his master had trained him to do so many times before. It felt terrible and cold—the first life he'd ever taken. And it broke something inside of him as he tumbled over an edge he hadn't known he'd been standing on.

Liam always knew he'd have to take a life someday; it was part of being a *real* warrior. But he hadn't expected it to come in this moment when he already felt so vulnerable and alone. The death around him was wasteful; the guilt and grief of just witnessing it was draining on the soul.

He paced the Dueling Arena under the barely risen sun and made thirteen strokes with his sword, took thirteen more lives. Then suddenly all was quiet.

He wiped his blade clean on the snow and headed toward the tall, iron gates.

Liam felt like he was floating as he walked, trying to erase the names of the lives that were now imprinted on his blade and his mind forevermore. Only one hour awake and his life would never be the same.

Slipping into the street, he expected to find guards or regulators patrolling, but no one was in the vicinity. It was eerily quiet on this side of town.

With a glance to the sky, he knew where he was expected to go. It was barely morning, so the district would just be waking to pay tribute to the High King.

He started toward the Square at a run, only slowing when

others came into view, lines of his peers marching obediently behind regulators who sat dutifully atop their horses. And elders from every district were already seated in the stands, claiming their spots to witness the finale of this year's Free Falls.

Glancing around the grounds, Liam spotted Noah almost immediately toward the back of the Square, his mess of red hair sticking out brightly against the dull heads surrounding him. Just the sight of his friend made him feel somewhat hopeful again, a bit of normalcy to help him find his bearings.

Liam searched for his trainer next; he found him leaning against the low stone wall near the base of the battered flag, hand on the hilt of his sword as he eyeballed the warrior-slaves lining up.

Liam pulled his hood up to cover his face and came up behind him, not wanting to attract too much attention just yet. Not until he begged for his chance to fight. He had no idea what to expect after what'd happened, but he had to trust Talis and try—it was the only option.

"Well, well, well, if it isn't Liam Black," hissed his master as he approached.

"Master Rondel," replied Liam, lifting his hood down and bowing low.

As he did, he felt the calloused hand of his master clasp tightly around the back of his neck.

"So you've decided to rejoin us, have you now?"

"Master, I beg your pardon for my absences. I'm fully healed from the first battle and request another chance to prove my worth. I know I can win for you. I know I can honor your teachings," he said.

"Black, 'course you'll be in the festivals today! You mad, are you?"

"Sir? I—"

"That dirty slave, *Belvedor*," he spat, taking him under his arm and walking him toward the gathering crowd, "almost robbed my star apprentice of the chance to earn citizenship. You've got every right at a second chance, and that's already been approved by the new general. Caretaker Cyn said you'd heal just fine, and so you have!"

He slapped him on the back.

"I've trained you well, boy," he added. "You'll be out of here soon enough. Just make me proud today."

"Yes, Master. I… I thank you for the opportunity," stuttered Liam. "But did I hear you correctly? Did you say we have a new general now?"

Master Rondel nodded. "You heard me all right. Glad to know that head of yours is still working. Try to keep it on this time." He threw his head back and laughed.

Liam could barely flash him a smile.

"The King will be here soon," Master Rondel added, his expression turning serious. "Better line up. It's his Farewell Ceremony and the regulators, or what's left of them anyway, are in downright sour moods since this year's Free Falls began. Justly so, losing General Ivo and all."

"Of course," said Liam, trying to keep up with all the new information.

"Now get going, and don't give 'em any reason to off you before tonight's festival!"

Master Rondel gave Liam a slight kick to be going, so he scurried toward Noah, even more baffled than before.

"Liam," gasped Noah, hands flying up to his cheeks as soon as he laid eyes on him. "I… I thought you'd died for sure!"

"I wasn't going to go that easy," said Liam, giving him a quick hug around the shoulders.

Noah pulled up his hood, trying and failing to hide the glimmer in his eyes. "They're going to let you fight again?" he asked, the worry plain in his voice.

Liam nodded. "Master Rondel just confirmed it to me."

"That's a miracle!" said Noah with a sigh of relief, throwing his arms around him.

Liam gave a slight chuckle. "All right, all right," he said, pushing him to arm's length and lining up beside him. "Try to act normal. Now's not the time to make a scene."

"You're right about that," said Noah, staring ahead. "These are crazy times, my friend. But I'm glad you're all right after what happened."

What happened? Liam was desperate to know.

"Have you heard anything about Ara?" he asked as he faced front as well.

Noah glanced to Liam from the side, a frown wrinkling his face. He lowered his voice to a whisper.

"Nothing since she ran off after killing Red Risso," he said. "I don't know how she could just vanish like that… but she did manage to escape. I just can't believe she attacked *you*, of all people, mate." He shook his head. "It's lucky you're even alive. She really lost her mind."

Liam's mouth fell open. "What are you talking—"

Then he remembered Talis' warning and quickly changed the subject.

"How have the festivals been since I've been out?" he asked. "How many people have earned citizenship so far?"

Then he dropped his voice low.

"And what of the *magic*… or whatever that was?" he added— he could think of no better term to describe what he'd seen occur the first festival night, so he pulled one from the prohibited fairytales he recalled from his childhood.

Noah sucked a breath in through his teeth.

"Don't be foolish!" he snapped, going rigid. "You shouldn't speak so freely. Now's not the time to be playing jokes. You're already on your second life, Liam."

Noah looked appalled, as if he had no memory at all of what had happened.

"As for citizenship cards," he hurriedly continued, "lowest

counts in history. Lowest counts. Seems your group is being made an example of. Arianna sure did make a mess of things, didn't she? Can't believe what she did, but I'm glad you survived."

He squeezed Liam's hand for a moment and then let go as the regulators called for silence for the ceremony to begin.

Liam had never heard the Square this quiet before, and he couldn't help but be intrigued. It seemed as if even the wind had stopped howling on this dead-cold morning just for the Farewell Ceremony—just for the King.

A royal sighting in these parts was a rarity. Maybe the first time in the last fifty years. Some people went their whole lives without ever laying eyes on King Devlindor, unless they made it to the High City of Saindora for some of the most sought out and competitive work placements. Liam fleetingly thought he'd be happy with any placement at all as long as it wasn't in the Tunnel of Tombs. He just wanted to live.

He focused on the stage as the historic scene played out—five guards, *real* warriors, walked across the stage in a tightly closed group. Their robes, the blackest of black, were unlike anything he'd ever seen before; the King's Crest shone at their backs in shining gold thread, and black fur speckled with gray and white lined their hoods. Dark chainmail and armors spread across their bellies, arms, and legs, and the handles of the swords at their hips were hissing snakes fashioned from pure gold.

If Liam didn't know any better, he would have thought them all royalty. But that's not how the Olleb worked.

He knew they were the official King's Guard.

One guard stood out among the rest. He was tall, slender. And a gold mask covered every feature of his face, save for the eyes… too dark not to be off-putting. His hood was pulled up over his head, and he wore no armor, carried no weapon. Just a pair of black gloves and a chain around his neck. Yet, somehow, he seemed like the strongest of them all.

Liam recognized him instantly from his lessons in the

Learning Center. He was staring at none other than Sir Vladamor, Head of the King's Guard, and notoriously known as the King's Shadow.

The guards parted, and King Devlindor was finally made visible. His back faced the crowd as he strode toward the seat normally reserved for the district general.

Who would sit there now? Liam couldn't believe General Ivo was somehow gone.

He fixated on the King's long cloak as it glided behind him, threads glittering in the early-morning light almost as finely as his crown. The deep gold velvet was embroidered with white, black, and red designs that came together in intricate detail to form his signature snake, one that stretched from the very bottom of this cloak to the nape of his neck.

An animal followed obediently at the King's feet, snapping at the guards' ankles as they walked; Liam was excited to see such a rare beast in person. Sleek, black fur stretched all across its body, and it had bright yellow eyes.

Then King Devlindor spun around to finally face the crowd. The High King of Olleb-Yelfra, the one he'd studied about his entire life—the one he had been taught to worship as a god—stood before him, a portrait come to life.

His face was stern and set in pale skin, and black hair hung loose over his eyes, kept in place by the rainbow-studded crown atop his head. Chains of precious metals hung from his fur-covered neck, and he held a white staff with a gleaming red jewel fixed to the center.

He appeared too young to be the High King and to rule the world. But he was over three centuries old, and Liam had to respect that.

The King raised his hand for silence, but the crowd couldn't have been quieter if they tried; Liam was so frightened of making a wrong move, one wrong look in the wrong the direction, that he couldn't even blink.

All he could do was stare, wide-eyed, at his king.

"Warrior's District—" he started in a smooth, commanding voice. It wasn't deep nor particularly loud, but it *was* to be obeyed by anyone and everyone who valued their lives. "—it's with great luck that I was in a neighboring city when I was brought the news of the… disruption. But today, I must bid you farewell. It brings me much sorrow to leave you on what will be such a joyous occasion, the final day of the 287th annual Free Falls Festivals. However, I have a long journey ahead."

He paused a moment, his eyes sweeping over the crowd.

"I swear, on all that we stand for, I'll do everything in my power to find number Twenty-Two." Liam's breath escaped him. "I'll bring her to justice for soiling this great kingdom's traditions and taking what others have rightfully earned. Arianna Belvedor, and anyone who aids her, will be nothing more than a small blemish on our bright history once in my possession. This, I promise."

He brought his fist to his heart.

The crowd began to clap wildly, cheering and screaming their support. Some even had tears in their eyes at the joy of seeing their ruler in person.

King Devlindor smiled approvingly, his cheeks reddening with delight.

"Now, now," he said. "Save your energy for tonight. There's still one last day of festivals, and you're to enjoy them. I command it! Banish this traitor from your thoughts, and soon it will be as if it never even happened." He winked, and Liam felt a shiver roll down his spine.

There were more scattered claps throughout the crowd.

"Few will earn their citizenship tonight, as few have in the past on the final days of the annual Free Falls, but we are to honor the sacrifices. Honor those who die to reveal to us the strong and worthy, the ones deserving of life in the Olleb and the ones who will continue to help her thrive," he said. "Oh, and don't worry. I leave you in good hands."

He gave a jolly clap of his own and waved toward the side of the long stage.

"Come, come, Princess. Don't be shy. Please escort our new general to the stage."

"Yes, my liege," came the soft, honeyed voice of Princess Elisa, the King's only kin and heir to the throne.

Liam stood on his tiptoes to get a glimpse of her as the regulators flanking the stage parted to make way. Then he saw her, the most beautiful woman he'd ever laid eyes on—or was it just her finery that made her so attractive to the eyes? In any case, he'd never seen someone quite like this.

Flowing hair, colored like the untouched snow at the top of the mountain peaks, fell down her back in waves, only outdone in shimmer by the silver tiara on her head. She donned dress robes of a deep, glittering blue with white fur trim, and wore some kind of leather lash around her neck like a scarf.

With her pink-flushed cheeks and striking green stare, Liam couldn't tear his eyes from her. Such poise. She walked up the stage, arm in arm with the new general.

He craned his neck to see the face of the person who would hopefully grant him his freedom this day, but there were too many regulators and guards surrounding them as they both walked to meet the King.

"Ah, come now," said King Devlindor, gesturing for them to hurry.

With their backs turned to the crowd, General Ivo's replacement and Princess Elisa bowed low to him.

"To your feet," bellowed King Devlindor, turning them both to face the crowd. He was very excited. "Warrior's District, treat your new general with respect! He's well-earned it, as I'm sure you already know. He's had my support for many years, but his retirement didn't last long. Seems he still has noble work left to do for our great land."

"Your Majesty," said the new general as he kissed the jeweled hand of the King. "You're too kind."

He lowered his hood and held his chin high to face the crowd.

"Can you believe this?" whispered Noah.

Liam stood frozen, his insides turning in circles as the people applauded their new general—Master Solomon Bell.

Solomon flashed his captivating smile at the district, and then he put a fist to his chest. "Hail to the King! Hail to Lord Devlindor!"

The district shouted the words back with a passion never before felt in the Jar. King Devlindor nodded his appreciation, graciously accepting their tributes.

Liam, however, still couldn't bring himself to move.

Master Solomon Bell… General of the Warrior's District? Arianna Belvedor's Master Bell?

He felt Solomon's eyes lock on his in that moment—they narrowed threateningly. Nothing to suggest he was anything less than General now.

It was then that Liam fully understood Talis' caution.

He would have to earn his citizenship on his own, and there would be no one there this time to save him if he failed. His memories would truly do him no good.

The King has somehow changed everything.

Noah and, clearly, the rest of the district had holes in their memories about the night Arianna had escaped. And Master Bell was no longer a trusted confidant; he was a general of the Four Corners now, and a general appointed by the King was no friend to a slave. There was no question in his mind, at least, about that.

VILLAGE OF DRAMINET

STOLEN FREEDOM WASN'T FREEDOM at all in Olleb-Yelfra. Arianna had learned this quickly.

She, Lessa, Jeom, and Demetrius had fought and won many battles in trying to liberate themselves from the mountains—but to what end? Escaping from slavery had only ensured that their freedom could never *truly* exist. Not in the eye of the law and not in a land riddled by regulations and tyranny. The four had no documentation of citizenship, no work awaiting them, and no place to call home.

The only thing they knew for certain was that their troubles were far from over.

Arianna forced her focus away from her worries and onto the air moving through her lungs, one breath at a time. Sweat rolled down her back and dripped into her eyes as she tried to hold on to the little energy she had left, running toward anywhere other than the place they'd just fled.

"Don't stop!" she said, feeling the pulse of the ground vibrate beneath her feet, hair whipping her face as she pushed her body onward. "Keep running."

Her voice swept away across the wind as she propelled toward the unknown, lungs burning with every breath while she tried to numb her mind to the growing ache in her legs.

Breathe. Just breathe.

She looked back for only a moment; a village lingered in the distance, growing smaller and smaller as it twinkled by the light of the moon. She pushed on, the Blancoren Mountains forever keeping watch as she willed her body to move faster.

With her friends at her side, she escaped across a frozen, grassy plain.

THE FIRST SIGN OF LIFE they had discovered after escaping the Vanishing Tunnels was the Village of Draminet. A cold, dreary place though it was, Olleb-Yelfra celebrated it as the 'Gateway to the World.' It was the only settlement between the City of the Four Corners and a future beyond.

Alas, the village proved to be nothing more than a town of bitter, resentful citizens, making up the only civilization on the edge of the mountains for miles in any direction. Arianna accepted the location as just an ill-fated passing to get to what she hoped would be a magnificent country. She daydreamed of what lay beyond the scope of the Four Corners—of warm winds and the ability to live a life without fear of an untimely or gruesome death.

The Village of Draminet was certainly not anybody's happy ending. It lacked any sense of cheerfulness except the shimmering sea of snowflowers creating the barrier between the village and the mountains. Even still, the flowers were forever frozen to the ground and the mountains shadowed their shine.

The people of Draminet were just as disappointing as the town itself, living each day like the one before. They followed an empty routine and an empty existence, nothing to be desired except for the remnants at the bottom of a whiskey bottle or the latest traveling gossip. Thus, the annual Free Falls proved to be the center of every conversation, the only excitement as the town took pleasure pondering the ghastly details of the festivals. And for the last three hundred years, the village ushered freshly freed slaves to their respective cities and work posts each and every year.

"Free at last!" they had shouted in welcome.

In keeping with tradition, the four had been greeted with gusto and without a lick of suspicion. Enjoying gossip with the local townsfolk over bread and ale, they were given lodging for nothing but the favor of their most enticing district festival stories.

After just three days, the horrible journey through the Vanishing Tunnels had started to fade from their minds. Instead, they focused on evading the onslaught of questions about where their first citizen assignments were located or what their job placements might be.

Though they needed a new plan—to think of their futures and to get as far away from the throes of the mountains as possible—a fake bliss hovered over them. The offerings of a soft bed, a full stomach, and friendly conversations satisfied them momentarily.

"That's a mighty fine weapon you got there," said the woman who ran the town inn, eyeing Jeom's black and gold axe procured from the City of Undor.

The four were seated next to her at the bar in the local tavern to take their dinner.

"You must've done *very* well in the Free Falls if you're able to craft such a thing as that." She tugged on Jeom's purple cloak, smiling up at him. "I heard the festivals in the Creator's District were the most excitin' in the last decade. How'd you claim citizenship? By a hair, I bet!"

She set her elbows on the bar and rested her chin in her hands, waiting for details.

"Yeah, I did great," he grumbled, taking a swig of his drink. "Still trying to get my best friend's blood off my blade, but it was an *epic* battle." Arianna didn't miss the curse under his breath—his temper had grown shorter each day they'd been holed up there with no good path forward.

"And where might your trainers be?" pried a man sitting on the other side of them. He pushed a plate of meat and potatoes into their reach, spilling his ale as he did so. His voice slurred. "You can't tell me you passed through the tunnels alone! I've never seen a slave come through Draminet without a guide."

"No, of course not. Mistress Serina guided us here," said Demetrius without hesitation. "She's been keeping to herself. Wants to rest before the long journey ahead."

A forced smile stretched across his face.

"We were never alone."

"You don't mean Mistress Isobel Serina, do you?" screeched the man.

Demetrius nodded.

"Why, she hasn't been around these parts in ages! I owe that one a drink, I do." He stood up from his stool, stumbling a bit as he went to lay his arm around Demetrius. "From the Agrarian's District then, eh?"

Demetrius gestured to his scythe leaning against the bar.

The man returned an understanding nod.

"Well, you lot have a tough time ahead, trying to pull anything from this wasteland. Luck will have placed you as *far* away from the north as possible," he said. "What'd you say your name was, kid?"

"Number um… Dem—"

Arianna kicked him in the shin before he could make the slip. *No numbers, no names.*

That was the first rule agreed upon. That would make them harder to track, if indeed someone searched for any of them—they prayed no one did.

Demetrius shoved a piece of bread into his mouth.

"His name is Dem," said Arianna with as much confidence as she could, taking his place in the conversation.

The man leaned around Demetrius to get a good look at her, raising his eyebrow.

"So, you lassies also from the Ag's District?" He eyed Lessa now too.

The girls shared a nervous glance, having stowed their elder cloaks from Talis and Solomon in order to avoid this very question.

"Yes… we are," said Arianna. They'd raise suspicion if people realized they traveled together—each one from a different district. They still didn't even have a proper explanation for themselves at how such a thing was possible, let alone to share with others.

"Funny, I never saw an agrarian with swords… *or* a bow on her back," said the woman next to Jeom. She craned her neck to get a good look at Lessa.

"Told you we should've left our weapons back in the room," whispered Demetrius to Arianna.

"*Hush,*" she said, giving him a murderous look. His lips closed tight.

No way I'd let my swords out of sight. And Jeom would have to die for anyone to pry his axe from his hands—he'd never even let one of them so much as touch it.

"And what kind of creature do you have there?" said the woman. She pointed to Sano's eyes popping out of Lessa's pack on her lap.

"What creature?" said Lessa in a shrill voice, quickly shifting her pack from her lap to the floor to hide their questionable miniature monkey companion.

"You must've had one too many," added Arianna, forcing a laugh as the woman took another slurp of whiskey.

They definitely didn't need to deal with explaining away Sano at the moment.

"I'm excited to meet the chumps who got placed in Draminet," interrupted a lanky man from behind the bar. "There's two or three this year, I hear."

He slammed his hand on the counter.

"We need some new blood! Been a while since we had a placement in these parts, and I could use a hand here."

"And what district did you come from, sir?" said Lessa, trying to sway everyone's focus in a different direction. "Let me guess, I'd say you were a fine healer in your day. Would I be correct?"

"Spot on!" The man smiled, showing off broken teeth and exclaiming all about his glory days in the Healer's District. Lessa even entertained him with questions about the district trainings and remedies—as if she weren't already a magnificent and sometimes magical healer herself.

For three days, they had suffered through this nonsense and managed to survive a myriad of interrogations while planning their next move. But on this particular night, everything shifted. All too soon, truly freed slaves began to trickle out of the tunnels alongside the regulators and the trainers who guided them. They showed off their papers, hard-earned identification that declared their new cities and work assignments. What's more, they brought with them surprising news from the City of the Four Corners.

"What do you mean *escaped?*" Arianna overheard one villager go into a tizzy, almost falling off her seat. "And the King… in the Jar? We didn't see him pass through here!"

Rumors of an epic battle between slaves and regulators in the Warrior's District spread faster than wildfire throughout the

Village of Draminet. And as all of the Olleb's newest citizens gathered together to celebrate their freedom, the former warrior-slaves had quite the unexpected story to tell about their Free Falls Festivals experience.

Arianna noticed her peers only spoke of the havoc *she* had caused during the first day of the Free Falls. They described in great detail how she disrupted a festival duel and threw away any chance at freedom in order to protect Liam Black. They even re-told of her escape and all those who were killed in the process, including regulators.

Strange though it was, Solomon's name and his undeniable treason never left their lips. And sure witnesses told no accounts of the extraordinary magic he'd used to help them flee, or of the powers she'd wielded against Grinda. Her fellow warriors seemed only to recall the panicking crowd, subsequent deaths, and her chaotic getaway.

"Listen up!" bellowed a lead regulator from the Warrior's District. "The King has joined us in the Four Corners to relay the following orders—"

"How could the King make it to the Jar so quickly? And without anyone spotting him from Draminet?" whispered Lessa, eyes bulging.

Arianna just flashed her a knowing look, the fear in her expression surely enough to communicate the answer.

He must've used magic… strong magic.

The new citizens were quick to quiet down, and the villagers responded equally obediently as this regulator demanded the busy tavern's attention.

"The tales you hear are true. The City of the Four Corners has been breached," he said.

Whispers snaked throughout the crowd as he held up a scroll painted with the portrait of a young girl. Long, dark curls, brown eyes, and a red cloak marked with the number twenty-two were the most distinct features in the picture.

The regulator moved around the tavern, passing out a stack of similarly painted parchments and hastily done sketches. The drunken tavern grew loud as they pondered the story behind the picture, wanting more information.

As more scrolls were passed around, someone pushed one into Arianna's hand, rendering her speechless—she stared down at a sloppy portrayal of herself.

"What we know," explained the regulator, "is that *this* slave escaped through the Vanishing Tunnels a few days prior." He jabbed his finger into her portrait. "Twenty-Two of Warrior's District. She goes by the name of Arianna Belvedor and has caused many deaths of respected citizens. She's a stain on the very foundation our Olleb has been built upon."

Arianna shrank back into the crowd as he paraded about the tavern, holding her portrait up high as everyone began to unite against her. *You know nothing!*

She wanted to scream out the truth—a tale of thousands of deaths, of a beautifully buried world, and of the pure betrayal King Devlindor had shown against his *beloved* Olleb-Yelfra when he'd tried to eliminate the magic from the land in his pursuit for power.

The crowd began to buzz, hungry for more.

"Be on high alert," said another regulator, her robes lined with purple. "This is… an unprecedented situation, but we've reason to believe that slave number Twenty-Three, Jeom Kane, of Creator's District may have also somehow fled after the festivals. It's unlikely he survived his attempt, but it's best to be cautious."

She held up a different sketch depicting a tall, dark, young man with chiseled features and purple robes.

"After his success in the festivals, his whereabouts are currently unknown. This is the first case in history of such an act, but I suppose even cowards slip through the cracks of the Free Falls sometimes."

Arianna stood up from her stool and squeezed Jeom's hand as the crowd began to tack their portraits to a column at the center of the dining area. Then discussions started up over their most memorable characteristics as their former peers provided detailed descriptions of them both.

"We need to leave. Now!" she said, tying her hair back.

Jeom nodded and gestured for the others to follow him.

The four slowly and silently slipped away from the bar and toward the back of the tavern, eavesdropping on the ranting crowd all the while. Hovering by a door, the girls took a moment to pull their cloaks back on. Then they all lifted their hoods up to hide their faces from view.

"But how could they get past the Vanishing Tunnels?" shouted one woman over the rowdy group.

"We can't know for certain, though we believe an elder's map was stolen," said a regulator with blue-lined cloaks. "The bodies of General Ivo's highest-ranking guards were found dead in the Vanishing Tunnels. A trainer from the Healer's District who led their first group of new citizens to Draminet made the initial discovery. Their designated navigator had no map on his person."

Shocked reactions from the tavern goers came in the form of obscene shouts and even more enthusiastic gossip.

"And what of General Ivo?" said another. "He was such a good mentor in my day. The best general the Warrior's District has ever seen, I'd wager!"

"His body was never found," said a Warrior's District regulator, removing his hood and bowing his head out of respect for their lost leader.

Other regulators scattered throughout the crowd followed the gesture.

"This day officially marks the first escape from the City of the Four Corners since its inception," said the lead regulator in his commanding voice, effectively luring back the crowd's attention. "When Arianna Belvedor is found, and she *will* be found, this slave faces charges of the highest account of treason this world has ever seen."

He jabbed a finger at her portrait.

"She's stolen what others have proudly and rightfully earned, so any who aid her shall face the same fate," he added. "And *if* she has truly made it past the tunnels, she'll not get far. It's up to us, and every citizen of the Olleb, to make sure of that."

His words hit Arianna like a punch to the gut, her fate sealed in some tacky town tavern on the borders of Blancoren.

"That scum isn't fit for our world," growled one man, shaking his drink in the air.

"Coward!" said another as others joined in against her.

The angered gathering grew louder in agreement, cursing Arianna's name for her defiance of the law. It seemed those who had earned their freedom by passing the Free Falls Festivals did not take kindly to one who deviated from that challenge and rite of passage. Had they forgotten the brutality of it all? Their peers who never made it past the mountains? Had their many years spent beyond the city's claws shielded their memories of the fear and suffering felt by all in their first seventeen years of life?

I'll never forget!

Arianna took one last look at the regulator as he raised his hand, calming the crowd.

"By order of the King, any who deliver Arianna Belvedor—dead or alive—to the High City of Saindora shall receive a high-life position in one of the great palaces of the Olleb, rewarded in riches for the rest of his or her days. We must work as one to rid Olleb-Yelfra of this unworthy filth. Hail to the King!"

The crowd mirrored him as he laid his fist across his heart. "Hail to Lord Devlindor!" they shouted in unison.

The celebrations started up again with a new kind of fervor. They were preparing for a hunt, their raucous voices echoing far and wide; the four fugitives took that moment to finally leave the tavern behind.

Arianna looked back one last time.

She spotted a young man in a red cloak, sitting at the bar in the seats they'd just left, who seemed wholly uninterested in the gathering, shoulders slumped and face buried in his drink. He turned his head just enough so that she caught the glimpse of a hazel eye, one she recognized instantly.

"Liam… you survived," she breathed, fighting the urge to call out his name.

But he couldn't see her, and she didn't have time to wait.

After quickly collecting the rest of their belongings from the inn, they ran through back alleys of the tiny town where distorted pictures of Arianna and Jeom already papered the streets, demanding their arrest. It wouldn't be long before the villagers began to piece the mystery together.

Someone would soon notice their sudden absence or remember the secretive slaves who had arrived too early and with no identified guide. Soon it'd be verified that she lived, and the entire Olleb would be searching for her and the others until their heads were on a stake.

Blinded by the promise of riches, they couldn't understand that Arianna was deserving of the life she had stolen. How could they when they didn't know the truth of why she had stolen it—the reality of a king they so readily worshiped?

She had justly earned her freedom in ways they couldn't possibly imagine, and she had faced dangers far more testing than anything the Free Falls could've ever conjured up.

Arianna and her friends were the *only* ones living a truth. And though a hard truth it was, she wouldn't trade her knowledge for anything. Everyone else lived a blind life in a harsh world, one built upon lie after lie.

These beliefs kept Arianna going until the Village of Draminet was far behind her.

Though, with the mountains still in view, it felt as if she ran forever in place.

"THERE'S A FOREST UP AHEAD," said Demetrius as a seemingly endless field stretched out before them. The blade of his scythe clipped every piece of grass it touched as he headed up the group.

"Where?" said Jeom, squinting into the distance to see the cover that Demetrius claimed was so near.

Arianna could barely see a thing through the haze of fog touching the ground. She glanced at Lessa, who squeezed Sano so tightly to her chest, she thought he might combust in an explosion of fur.

"Are we almost there?" Lessa called through clipped breaths, her pack, longbow, and arrows knocking together with every step. They were all weighted down by their belongings, and this muddy field was doing them no favors.

A howling wind carried the voices of the villagers off into the distance, chasing them even this far. The town would drink themselves into a stupor this night, entertaining the new citizens of Olleb-Yelfra. But tomorrow was a new day—a day of opportunity for those who lived shadowed by the Four Corners their entire lives. Arianna knew the town would surely rally for the hunt. The luxuries of a palace post made that promise quite clear.

She halted, gasping to catch her breath as the forest suddenly became visible, piercing the fog. Gigantic trees reached taller than the low clouds, their leaves a deep reddish-black that blended well with the night, and wide trunks shone like silver; they created a thick border against the field. And with the moonlight reflecting off the tree bark in such a way, the forest appeared like a vast, metal fence, blocking their means of escape.

Demetrius and Lessa stared ahead in astonishment, their necks craned back so they could look up high. This was familiar to them, probably a dream come true, and Lessa was the first to try to find a way through. The others followed at her heels as she searched for a clearing into the woodland, but wild bushes of all shapes and sizes barred their entry.

Jeom let out a loud groan after a few minutes of unsuccessful attempts. "Just move out of my way," he said, gripping his axe with both hands.

Everyone stepped back, and he hacked at the forest until it bent to his will and he led the way in. Branches and leaves rained to his feet with every step forward.

"You can stop now," said Demetrius after a while, placing his hand on Jeom's arm before he could take another swing—they had finally made it onto a path.

Jeom paused a moment but then swung his axe again anyway, letting out a loud yell as his blade sliced straight through a low-hanging branch.

Demetrius jumped back. "What'd you go and do that for?" he said, balking. "They have feelings, you know... spirits, I think."

"What do you mean *spirits?*" spat Jeom.

"The forest. It's alive, and it can sense everything you do."

Demetrius wagged his finger at his brother.

"You should be more respectful."

"Respectful?" said Jeom, his breath suddenly heavy. "What I respect is the value of my life and the little time I have left with it." His grip tightened around his axe. "Not some stupid shrubberies!"

He hacked senselessly at another tree, his inner anger rising to the occasion and the mighty Axe of Crissy aiding it.

Demetrius opened his mouth to protest, but Lessa interrupted what was sure to be an untimely fight.

"He just needs time," she whispered. "Come on, let's keep walking." She started down the trail with the others in tow.

"Where do you suppose this leads?" said Arianna as they walked along, dwarves among the trees.

"I don't know, but I'm sure this is one of the paths the new citizens will use to journey to their placements," said Demetrius, using the butt of his weapon to help him trek. "Look, there's more up ahead."

The wide trail they traveled twisted out in all different directions from this point onward, each path leading deep into the trees—rays of moonlight shot down sporadically throughout the canopy of the forest, spotlighting their options.

"What do we do now?" said Lessa, snuggling Sano close.

"I guess we just pick one…" Arianna looked back behind her, the trail they'd just taken disappearing to the darkness. "We shouldn't linger. They'll be looking for us soon."

They kept straight until the shadows of the woodland fully consumed them. But the way the trees loomed overhead made Arianna feel as if she were back in the Jar of Stone.

"I haven't heard any voices for a long time," said Lessa, breaking the heavy silence. "Maybe we should rest soon."

"They'll figure it out," said Jeom, his voice loud—it was the first time he'd spoken in what seemed like hours. "Sooner or later, they'll realize who we were."

He pointed at Demetrius and Lessa.

"They may or may not identify you both, but I suspect someone should be smart enough to realize that Arianna and I were in the company of others." He dropped his head back, staring at the treetops. "Stories *will* spread that more than one slave has escaped the Four Corners, and those portraits of us will reach much farther than just that forsaken village."

"I pray for better luck than that," said Demetrius, lowering his eyes to the ground. "Less than a week ago, everything seemed so… ordinary. And now—"

"And for now, we are alive and well," said Lessa, firmly.

"*Nothing* is ordinary about this life we were handed." Arianna stared ahead, contemplating their fates.

"Let's just try to remain positive." Lessa lifted her chin high and forced a lighter tone into her voice. "We're together, and that's what matters now. We have a chance at an extremely un-ordinary yet exciting existence. I'm sure everything will work it-self out."

"Sure, *you* can say that," said Jeom, stopping in his tracks. His voice pitched. "At least you and Demetrius have a chance."

He glowered at Arianna as they all faced him, but she refused to shrink under his scrutiny—she'd had enough of his attitude tonight.

"Jeom, you begged me to let you join us," she said. "I warned you not to come. You could be free right this very second and on your way to a normal life, so don't put that blame on me!"

She felt the itch for a fight creep under her skin, so many emotions tangling inside her in need of release.

"I still don't really understand why you even left with your freedom in hand." Her fists clenched at her sides, and she couldn't help it as her lip curled up over her teeth, her skin grow-ing hot.

"Why I *left?*" screamed Jeom, towering over her. His knuck-les turned white around the staff of his weapon.

Arianna didn't miss the intent behind his reaction; she reached for the hilt of one of the swords at her back.

"I left because I wanted to take my life into my own hands, but here we are again. On the run."

He took a step forward.

"And what would you have us do?" she retorted, meeting his challenge. "Would you have us march south to Saindora and wave our swords in the air? Challenge King Devlindor so you can sleep at night… so you can have your revenge? The entire *world* wants us dead, and we know nothing of it yet!"

Her voice pierced the hovering silence of the late night.

"Running is our only option right now. Or haven't you no-ticed?"

"Wants *you* dead," said Jeom, peering down at her as she stood on her tiptoes—they were eye to eye. "We're just the tokens that come with the grand prize. What a great leader you turned out to be, hmm?"

All Arianna could see now was red; her control slipped away to make room for the warrior's rage inside her. She couldn't help the word that fell into her mind—a magical, dangerous, and unbidden word.

Luzcora!

She hunched over, dropping to her knees as her insides burst with an overwhelming energy.

No... wait. I didn't mean it.

Digging her fingers into the cold ground, she tried to contain it, to hold this dangerous, defensive magic in the confines of her head. But it was only a matter of moments before it would explode out of her control.

"Arianna?" she heard someone say.

She strained to focus, the voice sounding so far away.

"Ara, are you all right?"

She felt the faint touch of a hand on her shoulder and looked up to find Lessa. And reflected in her friend's frightened stare, she recognized the silver, enchanted glow of her own eyes.

"Get back!" Jeom shouted, jumping in front of Lessa.

Arianna cried out, the energy releasing all around her in an exhilarating sensation; it was the same power that had ended Grinda Risso's life without remorse—the scene looked so familiar as Jeom moved behind his axe to block the attack, just as Grinda had foolishly done before she died.

But the blades of Jeom's axe glowed intensely, an effervescent shimmer expanding out from the weapon and shielding him from the spell.

As Arianna's magic collided with the Axe of Crissy, the resulting force knocked everyone to their knees, the grass and plants in the vicinity completely flattened from the blow.

"What in the King's name was that? Trying to kill us now too?" Jeom jumped back to his feet.

He stared at his axe with disbelief in his eyes, growing more angered by the second.

Arianna looked at her shaking hands, mouth agape. Her body felt suddenly weak from the exertion of so much power, and she struggled to even catch her breath.

"Well?" he shouted.

"I… I—"

Jeom turned away from her.

"You should focus some of that energy on the real enemy out there. Some *warrior*," he muttered under his breath.

"You know nothing of who I am!" said Arianna, shaking off her shock and standing to face him; it took everything she had to get back to her feet. "At least I didn't kill my friend for freedom and then throw it all away."

She regretted the words as soon as they left her lips, but still, she held her ground.

Jeom swiveled on his feet so fast that she thought he might attack—she drew a sword and took a fighting stance.

"Really?" he said, cocking his head to the side as he considered her, his expression stone cold. "And what of your master's fate, Arianna? Do you truly think he'd still be alive after such a traitorous act?"

"Stop it," she growled. *Master Bell is alive.*

Jeom shook his head.

"Or how about the girl who was tortured for a week. What was her name?" He twisted his mouth up, as if thinking hard, tapping his finger on his chin. "Oh right… Pippa. Her death belongs to *you*. Or have you forgotten them already? Do your friends really mean that little to you?"

He gestured to Lessa and Demetrius, still on the ground, remaining a safe distance behind Jeom—she could see the fear gleaming in their eyes.

"You don't know what you're talking about," said Arianna, taking a step back.

Her voice trembled, along with her sword.

"Don't I? You're quick to condemn, but I'll be making amends forever for my choices." He pointed at her. "You can't even *remember* yours. Or maybe you just don't care about anyone but yourself."

Arianna made to lunge, and Jeom readied his axe. But Lessa jumped up to thwart them.

"All right, stop this!" she said, pulling Demetrius with her to stand between the two of them—Demetrius sucked in a breath between his teeth as their weapons swung dangerously close before they pulled them back.

All the color had drained from Lessa's face, and Sano was wrapped tightly around her neck; she was trembling. "This is getting out of hand. Just stop this now."

"She's right," said Demetrius. "We can figure out a new plan, like we've done so many times before. You're both just scared. We all are, but we can't take it out on each other. Not now when we've come so far."

Jeom stormed off, down the forest path and ahead of the group, without another word. Arianna turned away, not willing to meet her friends' eyes.

"Let's just keep going…" said Lessa. With a deep breath, she took Demetrius by the arm to follow in Jeom's footsteps.

Arianna shadowed them a few paces behind.

"I SUPPOSE THE DISTRICTS MUST BELIEVE you and me dead," Arianna overheard Lessa say after a long time of walking in dreadful silence.

She'd been repeating her and Jeom's argument over and over in her head and couldn't help but think that maybe he was right.

Maybe they'd all fare better without me.

"Right," said Demetrius. "I fell through a hole in the earth…"

"And I was killed by my *ruthless* master," finished Lessa with a chuckle. "That's what they'll say. We were never counted missing because we're supposed to be rotting away somewhere in the ground."

"Precisely," said Jeom from up ahead. "Which means, you're in the clear. Arianna and I might as well hand ourselves in on a silver platter."

His footsteps were loud, weighted with his worry, and his next words came in a whisper, likely meant for himself—though the wind carried his voice back for all to hear.

"We'll see death before our due time."

Arianna's heart raced, silently agreeing with him.

This is my fault, my burden alone to carry.

Gazing toward the treetops, she continued to disguise her fear as poise. However, she knew with dreadful certainty that nowhere in Olleb-Yelfra would ever be safe for her or her friends again. They would always be hunted, pursued until their bodies were delivered to King Devlindor—dead or alive, just as the regulator had declared.

And despite Lessa's firm belief in remaining together, Arianna had a pressing feeling that maybe she'd be better off facing this next chapter alone; if they left her in their journey, the most wanted slave in the world, her friends might actually stand a chance.

For now, at least, they traveled together, following the forest path toward the same uncertain destiny.

WHAT LIES BENEATH

IRIDESCENT EYES GLEAMED DOWN from the broken limbs of the treetops above, as if the forest kept close watch on their every move. Rattles and screeches could be heard from all around, and the howls and hoots of unknown beasts filled their ears. The forest was alive—no doubt about that.

Just the wind rustling the leaves made Arianna twitch toward her swords, feeling vulnerable in the unfamiliar setting. There were too many dark corners where someone could hide, just waiting to attack them at any moment.

"Frightened?" whispered Lessa, slowing down to walk in step with her.

Her big, cerulean eyes peered out anxiously from beneath her robes, mixing perfectly with the eerie ambiance that was the woodland.

Arianna shook her head. They were all scared, all the time, it seemed. But no warrior would ever readily admit that.

After walking in silence for what seemed like hours through the night, they came to another clearing in the thicket, where large, moss-covered cliffs rose high in hills all around them. Covered in a golden dust, purple and red ivy snaked up and down the rocks, giving off a peculiar shine as the moonlight struck down. The dark seemed chased away in these parts by the sparkling setting, and Arianna instantly felt a sense of security wash over her as she explored the area.

We're finally free of the mountains.

She tempted her thoughts to stay positive now that her prison was no longer in view, obscured by the towering trees.

"Maybe we should rest here?" she said. "We need to gather our strength for what the morning might bring."

"You mean gather our strength for an eternity in hiding?" barked Jeom from up ahead.

Arianna ignored him, determined to hold on to this little bout of optimism. *We're free… for now at least.*

She turned her attention to Demetrius—he'd knelt down on the ground, placing his hands atop the rich soil.

"There should be water nearby," he said, sniffing the air and pinching the glittery dirt between his fingertips.

"Even so," said Jeom, pointing to his feet, "maybe we ought to keep moving."

Arianna followed his gaze and saw what looked to be a series of animal tracks peppering the dirt where he stood; they seemed to head away from the center of the clearing.

Demetrius considered this a moment but then shook his head. "No, I really think we should stay," he said with confidence. "Don't you hear that?"

As soon as all was quiet, the unmistakable bubbling sound of water could be heard from somewhere close by. And it was then that Arianna realized how thirsty she was; in the rush to flee Draminet, there had been no time to fill their canteens.

Jeom smacked his dry lips, and Lessa's eyes darted in every

direction to try to locate the sound.

"We need to find that water source," said Demetrius with a knowing expression. "Just like any other animal, we don't have a fighting chance without it. And who knows when we'll have another opportunity."

"I have to agree," said Lessa, hands on her hips. "We should rest here. Healer's orders."

"Fine, then it's settled. Let's set up camp," said Arianna. "We can think up a new plan in the morning now that Draminet is behind us."

"If you say so, oh *wise* leader," said Jeom, throwing down his things with a crash. "We need to keep up our strength if we're going to survive as outlaws of the Olleb."

Arianna let out a long, exasperated sigh.

"Look, I'm sorry for what happened back there! It was an accident, all right? I don't have a hold on my magic yet," she said, the tension between them no longer bearable. "And… I really *am* sorry for what I said. I didn't mean it."

Jeom pressed his lips together in a thin line.

Her friends all stared back at her in silence, their concern, anger, and sadness all etched on their tired faces. Seeing them in such a state, *really* seeing them now, made Arianna reevaluate every emotion she was feeling—she was humbled.

Her next words came softer, the confessions spilling out.

"Jeom is… right," she said; her whole body seemed to collapse in on itself as she let down her defenses. "I'm so sorry to all of you. If not for me, none of us would even be in this mess. You could probably integrate with the other freed slaves in Draminet if you head back now. If you want to separate, I'll understand. But we have to settle this."

She felt the betrayal of oncoming tears, but she wouldn't permit them to fall, wanting to appear strong as she said what was so hard to say.

"We're free of the tunnels. We completed what we originally

set out to do, so you all could start a new life somewhere far from here without being hunted." She looked back toward the way they'd come. "If that's your choice, I think it's time we said our goodbyes."

Arianna bowed her head low, unable to meet their eyes while she awaited their verdict; the last thing she wanted was to be alone in this cruel world, but her heart felt even more strongly about the safety of her friends. And they'd never survive if they kept bickering like this.

"Ara, I'd never leave you!" cried Lessa, embracing her in a hug. "You're mad for even thinking that. We started this journey side by side, and we'll end it just the same."

She pushed her to arm's length so that Arianna could see the seriousness in her expression.

"Besides, Talis would kill me if I let you out of my sight after all we've been through. I doubt you'd last long without me out here anyhow." She tossed her hair back, a forced smile on her lips.

Arianna felt a twinge of relief in her chest—no matter what came next, at least she could still count on Lessa.

"This is anything but simple," said Demetrius, getting to his feet and running a hand through his shaggy hair. "But as far as I'm concerned, I'm indebted to *all* of you for saving my life." He touched eyes with everyone. "We've been through a lot together in such a short time, and if I die tomorrow, I'll have no regrets. Especially now that I have my brother back." He smiled at Arianna. "I, for one, would love to stay in your company and explore this new world a little more, if you'll have me."

She returned a gracious nod.

"That being said," he added, "I... can't leave Jeom again. Ultimately, I have to leave this decision up to him."

He glanced to Jeom, something heavy in his expression.

"Our fate is in your hands, brother. What say you?"

Arianna envied Demetrius in that moment, his calm demeanor and ability to be so frank with his feelings. It took everything she had to let her guard down now, and she wondered which was the better trait.

As they all looked toward Jeom, awaiting his answer, an overwhelming sense of fear filled her chest; his decision would determine not just his but all of their fates.

To stay or to go?

Nobody knew for certain what the outcome might be of either choice, but this moment would undoubtedly impact the future for each one of them. *For better or for worse?*

There was no way of knowing until the end.

Jeom stood apart from the group, his brow furrowed as he considered his options for what seemed like an eternity.

Arianna couldn't stomach the suspense a second longer.

A little voice in the back of her head shouted warnings for her to speak up; if she wasn't brave in this moment, they might lose Jeom and Demetrius forever. And deep down she was completely frightened of that loss, even if she pretended otherwise—warriors had feelings, too.

Would they really fare better without me?

Although she and Lessa had only known the Kane brothers a short time, the handful of days they'd spent learning about one another, discovering the Golden Age hand in hand, and escaping the Jar with barely their lives made it seem like years had passed them by. Surely, a once in a lifetime shared experience.

Her thoughts flicked to Liam, thinking of what life in the Jar would've been like without a friend like him.

Friends like that don't come around often.

It was easy for her to blame herself for their troubles, to push people away when things got difficult, but her friends each had a stake in this adventure—they had all risked their lives for each other. Fought and bled for each other.

And if she let Jeom walk away now, something told her it wouldn't be for the best. After all, she was still torn apart inside by having to leave Liam behind, now twice over.

Putting aside her pride, Arianna spoke up.

"On my first day of training with Master Bell, he told me that things must get worse before they have any chance at getting better," she said. "At the beginning, I was *nothing*. A sorry excuse for a warrior-in-training. But I worked hard every day to become someone worthy of his time. Now I am a warrior by his standards, a sorceress of sorts, and free from the Jar despite all odds."

She took his hands in hers, feeling him relax; they needed each other, and she prayed she would hold on to that awareness for a long time to come.

"I didn't do any of that on my own. And I know we haven't known each other for long, but I don't want to find out what it's like to not have friends like you by my side for whatever comes next. This is the hard part for us now, but after all we've done, I know we can survive it. We've already accomplished so much that even the King had to take notice!" Her voice cracked. "But I can also appreciate if you'd rather go it alone. This is your life, and you have a choice now. That's the whole point of 'freedom,' isn't it?"

Arianna let go of his hands and stepped back to give him space to think.

"But, Jeom, no matter what path you choose, know that I *am* grateful to have met you."

He opened his mouth to reply but no words came out.

"In the tunnels you called us a family," said Demetrius, drawing his attention. "We don't abandon family. That's a loss I never want to feel again."

"Yeah, don't go," said Lessa—her cheeks were flushed, eyes rimmed with tears.

"Oh, all right," said Jeom with one look at her. He scratched the back of his head, shifting from one foot to the other as he gazed toward the sky. "Everyone can calm down now. We'll stay. It's not like we'd know where to go if we split up, anyway."

Arianna ran to hug him, and after a single second of

hesitation, he squeezed his arms tightly around her too.

"Demetrius is right," he said. "We're a family, and that's something we're lucky to have in this world at all, something to fight for. And I'm sorry too… for what I said back there."

He looked down at her, his expression pained.

"I just—"

"I know," said Arianna, softly. "You just want your *real* freedom." She hugged him tighter. "I know exactly how you feel. Let's not forget again that we're on the same side… even if we quarrel."

"I imagine we have a fair few ahead of us," said Jeom with a smirk. "But I won't forget."

Arianna gave a little laugh and then pulled away, looking to Lessa and Demetrius as they all came together.

"Whatever happens next, this is what we all signed up for," she said, feeling the weight of her words, heavy and true. *There's no going back.*

"We'll go down fighting if we have to," said Demetrius.

Lessa nodded in affirmation.

"Win or die," said Jeom with a resigned shrug.

There was a moment of silence among the group, everyone seemingly lost in the same thoughts of the future.

Arianna persuaded her mind to play their story out with a happy ending. But she knew now that the simple word 'freedom' seemed to have a lot of hidden layers. Every time they pulled one off, there was another challenge waiting.

And underneath them all was one unstoppable force—King Devlindor.

Just survive.

Startling everyone back to the present, Sano leaped from Lessa's shoulders and into the trees with an unnatural speed. His bright, orange eyes joined the unknown beasts' peering down at them from the blanket of leaves overhead.

"Sano, get back here!" screeched Lessa, her arms hopelessly

stretched toward the treetops.

"Did you see how *fast* he jumped up there?" said Arianna; she was sure her imagination had run wild into the night for how abnormal his agility had seemed.

"Oh, leave him be," said Demetrius, beginning to explore the area. "This is his natural habitat. He'll keep good watch on us from up there." He waved happily toward the trees as Sano flickered about the canopy.

"I'm sure you're right," said Lessa, staring longingly after him. "I suppose he did find me in the trees after all…"

She watched the tiny monkey dart about the branches with an envious gleam in her eye, just a blur of white fur—Arianna knew she yearned to join him in such height.

"Just keep close!" Lessa called, her words laced with worry.

Arianna had no doubt that the command would be heard and obeyed by Lessa's loyal friend, what Solomon and Talis had once called an avatar; they still had no idea what that actually meant, but Sano had already proven how special he was with healing powers that not even a master sorcerer could attain. He was not just *any* monkey, and Arianna sometimes wondered how far Lessa would go to protect him from harm—it would seem they were deeply connected.

"Shall we set up camp now, then?" said Arianna, her growling stomach one problem she had a chance at solving. "I'm starved."

She removed her pack and swords, tossing them into the center of the clearing. The others followed suit, arranging the area so that they could try to get a good rest before the sun came up.

"Think it will be safe to sleep?" said Jeom.

"If we can make a small fire, surely nothing will bother us?" said Lessa, laying out the last scraps of food they'd managed to save from their journey.

"Good idea. That should keep the animals at bay," said Demetrius. "How do we get one started?"

Everyone looked to Lessa, waiting for direction.

"Well, how should I know?" she said, shrugging.

"Oh bother!" grumbled Jeom. "None of you know how to make a measly fire?" No one spoke up. "What nonsense did you learn in those districts of yours anyhow?"

Lessa smirked.

"Talis always took care to make the flames for our potions," she said. "In retrospect, I suppose he thought I might burn down his home."

"Well, he was right to show caution!" said Arianna with a laugh. "My district didn't play with fire. We wielded weapons. No time for much else."

"And what's your excuse?" said Jeom, ruffling up Demetrius' hair.

"I practiced *growing* life in the Agrarian's District. Not burning it to ashes," he said, playfully shoving him off. "They didn't teach us that."

"Well, you all had better learn," said Jeom. "As a creator, I was always welding. The flame is something I know well. Fire is a fantastic tool."

"Right, so why don't you handle that, and we'll get everything else ready," said Arianna, feeling happier by the second with the group in better spirits.

"Very well, madam," said Jeom, hopping up. "Les, you're with me since you love climbing so much. We need to collect a bit of wood." He pointed to a tree that looked like it had been dead a while, its branches all but falling off. "That one should do!"

Lessa followed in his footsteps toward the edge of the clearing, and Arianna could already hear them discussing the Axe of Crissy's timely display of magic in protecting them earlier—another mystery to add to the pile. Demetrius went to scout in the vicinity for edible berries and plants to make a stew, and Sano returned from the trees just in time to accompany him.

That left Arianna to refill their depleted water supply.

Wanting to keep her load light, she left her swords at the campsite and filled her rucksack with their empty canteens.

"Just don't wander too far off now," sang Lessa in a jolly tone as the four split off into different directions on the outskirts of the clearing. "It's getting darker by the minute."

"We'll be fine," called Arianna as the voices of her friends died away. She, for one, was confident in her ability to follow her footprints back— she'd had such practice before.

Happy to spend a bit of time alone to clear her head, she set off through the woods to find the source of the water, tracking the sound of a bubbling stream in the direction Demetrius had sent her. A comforting tune popped into her head as she walked, an old battle song from her district:

> *When the sky is clear,*
> *And the moon is bright,*
> *Be brave, little slave.*
> *Fear not tonight.*
>
> *And if the light falls down,*
> *Darkness all around,*
> *Be brave, little slave,*
> *There are monsters about.*
>
> *Though some shadows are kind,*
> *And fear's controlling your mind,*
> *Still be brave, little slave.*
> *Don't let your guard down.*
>
> *But, when the last of the moon disappears,*
> *Death whispers much too near.*
> *Don't be brave, little slave.*
> *Be a warrior.*

Alas, 'The Song of the Brave', as it had been aptly named by young warrior-slaves long before her, may have had the opposite effect on Arianna this night as she wandered this unknown path all alone. The melody struck something deep in her soul, the words resonating with her innermost fears and her most intoxicating imagination as her mind homed in on all the horrific likelihoods of the life she'd chosen.

Her fears were many, always accumulating and never lessening. And in this foreign place, she quickly wished again for the company of her friends. She laughed to herself, thinking that if they *had* split up, she would have regretted it immediately.

What was I thinking? No one's best chance of survival is ever 'alone.' A warrior should know better.

She squared her shoulders and kept walking, keeping her eyes peeled for the water. After just a short time, the sky turned an intense black. The clouds hovered like an impenetrable shield over the brilliantly bronzed moon, and the rumble of an oncoming storm resounded across the night.

Arianna quickened her pace, wondering what horrors might be lurking in the shadows here as her path became veiled in the thick blackness. Not moments later, a noise reached her ears.

Thump, thump, thump.

"Who's there?" she called, hand reaching for her dagger. "Les, is that you?"

Arianna tried to adjust her eyes to the sudden, complete darkness, but it had come on so fast; the silver sheen of the tree bark was the only thing she could really see now, and it wasn't enough—the sound was growing louder.

Thump, thump, thump.

Whatever it was, it didn't sound human and it was getting close; Arianna regretted leaving her swords in the clearing as she considered which of her fears might come true. She knew now that monsters *did* exist, the memory of the lavahounds flying into her head.

Thump, thump, thump.

She could see nothing at all as she squinted toward the sound. Then the culprit ran right up to her. With a shriek, Arianna stumbled backward and fell.

A horse—black as the blanket of night that surrounded her—had burst through the trees and reared onto its hind legs with an awful cry at her presence.

"Thank the gods… it's just a horse," breathed Arianna, her hand resting over her racing heart.

The huge animal anxiously paced back and forth, so she slowly got to her feet, grabbing hold of its reins.

"Whoa, calm down there," she said.

Arianna welcomed the appearance of the beautiful beast. Suddenly, she was no longer alone.

She had never ridden a horse before, but it seemed easy enough. She inspected the saddle across his back to see if it was secure and felt large grooves in the side; they were letters carved into the leather.

"*Phantom*," she said as she traced them with her finger. "That your name? Suits you well enough. You gave me quite the scare."

The horse offered a slight whinny, seeming soothed by her words.

"You must be a runaway too, huh?" She caressed its head, still studying its features. "I know the feeling."

Just then, a loud clap of thunder—followed by a streak of lightning so bright that Arianna thought a fire had caught alight in the forest—startled the horse into another frenzy. It reared again, bucking its hind legs and knocking Arianna back to the ground.

Her hands became entangled in the reins, and she tried to get to her feet. But the horse, so frightened, raced back in the direction it had first appeared, dragging Arianna along for the ride; a bloodcurdling scream escaped her lips as her body tore through the thick of the forest.

The gleam of eyes above melted into sparkling strings of light as she scraped over the ground, her limbs flailing about. Her body bounced over sharp rocks and sticks, adding her own flesh and blood to the living woodland.

Then, she blacked out.

I OPEN MY EYES and slowly sit up… Ouch.

My whole body is stiff and sore from the abrupt abuse of the forest floor. Luckily, I'm still in one piece.

"Damn horse."

I'm pretty sure my wrist is sprained as I carefully untangle my hand from the reins. And my head is pounding like I've been hit on the head with a hammer.

Nothing I haven't suffered before in the districts.

Solomon made sure of that.

As I get to my feet, my whole body sways and my stomach lurches. I throw my hand out to the tree to steady myself before I can black out again.

"Deep breaths. Just breathe."

I turn in circles to try to find my bearings, pulling twigs and leaves from my matted hair as I go—no use.

"Be brave, little slave," I say, spitting the dirt from my mouth. "You're a warrior."

The horse gives a weak whinny and steps a few paces forward.

"Oh, where do you think you're going? Get back here!"

This animal will feel my wrath if it's the last thing I do. I stumble after it, but it stops, lowering its head to the ground. The earth feels strangely squishy under my boots, so I look down too.

"Water!" I would jump for joy, but my ankle is definitely injured.

I pat the horse on its head, momentarily forgetting that I hate it. "Demetrius was right about the stream. Our friends won't be far off then," I say. "He can figure out what to do with you, I'm sure."

The horse whinnies again, its intentions of drinking impeded by the layer of ice touching the shore of the stream, barring the water from reach. The ice reflects the soft glare of a snow-covered shore, making this part of the forest seem less ominous. With ease, I press my boot down on the frozen water. It cracks under my weight, and a pool of clean water spills out.

Following the horse's lead as it hastily drinks, I kneel down by the shore and cup my hands in the cold river. The water burns through the cracks of my calloused hands, but it feels so good, refreshing. I splash it on my face and in my mouth, drinking greedily. It seems there's not enough water in the world to quench my thirst right now… I wonder how the others are faring.

"We should leave soon."

Great, now I'm having a full-blown conversation with a horse…

I dip my hands in again for another drink, but something makes me take pause, a movement in the stream; there was a face, flickering through the ripples.

"That can't be real." I blink my eyes a few times, thinking I must've hit my head too hard.

But my heart is pounding, like it saw something too—how many times will I ignore it?

I stare intently into the water, trying to see, but only my blurred reflection stares back, moving slightly with the waves I created with my hands.

"Oh well." I sigh, pulling the canteens from my pack; with luck, it wasn't lost.

I plunge my hands back into the water and begin filling the containers. As I do, something heavy and hard latches onto my wrists from beneath the surface, squeezing my wounded hand.

I scream, and the sound seems to echo on forever.

The water containers slip to the depths of the riverbed, and my knees sink to the muddy ground as an unmovable force holds me down. The weight on my hands is growing stronger, pulling hard—though I struggle—until my arms are almost completely engulfed within the water.

"Help!" My face is nearly touching the water now. I focus my eyes, and my voice catches in my throat—a figure beneath the water becomes clearer… alive. Silver eyes glow up at me from the depths below, plastered to a pallid, ghost-white face.

I scream again. "This isn't real. Wake up. Wake up!"

The face, the figure, becomes clearer.

A shiver shoots through my body as its lips begin to curl up into a wicked smile.

I know that smile.

Then I'm plunged beneath the surface, my screams lost as the frigid water rushes down my throat.

I'm free of restraint now, but I'm so scared, I can't even think straight. I thrash around in a tangle of robes, my arms and legs entrapped in a white and crimson blur.

I open my eyes, fighting the water to try to find the surface. Instead, I see the frightening figure drifting right along with me, distracting me—it takes pleasure in watching me drown, like a sinking rock.

A sense of clarity washes over me in a sudden, sobering wave. I'm completely frozen, but my mind is free. And I can see so clearly, as if I look upon a mirror.

The ominous figure stares back at me with the same eyes and stern expression that I know I've seen on myself before, in mirrors just the same. Translucent clothes cling to its body as it floats—rigid yet smooth, as if made of a weightless stone. All at once it looks magnificent, mysterious, and terrifying, long hair suspended out behind her in a dark train.

Stretching out a hand, the figure seems to move at a glacial *pace until its hard fingers are clinging to my neck. She pulls me toward her, yanking me so close that I can focus only on her piercing eyes. My eyes…*

They start to glow again—that striking blue-silver.

"I'm not your imagination," it purrs in a sound so threatening that if I weren't already cold as ice, my very bones might have shivered. "I am you."

It smiles… a sincerely sinister smile.

Wake up!

The figure vanishes just as suddenly as it appeared, and the weight of the water comes rushing back in full force.

I can feel again, all at once.

The burn in my throat, the sting in my eyes, my mind struggling to stay conscious with no air to feed it.

I kick my arms and legs with the last of my energy, soaring to the surface of the stream.

ARIANNA AWOKE AS IF FROM A DEEP SLEEP. The sky had broken now into a complete downpour, and she was soaked from head to toe. Strangely, though, she found that she was still entangled in the horse's reins, and there was no river anywhere nearby, as far as she could tell.

After untangling herself, she checked her pack and saw the canteens still inside, empty, just as they had been at the beginning of her walk—none of it made any sense.

She seemed so real.

Arianna rubbed her hand at her neck—sore, as if she'd been nearly strangled.

That much was real. *Wasn't it?*

As she appraised her injuries further, she found that her wrist and ankle were, in fact, sprained and a lump on her head gushed blood. She supposed it reasonable enough that the jarring ride had knocked her into an unconscious state and caused all this damage; she had no clue how much time had passed and where she was right now, but it was still dark.

She just couldn't shake the vivid images in her head.

What does 'real' even mean, in a world with magic?

The definitions were endless now with her eyes opened to the truth of the Olleb.

One thing Arianna knew for certain was that she'd been attacked by the girl in the mirror many times before. But she'd never awoken with any injuries from her nightmares in the Jar…

She shook her head at the thought. *It's not real.*

She gently stroked her neck again; it tingled with pain.

4

NATURAL SELECTION

ARIANNA SLOWLY WALKED up the nearest path, guiding the horse carefully along with her as she tried to locate their campsite. Her teeth chattered uncontrollably and a numb sensation began to settle into her muscles, delivering a false sense of warmth—she'd felt like this before.

This kind of cold was familiar growing up in the Jar, and she knew that if she didn't dry off soon and warm up, she could be in real trouble.

In her search, she eventually found the path that led to the *real* river.

"Hopefully our friends won't be too far off now," she said to the horse, trying not to notice the wet ground beginning to freeze over as the icy rainfall turned to snow. "I'm sure they found a way to get that fire going, and we can warm up soon."

Just thinking of this gave her motivation, but she didn't want to go back empty-handed.

Arianna tied the horse to a nearby tree and went to the stream, determined to fill the canteens. But before she could even make it to the stream, there was a rustling in the bushes. Fearing the girl from her nightmares had reappeared to finish her off, Arianna dropped the canteens on the ground and used the last of her strength to pull out her trusty dagger, Aurora, from its sheath at her thigh.

The vibrant stones that made up the weapon gleamed and glittered in the dark. And the slash of yellow through the black jewel on the pommel seemed to glow brighter than usual—electric and alive.

Arianna listened for the sound once more, pointing the dagger in every direction. Then she felt that prickle on her neck, a warning that someone—or *something*—was watching her; she knew to trust in that instinct by now.

She turned in a slow circle and spotted the culprit not far from the riverbank. Eyes they were, but not any that she recognized and certainly not human.

The creature that watched her made Arianna's hair stand on end, the way it had when she'd first discovered the jade-riddled labyrinth within the Vanishing Tunnels. She stowed her dagger back at her thigh and called to it—a snow leopard cub come to life from the portraits of her teachings in the Learning Center; it was caught in a thorn bush.

"Come now," said Arianna through chattering teeth. "Let me help you." She moved closer.

Blood dripped down its side from where the long thorns had punctured its body, showing bright crimson on snow-white fur. Mesmerized by the creature, Arianna couldn't help but appreciate the moment. The only real animals she'd ever been privileged to see within the Jar were the ones they ate or the flocks of birds that flew well clear of her prison. Besides Sano and the occasional wolf, this was the most magnificent living thing she'd ever laid eyes on.

Small spots of the blackest black covered its head, growing larger with the natural pattern of its body. And flecks of gold could be seen here and there in its fur, as if someone had accidentally splattered a bit of paint on it. Its presence was intoxicating and much more impressive than any painting or sketch could ever portray.

Arianna had learned from her studies that wild animals such as these were rarities in the Olleb, nearly hunted to extinction for their furs in the cold regions. Uncommon though it was to find one, they weren't extinct yet. Such beasts still lingered near the Blancoren Mountains where people were scarce and the snow was never in absence.

Tempted to touch, Arianna stepped closer.

"Careful now!" she said, jumping back as it snapped at her fingers.

A deep, rumbling growl and a mouth full of sharp teeth kept her at a reasonable distance.

"You just wanted a drink, didn't you?" she cooed in a voice unknown to her, shivering all the while. "Well, the water in this part of the woods isn't worth much. *Believe* me."

The animal tilted its head with wary recognition, and Arianna approached with caution.

"I'm just going to get your legs free and then be off to my friends," she said. "And not that you understand a word I'm saying, but try not to bite me. I could use better luck tonight."

The cub's tail twitched, its fur standing on edge. And low growls merged with a wounded whine every time the animal tried to adjust its defensive stance.

Arianna now stood at the side of the bush, safer from harm at the rear of the animal. Then again, as its back paws flexed, long claws scraped at the ground and seemed just as lethal as the weapons in its mouth.

Arianna carefully leaned over the animal to help.

"Such beautifully strange eyes you have. I've never seen such a thing in my time," she said, overwhelmed as she became lost in its marble-like gaze.

She saw a scar striking through its left iris that looked like a flash of lightning etched across a clear blue sky. It seemed oddly familiar somehow—but she couldn't quite place it.

The animal began to thrash wildly, wounding itself further as the thorns pierced deep into its flesh.

"Just hold still," said Arianna, trying not to get scratched.

But before she could free its leg, a new noise made her stop dead in her tracks, one that didn't come from the cub.

Arianna turned around, ever so slowly, already knowing what she'd face. A ferocious animal met her gaze, a warrior in its own right—maybe even more so than she was.

Its eyes bore down on her, and Arianna felt as if she'd seen that look before. Hidden somewhere deep in her memories and just within reach, the same protective glare of a mother looking upon the predator there to take away her child had most definitely been stored.

Arianna backed up. Her fingers felt weak, frozen as they clasped back around the dagger; this was not a battle she could win in her current state.

The giant snow leopard was still and quiet, contemplating its next move as it watched Arianna. After a long while, it sat back on its haunches, just studying her.

"See… it's fine," said Arianna in the gentlest tone she could muster. "I'm not going to hurt anyone. Leaving now."

She tried to inch away, but a twig snapped beneath her boot, shattering the unstable silence.

The snow leopard let out a roar so loud that the force of the sound nearly brought Arianna to her knees.

She stumbled backward, slipping on the icy ground and into the thorn bush. She couldn't help but cry out as the sharp spikes embedded in her skin, ensnaring her.

The cub took this moment to attack, swiping at her shoulder;

its claws scraped across her arm and dug deep into her skin.

Crawling away from the bush, Arianna kicked through the mud with one hand on her wound from the cub and the other on her dagger, blood dribbling down her arm. Her screams never stopped as the pain from the scratch began to trickle throughout her body. It was as if the electricity she'd seen in the animal's eyes pulsed within her veins, burning like flames across her flesh and attaching an inexplicable agony to her very existence; she could have never imagined a moment more painful than this.

Even the night she died—a sword to her stomach—had been less excruciating.

Make it stop. Please! Make it stop.

She wasn't sure if her words were being screamed out loud or just echoing within her mind. Her vision blurred and time became distorted.

What dark magic is this? What's happening to me?

It was the first thought that came to mind.

Her own blood warm against her ice-cold skin was the only comfort she felt in what were sure to be her final moments. She held on to that simple, pleasant sensation—*warmth*—the only thing keeping her from letting go.

As she lay helpless in the mud, praying for relief, she saw the mother leopard creep nearer to her through a now heavy snowfall. Clearer, though, was the distorted voice of a woman crying. Surely conjured up from her memories, it eventually filled her ears over her own screams as she went in and out of consciousness.

'Please, please don't take her from me. Arianna!'

She could feel the woman's grasp wrapping around her body, clinging to her, calling out to her as she was pulled from her arms.

The voice grew distant until it was replaced by another.

"Get up. Do you hear me? You need to get up, now!"

Arianna pulled her mind back to the present as the firm voice of a man filled her ears. And he was definitely not of her memories or any dream. He was *real.*

"Help," she muttered, trying to lift her head off the ground, tears warming her cheeks. "It feels like… fire."

"YOU'LL BE A WARRIOR SOMEDAY," said the Opall Mother.

The woman smiled, but it didn't seem to reach her eyes when she handed Arianna a small cloth stitched with the number twenty-two.

Arianna took the cloth from the Mother's hand, studying the grayish thread, as if it held the reasoning behind the woman's words—it didn't.

She looked around at the other children receiving their placements, all with the same fresh, clueless faces; some would become healers, creators, or agrarians. But Arianna had been labeled a future warrior of the Olleb after five years of observation in her Opall, the only place she'd ever known.

Her heart swelled at the thought, and she put the numbered cloth safely within her robes.

A few days later, the Warrior's District became Arianna's new home. She looked around and realized the promise of any future held little truth. Melting into the lifeless crowd as a warrior-slave in training, she faced her first day as a prisoner of the Jar of Stone.

A VICIOUS GROWL and the shouts of the mystery man snapped Arianna back to reality. A blurred image of a figure in black robes stood over her, waving a thick sword and shield as the mother leopard pawed and snapped its teeth.

"You have to move!" he screamed down at her.

"Who are you?" slurred Arianna as she focused in on the golden snake sewn onto the back of his cloak and crested on the shield's metal.

She couldn't see his face with his hood raised, but she could tell he was good with a sword.

"The name's Elijah," he said between breaths, dancing around the clearing as the animal attacked.

"Are you going to kill me?" she replied in a daze.

Even in her current state, she'd recognize the mark of a regulator anywhere.

"Right now, I'm *trying* to save you," he said as the leopard lunged again.

She attempted to move her tongue further—or move anything for that matter—but her body was weighted like stone; the strike of the cub had somehow paralyzed her, as if an incapacitating poison laced its claws.

'By the Earth, Air, Fire, and Sea, please let this child survive. Gods, I beg you only for this. I ask of you nothing else!'

The voice of this woman from her dreams—from her memories—lingered for a moment again and then faded as Arianna came back to her senses. Hazy images of her frightened friends hovered around her this time, and Elijah was nowhere in sight.

Before the darkness could overcome her completely, Arianna saw an arrow flying overhead and the mother leopard pouncing toward her motionless body on the ground. Then Aurora slipped from her hands, the pommel still glowing bright as the depths of her mind consumed her.

5

REUNIONS

ARIANNA BLINKED OPEN HER EYES, the sun warming her face. The light fell against her cheeks in sporadic rays, and rain sprinkled down alongside it, pattering a glass-paned window above. *Where am I?*

She was naked. A cold sweat covered her skin, and she felt so disoriented. Bringing her hand up to massage her pounding head, she suddenly realized that there was no more pain—not on her wrist, not on her ankle, not anywhere.

She'd been healed.

For a moment, she thought herself back in her private well room… back in the Warrior's District. Her breath came rapid, panicked.

No, no, no!

She thrashed a bit, fighting the white sheets that had been snugly tucked around her. Eventually freeing herself and sitting up, she realized that this certainly was *not* a place she recognized;

dark curtains draped across a four-poster bed, concealing her from the rest of the space.

She yanked them back to search for her weapons.

"You're awake!" sang Lessa, running over to her from across a wide room. "It's about time. Glad to have you back."

"Les… oh, *thank* the gods. I thought—" Arianna let out a loud sigh, shaking her head, her curls bouncing every which way. Then she looked around, fixing her sheet so that she wasn't exposed. "Where are we?"

She couldn't have been more relieved to see a friendly face, but things weren't quite right. Lessa appeared exceptionally clean and well-rested for having just trekked through a forest during a storm. And her mood had lightened about ten notches since they'd parted back in the clearing. Clearly, she'd missed out on a few things since…

What happened to me?

There were holes—gaping chasms—in her memory.

Lessa handed her a cup filled with a dark liquid before she could utter another question.

"Drink this. All of it," she said.

Sano hopped up beside Arianna on the bed; he gave one sniff to the drink and then scurried away.

Arianna pinched her nose, knowing better than to trust the taste of anything Lessa handed her after an injury. She shivered as the rancid fluid slid down her throat, taking the drink in one gulp.

"I think your prillyberry juice has spoiled," she said with a gag as the remedy threatened to come back up.

"That's not prillyberry juice," said Lessa. "You won't believe it! There are so many new tonics here that my head is spinning. If I didn't know any better, I'd say some were laced with a bit of magic, too." She winked.

Then she took the empty cup from Arianna's hands and set it aside.

Already Arianna felt her stiff muscles relax, and she could see the color returning to her skin, her heart rate normalizing. Lessa was right. There was definitely something special about this concoction; it worked throughout her body at a much greater speed than would be expected—it was more sophisticated than the ones she'd been treated with in the Jar.

"Where are we?" she asked again, looking around.

"Just don't be alarmed," said Lessa, patting her leg.

She struggled to find the right words.

"We're in the City of South Luose."

Arianna felt that familiar flutter of fear well up inside her chest—taking refuge in a city had been their original goal. Having a life somewhere had *always* been the general plan, but now any city would be a deathtrap. They could no longer hide in plain sight without considering the highly probable outcome that someone might recognize them; the entire Olleb would be on the lookout for someone with her face.

They needed a proper strategy, and stepping foot in any major city was far from it.

"How long have we been here?" was the only one of a thousand questions that Arianna could bring herself to voice.

"A few nights," said Lessa. "About four days to be exact."

She left for a moment and returned with fresh robes and a wrinkled scroll. Uncoiling the parchment, she laid it flat across the bed between them.

Arianna immediately recognized it to be the map Solomon had gifted her as his last act of guidance. It was decorated with a myriad of colors highlighting every livable corner of Olleb-Yelfra. Strange names that she did not recognize were scribbled all over, marking each elaborate area.

Lessa gently smoothed out the parchment. "Solomon's last advice was to go to—"

"The City of Luose and find someone by the name of Ferlon Ragaric... I remember."

"This map is a bit difficult for me to read, but we learned that there's actually a North *and* South Luose," said Lessa, pointing to different sketches on the scroll.

Arianna nodded, her eyes drifting over the old parchment. But above the portion Lessa was focused on, gray, jagged lines that could only symbolize the Blancoren Mountains drew her attention—they were still so close to the Jar.

"You can see that North Luose looks barely inhabitable, so we thought Solomon must have meant here." She jabbed her finger at an area portrayed with trees on all sides. "We're in the northeast now, just south of the Jar."

She gestured to the room around them.

"And where is 'here,' exactly?"

Arianna took in the new setting.

The room they were sitting in had gray walls and shining fixtures, a bulky cabinet one of its only centerpieces; it held an assortment of bottles filled with strange liquids and gels, making a colorful addition to the otherwise lackluster surroundings. There was a dusty air about this place, stifling, like it hadn't been used in quite some time.

Cobwebs had formed in corners, hung like decorations from the ceilings, and filled the cracks of the stone floor. The only thing for real enhancement was a dreary painting pinned to the far wall, depicting a city she didn't know. And there was another large bed in the corner, the curtains drawn on all four sides, as hers had been before.

Chills ran across Arianna's skin in the drafty place, so she slipped on her cloak. The freshly washed fabric glided on smoothly. But as she pulled her arms through the sleeves, she noticed something on her skin. Her mouth fell open at the sight of a rather large scar streaking across her right arm; it extended from the front of her collarbone all the way down to the back of her shoulder blade. And unlike any wound she'd ever earned before, this one had healed in a coat of silver, raised skin.

"What the...?" She twisted around to try to see the full breadth of the mark—it was made up of four, jagged lines that would definitely be prominent forever.

"You tell me," said Lessa, a knowing look on her face. She lifted her blond locks to show off her own silver mark on the back of her neck—it swirled like the clouds just before a storm. "I'm still trying to figure out what mine means."

"I don't—" Arianna swallowed the growing lump in her throat, thinking of Liam and how he'd been healed in a similar fashion. "Sano?" she stuttered, glancing to the monkey.

Lessa shook her head.

"I'm not sure how his... powers work, exactly, but it wasn't him," she said with certainty. "And your body rejected everything I did to try and help. You just wouldn't wake." Her mouth scrunched up and she averted her eyes. "I even took a stab at stronger healer magic, but it was an embarrassing failure."

"This is too much, Les," said Arianna, her headache returning.

"I know," said Lessa, gently. "We'll go over everything. Let's just take it slow."

Arianna gave a reluctant nod and closed her eyes, trying to remain calm. Nothing was in her control right now. She remembered *nothing*, so she took a deep breath and tried to pin down her memories.

"Can you recall anything from before you blacked out?" asked Lessa. "Take your time."

Arianna pressed her hand against the scar, the healed skin somehow warm to the touch. With a jolt, she was reminded of an unending pain and the culprit who'd given her this mutilation; her memories flooded back, and she opened her eyes.

"I got lost searching for the water. There was a horse, and..." She pressed her fingers to her temples as the girl relentlessly haunting her dreams flashed across her mind—Lessa would never believe her. "... Then that *beast* attacked me."

Lessa was nodding along, as if to verify these details.

"And someone else was there, too, trying to protect me. He called himself Elijah." Arianna's hands fell back to her lap, and she pulled at a thread on her cloak. "That's about the last thing I remember before you showed up. Did he help you fight off the snow leopard?"

Lessa had the most incredulous expression on her face, staring at Arianna as if she'd gone mad.

"What? Why are you looking at me like that?"

"There was no one there with you, Ara. You must've been hallucinating," said Lessa, matter-of-factly. "You weren't in your right mind when we found you."

"But I'd swear it…"

Lessa just shook her head.

Have I gone insane?

This, paired with the maybe-not-real near-drowning experience, made Arianna really start to worry. Then again, the more she thought about it, the more it did sound ludicrous that there'd been anyone else trying to save her.

With four days gone by since fleeing Draminet, hundreds—maybe *thousands*—of citizens would know her name by now, already seeking the highlife reward that came with her capture. Had she possibly had her first encounter with being hunted by a man? Had a regulator recognized her, only risking his life to save what he thought would be nothing more than an enormous payoff? Or, maybe, he *really* hadn't existed at all, as Lessa seemed so sure of.

Arianna tried shoving her overwhelming thoughts aside to focus on the immediate question. *How did we get here?*

It was as if time had skipped ahead since entering that gods-forsaken forest.

"Tell me everything that happened from the time you found me, please," said Arianna, leaning back on her pillow. "I can't stand being so lost."

"Of course," said Lessa, a smirk on her face. "But you're not going to believe what we did!"

After Lessa had finished relaying the successful fight against the mother snow leopard, she went on to describe how fortunate they'd been to find the horse tied up by the riverbank.

Arianna scoffed.

Wretched animal. If only she knew.

With Arianna laid across Phantom's back, Lessa, Jeom, and Demetrius continued the trek through the forest in search of help.

"The boys and I were so panicked," said Lessa. "We knew if we didn't act immediately, we'd risk being seen by the new citizens and trainers approaching the city. And we'd risk losing you." She tilted her head to the side, considering the room. "Lucky for us that South Luose was even so near our campsite… otherwise you would have died."

"Ouch," muttered Arianna, feeling her cheeks redden—it was hard to listen to this sad story that painted her as some kind of helpless damsel when she'd spent her whole life training to be anything but. "How did you even manage to get in without causing a scene?"

"The city walls are bordered by the woodlands, so it was easy enough for me to climb one of the taller trees and sneak in over its branches," explained Lessa. "Everyone in the city was focused on receiving new citizens at the *front* gates, so I located an unguarded entrance and opened it from the inside for you and the others. We got through without anyone questioning us, horse and all!"

She beamed.

"And once we were in, we didn't seem out of the ordinary… word hadn't reached here about escapees, yet."

A flicker of a frown crossed her face, but she quickly put back on a smile—not quite fast enough, though.

What's she not saying?

"Then we took you straight to the city well center. This place is massive, Ara! You'll see soon."

"I'm… in the South Luose Well Center?" said Arianna.

We shouldn't be here, in the open like this.

"You're welcome!" Lessa shimmied her shoulders, a prideful look on her face.

Arianna didn't know how to react, unable to stop the negative thoughts from seeping into her brain—all she could think of was how she and her friends would never be welcomed anywhere in this world; it didn't belong to them… they'd stolen it. And now they were paying the price, forced into a life of running and hiding forever.

Why had they fled, broken all of the rules, when every action and each decision had only led more toward a life that would always be darkened by limitations?

Her wildest imagination couldn't have foretold all they had done in order to achieve some sort of liberty from the Jar. And now everything seemed so preposterous.

This will end badly for us all.

"I don't quite understand," Arianna finally said, running a hand through her tangled hair. "How could we go unnoticed all this time in the city well center?"

She felt herself getting worked up but could do nothing to stop it.

"Solomon said we'd need citizenship proof, *papers*, when we were first making plans. We don't have proof of anything! How?"

Her breath became ragged, and she was suddenly aware of how weak her body felt after not moving for so many days.

"Try to relax," said Lessa. "You've been through a lot. Believe it or not, we just ditched the horse and dragged you right through the front doors that very night. With everyone occupied preparing for the first wave of new citizens, it was easy enough to get by. It's called 'Transition Week,' and it's *absolute* madness in the city." She shook her head. "There are big celebrations and gatherings every day."

She placed a hand on Arianna's knee.

"You were nearly lost," she said, more serious now, "ice-cold and barely breathing. Jeom carried you in his arms and Demetrius grabbed the first caretaker we saw to come to your aid. We didn't have any other choice but to try our luck, if we were going to save your life."

"But—"

"It's him you should thank, really," interrupted Lessa. "*Demetrius.* He's the one who got us out of showing documentation. He lied saying we were attacked in the forest and became separated from our guides on the way to the city." She chuckled at the memory. "He's quick on his feet, that on. The caretaker saw you were in such a bad state that he told him not to worry and brought you in to be treated right away." She gestured around the room. "We moved to this secluded room shortly after."

Arianna could only stare at her friend, wondering if she was still dreaming.

"It was the only option!" said Lessa with a snort at her reaction. "We needed to find an experienced caretaker for you, and no one would be expecting runaway slaves. Not just yet anyway."

Lessa threw her hands up after Arianna still didn't speak.

"Well, you're alive, aren't you? What might you have done in my shoes?"

That got her attention—she couldn't help but smile.

"I guess… something crazy," she said after a moment. Then she narrowed her eyes at Lessa.

"But you're not telling me everything. Are you?" An inkling told her things didn't quite add up, but Arianna couldn't put her finger on exactly what.

Lessa blushed a bright pink almost instantly, and Arianna pressed further.

"How could we have stayed here for so long, unquestioned? Surely rumor of my escape has reached here by *now.* And with

Sano… and the boys." Her heart skipped a beat, and her voice pitched. She looked around. "Where are Demetrius and Jeom?"

Maybe that had been her funny feeling; with her memories and thoughts flooding back to her all at once, she hadn't realized they weren't accounted for yet.

"Calm *down*," said Lessa, a finger to her lips. "They're sleeping in the bed over there. It's still quite early."

Arianna let out a long sigh, eyes flicking to the bed in the corner, its curtains drawn around it.

"And this room we're in has been unused for years, so no one will check for us here. We're all safe, for now," she assured her. "You'll understand everything soon enough."

Arianna let out a groan, glancing up to the ceiling. Eyes set on the window, she felt as if she had listened to a banned bedtime story as a young slave, a fantasy of sorts. She just couldn't quite connect the words to reality.

Lessa leaned over and gave her a long hug, taking Arianna by surprise. "I'm really glad you woke up, Ara. For a minute there, I thought you might take the easy way out."

Arianna returned a weak smile.

"Never," she said, relaxing a bit. "So, what now then?"

"Come with me." Lessa held out her hand.

"Where are we going?" Arianna was reluctant to even plant her feet on the floor—all of her instincts told her to remain cautious.

"Oh, by gods, Arianna, will you just trust me already?" Lessa tugged at her arm. "There's so much more to tell. Days' worth, but we can't pack it all into this very second! I know you must feel confused, but just follow my lead and I promise you'll get more answers."

"Yes… all right," she said, letting Lessa pull her up.

Arianna quickly dressed and then yanked up the hood of her robes, as if hiding beneath the cloth might protect her from the unknown. She found her dagger on the bedside table and sheathed it in its proper place at her thigh. Then Lessa led her out into the hall, closing the door behind them.

THEY WERE STANDING in a dark corridor with shiny brick walls of a deep blue—almost black.

"See, no one has come down to this wing of the well center in quite some time," said Lessa, swiping her finger on the glass of an unlit lantern fixed to the wall.

Squinting in the dark, Arianna could just barely make out an opening a few feet ahead to what looked to be a hallway. From where she stood now, she saw three other rooms, none of which seemed to be occupied either; this corridor had truly been forgotten with time.

"We'll need some light," said Arianna, her arms outstretched in the darkness as she grasped for Lessa; there were no windows here to let in the sun.

"Here, let me," said Lessa, slipping the lantern out of its frame on the wall. "*Solza ven immito.*"

She waved her hand over it, and a flame grew where before there had been nothing but dust; it washed away the dark with a soft, glowing light.

"Where did you learn that?" gasped Arianna as a pink flame danced before her eyes.

It wasn't *really* the magic that had startled her but rather the fact that she wasn't privy to this particular spell herself. What's more, the control with which Lessa had conducted the spell left her completely baffled—Arianna saw they were no longer equals in their newly discovered powers, and a twinge of jealousy crept into the empty parts of her that had been created after four days lost.

"I've been practicing," said Lessa, casually—Arianna saw the satisfaction twinkling in her eyes. "There wasn't much to do cooped up in that room while we waited for you to wake, so I've been studying the Golden Age scrolls next to a few quiet duels with the boys, of course. Your sword training has really been coming in handy for me!"

Lessa feigned an attack, but Arianna just stood there. She could feel herself growing more frustrated by the second, no energy to reel her darkening emotions in or put on a fake smile just for her friend's sake.

Lessa straightened and cleared her throat.

"We just wanted to stay sharp and at the ready while you healed. And I thought it wise to work on conjuring fire, since we had quite the time starting one without magic during that freak storm back in the woods." She offered a shaky smile and started down the hall.

They made several turns throughout the winding building, turns that Lessa was clearly familiar with. And she'd been right— this well center was massive.

But Arianna was awed by more than just its size, drawing comparisons to what she'd been accustomed to in the Warrior's District with every step; the halls were lined with door after door, and more healing instruments and concoctions than she could've ever imagined existed.

If this is just the South Luose Well Center, I wonder…

What other luxuries did the city hold for it to be afforded such a large, sophisticated medical division?

As they entered into a main hall, the walls curved into an oval-shaped ceiling high above her head, hanging with low lanterns that reminded her of the firebugs buzzing in the Vanishing Tunnels. Dark blue bricks shifted in shades with each and every turn, an azure ombre that made for an eerie yet calming setting; it was as if they walked through a tunnel of water.

Arianna thought it strange, though, the lack of bloodstained floors and grime-covered walls, as was customary in the Four Corners. Where were the crying victims or the bodies piled haphazardly in the corner until they could be properly discarded in the Tunnel of Tombs? Where were the caretakers running about in a frenzy, their robes stained with the gore from the latest Warrior's Challenge gone wrong?

Arianna peeked into every open door as they walked, growing angrier by the second as she counted hundreds of shelves lined with more supplies and curatives than she'd ever seen in all her district life. The sheer number of available remedies was staggering. Her hands clutched at her robes as she tried to hold in her scream.

Countless young lives might've been saved had there been access to such supplies in the Jar.

Mere colds had taken out droves of her peers because their well center had run low on stock of the proper ingredients for the known remedy.

But, clearly, it wasn't a matter of supply.

Just another way to weed out the weak.

Arianna could almost imagine King Devlindor's voice stating his cruel intentions; she realized how lucky she'd been to have Caretaker Cyn to herself and access to Solomon's private well room.

Lost in her thoughts, Arianna hadn't even noticed they'd entered a new wing.

"I learned these are called Birthing Chambers," whispered Lessa. "Where caretakers help deliver newborns before they're taken to the Opalls."

Arianna shivered, staring into a room filled with a shallow pool of water and peculiar plants. For maybe the first time in her life, she wondered where in this larger world she'd come from.

They turned down another hall, one with soft, welcoming palettes of color. Arianna saw it was labeled the 'After Ward.'

Curious, she peeked into the last room at the end of this

corridor and found an old man covered in a thin blanket. His hands and feet lay in shackles, and his mouth hung slack as drool dribbled down his chin; he was unmistakably dead. It was, sadly, the most familiar thing she'd seen thus far.

They passed by many more rooms, some just storages for caretaker supplies and others waiting at the ready for those soon to need healing. But there were also chambers with frightening instruments laid about, stone slabs for tables, ones certainly not meant for healing—Arianna took a closer look at one of these rooms and noticed fresh blood pooled on a table, chains dangling down over it like restraints.

"That's different," she murmured.

It was named the 'Study,' and she hoped that whatever this place could possibly have to do with being a citizen never played a part in her future.

Hurrying along, they tiptoed through a hall that was clearly at full occupancy. The sound of moans from the wounded trickled past closed doors to their ears. And caretakers shouted over each other in one room, sounding like they may, in fact, lose someone this morning.

This is more like it.

For a moment, Arianna felt right at home. But it made her wonder more about the world outside of the Four Corners— about the world she'd so tirelessly fought to have access to.

What dangers could citizens possibly encounter after finding freedom?

There was a lot to learn about adulthood in Olleb-Yelfra. From her first real glimpse of this society, it was clear there was still plenty to fear. Ashamed though she was to admit, a piece of her couldn't help but envy the youth she'd been so eager to leave behind in the face of the unknown. Before she knew about the Golden Age or King Devlindor's real story behind his claim to the throne, living had been easier to bear.

Now she had to walk around always knowing too much about

everything, knowing that none of this was right.

It wasn't just her who'd been wronged—it was *everyone*. The King had cursed the entire world into the Dark Ages, and no one knew it but them.

Arianna was reluctant to keep going as they snuck through this busy hall, past the shouts of panic and onward to their destination. But Lessa insisted—the caretakers didn't bat an eye as they ran past, too preoccupied with the wounded and sick.

Then Arianna heard the echo of footsteps nearing from behind, and she panicked.

"I think we should hide," she said, pulling Lessa around the corner without waiting for her to reply.

Lessa didn't protest.

"Quick, in here," she said, placing her hands on a doorknob as the footsteps grew closer. "*Operium undrio!*" A streak of silver flashed across her eyes.

Arianna felt a knot twist in her stomach again—how comfortable Lessa had grown with magic.

The door opened, and she and Arianna fell into a musty-smelling room with sunlight spilling in. It had a small window to the hall, so they cautiously peered out and spotted what looked to be a man mopping the corridor.

Arianna let out a low whistle.

"That was *too* close," she said. "I thought he was trailing us." She turned a sharp stare on Lessa. "Why don't you just tell me where we're going already?"

"You wouldn't believe me if I did," said Lessa, seeming a bit shaken.

Arianna followed her gaze and froze, eyes adjusting to the contents of the room.

The soft light of the sun bounced eerily off jars filled with strange-colored liquids all around them, but the contents of the jars were… they looked to be showcasing body parts that Arianna was more accustomed to seeing *attached* to people. Unless it was a Free Falls Festival or a particularly nasty practice duel, free-floating limbs were, thankfully, not normal.

As Arianna surveyed the room further, she saw human bodies—somehow preserved well after death—laid out on tables. Descriptions flanked their sides, and they were purposefully arranged for display. Moving for a better look, she spotted a plaque that read:

Lessa took one look at the tables and immediately let go of the contents of her stomach, adding to the already sour stench in the air.

"Come on," she said, wiping her mouth on her sleeve. "I can't be in here a moment longer." She tugged Arianna toward the door when they saw the way was clear.

They each took a deep breath of the somewhat fresher air as they stumbled out of the Gallery. But Arianna couldn't help herself and looked back one last time.

Her breath caught in her throat as the ghost of a man preserved on display stared straight back at her. His look, such a sorrowful one, said more than his words ever could. She knew he'd never move on this way—another cruel curse of the King.

"Just a little farther," said Lessa, walking off.

Arianna didn't look back a second time as she continued to follow Lessa, but she thought she heard a wail coming from the Gallery.

Why me?

Arianna wished she could return to a moment in time when ghosts weren't real; seeing them would never *not* be scary—but feeling completely helpless to aid them was an even worse burden to bear.

They came to a stop in front of two tall double doors. Lessa pulled one open with a creak and slipped through.

This wing of the building seemed isolated from the well center altogether—the sickness was completely wiped away and replaced with delicate décor and sun-filled corridors. Vibrant paintings hung on the walls, and corner tables were adorned with fresh-smelling flowers. Arianna could almost imagine she had stepped through another wall of green light to discover an entirely new city, like the City of Undor (although this was *much* less extraordinary).

Following in Lessa's footsteps, Arianna scrutinized the paintings of the outside world. Sprawling cities, extraordinary castles, and vibrant landscapes of oceans, forests, and deserts alike dotted the walls. Alas, the next one she laid eyes on made her recoil—it was a large portrait of King Devlindor in his signature robes of black and gold. And positioned next to it was a slightly smaller portrait entitled 'Hon. Keeper Helix Kassime.'

The man had a frigid look about him. Dark brown eyes and smooth copper skin first drew her in. Then she noted his dark hair streaked with gray, perfectly trimmed and tucked behind his ears. The image depicted a manner of confidence and cruelty—as to be expected from one of the King's trusted city keepers.

Painted into beautiful robes of blue and purple, he proudly wore a humble crown made of thin, intricately designed silver. And his hands lay folded across his lap, showing off a stunning ring topped with a medley of stones she definitely recognized. *Aura and Ora!*

"But how can that be?" she whispered.

"I wouldn't like to meet him," said Lessa, contemplating the portrait alongside her.

Arianna just nodded, only half-hearing as her eyes fixated on the brilliant ring. As she leaned closer in to see the details that were also present in her dagger, she was distracted by the sound of a soft knock.

Looking up, she saw Lessa standing at one of the many doors lining this hall, her ear pressed to the wood.

"Have you gone mad?" said Arianna as she rushed to pull her away. "We can't draw attention to ourselves!"

"Can you just *trust* me?" whined Lessa, holding up her hand. "I know what I'm doing."

"Someone's coming!" whispered Arianna, looking around the hallway for a place to hide.

Too late—the door creaked open and a blob of curly, reddish brown hair peeped out.

"Ah, she's finally awake," said a woman. "Quick, inside."

The two girls slipped through the door before Arianna even had a chance to look at who had greeted them.

That voice…

It was one she surely knew.

The door shut with the click of a lock behind them, and Lessa held up the lantern to chase away the dark. As the woman's face became illuminated in the low light, Arianna nearly broke down in tears of joy.

"Well, don't be shy, dear. Come now! Give your caretaker a hug."

"*Cyn*, is that really you?"

Arianna stared on, unable to blink, as the caretaker she'd known since childhood loomed by the doorway, arms wide open and waiting, gazing down at her with the warm smile she'd always adored.

"Not possible," Arianna finally said, flying into her arms.

"Anything is possible." Cyn chuckled. "You proved that!"

Arianna looked up at her with such a renewed hope, safe in her healer's arms. "And what of Master Bell and Master Churry?" She couldn't wait to hear news of what had happened after they'd fled. "Are they well, I hope?"

Tears began to well in Cyn's eyes as she stroked Arianna's hair, pressing her head into her bosom.

"Talis is in good health," she said, glancing to Lessa with a soft smile. "But... I'm so sorry, dear. Solomon is lost to us now." Her words quivered, struggling to leave her lips. "Lessa thought I should be the one to tell you."

Cyn shook her head back and forth as if to rid the words from her mind.

"No," said Arianna, glancing back to Lessa—any trace of lightheartedness had fled her face, her expression confirming the truth of the statement.

"No, that *can't* be."

She pushed away from Cyn and let her body sink to the floor. She felt as if her heart might stop beating as a huge pressure weighed down on it.

"It's the truth," said Cyn. "You must remove him from your thoughts now. There's nothing more we can do."

"But he's just too strong," said Arianna. "He can't be gone." She couldn't accept this truth, yet deep down she knew she'd finally figured out what Lessa had been so reluctant to say.

"That's why I'm here," said Cyn. "I couldn't bear to stay in that dreadful place without his support... his friendship. I left immediately after you all fled. Without Solomon—" She let out a terrible sob. "Well, without Solomon, I would've left a long time ago. Let's just leave it at that."

She took Arianna's hand into her own.

"I'm so sorry for your loss," she said again. "He truly loved you. I believe he truly did, and you must never forget the man and the teacher that he was to you. He *really* fought for you, but things are different now."

She locked eyes with Arianna as if to make certain that she understood every word.

"He can't help you any longer, but I'll do my best to help you survive. I'll try my best, dear. I really will. I wish to honor his memory."

"Master Bell is... *dead?*" She needed to hear the words aloud before she could truly accept any of it.

"Yes. The Solomon Bell we know is dead," said Cyn, firmly. Arianna began to weep.

The brief joy of seeing Cyn was lost, instantly swept aside in a moment of agony. She had never before felt her body give in to such intense emotion, but the tears came unyielding now as all of her sadness and fear exploded out from the surface.

Lessa knelt down beside her, and together they mourned for the loss of her trainer, legendary warrior, and friend—the Great Wolf of the East, Master Solomon Bell.

A SPARK OF FIRE

"SOLOMON IS DEAD." Arianna could think of no better wish than to have one more night without memories, but there was no way she'd ever be able to sleep again.

Her mind was tired of all the thinking and thoughts, her eyes bloodshot and dry from the river of tears she'd shed for her fallen mentor—he'd given his life for her, a slave.

Solomon is dead.

She would cry more for him now, if she could. Who else would have to die for her freedom?

No one else will die for me.

Lessa led her back to their secluded well room as Cyn had to take care of some work, but Arianna hardly noticed the walk. She felt like she was floating the entire time.

"Is there anything I can do?" asked Lessa, her tone somber as they entered the room. "I'm sorry… I just didn't know how to tell you."

Arianna just stood there a moment, staring at the walls—it felt like they were closing in on her.

Her fists remained balled at her sides, her knuckles turning white as she struggled to keep an angry, destructive, and unforgiving piece of herself buried deep down inside; it was clawing itself out.

"I just need to take my mind off of it," she said. She looked to the bed where Demetrius and Jeom still slept. "How can they possibly sleep so late? I'm conditioned to wake up at the crack of dawn." She tried to laugh it off, to smile, *anything* that would dent the darkness shrouding her from the inside out. But her voice remained rigid, cold.

Solomon is dead.

She was desperate for a distraction, so she pulled the drapes open to wake them up.

It was already late morning, nearing the afternoon, and the sun spotlighted the boys from another high window—they were both still in a fit of snores. Then Arianna noticed something in the bed with them, tangled in the blankets.

"Is that—" She stumbled backward, away from the bed and in search for her weapons. "What have you done?" There was no focusing her thoughts now. "Where are my swords?"

Her voice came at a crescendo, and Jeom and Demetrius were startled awake, confused expressions on both their sleepy faces.

"What's going on?" muttered Jeom, wiping the sleep from his eyes.

Arianna located her swords leaning up against a wall, piled with the rest of their weapons; Lessa was standing in front of them, trying to block them from view.

With one quick maneuver, Arianna had pulled Lessa away from the wall and grabbed a sword—the weight of the weapon, *Solomon's* weapon, made her feel centered, justified in what came next. She lifted the blade, pointing it at Jeom and Demetrius. "Get out of the bed!"

She was staring past them to the sleeping snow leopard cub that had almost claimed her life; it was camouflaged in the sheets.

"It's okay, Ara. Really," said Demetrius, slowly moving his feet to the floor as he stared wide-eyed at the sharp end of Arianna's sword.

He blocked her path, hands raised in peaceful protest.

"That *thing* is the reason I lost four days of my life." Her cheeks grew hot. "I almost died trying to help it!" She took a step forward. "Demetrius, move out of my way. *Now.*"

"You don't understand," said Jeom, sitting up. "We found the animal unconscious, just as we found you. It has yet to even wake… maybe it won't. It can't hurt you now."

He stood, gently placing a hand on Arianna's in an attempt to lower her weapon.

Without thinking, she used her free hand to grab a hold of his wrist, twisting it around so much that he was forced to his knees with a yelp. Her weapon was now pointed at his eye level; he stared up at her in disbelief.

"Arianna!" shouted Lessa. "Let him go."

Demetrius prepared to intervene.

Arianna gritted her teeth, wanting so badly to just fight. Then, she remembered the last argument they'd had and relinquished her hold over him—her family.

"Sorry, Jeom," she mumbled as he toppled forward. "But you don't know what you're talking about."

She yanked up the sleeve of her robe, and everyone gawked at her remarkable scar, a permanent reminder of her constant fear and failure as a leader.

Arianna turned her attention to Demetrius now, her sword hand still raised, shaking—the rage she felt in her soul visibly pulsated all the way down to the tip of the blade.

"I won't ask you again," she said, narrowing her gaze. "Move out of my way."

Demetrius reluctantly slunk away from the bed, leaving the

cub defenseless at Arianna's mercy.

"Now, just hold on a second," said Lessa, inserting herself between them. "I know you're upset about Solom—"

"Stop!" Arianna scrunched her eyes closed, sensing a whole new bout of tears coming on.

Just hearing his name made her mind erupt in an overpowering wave of anguish. It was like an emptiness inside of her filling up to the brim with sorrow—a bottomless pit with no way out. And with each and every excruciating thought, the emptiness kept spreading until it eventually overflowed and eliminated her ability to rationalize on any level.

All she wanted in this moment was revenge—revenge for her dead master, her useless freedom, and the future stolen from her and her friends.

Alas, the only opportunity she had within reach was to retaliate against this creature for the torment it'd caused her, even if the memory of it now felt like a mere sting in the face of losing a friend.

The cub's long, furry tail twitched from beneath the blankets, and Arianna closed the distance between her and the bed. Carefully, she pulled the covers back to find the animal that she had risked her life for fast asleep and purring.

It looked so innocent.

Lies! It's a monster.

Arianna was no stranger to taking a life; she'd killed before and not by accident. Grinda Risso, nameless regulators, all dead by her hand. And though she could never say no to a good battle, she hadn't much enjoyed the ones that had ended so… finally.

Solomon is dead.

And yet, it was a consuming thought, that revenge might bring her the relief she so desperately desired.

She toyed with the idea.

Would it be so wrong to destroy something that had caused her such suffering? In a world in which she'd witnessed death far more often than life, would it be so sinful if the act made her feel good again?

The longer she contemplated killing it as it lay sleeping, the more disgusted she felt by herself—and the more mesmerized she became with the beautiful creature before her.

But it's not even a human life. It's just, just… an animal.

Her eyes flicked to Sano, the only other animal in the room… one beloved by all in their group.

What am I doing?

Arianna stood there for a long moment before inevitably dropping her sword. With a loud groan of frustration, she slid to the floor in a crumpled mess, wiping her tear-stricken face on her robes.

Jeom, Demetrius, and Lessa simultaneously let out sighs of relief.

"Don't you get it?" said Lessa, crouching down next to her.

"No, I don't *get* it," said Arianna, choking on her words. "I don't get anything anymore."

She put her head in her hands.

"Stop thinking of everything that's outside of your control," said Lessa. "You've been conscious for all but a minute, and you've had a lot of information." She took Arianna's hand, forcing her to stand up and face her fears—they were standing over the cub. "Calm down now and just look at what's in front of you, at what you *can* understand."

Lessa gently grasped the animal's hind leg and turned it over so that its paw was clearly visible.

"Be careful!" said Arianna, throwing herself in front of Lessa as the cub's sharp claws flexed.

"Just look."

Arianna saw its upturned paw, the padding of the skin bright silver. Her mind flip-flopped as a revelation gripped her; she glanced again to Sano who was now perched on Demetrius' shoulders. "It's an…"

"An *avatar*," said Lessa, grinning. She stood back with the boys at the flanks of the bed to give her room. "I'm certain of it."

"So, it… healed me?" said Arianna. She looked to her friends, all wearing eager expressions. "That's what you all think, isn't it? Like with Sano's magic."

Lessa was nodding emphatically, and Jeom just shrugged his shoulders, a bewildered smirk on his face that told Arianna he was just as surprised as she was.

"*She* healed you," said Demetrius with sureness. "I checked."

"I see." A dream-like state settled over Arianna then, a fog that at least numbed some of the sadness, temporarily replacing it with new excitement and wonder.

Ever since they had escaped the Vanishing Tunnels, it seemed as if they'd entirely left the magical world behind, forgotten and locked away in the labyrinths under the Blancoren Mountains; the real Olleb didn't appear to have any of the enchantment they'd unveiled back in the Four Corners. In truth, Arianna had *almost* grown to doubt in it herself… to distrust herself and her choices.

But this… another avatar?

This was unquestionably real. Just like Sano, this creature was a tangible piece of the Golden Age that King Devlindor had tried to wipe away with the passing of time. And now they couldn't even rely on their masters to help them understand what such a finding meant—with this heightened awareness, a new fire ignited in her heart, and one that wouldn't be easily extinguished.

Never forget.

She and her friends were alone in this bizarre world, and that was *nobody's* fault but the King's. If anyone deserved her wrath, it was him.

"This is truly an avatar?" she said, tasting the word again. How strange it sounded. "And it healed me… with magic?"

"Yes," said Lessa, twisting a lock of hair around her finger as she thought. "Although, I don't believe she healed you on purpose, really. When Sano healed me in the tunnels and when he healed Liam, it happened much quicker and with intent. We visibly *saw* the magic as it worked. But, Ara, you've been out for the better part of a week. It can't have been quite the same."

"Nonetheless, it definitely was magic," said Demetrius with the clap of his hands. "Can you believe it?"

Arianna shook her head.

"How else could it have left such a marking?" added Jeom, studying her scar.

Arianna pulled her sleeve down to hide it.

"She definitely had *something* supernatural to do with your recovery," said Lessa, touching the back of her neck with a distant look in her eyes.

Arianna scoffed. *Recovery.*

"Let's not forget that it attacked me," she said, sternly. Avatar or not, she wouldn't be forgetting what it was capable of.

"Regardless of those specifics, she's also to thank for your survival," said Lessa, hands on her hips. "Whatever happened to you that night, it wasn't just well center remedies that healed you. This animal had something to do with it."

"*Avatar,*" whispered Demetrius, gazing at the sleeping cub in admiration.

Lessa called to Sano, scooping him into her arms.

"Do you remember the story I told about falling from the tree?"

Arianna recalled it very vividly; it was the reason she'd been tempted to go searching for Lessa in the Healer's District in the first place, the catalyst to their entire escape from the Jar. "Of course," she said.

"Well, when I awoke, Sano was there." Lessa tickled the monkey under his chin. "He's stayed by my side ever since. Talis could *not* get rid of him. Believe me, he tried!" She laughed. "Anyhow, it was a miracle I didn't die. And after the incident, I was out for an unusually long time as well."

"Yes, nearly two weeks if I remember right," said Arianna. "You woke up on a Sunday."

She couldn't help but smile at the memory.

"That's right," said Lessa. "But the accident was so... *strange.* I'll never forget the moment I hit the ground. It was the most painful thing I think I've ever endured. And mind you, that wasn't the first time I've fallen out of a tree." She trembled. "It felt like I had broken nearly every bone in my body before passing out."

Arianna winced.

"Yet, Talis told me there were only a couple breaks, normal injuries that should've healed much more quickly, especially with his skill as a healer *and* sorcerer. It wasn't natural." She looked to Arianna, a knowing in her eyes. "Can I assume this is similar to what happened to you?"

Arianna returned a reluctant nod.

"I thought as much," said Lessa. "Just a scratch and a bump on the head were all you had, easy fixes with superior remedies such as these—" she gestured to the cabinet stacked with vials of medicines "—and nothing compared to injuries you've battled before. So, whatever an avatar is, I believe the initial contact or connection with one is meant to be painful... a test of strength or merit, perhaps?"

She shrugged.

"Whatever the case, I'm glad we survived our encounters. And I, for one, think the pain was worth it." She hugged Sano to her chest. "You'll see."

Arianna pondered this theory, letting the idea roll around in her mind.

"Magic *is* sometimes rejected by the recipient," she said after a moment. "Talis told me so on our very first meeting. Even when conjured, it can have a mind all its own, no telling the conse-quence."

"Then this would be the same sort of thing?" said Jeom,

gently stroking the cub's spotted fur—even Jeom, easily the most distrustful of the magical world in the group, could recognize the importance of another creature like Sano in their midst. He glanced at Lessa, curiosity in his eyes.

"It's just my guess," said Lessa, chewing on her lip. "That would explain the pain. *And* the struggle to accept or reject whatever magic is at play when an avatar connects to a human."

"But why us?" Arianna found herself again drawn to the cub, drifting closer to the bed.

Lessa shook her head.

"Honestly, of all the curious things I've read throughout the scrolls, avatars are barely mentioned. I think even in the Golden Age they must've been a rarity. But this…" She bent down next to Arianna and gently touched her sleeve with the scar. "This is the first step in forming a bond, and the avatars battled with the same pain, too."

"What do you mean?" said Arianna.

Demetrius ran a hand through his disheveled hair. "She was just as bad off as you when we found her. She's been asleep all this time."

"It's an equal connection on both sides," said Lessa. "I just know it."

Arianna pinched her fingers to her forehead, trying to grasp everything.

"Solomon and Talis told us to care well for Sano," she finally said. "They knew he was something special and now another shows up? What are we supposed to do with it? We can barely take care of ourselves."

"You'll bond with her as if she's your own life," said Lessa as she coddled Sano. "We owe them to at least try and figure out how that bond is formed and why."

Arianna was hesitant. "But why does he mean so much to you?" she asked. "At least, tell me that."

"It's hard to explain," said Lessa. "But soon after he came into my life, I just felt like… like he became a part of me. I don't know what I'd do without him now."

Arianna looked down at the cub, an entity she couldn't help but loathe, and was certain she'd never feel the same. But if this was *truly* an avatar, an endangered remnant of the Golden Age, no matter her negative feelings toward it, she knew she must protect it.

She had to obey her master's wishes and honor his wisdom; this was a special creature of a good and magical history nearly lost to the Olleb—and it was now her responsibility, whether she liked it or not.

The animal's eyes shot open, a flash of that brilliant blue and a strike of yellow.

"Oh!" said Arianna, catching her breath.

"She's awake!" squealed Jeom with a clap, his excitement shocking everyone in the room into a momentary silence.

Demetrius cleared his throat, trying not to laugh.

"Erm… I'll just give you some room," said Jeom, scooting away, a blush rising in his cheeks.

The cub stretched its legs and flexed its paws.

A little hesitant at first, Arianna held out her hand in a gesture of forced friendship. It studied her for a long moment and then pressed its forehead into her palm. At the touch, a jolt of energy passed through her, engulfing her entirely in a wave of warmth and calm.

Arianna gasped, quickly pulling her hand back. "Well, I wasn't quite expecting this. Ferocious, aren't you?"

She reached out again to stroke its cottony, speckled fur as some of her resentment dwindled to make room for her curiosity. Looking toward Lessa, she gave a deep sigh, resigned to her duties to the snow leopard cub. Still, she wasn't quite convinced they could ever form an attachment as strong as Lessa promised.

"So where do we begin?" she asked, hesitantly.

Lessa laughed, dumping a pile of scrolls at their feet—she'd already spent quite some time marking instances where avatars had any mention. And while the boys occupied themselves, the girls pored over the ancient texts well into the night to see if something had been missed.

Arianna was thankful to occupy her thoughts with anything other than Solomon for a while. Sadly, though, there just wasn't much to decipher.

Throughout the references to magical creatures and even ancient myths, there was not one definition—not one story—indicating what an avatar might actually be.

After hours of reading, they knew the same amount as they had started with from the mouths of their masters.

'There's more to them than meets the eye.'

"This is hopeless," said Arianna. "We know just as much about their magic as we do of our own. Absolutely nothing!"

She plopped back on a pillow, spreading out on the floor.

"Maybe someone in the city will know something?" said Lessa, looking exhausted as well.

"Don't be foolish," said Arianna, fed up with the endless mysteries to be solved. "No one but us knows anything or *can* know anything. We can't exactly go running out onto the streets asking strangers about avatars. I'm surprised we even made it this far. Who could we trust?" She gazed at the ceiling. "We need to get out of here."

Lessa rolled up the parchment she was reading. "We can trust *Cyn.*"

"No, we can't," said Arianna, firmly, pushing up on her elbows to look Lessa in the eyes. "Not with this."

She wasn't about to drag her cheery caretaker into this mess, not after what had happened to Solomon.

Solomon is dead.

Arianna shook her head and put her attention on the cub; it was sniffing around the room, probably looking for food or performing any number of normal animal behaviors—it appeared a *normal* beast in every way, and yet was anything but.

Such a mystery. A baffling, magical mystery.

"You need a name, I suppose," she said, eyeing it warily as she tried to shift her thoughts to something more positive. "We'll just start there."

"I'm glad we could save you both," she heard Demetrius say with a yawn. He came to sit beside her. "I'm sorry though… about your master."

He laid a gentle hand on hers and Arianna looked away, her shoulders slumped. "Thank you."

"Ara, have you finally calmed down now?" called Jeom from across the room—she was thankful for the timely change of subject. "Is it safe to join you?"

She chuckled. "Do so at your own risk," she said, trying to keep the dark thoughts at bay.

She just couldn't believe she'd awoken in a new city, an avatar to her name, reunited with Cyn, and learned of her master's passing—all in one day!

So much can happen in just a single moment.

Time humbled her then—its destructive capabilities neither enemy nor friend.

"It'll take more than just a scratch to get rid of me. Disappointed, are you?" she said.

Jeom let out a booming laugh—it reminded her so much of Solomon, and it always would.

Dead.

She was obsessing, so she focused again on a name for the cub, on anything other than her departed master. "I think I'll call her 'Solza' like I've seen written in some of the scrolls. It has a nice ring to it," she said, glancing to Lessa for approval.

It felt oddly empowering… to grant this creature a name; she'd never done anything of the sort before.

"From what I've learned, *Solza* translates to the meaning of light or fire," said Lessa, matter-of-factly. "Fitting. She deserves a name reminiscent of her world."

"She does have a fierce spirit, too," said Demetrius.

"Sounds good to me!" said Jeom, coming over to join them.

The cub's ears perked up with the sound of his thunderous voice, and she turned her gaze on them.

"And her eyes are full of fire," mumbled Arianna, staring in wonder at the yellow streak slashing through the blue.

She touched the rigid lines of the silver scar on her arm, remembering the burn that put them there.

"Yes, very appropriate," she said.

"Solza and Sano!" sang Demetrius, solidifying the choice. "What a perfect pair."

Everyone looked toward the two enchanted creatures in their midst; they'd taken to each other quite quickly and had begun to playfully explore the room side by side.

FACING THE FUTURE

"CHILDREN," SAID CYN, bursting into the room the next morning. She looked terribly flustered and black circles shadowed her eyes. "I'm afraid you can't stay here any longer now that you're well. I've been up all night trying to figure something out, but there's no other way. People are beginning to become suspicious of me always sneaking away with extra food and such."

She closed the door behind her.

"It's all but a miracle that I was a caretaker on duty the night you stumbled through the doors, but I think you ought to make new arrangements now."

Arianna stood to greet her. "Did you manage to get us some kind of registration, at least?" The look on her caretaker's face told the unfortunate answer.

"I'm afraid I wasn't able to, dear," Cyn said with a sigh. "But I've brought you some things to help you blend in with the public so I can get you safely out of the city." She set a stack of silver cloaks on the nearest bed. "This is the attire new citizens are required to wear during Transition Week."

"When?" said Lessa, holding one of the robes up to her chest. She frowned.

"Tonight," said Cyn. "I'll need to sneak you out of the well center immediately, in case I'm being followed. I think I can accomplish that much." She gazed at Arianna, her face full of sorrow. "I would do that for you."

"I know you would," she said, not letting Cyn or the others get a whiff of her fear.

Arianna forced a smile for her caretaker's sake and went to inspect the robes; they represented a life she'd once spent every waking moment aiming for, but now she saw them for what they truly were and always had been—meaningless.

"But… maybe there's a way we can stay here somewhere," said Jeom, worry wrinkling his face. "This city is huge, after all. Do we have to leave? Where are we to go?"

"Don't be naïve," said Cyn, cocking her head as she considered him. "The City of South Luose may seem like the golden end of the world, but the ruler here is just the same as the one who built the Four Corners. You should know better. Even here there are rules that if disobeyed will leave you headless, and you've made a point to break them all."

She placed her hands on her hips, turning her attention back to Arianna.

"You just can't stay within these city walls if you want to live." She shook her head. "I'm so sorry for this mess that Solomon dragged you into, but I'm sure you'll find a home soon enough. Just not here, I'm afraid."

The boys started to whisper about other options and Lessa reluctantly began to pack up their things, everyone too accepting of their bad fortune.

Arianna couldn't take it.

"No!" In a bout of anger, she swiped the clothes off the bed;

they hit the floor, and the room grew quiet. "We aren't running anymore. *Please*, Cyn. You have to help us find another way. We deserve a life."

If they ran now, they would forever be running, just as Jeom had predicted back in the forest. Every city would be the same, and Arianna couldn't face her friends, *herself*, if this was the destiny she'd brought upon them all.

"But what more can I do?" said Cyn, looking terribly defeated. "I don't know how else I can aid you in this."

An idea came to Arianna then, like a burst of light in her mind's eye.

"Master Bell has helped us already!" she said. "With his last words to me, he led us to *this* city." From the corner of her eye she saw Lessa bring her hands to her lips as if in prayer, and Arianna knew they were thinking the same thing. "He urged us to find a man who goes by the name of Ferlon Ragaric. Do you know of him? Maybe if we can find him, he'll be able to help us."

Cyn scratched her head, looking to the ceiling. "Hmm… Ferlon Ragaric." Her face scrunched up in concentration. "I don't know, but maybe you shouldn't trust what Sol—"

"Cyn, I'm begging you! It's our only chance," said Arianna, grasping Cyn's hands in her own, forcing her to meet her eyes. "Please."

"Oh, all right," said Cyn, her cheeks turning a bright red. "I don't know what that Solomon was up to or who this 'Ragaric' is, but if there's anyone who can find him, I think I know just the man."

She began to pace the room, unable to stop herself from tidying up. Arianna and her friends all shared glances, realizing that their future lay in Cyn's hands—they needed her to talk.

"Who is it?" said Demetrius, the hope clear in his voice.

"There's a citizen here who goes by the name of Godfrey, and he knows *everyone* who comes and goes in South Luose," said Cyn, picking the robes off the floor.

"How did you learn of him?" asked Jeom, arms crossed at his chest—Arianna knew he was trying to seem collected, not hopeful nor scared; they were alike in this way.

"I spent many years training in this city before my transfer to the Warrior's District Well Center," said Cyn. "Word of him gets around. If there is, or ever has been, a Ferlon Ragaric in this city, he'll know of it."

"Well, we must speak with him, then!" said Lessa, clapping her hands. "Where can we find him?"

"Quite fortunately for you, he's always checking into this well center for mischief that you want *nothing* to do with. He's here now in the east wing. I treated him only last night for a broken leg."

"He can't be more mischievous than us," said Demetrius with a chuckle, his positive energy never waning. "I think we can handle him."

"How did he get injured?" asked Lessa.

"He has a talent for making enemies," said Cyn, her expression darkening. "You see, he's a trader of sorts. He deals in secrets and has a habit of twisting your words… using them against you to keep you indebted. He's really a cunning man. His reputation precedes him here."

Cyn looked far away in her thoughts as she folded the cloaks in a neat stack atop the bed.

"He can be trusted to give you what you want, but he can't be trusted to care for what you give him."

"We can work with this… thank you, Cyn!" said Arianna, relieved that they weren't at a dead end just yet—though she couldn't help but wonder what dark past might've brought her gentle caretaker to know such an unpleasant man in the first place.

"Don't thank me just yet," said Cyn, her voice unnaturally firm. "Now, you might not like this, Arianna, but I will not permit any of you to see him. For your own safety, I believe." She nodded, as if reassuring herself of the decision. "I'll go to him in the morning and find out the information you seek. And if he doesn't know, you must let me guide you from the city by tomorrow's end."

"But—"

"No buts! I won't have Solomon's last noble sacrifice be in vain. Your faces are already plastered all over the city streets, and you can't risk being seen. It's not safe for you here. I'm going to handle this my way."

She made to leave, holding her head up high and not even looking Arianna's way; if she did, Arianna was certain she'd crumble.

Arianna let out an exasperated sigh. "Oh, Cyn, just *wait* a moment." Before Cyn could object again, Arianna had wrapped her arms around her in strong hug; they remained like that for a long moment. "I'm so lucky to have you as my caretaker."

She felt Cyn relax.

"I'm lucky to have you to care for, dear." She gave Arianna a tight squeeze. "Quite lucky, indeed."

Then she left the room.

Arianna watched the door shut behind Cyn. The words she said next were hollow and cold.

"We can't trust her with this," she said, addressing her friends as she leaned her back against the door. "I care for her deeply, but this is *too* big. Who knows what this Godfrey is like, and I don't believe Cyn fully registers the extent of the mess that we're in. We need to handle this ourselves, and I don't want her tied up in it any further."

"Are you sure?" said Lessa, sitting down on the bed.

"Positive."

Arianna had spent enough time with Cyn to know that she had no place in the battle they'd found themselves in. And from what she'd described, the one man who possibly held the answers they sought may put up a decent fight.

"Then we'll need to go tonight," said Jeom. "Before she comes back."

"Tonight it is," said Arianna, looking to Lessa and Demetrius to make sure they agreed; they didn't protest. "Great... we have *something* of a plan. Now, does anyone know how we might locate the east wing?"

"Lessa is a walking map," said Jeom, winking at her.

They all looked her way.

She tried not to blush. "I do think I've seen it marked," she said, tapping her finger to her lips as she thought. "I'm sure I can find it."

"I just wonder, though..." said Demetrius, staring at Arianna.

"What?" she said, shrinking back from his scrutiny. "Why are you looking at me like that?"

"Well, it's just... what if Godfrey recognizes you, Ara? It might not do us any good since the city's been cautioned to keep a lookout."

She opened her mouth to respond but Jeom cut her off.

"That's a fair point," he said. "I hadn't thought of this. Maybe she shouldn't join us when we go to him, then."

"I suppose she can just wait here," said Lessa with a shrug. "We can fetch her when we're finished."

"You expect me to stay behind?" Arianna's voice cracked on the last word as she walked to the center of the room, demanding her inclusion—they were speaking as if she weren't even present, a helpless creature still bedridden.

"I do think it's best," said Demetrius, choosing his words carefully. "Your portrait is probably everywhere in the city by now, as your caretaker said."

"And what of Jeom's portrait?" she retorted. "They're looking for him, too. They could've identified all of us by now, for all we know."

Jeom frowned, hands in his pockets.

"But it's you they're *really* after," he said. "The rest of us are just collateral. You're the only one anyone is completely sure about."

Arianna was taken aback as Jeom stared at her with the look she'd been dreading to see again since the night they had their fight—and to her, it felt like no time had passed.

"Also, his portrait doesn't really do him justice," said Lessa. "There aren't any defining features to single him out of a crowd like yours. Just a muscular guy with dark skin, but that's half the world, right? Here, take a look." She rummaged in her bag and then pushed a parchment into Arianna's hands. "I saved it from Draminet."

With contempt, Arianna stared down at a perfect portrait of herself labeled 'traitor.' And whoever had instructed the artist about *her* features had an impeccable memory and very good descriptive skills; her long curls had always been her most recognizable feature, and there they were, a perfect resemblance—anyone would identify her next to this, slave number Twenty-Two of Warrior's District.

My name is Arianna Belvedor, and I'm no slave!

She couldn't help herself as her fingers curled into a fist around the parchment, the paper tearing to shreds in her hands. Then she stormed over to the cabinet that contained all of the medical equipment and rummaged in the drawers.

"Perfect." She held up a pair of sharp shears, grabbed a chunk of her hair above her shoulder and cut.

"What are you doing?" cried Lessa, her hands flying to her cheeks.

Demetrius had a huge grin on his face.

Snip, snip.

"Boy, you've really gone mad!" said Jeom.

"Maybe." A few more cuts and Arianna felt so much lighter, her curls covering the floor at her feet.

"There. No one will recognize me now," she said, a sort of

calmness washing over her. She kicked the hair aside. "I don't want to hear another word about me staying behind. That's *never* going to happen."

Lessa, Demetrius, and Jeom could only gawk.

"*Well?*" she said.

"We'd be fools to try and stop you," said Lessa with a resigned sigh.

Jeom wore a dumbfounded expression, and Demetrius put his hands up in mock surrender.

Arianna set the shears aside. "Glad we're all on the same page again." Then she considered the pieces of the parchment on the floor. "Those sketches aren't so good anyway... Lessa could draw something better with her eyes closed."

Lessa shook her head, an incredulous smile stretching across her face. "At least let me fix this mess so you seem somewhat normal," she said, picking up the shears. "I had a lot of practice on Talis over the years, and the way you've gone about it makes you look absolutely nuts."

Jeom snorted. "As I said."

"I suppose it's fitting then, for how the Olleb sees things," said Arianna—a dangerous thought crossed her mind. "I guess this is me now."

She smiled at her reflection in the glass of the cabinet; the reflection smiled back, a flicker of silver in her eyes.

Demetrius and Jeom took charge of packing their things as Lessa made the last of the cuts, Arianna's long hair littering the floor in a big, fluffy pile.

"There," she said, brushing the clippings off Arianna's shoulders. "All set."

"Thanks, Les," said Arianna, feeling strangely excited as she considered this new version of herself.

"Ready then?" said Demetrius after they were all packed. "On to the next adventure?"

Arianna took a broom from the corner and swept the pile of

hair into a bin. After wiping her hands of it all, she gathered her swords. "More than ready," she said.

AS NIGHTTIME FELL, they gathered their belongings and prepared to depart their short-lived sanctuary inside the South Luose Well Center. With Sano curled on Lessa's shoulders and Solza's head sticking out from Arianna's rucksack, they left the safety of the well room behind. The only evidence that it had ever been occupied was a farewell note addressed to Cyn and the remnants of a bad haircut; Arianna hoped her caretaker could find the heart to forgive their decision when she came to find the room emptied in the morning. But she didn't have time to worry about that just now—she put her focus on their futures and on the role this Godfrey might play in them.

With Lessa leading the group, they made their way through the maze of halls in search of the east wing. Dim fires burned in lanterns all the while, lighting a path toward the unknown. Every footfall seemed to echo indefinitely across the stone floors. And Arianna felt like they marched head-on into danger, her nerves spiking with each step.

"This way," said Lessa, turning down an unlit corridor.

The east wing swallowed them in darkness.

"Watch it!" said Jeom, sucking a breath in through his teeth.

"*Sorry*," said Demetrius, arms outstretched. "I can't see a thing."

"The caretakers must've already turned this hall down for the night," said Lessa. "They shouldn't be through here until morning, so at least we don't have to worry about being caught."

Arianna was at the rear of the group, relying on the glistening of the watery-blue bricked walls to steer her in the right direction.

There was a clang from up ahead. "Argh… we don't have *time* for this," muttered Jeom.

"He's right," said Arianna, focusing on the glint of his axe as he stumbled ahead of her. "Les, can you do the spell from before? We could use some more light."

Arianna couldn't help the bite in her voice, and she knew the jealousy restrained behind her words wouldn't be lost on Lessa— it wasn't that she withheld support for her friend, and she wasn't *proud* of her emotion, but she was eager to learn more about her new powers, too.

With the missing days from her memory, she felt as if she'd always be one step behind.

Lessa came toward her, big blue eyes bouncing about in the shadows.

"Why don't we try it together this time?" She reached for Arianna's hand. "I can teach you. You only need three words."

Arianna was grateful for the dark in this moment so that Lessa couldn't see how red her face had turned, a mix of shame and embarrassment taking over—but she admired her Lessa that much more; even at a time like this, her generosity remained steadfast.

"You just need to light one torch," said Arianna, hesitant. "We don't need the power of two for that."

"Even so," said Lessa. "Using just a little magic takes quite the effort. That much we know. Together we're stronger, and none of us can afford to be weakened right now."

She whispered the spell in Arianna's ear before she could object.

"Let's try for this one." Lessa placed her hand on the nearest torch along the wall.

Excited by the challenge and finally feeling useful, Arianna followed her lead.

"*Solza ven immito!*" they said in unison.

The words felt so right, sliding smoothly off Arianna's

tongue, yet the result was completely unexpected—as if the lifeforce had drained from her in an instant, the magic jolted through her arms and coursed to her fingertips until there was nothing left; one by one, the hallway was swept over in a bright pink glow, the flames of a hundred lanterns radiating down the long corridor.

Then her legs gave way, unable to hold her weight any longer, as she slowly sank to the cool floor. Beside her, Lessa had gone as pale as a ghost; she teetered backward into Jeom's open arms, and he carefully lowered her down as well.

"Thanks, Jeom," she said, trying to catch her breath. "That *wasn't* supposed to happen."

"This is why we can't trust magic," said Jeom. "You shouldn't use it so freely. You don't know what you're doing." He brushed Lessa's hair from her eyes.

"It's unpredictable, that's for sure," said Demetrius, kneeling down to check on Arianna. "Is there anything we can do to help?" He looked down the hall with an anxious expression. "We need to keep moving."

"Just give us a moment," said Arianna, leaning her head against the wall—she'd forgotten Solza in her rucksack, not quite used to this new addition yet; disturbed by the impact, the cub wriggled out and came to her side, purring loudly.

"Go *away*," she said, pushing it aside.

"She's just worried," said Demetrius.

"Somehow I doubt that," muttered Arianna, staring at the animal with disdain. As their eyes locked, she swore Solza's began to gleam more brightly than usual.

"Here, let me get you both some water," said Demetrius. "Maybe it'll help." He swung his pack down and began to look for the canteen.

Solza was still purring, and Arianna couldn't look away, entirely mesmerized by the animal.

Avatar.

Then the fog in her mind lifted, the vacuum of energy the spell had created inside of her beginning to fill with a completeness she just couldn't comprehend. Within seconds, she felt entirely recharged, as if she could perform the same spell twice over. *What in the world...?*

She looked at her hands with confusion.

"Here you are," said Demetrius, handing her the water.

"Thanks." She took it with a shaking hand, trying not to let him see her miraculous recovery. "I'm feeling... a lot better. Why don't you give some to Lessa? She looks a bit more affected by whatever that was."

"Sure thing." He left her alone with the cub.

Arianna studied Solza warily; she sat on her haunches and never took her gaze off her.

"Strange beasty you are," she whispered, not allowing herself to become sucked into its charm. She scooped her up and placed her gently back in the rucksack.

Then she went to check on Lessa.

"I don't know how that all happened," said Lessa as Jeom helped her to her feet; Sano stayed firmly on her shoulders. "You only focused on the one lantern, right?"

"I think so," said Arianna with a shrug. "Maybe I was just overly excited?"

"*Maybe*," said Lessa, clearly not convinced. She pressed her hand against the wall for support. "Whatever it was, we need to be more careful. I feel completely depleted."

"You shouldn't read off those scrolls anymore until you know *precisely* what you're doing," said Jeom. "What if this entire place had gone up in flames?"

"Oh, you're one to talk," said Demetrius. "We have yet to properly examine that axe of yours. Let's not forget what happened back in the forest."

They all eyed Jeom's weapon, its brilliant blend of gold, black, and silver metals sparkling under the firelight.

"What? This old thing?" he said, holding it up with a smirk.

"May I?" said Arianna in her nicest voice, curious to hold the enchanted weapon; it had impeded the dangerous magic she'd accidently let escape, yet none of them had any answers as to how or why.

"Oh, I suppose," said Jeom, though reluctantly—he'd yet to let any one of them touch his precious finding. "You did take one for the team."

He tossed it to Arianna, and she caught the staff with a warrior's precision.

"Ah!" She released her grip, the clang of the metal reverberating through the hall like a bell meant to signal their whereabouts. "Damn, it burned me."

The sound seemed to continue on forever, making her wince with each echo. She held her shaking hand at the wrist and saw it glowing a bright red.

"Of course it did," said Lessa, still seeming quite unwell.

"Of course it did, *what?*" said Arianna through clenched teeth as a blister immediately began to form on her skin.

"I'm just not surprised," said Lessa. She set down her things and began sifting through her rucksack. "The Axe of Crissy has been willed solely to Jeom, its rightful heir, and the inscription from Undor said it held peculiar powers. It's been welded with the 'essence of a dragon.'"

Jeom picked up the axe, gaping at it. "So..."

"So I'm not surprised that it's been enchanted to *burn* anyone but you. Another precaution to keep it from falling into the wrong hands."

"That makes one of us," said Demetrius. "Ara, are you all right?"

She shook her head, trying to hold back tears. "It *really* hurts. If I'd held on a moment longer, I think my hand would've fallen off."

"Here," said Lessa, pulling a tiny vial from her pack. She took a deep breath, visibly exhausted with every movement. "Let me see your hand."

She placed a droplet of liquid on Arianna's palm and began to speak the strange chants Talis had taught her. "*Helthra saludis emencia.*"

Arianna tried not to squirm as the magic mended her scalded skin. "Thank you, Les."

Lessa barely acknowledged her as she sank back down to the floor. Then she took out some of the food from Cyn they'd packed and shoveled it in her mouth.

"Sorry," she said with her mouth full. "It's the only thing I can think of to boost my energy back up." She pushed some of the food toward Arianna.

"No, I feel… fine, actually."

Lessa raised an eyebrow at her but didn't press.

Jeom and Demetrius were hunched over the axe, even more intrigued with it now than ever.

"We should probably hide this somehow before we meet Godfrey," said Demetrius. "Remember the attention it was getting in Draminet?"

"He's right," said Arianna. "We could benefit from being more discreet."

"Says the woman who just signaled to the entire well center that something's amiss in the east wing?" Jeom pulled the axe to his chest. "I'm not letting this out of my sight," he said.

Arianna scoffed but then glanced around, anxiously, listening for footsteps—so far, all was quiet. "Well, what do you reckon we do, then?"

"I have an idea." They all glanced to Lessa; the color was returning to her skin now and she seemed more awake.

"The axe seems to have a knack for protecting itself," she said, brushing the food crumbs off her robes and repacking her bag. "We saw its protective magic in Undor. Also when it fended off Arianna's spell, and just now when it burned her hand. Jeom just needs to learn how to control this power for himself, how it responds."

She held her hand out to him, and he pulled her up.

"What's the word for 'disguise' or 'hide' in the dwarf language?"

"It can't be that simple," said Arianna.

Lessa held her hands out to the side with a shrug. "We don't know unless we try. Besides, it seems magic can be just as simple as it can be complex." She pointed down the firelit corridor.

Jeom looked to Demetrius, unsure.

"I say give it a go," said Demetrius.

"Here goes nothing, then," he said.

The familiar heavy, low tones of the dwarf language rolled off his tongue—Arianna hadn't heard Jeom test these foreign words since the tunnels.

"*Hydfrömeh.*"

They all stood back, waiting.

Jeom huffed. "Anyone else have any other bright id—"

A ghostly wind suddenly poured into the hallway, and an unseen force ripped the Axe of Crissy from his grasp.

He shrieked, jumping back to stand with the others.

The axe began to spin, faster than the eye could keep up with, a whirl of golden dust surrounding it. Moments later, a plain, black, metal tube dropped out of the glittering cloud to the floor.

They all bent down for a closer look and saw a word scrawled in translucent ink.

"What does it say?" asked Arianna in a daze.

Jeom carefully picked up the tube, bringing it close to his face. "It says 'Reveal.'" He gazed at Lessa, admiration twinkling in his eyes. "How are you always right?"

She smiled.

"It's just a bit of logic," she said, tossing her hair back with a blush. "Every time you spoke that language back in the tunnels, the City of Undor reacted. And that axe seems to be the city's greatest treasure." She grew serious, thoughtful. "You shouldn't fear that side of you, you know? That's what the King wants."

The words hit home for Arianna… for all of them, it seemed, as a silence hovered in the air.

Never forget.

"Better not lose that now, brother," said Demetrius, handing him a small sack.

"Thanks," muttered Jeom, a bewildered expression on his face. He slipped the tube into the bag and tied it tightly to his belt. "Don't worry, I won't."

"*Maybe* we should be on our way, then," said Arianna, grabbing a lantern off the wall.

"Right," agreed Demetrius, "before one of these magic tricks wakes up the entire well center."

"Godfrey has to be down one of these halls," said Lessa. "Keep your eyes peeled for any clues."

They set off through the east wing, in search of a sign that Godfrey was near. After inspecting several corridors and well rooms to no success, they reached a door labeled '375.'

Like many of the occupied well rooms, a note had been nailed to the front of the door, scrawled in barely legible calligraphy; Arianna recognized the handwriting on sight.

"That's definitely Cyn's hand!" she said, stopping in front of the door. Her heart started racing.

Lessa squinted to read the messy note. "She left instructions to other caretakers that an occupant received healing for a broken leg." She did a little dance. "This has *got* to be him."

"Let's not waste time, then." Jeom made to open the door.

"Wait," said Arianna, putting a hand on his shoulder.

He tensed but turned back around—it was evident Jeom was eager to face this next chapter in their journey, but Arianna wondered if he wasn't even a bit scared at what they might encounter behind that door. *I'm terrified.*

Luck had guided them to Cyn, a friend, in this unforgiving land; what would exposing themselves to a complete stranger with a reputation for trouble offer as consequence?

Alas, it was their only lead to finding Ferlon Ragaric.

Arianna addressed her friends.

"I want to remind you all that this man may seem weak now, lying asleep in his well room, but let's not take Cyn's warning lightly. We can't let our guard down, not for a second. We're risking a lot here."

"You're absolutely right, Ara," said Demetrius, tightening his grip around his scythe. "Let's stick with what we agreed back in Draminet. Best not relinquish our true names. We've only just earned them."

They all nodded their agreement, and Arianna racked her brain for a new identity to use—nothing came to mind.

She considered each one of her friends then, their eyes glowing fierce by the light of the torch in her hand. She was certain they all felt it… that they were about to enter the maze of doors once again.

Jeom spoke the words they were clearly all thinking. "And if he deceives us? If he finds out who we really are?"

"Then, we kill him," said Arianna, without hesitation.

Just survive.

No one in the group so much as flinched at the statement. Backs against the wall, with no other option but to move forward through yet another door, they pushed it open and stepped inside the well room.

Shuffling into the tight space, the four gathered, shoulder to shoulder, at the foot of a single bed, the only furnishing save for a small shelf and bedside table; and the room would've been pitch black, if not for the torch washing the area in a dim light.

"What do we do now?" whispered Jeom, towering over the tiny bed.

Arianna maneuvered the torch so that they could see the face of the occupant—a scrawny man lay fast asleep and was snoring loudly, filling the entire well room with a deep, unsettling sound. His blankets were tangled around him, so much of him visible, and his black skin did nothing to hide the several shining bruises up and down his body; he looked *so* fragile, weak, skin hanging off his bones.

"*This* is Godfrey?" said Demetrius, stifling a laugh.

Arianna looked at him. "Remember what I said."

He nodded, but his expression remained skeptical.

"It looks as if they've heavily sedated him," said Lessa. "Likely in order to properly attend to his wounds."

"How can we wake him up?" said Arianna.

"Let me see…" Lessa shuffled through the vials on the shelf, muttering to herself. "Ah, *perfect.*" She picked up a green glass jar and poured its powdery contents into the palm of her shaking hand.

Then, she knelt down in front of Godfrey's face and blew. The powder instantly formed a cloud of green smoke, engulfing Godfrey from the neck up and settling on his wrinkled face.

"Wake up," she whispered.

On Godfrey's next inhale, the powder was sucked into his lungs, and he jolted awake; beady eyes popped open, taking them all in, alert.

Arianna opened her mouth to speak, preparing to try out a false identity. "Are you Godfrey, sir? My name is—"

He plugged his ears.

"When I want to know your name, I'll ask for it," he said in a tired, squeaky voice. "All I need to know from you now is what you want from *me.* Then I'll tell you my price."

This is definitely the right man.

He looked them up and down, calculating. His probing eyes settled on Arianna, and she wondered what he was thinking.

"And, from the looks of it, your *names* will be only a fraction of the payment."

Instinctively, Arianna stepped back to hide her face in the

shadows—she could've shaved her head for all she cared; she was still Arianna Belvedor.

Taking a deep breath, she answered him. "We need to find a man who goes by the name of Ferlon Ragaric. Do you know of him?"

Godfrey smiled, his eyes burning with curiosity. "Don't insult me," he said. "Of course I do."

"Well, can you help us find him?" said Demetrius.

"I certainly am able."

Arianna wasn't yet convinced.

"But first things first," he said, slowly sitting up. "I need to get some food in me. Have anything?"

He looked at them hungrily, lanky limbs and all; Arianna could hardly believe people feared such a fragile person as Cyn had suggested. If she wanted, she could snap him like a twig without even touching her weapons.

No one spoke.

"Right stiff bunch you all are! Well, we better get going then before that bloody caretaker tries to prod me with more needles. This place is worse than the Jar."

Arianna let out a snort—clearly, he'd forgotten what the districts were like if he truly thought as much. And if he spoke ill of Cyn again, he'd earn another broken leg.

"Mind stepping out while I dress?" He threw the blanket back with no shame at his nakedness.

They all shielded their eyes, stumbling into the hall as his laughter trailed behind them.

"This is it," whispered Arianna outside of the door. "We're going to finally find *real* freedom. I can feel it."

Alas, her lie didn't even fool her; they all stared at each other in silence as they waited, the fear palpable at what other dangers might lay ahead for them. Without even knowing, this mysterious Godfrey held their lives in his hands—and they hoped he'd never find out.

Finally, he exited the well room, wobbling slowly with the help of a crooked cane; Arianna noticed the way his legs contorted. She wondered how on earth he had made it past the Free Falls alive—not to mention years of training.

It was common knowledge that people born *different* could survive in this world; King Devlindor didn't discriminate, as long as one proved their worth when thrown to the ultimate test. But it just seemed so unlikely that someone like him could've endured such a challenge.

Then again, Arianna had to admit there were other things to value beyond just physical strength and skill with a weapon. She was quickly learning that the human body was capable of so much more than what had been taught to her in the Warrior's District. And here they were, asking this fragile-looking man for help.

Does that make us the weaker ones?

"Follow me," said Godfrey in a sharp voice. "We can discuss your request after we're out of here."

Arianna nodded, taking the lead for her friends as he guided them past two snoozing regulators at the well center entrance and onto the street.

Arianna savored the cool night breeze, the fresh air awakening her senses and reviving her from what seemed like a sleeping death. In the mere two days she'd been conscious, time had passed in a sort of surreal fashion. She hadn't *really* registered where she was in this world. Though, now, it was made perfectly clear—she and her friends had escaped the Four Corners, and the secrets of the City of South Luose awaited them.

ALL THE ILLUSIONS

IT WAS DARK, but lamps lined the narrow, cobblestone streets and flames flickered in windows with pearly white shutters; they could see the shadows of the city as they walked. Arianna wondered how far the paved paths went and what mysteries lay behind each one of the doors they passed as they followed in Godfrey's footsteps.

So this is South Luose...

She wrinkled up her nose as a mixture of strange, new aromas scented the air. Brown grass crept through cracks in the pavement, nature's growth halted by the city development; and some of the buildings lining their path, mostly made of beautiful burgundy blocks and overhanging roofs, were so tall that Arianna couldn't see anything of the forest (though she knew it lay just beyond the city gates).

While some of the city structures stood tall, towering over their heads, others remained at ground level, decorated with flowers and greenery from the forest; it was evident, eventually, that the taller buildings were sleeping quarters and the smaller ones reserved for various functions—workshops, eateries, markets, and the like.

The wind caressed her cheeks, and she embraced it. Cold, yet not so frigid as her former home had been. And the subtle sound of music and voices trickled to her ears from somewhere nearby.

Looking toward the noise, Arianna spotted two women sneak a kiss in an alleyway before going their separate ways. She stared after them, wondering what it was they were hiding from… citizens were free, after all, to do what they pleased.

She glanced back to take in the well center from a new perspective. It was monumental compared to the crumbling building in the Warrior's District she'd grown accustomed to. But, as she drew her gaze all the way to the top, another structure in the distance caught her attention—a grand building, with towers stretching into the air, stood watch over the entire city, high upon a hill.

It looked to be at the other edge of South Luose, far enough away that Arianna couldn't even see where the city walls ended on that side. And a line of trees encircled the towers, as if the forest had broken its way back in, crowned roofs peeping out through a canopy of red leaves. She recognized it from the portraits in the well center: the Palace of South Luose.

"This place is massive," said Arianna, realizing she hadn't a clue at just how big Olleb-Yelfra might actually be. "Think we'll ever get to see the palace? It looks so grand."

Lessa chuckled, slowing with Arianna so that they fell to the rear of the group.

"Not likely," she said. "That's where the city keeper lives, Honorable Helix Kassime. Other noble citizens will have palace positions, too… councilmen, prominent elders, masters of their trade, and the like. The South Luose highlifes."

"That's what my life can be redeemed for," whispered

Arianna. It was surreal to see what it meant for herself.

Lessa nodded. "Though, it won't."

Arianna wanted to smile, to pretend she was as optimistic as her friend, but her gaze settled upon a large poster of her own face, tacked to the side of a building. 'Wanted: Dead or Alive,' it read.

Lessa grabbed her hand and they hurried past it, trying to ignore its looming threat. Arianna pulled up her hood and cast her eyes down.

Wanted—dead or alive.

The words bounced around her head for the rest of the walk, her thoughts jumbling along with them.

What would I have done if I were on the other side?

Her head was worth a palace position, a life full of ease and riches, and a part of her empathized with the people hoping to claim that reward. She wanted to say she would've looked the other way. But it was hard to really know how desperate she might've been if the situation were reversed... if she'd never learned the incredible secrets they'd uncovered in the mountains and if she'd walked the normal path of a citizen of Olleb-Yelfra.

Arianna had once been excited to discover more about that life beyond the Jar—the Learning Center hadn't covered much on the neighboring cities or their leaders, her teachings restricted to what were deemed 'basic human skills.' She'd sat through a lifetime's worth of lessons about King Devlindor and his rule over the world from the High City, but only citizens were privy to knowledge beyond him; upon receipt of citizenship and a work placement she would have been finally allowed to know 'everything.'

She laughed to herself, knowing that she'd already learned much more about the world than she'd bargained for, *far* more than any citizen here could ever understand.

Her thoughts shifted to Lessa, who always seemed to have the answers to everything. "How did you come to learn so much about the outside world while in the districts?"

"Talis and his books," said Lessa. "I know a lot of things, about a lot of people, that I guess I shouldn't."

"Like what else?" Arianna was hungry to learn as much as possible—it felt as if the world was unfurling wider before her with each step down this new road, and she desperately wanted to keep up.

"Actually, while you were sleeping, I studied a bit more about the Golden Age from the scrolls," she said, slowing her pace to be sure Godfrey couldn't overhear. "Did you know that all the major provinces of Olleb-Yelfra, including this South Luose, used to be actual kingdoms? Before Devlindor instated himself as 'High King,' all these cities used to be governed by their own kings, and even *queens*, with entire royal family bloodlines."

Her eyes sparkled with the information.

"There was a time where they all ruled peacefully, as neighbors and friends."

"What happened?" said Arianna, hardly able to comprehend that she walked as a fugitive through the streets of a once glorious kingdom.

"You know what happened." Lessa turned serious. "King Devlindor took control by force with large armies and black magic. Magic forbidden even then. All of the royal families were wiped out until the only one left was his. Then he chose people to put in power that he knew he could control. He completely changed the natural order." She looked to the sky. "And so, here we are."

Arianna let out a long sigh. "Yes, here we are."

Never forget.

Knowledge was a powerful, valuable thing; she knew now that the world had not started with King Devlindor. He'd restricted their lessons in the districts and told half-truths to those deemed citizens, trying to erase a history written in blood—there was value in 'knowing.'

But Arianna had also come to find that, just like anything else of value, knowledge came at a price.

Solomon is dead.

He had died to protect not just her but the truth. And such sacrifice was more valuable than anything.

While under his tutelage, Arianna had lived and breathed a rigid plan, one defined by the goal of belonging to the world outside the Four Corners—that plan, one never realized, ran through her head now as she walked the streets of a city she was not welcome to.

Earn a placement as a regulator in a reputable city. Work from there to be instated as a palace guard or personal protector for high-ranking citizens... highlifes.

An inflexible checklist of achievements she had to attain in order to feel worthwhile; not everyone did, but most stayed the course they were trained to do. And so would she. Rising as a known warrior of the Olleb, the grand plan ended with her titled as a master, just like Solomon Bell.

"*Pff.*" She couldn't stop the sound blowing out of her mouth. *What a fool I was.*

She had wasted so much time following the crowd, dedicating her life to a path that had been laid out for her by an evil and undeserving king.

But what path was she on now?

Arianna felt as if the streets began to close in on her as they walked, the beautiful buildings suddenly looming like monsters from a bad dream. Somewhere deep down, this strange world, this façade of freedom, was something she wished to turn real.

She sensed the child she used to be struggling to return and melt back into the structured and simple way of her past, to stand in these streets proudly and free. But life had drastically shifted now, and this peaceful moment in time was nothing more than an illusion.

Arianna didn't have ownership of the polished buildings or

the paved pathways under her feet. She didn't have a work placement or advanced training to look forward to. And she couldn't
even be herself or use her own name in a place that seemed to
promise such a lovely life. *Don't be daft! That life isn't real. It's a
lie… all a lie. Never forget.*

The old Arianna wished to turn back time, to never have
veered off track in the first place, but her present and future self
just couldn't allow it. Although it would've been an easier existence to have stayed blind to the truth, the lure of the sparkling
tunnels and the strange magic she'd uncovered within herself
called to her now; and she yearned for the thrill of learning a new
enchanted secret.

I'm a warrior… and I'm a witch. That is my truth.

With her fists balled at her sides, eyes to the star-studded
night sky, she embraced her new path and let the ignorance of
her childhood drift away.

"Pick up the pace!" barked Godfrey, snapping her out of her
daze. "We don't have all night." He hurried ahead, surprising
everyone with his speed—cane, crooked legs, and all.

"You all right back there?" said Demetrius, glancing over his
shoulder.

"Yes, everything is as it should be," said Arianna, gripping
tight this realization.

"Well, come on then," said Jeom, waving them forward. "I
want to get to where we're going."

The girls hurried along behind them, but Arianna could
hardly keep up for how heavy a load she was carrying—Solza
wasn't exactly light. She stayed at the rear, watching her friends
closely, their silver robes sweeping at their feet.

Just then, several sets of hooves came into her line of sight
from up ahead. She looked up to find a herd of city regulators
patrolling the streets on the backs of large horses. She was about
to draw her swords when Godfrey spoke.

"Nice night." He tilted his hat to them as they passed.

Jeom froze, his fingers cupping the concealed axe at his belt. Lessa twitched toward her arrows, and Demetrius' grip on his scythe stayed sure.

"Hope you're not headed into any trouble," said the lead regulator, barely paying him a glance.

"Me? Trouble?" said Godfrey with a sly grin. "Why, I wouldn't dare."

The others in the group chuckled under their breath, but the lead regulator chose not to engage. He looked past him to Arianna and her friends.

"It's good to see some fresh faces in the city," he said—Arianna wished hers would melt away under his scrutiny.

Please don't recognize me.

"Enjoy the end of Transition Week. And don't drink yourselves silly now."

There was an uncomfortable moment of silence.

"We'll try not to… sir," said Jeom, in a squeaky voice.

The regulator smiled, gave a courteous nod, and then led the group away down the street.

Jeom sounded as if he'd been holding his breath the entire time for how he deflated once they'd gone. And Lessa's hand was shaking when she let it fall back to her side.

Arianna let out a silent sigh, not wanting to alert Godfrey to their situation. But she just couldn't get used to this topsy-turvy version of the Olleb.

What dangers could be hidden in the streets of a city that seemed to be exempt from the brutality of the Four Corners? Where was she in the world that even regulators proved cordial now?

Demetrius caught her eye, his own wide and nervous. She offered him a calming smile, fixed her hood so that even more of her face was covered, and walked to the front of the group; Godfrey continued to lead them through the streets without hardly a pause in his step. Then, finally, he came to a stop somewhere in the center of the city.

The South Luose Well Center had vanished from sight, and high buildings on either side of the narrow streets surrounded them.

"This will be it," he said, showing off a rickety door to a small building in a somewhat hidden alleyway.

Arianna studied their final destination; barrels stacked upon barrels at the entryway, and the sound of music became apparent as a band played to a lively crowd. She noticed it leaned up against a taller building with small balconies sprouting out at every level, and candlelight spilled onto the street from a few open windows.

"A tavern?" said Lessa, warily, looking it over.

"Don't be shy," said Godfrey, reaching for the door handle. "We can have a chat inside."

He disappeared through the door, leaving them alone to follow, or...

"We can still turn back and flee the city before sunrise," said Lessa, chewing on her lip.

Arianna knew she must be thinking of the last tavern they'd fled, the villagers of Draminet rallying against them in their wake.

"No," said Jeom, stamping his foot. "No more running."

"Maybe we can make a life here?" agreed Demetrius, clearly tempted by the city. "We have a chance here... if he helps us."

Arianna still wasn't completely convinced by Godfrey's promise—the 'if' not comforting in the slightest. But she stood by their earlier decision; they had to try.

"I don't know if this is right," she said. "I don't know what's right or wrong anymore these days, but I do know that if we leave now, we'll never know if Godfrey is telling the truth or not. We may have an opportunity to find Ferlon Ragaric."

"It may be the *only* opportunity," added Demetrius.

Lessa still seemed so unsure. "And what if he lies? Right now, he's got the upper hand. He knows more than we do. We just can't trust him."

Arianna put a hand on Lessa's shoulder. "Nobody knows more than we do," she said, "but that doesn't mean we can do this alone."

"He may lead us to Ragaric for only a payment of silver," said Jeom. Arianna remembered the coinage from Undor still in her pockets. "This is a risk worth taking."

"Or he may give us up to the King for a much bigger reward," said Lessa. "I just want to make sure we appreciate the entire picture before we move through those doors. I didn't... until now." She looked to Arianna. "Are you *sure* you want to do this? I'm with you either way."

Arianna gave a firm nod. "Solomon's guidance is our last hope, and this man is the one thing that possibly connects us to that hope," she said, a passion behind her words. "If we leave now, who can we trust? Where will we go? Ferlon Ragaric is here, somewhere in *this* city. We must go and find him."

"Yes, you're right," said Lessa, her shoulders slumping. "I know we have to, at least, try. But, if anything happens—"

"If anything happens, then we fight back," said Arianna, hands on her hips.

Her courage never faltered; she'd already accepted the risk they were about to take back in the well center.

"We'll figure it out. Just like we always do." She glanced to the door. "Besides, Godfrey doesn't scare me one bit."

"Really?" said Demetrius, raising an eyebrow. "He scares me enough."

Lessa nodded her agreement, making sure Sano was properly tucked away in her robes. Then, she fixed Arianna's pack so that Solza couldn't be seen.

"Let's get this over with," said Jeom, puffing up his chest as they all readied themselves for the future. It was here now, no stopping it.

Arianna pushed open the doors to the tavern. Light flooded onto the dark street, placing them in a spotlight as they lingered in the doorway. Wooden tables and benches were scattered all about the room, and groups of men and women gathered over mugs of ale and wine, the stench of smoke and alcohol overwhelming.

There was music, too, alluring sounds that Arianna had never heard before in her life (though her own singing voice wasn't *that* bad compared to some of her peers in the districts). Her eyes were drawn to where a small band played in a dimly lit corner, offering the final note to their performance. They gave the floor to a handsome young man with a shoddy guitar—as soon as his fingers touched the strings, slowly strumming the instrument, scattered couples rose to their feet and began rocking back and forth in each other's arms, lost to the music.

Arianna became lost, too, the somber sound unnerving yet intoxicating as he hummed to a familiar melody.

"Don't be brave, little slave…" he sang.

Arianna's heart skipped a beat, feeling his voice as her own.

Be a warrior.

9

EDUCATION

THE MUSIC CAME TO A SUDDEN HALT as the boy with the guitar caught Arianna's eye. Then she felt all the blood rush to her face as the entire bar turned to look them over.

"Eh, look what we got here. Fresh meat in town! Is it still Transition Week?" said a woman, slurring every word.

"'Course it is!" said her friend, swiping the drink from her hand. "You've been drunk the entire time. Still two more days left."

The woman cackled, snatching back her mug and raising it to Arianna and her friends before she drank. Several others also lifted their cups to welcome them, and then the music and chatter began again.

"Over here, kids."

Arianna almost hadn't noticed Godfrey, standing in the shadows. He ushered them to a table in the back, so she led the way across the room, trying not to look anyone else directly in the eyes. A husky man stepped into their path just as they were about to approach the table.

His muscles seemed too big for his body, and he was clearly drunk from the way he swayed back and forth on his feet. He pushed straight through their group, angrily waving his fist at Godfrey.

"You got no business being here, snake!" he shouted. "Best move along before you find yourself back in the well center."

"Is that a threat, Harrin?" said Godfrey, moving to face him. "The snake is the *King's* mark, so I take it you were offering me a compliment."

Harrin's face turned the same dark red as the wine in his cup. "You little bastard! Why I ought to—"

"Best not forget what I know about you." Godfrey smiled with cracked lips, his words quiet but sharp. "Would be quite the shame if I let something… slip."

"Can't talk if I rip your tongue out!" Harrin made to lunge for him, but a young woman lingering nearby chose that moment to intervene.

"That's enough, Harrin! Time to get on home." He immediately calmed in her presence. "That's it, go on. I'll see you next week."

He tipped his hat to her and stumbled out the door, though not before flashing Godfrey one last glare over his shoulder.

"My, my," said Godfrey, clicking his tongue at the woman after he'd gone. "That was quite unexpected. And in front of my guests, no less." He gestured to Arianna and her friends.

"Sorry about that," she said, fidgeting with her apron. "He's just had one too many tonight. Wasn't in his right mind." She laughed it off, though Arianna didn't buy it—her voice shook on every syllable.

Lessa tried to speak up. "It's really no prob—"

Godfrey held up his hand, narrowing his gaze at the woman. "*Don't* let it happen again."

She looked to her feet. "Certainly… very sorry, sir."

"Wonderful," said Godfrey, sounding much too cheerful for how uncomfortable everyone looked. "Now, Myrisa, be a dear and bring us all your finest ale and bread. On the house, of course."

Even now, his words were threatening, but Arianna just couldn't understand why this poor girl quivered so much in his presence; Myrisa was extremely tall, maybe twice the size of Godfrey, yet she was too nervous to even meet his eyes.

"But…" she said in barely a whisper.

"But nothing unless you want to lose your placement," he snapped, stepping closer to her. "We both know I've been paying your dues to keep this place afloat. What would Gabriel say when he gets back and finds the tavern has gone out of business? Better yet, what would our keeper say about you neglecting payment to the Crown? Probably worth a *few* nights in the dungeons, I'd wager."

Myrisa nodded without another word and hurried to wipe down the table, Godfrey's eyes on her the entire time.

"I'll bring everything right out," she said after the table was cleared.

Godfrey sat first, followed by Demetrius and Jeom. But as Arianna and Lessa made to sit down, Godfrey put his cane out to stop them.

"Not you," he said. "This is a man's conversation."

Arianna was so stunned by this blunt segregation she didn't immediately react, but Lessa looked ready to pummel him in the face.

"Follow me," said Myrisa, gently guiding them away before another fight could ensue.

Arianna clenched her fists at her side and was about to say something off color, but Demetrius caught her eye, shaking his head.

"Don't make a scene," he whispered through a smile.

Jeom swiveled around to face her. "We'll be fine."

His expression told her they would be *very* careful in this conversation; she needn't say it.

She and Lessa, reluctantly, followed Myrisa to the bar on the other side of the room, the boy's conversation with Godfrey lost to the muddled hum of the tavern.

"Please, have a seat," said Myrisa, pulling out two stools.

Then, she went around the bar and cleaned off a couple glasses. With shaking hands, she poured Lessa and Arianna ale and offered them plates of warm bread and stew.

"You don't have to do that," said Lessa, clearly feeling sorry for her.

"It's my pleasure," she said, pushing the provisions forward with a smile—it was insincere; Arianna saw her gaze drift behind them to Godfrey's table.

"Well, thanks… I guess," said Arianna, nudging Lessa to dig in. She wasn't about to turn away free food, unsure of where their next meal would even come from.

Myrisa hovered near them as they ate, absentmindedly preparing food and drink to serve to Godfrey, Jeom, and Demetrius. She had a gentle demeanor about her… weak, Arianna thought. Certainly not a warrior's make.

I wonder what district she's from?

"So… Myrisa is it?" said Lessa in her kindest voice, trying to start a conversation; Arianna could tell this whole situation sat very uneasily with her.

"Myrisa Lang," she said, quietly. Then she looked up, finally meeting their eyes. "But… friends call me Mya. Yourselves?" She smiled again, more genuinely this time.

Lessa returned a bright smile of her own. "This is Ari—"

No numbers, no names!

Arianna immediately interjected with the first thing that came to mind. "Pippa. My name is Pippa," she said, kicking Lessa underneath the bar. "Pleasure to meet you, Mya."

This is going to be harder than we thought.

Arianna shoved a spoonful of stew into her mouth, and Lessa looked ready to drown herself in her drink as Mya looked to her for her name.

"Uh, my name is… *Grinda*," said Lessa, wincing as the word popped out of her mouth.

Arianna resisted the urge to kick her twice, taking a big drink instead.

"Pleased to meet you both," said Mya, too distracted by what she was doing to notice how oddly they were acting.

"So, do you run this place alone, then?" said Arianna, wanting to change topics.

She shook her head.

"I'm just keeping watch for my partner, Gabriel, right now. He's traveling to learn more of his trade, but he's supposed to come back soon." She glanced toward a calendar on the wall. "We were paired right before he was due to leave."

"What district are you from?" asked Lessa.

"I was placed here from the Ag District just a few years ago," she said, drying off three mugs. "The first owner of the tavern was Gabe's advanced trainer for several years, but he became too old. He fulfilled his time and was taken to the After Ward just recently."

A frown crossed her face at the memory.

"He left this dreadful place to Gabe, and now I'm stuck with keeping it afloat until he returns." She slammed the mugs down on a tray and filled them to the brim with ale.

"What exactly happens at the After Ward?" whispered Arianna, recalling that frightful corridor in the well center.

Mya lowered her voice, as if out of respect.

"It's where we all inevitably end up in old age," she said, "after we're no longer useful to the Olleb. Gabriel's master was a great man, and he worked hard his entire life to train others in his craft. He deserved a good, fair departing like that." She was nodding to herself. "It's hard-earned, you know, to make it that far in this world."

Arianna pondered her words, chilled by the inevitable ending that was certain death—no matter how far they ran to avoid it.

"But what does *this* have to do with your training in the Agrarian's District?" said Lessa, looking around the crowded bar. "I mean, serving drunken folks doesn't exactly seem to connect for me."

"Oh, you are so new, aren't you? Someone has to do this work," Mya said with a laugh. "You'd be surprised where some people are placed outside of the Jar. The Olleb isn't as black and white as the districts make it seem." She topped off their drinks. "Think of it as a 'Forty-Four *Hundred* Corners,' if you will, with even more variety and rules than before."

She rolled her eyes at her own statement.

"But I actually do use a lot of my district training, I'll have you believe." She was growing excited at the conversation. "I tend a garden just out back that serves as the produce for this tavern, and I can sell it in the markets or use it for trade. We ag-slaves also learned patience better than any other district, I'd wager." She began scooping steaming stew into three bowls on the tray. "*Trust* me. That really comes in handy when dealing with sloshed patrons like Harrin."

She sniggered, surveying the crowded bar and its rowdy regulars.

"You'll see when you start to integrate into the city," she said, lifting the tray. "You may not immediately understand how your talents tie into what your assignments are, but you will soon. Things just fall into place how they're supposed to, and you'll continue to learn."

"I see," said Lessa, sipping her drink. She and Arianna exchanged glances. "I sure hope you're right."

"Excuse me a moment," said Mya. She took a deep breath and then carried the tray over to Godfrey's table.

When she returned, she seemed a lot more at ease.

"So what placements did you lot earn, then?" she asked, busying about the bar. "Hopefully you'll pass your placement tests and not get demoted to a lower station in your first weeks. If you get demoted more than three times, well… you know."

"No, I don't know," said Arianna, listening intently. "What happens?"

This was really the first taste of true citizen life she'd had, and she was glad Mya couldn't seem to stop rambling.

"The festivals just aren't as foolproof as they'd have you believe," she explained as she wiped down the counter. "Sometimes weaklings do slip through the cracks. But they don't last too long in the real world."

Mya slid a finger across her neck, and Arianna was a little taken aback.

Mya didn't miss her reaction. "I'm quite surprised they haven't covered that bit yet during the new-citizen ceremonies." She cocked her head to the side, studying her.

Arianna looked away. "Yes, um, maybe tomorrow they will," she said.

She knows!

It was hard enough to lie about a fake identity as a fugitive, but Arianna hadn't realized how many details they were missing out on about being a citizen from not taking part in Transition Week; they needed to catch up fast.

Lessa chimed in, trying to steer the talk in a different direction as Arianna stuffed a chunk of bread into her mouth.

"So when will he return… your partner, Gabriel was it?" she said. "How do those pairings work, exactly?"

Arianna had heard the concept of 'pairings' before in the Learning Center. She knew, at the very least, it was how people were expected to reproduce, how she came to have life in the first place. But this was the first time she ever had a glimpse into a real partnership; she leaned in to listen, knowing well that the more they learned, the better chance they stood at survival.

Alas, Mya clammed up, abruptly excusing herself to tend to other customers.

"What do you suppose that was all about?" said Arianna as she and Lessa watched Mya buzz around the tavern.

Lessa just shrugged, tearing off bits of bread and sneaking them to Sano.

"Maybe I struck a nerve?" she said. She pushed a napkin toward Arianna. "Better save some of that meat for Solza."

Arianna sighed, swiftly wrapping up some of the chunks and setting it aside for later. Then they turned their attention to the boys, still deep in conversation.

"You shouldn't have that animal in here!" said Mya in a low voice, taking them off guard as she came back to the bar.

Lessa jumped, swiveling back in her chair. "Oh… you saw? I didn't… he's harmless." Her smile wavered as Sano's head disappeared back into her bag.

Arianna froze with her drink to her lips, hoping Mya hadn't noticed Solza sleeping inside her rucksack; she certainly wasn't harmless.

"That's *not* what I meant. It's against the law."

Her eyes were practically bulging from her head, and she nodded behind the bar where a plaque hung as a centerpiece on the wall—the golden snake of the King's Crest glistened bright on the engraved metal.

Lessa's mouth formed an 'O'.

"You should know the laws," said Mya, firmly. "They're given to you at the commencement of your citizenship. Animals are not tolerated as companions… as it should be."

She stood there with an accusatory glare, hands on her hips, awaiting an explanation.

"Oh, of course not," said Lessa with nervous laughter, hiding Sano away. "I only… forgot. Found him in the forest just tonight and don't know what to do with him… *it*."

Mya sighed, nodding as if she understood.

"Sell it, skin it, *anything*. Just get rid of it," she said. "If anyone even suspects that thing is more than money in your pocket, you're going to be in for some hurt. Punishment is worse here than in the districts, so best not get in the habit of breaking the laws just because you're feeling invincible after the Free Falls."

She lightened up her tone.

"Listen, I get that you're new here. I get you're fresh from the Jar thinking that now you can finally relax and bend and break the boundaries a bit. I was new, too, and it's only been a few years since my festivals," she said. "It feels like you can do anything now that you've earned your freedom. But… you never *really* forget, do you?" She looked down to her hands. "Nothing's much changed."

Then she leaned over the bar, eyes wide and serious.

"Don't disobey the rules," she said, "and if you must, don't get caught."

Her voice trailed off as her mind wandered elsewhere, her eyes flicking to Godfrey. Then she turned away from them, standing on her tiptoes to reach for glasses on a high shelf; Arianna couldn't help but stare as her shirt rose up to the middle of her back—bright red scars showed clearly on her olive skin, painting a better picture of the true South Luose.

Never forget.

Contemplating Mya's warnings and this city with new understanding, Arianna zoned into the guitarist's tempting tune. For a moment, they both locked eyes again, and he seemed to falter cords. But then he played on flawlessly.

Arianna studied him, wanting to distract herself from the fear that was rising again in her stomach—he looked a bit rougher than the rest of the crowd, with short hair and a little bit of stubble on his face. His tan skin reminded her of her own, except with the addition of warm, golden tones that could only come from healthy doses of sunlight. And his piercing green eyes were almost as hard to ignore as his music.

As the melody grew louder, his voice and his words seemed to actually penetrate Arianna's fears, strengthening her against an uncertain tomorrow.

Just survive.

She felt a hand against the middle of her back, and the good feeling vanished.

"Three whiskeys, please." She turned to find Jeom hovering behind her.

"Coming right up," said Mya, disappearing behind the bar without so much as a glance in his direction.

Arianna was impatient to hear all that had been discussed with Godfrey this past hour. "So, what's going on, then? Hurry, before she comes back."

Lessa leaned in, too.

"He does know where we can find Ferlon Ragaric," said Jeom. "He says he can take us to him at the end of Transition Week, when the fuss of the festivities dies down. Apparently, he's in a bit of a high station, but that's all he'd say."

Arianna felt her hopes soar with Jeom's words.

Thank you, Solomon.

"That's just a couple more days!" said Lessa, quietly clapping her hands.

Jeom gave a tight smile, tapping his fingers on the bar.

"What did he ask for in return? What's the price?" said Arianna.

"He didn't ask for anything… *yet,*" he said. "Not even our names, oddly enough. He just suggested that we stay in the inn above the tavern while he gets a message to the bloke."

"Really, that's all?" Lessa cocked her head to the side.

"It does seem odd," said Arianna, pursing her lips.

"Well, he did also ask why we weren't staying in the new-citizen dwellings," said Jeom. "We just told him that we weren't placed anywhere yet while you healed at the well center. He seemed to believe us, but it's hard to tell. He's definitely a shady character."

Mya came over with his drinks at that moment, so they lowered their voices.

"Demetrius and I are just trying to stay on his good side right now," he said, clearly annoyed. "And that means drinking with the brute, unfortunately. We're done talking business for tonight. He said the price will come later, once he's kept up his end of the bargain. We don't have much to work with here, so we just accepted to be in his debt if he gave us access to Ragaric."

"That seems… fair enough," said Arianna, unsure. "We won't pay until he delivers."

"That's the deal," said Jeom, though his frown didn't help ease her worries.

"Well, just be careful," said Lessa, poking him in the chest. "And don't get too drunk! Keep your head on straight."

"Same goes for you girls," he said, nodding to Mya as she refilled their drinks. "Right, and he said to talk to Myrisa about lodging for the night."

"Thanks for taking one for the team," said Arianna, patting him on the back.

He grumbled something unintelligible and then returned to his table with the drinks.

"You can stay in the inn as long as you like," said Mya, overhearing the last of the conversation. "I've got a few rooms available, and if you're mixed up with that one—" she glanced at Godfrey "—I'm sure you could use a helpful hand."

"Oh, that would be lovely!" said Lessa.

"Yes, thank you very much," said Arianna, suddenly realizing how exhausted she was. "We should… um, be placed in regular city dwellings soon, so we won't be in your hair for too long. I think we'll just need two rooms, and we can pay you, of course."

She pulled out one of the silver coins they had plucked from the City of Undor and handed it to her.

"That's strange coinage," Mya said with a gasp, turning it over in her fingers. "Where does it come from?"

"We... found it," said Lessa. "In the forest outside the city."

"It must be rare, then!" said Mya. "Certainly worth more than a few nights' stay. Are you sure you want to part with it? I can include provisions as well."

Arianna didn't miss the enthusiasm in her voice, and she wondered how much just one coin might *actually* be worth in this world. But that was a question for later. Right now, they just needed a safe place to sleep.

"Certainly, please take it," said Arianna, knowing they had more than enough to spare. "It's yours, if you can take care of us for a little while... until we figure out the city."

"We had an unusual beginning to Transition Week," said Lessa, "as Ara... *err*, Pippa was injured in the travels."

Arianna wanted to slap her hand across Lessa's mouth.

"Oh, my! No wonder you seem so lost," said Mya with bright eyes. She pocketed the coin happily. "Don't worry, I'll take good care of you, then."

She leaned across the bar, waving to try to get someone's attention. Her voice carried over the loud buzz of the tavern.

"Eli, can you come here a second, please?"

The music ceased.

Arianna turned on her stool to see that Mya was calling to the guitarist; he had the stride of a warrior as he walked over to them, and Arianna knew instantly he must be a former slave from her district. He handed his instrument off to another in the tavern, and soon a much more upbeat tune filled the room.

"Mya, I was right in the middle of some of my best work!" said Eli, jokingly, a wide grin on his face. "What's all the fuss for?"

His speaking voice held the same allure as it did when he sang, and Arianna found his looks to be just as beguiling now that she saw him up close. He glanced her way and she shifted her eyes down, trying to hide her reddening cheeks behind her hair—though her short, new style proved a lot less practical for this move.

"I know, I know. It was *beautiful*," said Mya, too excited by the silver in her pocket to care. "I want to introduce you to Pippa and Grinda. They'll be our *very* special guests for a few nights since they had a bit of a funny start to Transition Week. They're with the two new citizens over there… and Godfrey."

Eli groaned at the mention of his name, assessing Arianna and Lessa with something more like suspicion now.

"Can you please see to it that they have a couple of rooms made up and show them around a bit? They've paid upfront," she said. Then she narrowed her eyes at him. "Treat them well, Eli."

"Sure thing," he said, leaning over to give her a polite kiss on the cheek.

Mya blushed, bidding them goodnight as she scurried back to her duties.

"Follow me, ladies," said Eli, leading them out of the bar and around the corner toward the lofty building that overhung the tavern.

Reluctantly, Lessa and Arianna left the Kane brothers to handle their futures and went with Eli to inspect their sleeping situation.

"So… *Pippa*, is it? Funny name." Eli pushed open a door.

"Yes," snapped Arianna, feeling a pang of guilt for her slain friend.

"And Grinda?" His voice sounded skeptical.

"That's right," said Lessa—her nerves were practically radiating off her body as they followed him inside the building.

"Well, if you need anything at all, I'll be around," he said after a moment. "Mya saves me a space here in exchange for help at the bar. I'm normally traveling, but I'm at your beck and call for now, I guess."

He looked over his shoulder at the girls as he led them up a tall stairwell, flashing a disarming smile.

Arianna wouldn't let her guard down, though. She hated that they had met so many new people before reaching Ferlon or before they had some sort of plan.

"Thanks," she forced out. "And what do you do when you're… traveling? You're free to just leave at your leisure?"

"Of course!" he said with a laugh. "We're citizens now. You can do whatever you want within the bounds of the law. But most people don't travel unless their placement requires it. Life's just easier that way, I think, for some."

He shrugged his shoulders, running his hand along the railing as they climbed past several floors.

"That kind of life bores me, though. I *crave* adventure."

"And what's your placement then, to require so much travel?" said Lessa.

"I *was* a city regulator, but I'm not anymore," said Eli, casually. "Not really, anyway. Sometimes I'll take a post here and there, though, as necessary to maintain my lifestyle."

Arianna almost stumbled backward, clutching the railing tight for support.

"Oh," was all Lessa thought to say in response.

She and Arianna locked eyes, both surely thinking the same thing.

He won't be earning our trust for one second.

"I just love to travel," he continued, not noticing the change of atmosphere. "Not too far, but I'll visit other cities, looking for work where I can. I want to see the world, you know? But I haven't made it *quite* past the Nicora Forest yet."

He stretched his arm out, pointing to some unseen place in his thoughts.

So that's the name of that gods-forsaken place…

"There are a few cities just within a few days' walk in either direction. After that, there's nothing but desert and dry land. Not too many are known to cross it without an expert guide, and that takes gold." He sighed. "I think I'm almost ready to do it alone, though. A few more preparations and then I'm gone."

He seemed proud at the declaration, puffing out his chest and leaping the stairs two at a time until he was standing at the top.

The girls hurried to meet him. "Wait, so you can just quit your placement whenever you want?" said Lessa.

"You *can*, but I wouldn't recommend it to just anyone." He searched in his pocket for a moment and then pulled out a key. "Those who don't stick to their placements willingly are called 'drifters.' You can call me that if you want," he said, flashing her a wink. "I don't mind it."

"A drifter?" said Arianna, not having a slightest clue as to what that meant.

Eli chuckled to himself. "I forgot how much there is to learn after leaving the Jar. Yes, a drifter, but it's not really a *good* label, if you follow. Not everyone is as lucky as me, as respected as me," he said. "I can find work here and anywhere to survive. I was top of my year in Warrior's District."

He spoke evenly, as if he wasn't gloating, but Arianna thought he most certainly was.

"Most drifters are poor and travel at necessity, removed from their placements. If they don't drift, they're put to rest. No use for them in the city."

"Put to rest," said Arianna, scoffing. "How eloquent."

Eli shrugged.

"Life is what you make it," he said, leading them down a hall at the very top of the staircase.

There were only two sleeping quarters at this level, and he gave Arianna the keys to both.

The girls peeked inside what would be their room for the night; it was dusty and had an old smell to it, much like the last room they'd slept in, but it was more than they could have wished for at a time like this. Seeing fresh linens and separate twin beds,

Arianna was more than willing to accept it.

"This will do?" said Eli.

"This will do," she said, trying not to seem overly excited. "Can you please send the others up when they're done with Godfrey?"

Eli tensed but nodded. "Good night, ladies," he said with a confused grin, their obvious delight not lost on him. "See you in the morning."

He seemed kind—very much a gentleman with a pleasant personality—but Arianna didn't trust him at all. She didn't trust anybody anymore. He left, closing the door behind him, and she immediately locked it from the inside.

"At least we're safe for one more night," said Lessa with a sigh of relief.

She placed Sano on the floor to explore, shed her belongings, and immediately stripped down to her undergarments.

"For now," said Arianna, setting aside her swords and unloading a sleepy Solza from her pack.

The avatar gave a slight whine as she laid her, ever so carefully, at the foot of the bed—Arianna flinched, still wary of the sharp claws that had forever marked her skin.

Too tired to even fully undress and too mentally drained to discuss anything she'd learned from tonight, Arianna plopped down next to Solza. Sleep overcame her almost instantly, though it wasn't a peaceful one. Her brain kept repeating Cyn's warning on a loop.

'He can be trusted to give you what you want, but he can't be trusted to care for what you give him.'

There was *always* a price for knowledge, and Arianna had a terrible feeling that they might not be able to afford the impending cost.

10

SOUTH LUOSE

STARING UP TO THE CEILING, Arianna could have easily convinced herself that everything that had occurred since the Jar had been nothing more than a delusion, her mind playing tricks with an imagination run wild after being bottled up for much too long. Wooden beams stretched from wall to wall, cobwebs forming out of reach where no one could disturb their owners. And dust gathered on the slabs where for certain no one would risk their necks to clean so high up.

Arianna felt as if she looked upon the ceiling in her sleeping quarters back in the Warrior's District—or up toward the bottom of the bunk bed she had once shared with Pippa. She imagined the sound of the bell, ringing loud throughout her district to signal the start of another day. Only, this time, she awoke not with the wailing of an abrasive noise but with the gentle rays of sunlight willfully trying to break through the curtains.

As her mind pulled away from sleep and the haziness lifted,

Arianna looked around and reminded herself that her future started here and now. *This* was the beginning of a new life for her and her friends, the beginning of their eighteenth year. And their past, caged to the districts, was long gone.

She found Solza, still asleep, on top of the covers… a creature so impossibly beautiful and mysterious that Arianna could hardly believe she existed. Then, she glanced to Lessa, sleeping soundly with yet another magical creature by her side.

The room itself may not have been clean nor quiet, the noise of the city seeping in, but it was theirs for the time being—a place to feel safe and, somewhat, welcome.

She contemplated this strange feeling of waking at her own leisure, no one there to force her from her bed; her body reveled in the holistic energy that could only come from the magic of a good night's rest. Though the Warrior's District early rising routine would be forever impressed on her, Arianna enjoyed the liberty to just continue staring at the ceiling forevermore, if she should choose. With no regulators around to punish her or to tell her otherwise, she wasn't compelled to even plant her feet on the floor.

This is the meaning of freedom.

Then came a sharp knock at the door, shattering Arianna's peaceful state of mind. She cursed under her breath and slipped out of bed, careful not to disturb Solza.

Slowly, she opened the door to meet whoever stood on the other side, reluctantly letting go of the shelter this room provided—she had to become Pippa again. With the door only slightly cracked, she peeped out. One hand remained behind her back, clutching her dagger… just in case.

"Yes?" she said, finding Eli on the other side. Her voice came out hoarse, so she cleared her throat.

"Morning!" he said with a chuckle. "Sounds like you could use some water."

He looked her up and down, surely smirking at her

disheveled appearance—Arianna couldn't care in the least bit what she looked like right now, as long as he didn't recognize her. But she was sure it wasn't pretty.

She yawned in response.

"Or coffee, perhaps?"

She perked up, never having been offered such a delicacy before.

Eli smiled. "I thought as much." He gestured to a tray in his hands. "I've brought everything you could desire for breakfast, on Mya's orders. She said you'd be hungry by now. It's nearly noon, you know?"

He leaned against the doorframe, showing off the body only a warrior could possess.

"Noon… already?" Arianna rubbed the sleep from her eyes.

He beamed. "Oh, you and I will get along *just* fine. I like your style," he said, pushing open the door to set the platter down on a small table.

Arianna let him pass, quickly sheathing the dagger at her thigh before he could see.

"Well, listen," said Eli, removing the tray lids; the delicious scent of eggs, bacon, and what Arianna presumed to be coffee filled her nose. Her stomach reacted immediately to the promise of breakfast, the platter of food filling the room with a sweet aroma. "If you're not *too* busy today, I'm to show you around South Luose. Mya says you've been holed up in the well center for the better part of Transition Week! Dreadful start to your new life. You must feel so behind."

He finished arranging the food and turned to face her.

"I'm happy to give you the grand tour. You'll need to learn your away around here quickly… before you break anymore rules."

Arianna crossed her arms at her chest. "What do you mean to say?" she said, trying to seem unperturbed.

Eli glanced around her, taking in the snoozing Lessa *and*

avatars strewn across the beds—Arianna immediately turned red at her own carelessness.

Why on earth did I let him in?

"The animals for a start," he whispered. "It's not the smartest idea to be caught with beasts in your bed during your first week as citizens. Animals as anything other than sustenance, fur, study, or transportation are strictly prohibited, according to citizen law. So, unless that cat is going to be your dinner tonight, best be rid of it."

Arianna wanted to laugh out loud; that 'cat' was a magical creature, unbeknownst to him, and she had a duty to protect it. Just two days ago, she would've been more than happy to cook Solza up for a hot meal—but that was then. Now, anything, or anyone, that tried to cause the avatar harm would have to go through her first.

"And that's just the one," said Eli. "You're obviously in need of a quick lesson."

He waited for a response, rolling the sleeves up on his shirt so that his arms showed. Beautiful black markings, like an intricate, abstract painting, wrapped all across his skin.

"Um, right," said Arianna, distracted a moment as she tried to block his view from noticing anything else out of the ordinary. "I—"

"I take that as a yes," said Eli, excitement in his voice. "Meet me downstairs in the tavern in an hour. And don't be so tense!"

He grabbed her by the shoulders then, as if to jokingly shake the stress from her; Arianna went rigid, stifling the urge to break his fingers.

Eli let go, hands in the air with a sheepish grin on his face. "Sorry, miss! Just try and loosen up a bit," he said. "You're going to love it here. Anything is better than the Warrior's District, right?"

"How'd you know my district?" Arianna was taken aback— it scared her to no end that this person she barely knew could peg down such a defining characteristic of her true self, and so quickly.

Could he as easily guess my real name with the whole world searching for me?

"You always know one of your own," said Eli, softly. "See you later, Pippa!"

She didn't like the way he said her name—mostly because a chill ran down her spine every time she remembered she was walking around with someone else's identity, playing the character of her dead friend, no less.

He waved her off, bounding back down the stairs, and she slammed the door behind him.

"What was that all about?" said Lessa, shamelessly migrating to the food as if it had summoned her out of bed.

The avatars followed at her feet, begging for scraps.

"That Eli," said Arianna, her face scrunched in concentration. "There's something… off about him." She mindlessly stroked Solza, starting to grow more comfortable with her company each day.

"Well, what did he say?" said Lessa, biting into a piece of cold ham.

She threw some to Solza as she struggled out from under Arianna's grasp, pouncing on it before Sano could.

"He wants to show me around the city today," said Arianna, pulling on her robes and combing her fingers through her unruly hair.

"How's that strange? You should go," said Lessa through a mouthful of food. "Maybe you'll learn something useful while we wait for Godfrey to come back with news."

"True," she said, pouring them both a cup of coffee to taste—they both spat it out on their first sip. "And he was adamant that we need to study the rules here."

"I suppose… we do." Lessa had a puzzled look on her face, and Arianna knew she was probably struggling with her own realizations at the moment. "Yes, you should definitely go. It's imperative, in fact. The more we know about Luose, the less vulnerable we are as long as we stay here."

"But what about you?" said Arianna, helping herself to some fruit and chugging a cup full of water.

"I'll check in with Jeom and Demetrius," she said. "I'm sure they've got news for us after last night. And maybe I can get more out of Mya. We can cover more ground if we split up. Tonight we can fill each other in on everything to make a better plan."

Arianna nodded, agreeing to this adventure for the day—though wholly unenthused by the task.

While Lessa stuffed her face full of breakfast, Arianna went over to the window. The eclectic noises of the city began to pour in as soon as she rolled the curtains back; she peered out, her short curls swaying in the breeze in an unfamiliar fashion, enthralled by this bird's-eye view of South Luose.

The burgundy buildings she had noticed last night showed their true identity under the sun—a dark, dirty brown with nothing beautiful about them. And people buzzed about below, swarming the empty streets they'd journeyed through last night, dressed in flowing robes and garbs of many different colors; Arianna was instantly opposed to the sight.

It had an unnatural look after seventeen years staring at the monotonous blend of red robes, as if the districts had truly merged together as one.

She spied on people laboring through their chores, various tasks at hand. Working men and women shed their robes, too warm with the sun beating down on their backs. And she could spot the city caretakers from a mile away, moving about in robes of a gentle yellow, the same as Cyn had always donned in the Warrior's District.

But, unlike in the districts, not everyone was hard at work during this time of day. Some leisurely explored the surrounding storefronts or were completing simple errands, seemingly not a care in the world. *This is freedom.*

Citizens also appeared to cluster together in groups of their own defining characteristics, moving as one with the same goal at hand. It reminded Arianna, in the most unpleasant way, of how Grinda Risso once led a pack of submissive peers—easy to spot the leaders versus those who just followed along.

Next, her eyes glued to a caravan of regulators in their unmistakable black cloaks. Nothing seemed much different about them at all, except for that each sat atop beautifully groomed and healthy horses. Banded together, they guided a decorated horse-drawn carriage up a narrow path, and citizens excitedly waved at whoever sat inside as they stepped out of its path.

Alas, the most fascinating thing about the city life she spotted were the newest slaves-turned-citizens, scurrying frantically about the streets in robes of bright silver, pointing to everything with such excitement as they rushed to discover their place in this new world—she glanced to her own silver cloak, *stolen*, pondering her place among them.

As the streets became more and more crowded, Arianna found it strangely impossible to discern the different districts represented in each cluster.

Do their pasts even matter in this new world?

She thought not.

After all, she knew from Mya that not everyone ended up with a placement directly related to their former trainings. Strange though it was to consider, it did make sense that a world couldn't tick on just four basic skills; she now saw it expanded into many more complicated parts than that.

"It's as if the Free Falls never even happened to them."

So content they seemed.

Lessa joined her at the window, peeking out with a fresh outlook on life, delight plain in her expression; she could've fit right in with the freed slaves during Transition Week for how eager she seemed.

"Look at all of the colors, all the people!" she exclaimed, smiling down at passersby. "I suppose it's much easier to live outside of the Jar."

Arianna couldn't help that sharp pang of guilt welling inside her chest again.

We deserve our freedom, too.

And with it nearly in reach, suddenly, it seemed that soon they might get it.

AN HOUR CAME AND WENT, so Arianna halfheartedly donned her silver cloak and went downstairs to the tavern. After she greeted Mya, Eli didn't waste a single second to drag her out into the unknown. He scooped his arm through her elbow and forced her out the door.

A crisp and refreshing breeze kissed her face as soon as she stepped outside, nothing like the biting air which eternally filled the Jar. This morning welcomed her, the wind swirling her robes about in nothing less than a magical fashion. People also bustled back and forth around her, accepting her as one of their own, for now, each with their own purpose that she didn't fully understand.

Eli pointed everything out with much enthusiasm, happy to impart his wisdom.

"Over here is the Garden," he said, guiding her down a hill and away from the tavern until the streets opened up into a wide, central area. "This is where you'll come for the morning commendation to the King."

Arianna scanned the massive grounds. They were beautifully maintained, with a colossal white statue of King Devlindor as the centerpiece and a bronze snake draped elegantly about his shoulders. Directly elevated behind the statue stood a podium, much like the one she was so accustomed to seeing General Ivo parade upon. And although there were no seated steps surrounding this stage, she knew where her place was meant to be here.

The cobblestone path weaving about the Garden was expertly designed to match the Four Corners symbol. Stretching into a massive circle with the statue at the middle, symbolic blue, green, purple, and red sections glittered under the glaring sun. And a lovely trim of flowers and bushes interwove it all for a flawless effect.

"You missed today's ritual," whispered Eli so that only she could hear. "I would advise you to let that be your last gamble with breaking the laws."

He walked her about the Garden, arm in arm, head held high as if they had done this stroll a thousand times before.

"If someone found out—" He seemed genuinely concerned.

"Of course," said Arianna through gritted teeth, lifting her hood up.

As they walked past the Garden and deeper into the city, Arianna noticed a group of new citizens huddled around an older man dressed only in beige slacks. His robust chest glistened with sweat as he worked around what looked to be a welding fire. He pulled an iron stick from the flames, eyes gleaming as he addressed the fresh crowd.

"As your new master of creation, do not accept this mark if you're unwilling to prove your worth," he said, sternly. "You may be the most talented lot from the Creator's District this year, but you've a long way to go to earn the 'Master' title from me."

He paraded about the young spectators, the tip of the iron stick glowing a bright red.

"I don't tolerate laziness or disrespectfulness. And I *will not* tolerate weakness." He touched eyes with each of them. "I expect greatness in every possible capacity. And that means to always compete against your yesterday's best."

His voice grew more passionate with every word.

"Don't disappoint me like so many others have! This city was not built in a day, and it's our duty to ensure that it keeps on standing for the generations of tomorrow."

He lifted the hot iron stick into the air, and the young citizens applauded, holding out their arms with anticipation. The master creator then pressed the metal rod into the side of their shoulders, one by one—each young citizen on the receiving end cried out from the pain at their turn, but none looked fearful or wronged. Instead, they studied their new marks in reverence, chatting devotedly about their placements under him, and trying with every effort to hold back their tears; and a caretaker on duty tended to the fresh wounds so they'd heal properly.

Arianna had to look away, repulsed by the tradition, but Eli explained the man to be a great creator tasked with teaching a select group of new citizens with a proven talent for building, welding, and anything in between.

"They're very lucky to have snagged advanced training under him," he said, seemingly impressed. "They've got a chance to make a name for themselves in this world early on. A handful of this lot will probably even be invited to train further in Saindora, eventually earning master titles, too, one day."

Arianna frowned.

"I know how it works," she said, thinking of her former, perfectly laid out, plan for such a path. "Are there many more master trainers like him here?"

"Oh, surely, yes," said Eli. "Every new citizen is placed under the expertise and watch of a new master or elder for advanced training. As you can imagine, some placements are more… *coveted* than others."

He pulled her along, pointing out another group of new citizens being led around the city by a man in dirtied, brown robes. The young faces that trailed him looked downtrodden, miserable, observing other groups with what could only be described as envy; they carried brooms and buckets of sloshing gray water, following their master with heads hung low before turning a corner and moving out of sight.

"Those are some of the unlucky ones," said Eli with a shrug. "They would've earned the lowest marks at their Free Falls, and now they're tasked with city preservation."

He shrugged.

"Someone's got to do it, I guess. The creators build our cities up, and the preservers keep it clean. I think it's a duty to be respected, but I doubt it was their dream placement in the districts. Doesn't exactly lead to a glamorous future, if you ask me."

"At least they're alive," said Arianna.

"Hail to the King," said Eli. "Speaking of placements, what did you earn? Were you marked well?"

Arianna laughed nervously, averting her eyes. "Only average. Nothing to complain about." She pointed up ahead to a large building on their path. "What's that over there?"

After unlinking her arm from his, she ran up to it, pretending to be enthralled; it stood out like a blemish among the city grounds, and the doors were flung wide open, releasing a strong stench into the air.

Eli caught up to her. "Ah, this is one of my favorite places by far! The Stables," he said, leading her inside.

Arianna was barely listening, focused instead on controlling her onset of nerves—hoping he didn't notice and hoping desperately that she played the part of Pippa well enough to fool him a while longer.

"Come on, I'll show you," said Eli. "It's huge, and not just meant for elders or regulators, like the one in the Warrior's District. It's open to everyone who cares to look."

He led her through the doors, and she saw people inside, tending to horses and other animals of all shapes and sizes.

"When you've had some years under your belt, some decent earnings, you can buy your own horse or pig, what have you," explained Eli, pointing out the various animals. "Most citizens usually don't unless they need to for the purpose of their work, but if you know what's good for you, you'll learn to ride young and save up for one of these beauties."

He patted a horse on its hind leg.

"There's such a thing as freedom in riding, truly!"

"I'm not very fond of horses," muttered Arianna, recalling the night that led her here in such shambles.

"No?" he gasped, his hands flying to his cheeks. "I'll have to try and change your mind then, teach you to ride someday." He gestured for her to follow, continuing his tour.

"That… might be nice," she said, trying to hide her smile; little by little, Eli was beginning to gain her trust—he was just so kind and so full of joy, it was hard not to let her guard down around him.

Arianna turned her attention to the countless penned animals, and she couldn't help the look of awe spread across her face. Her mind raced at all that one city held and all that was available to her now; it was a difficult task not to fall into the trap of letting Pippa's identity take over.

This is freedom.

"Everyone's fond of horses," said Eli, prattling on as she attempted to keep a low profile and minimize her reactions to all this new, exciting insight. "Well, mostly agrarians and warriors are the ones who find an interest in the end. I was a warrior-slave once, but I never thought in my wildest dreams that I'd have my own someday. That type of imagination had no place in the Jar, did it?" He chuckled at his own memory. "Come see. I'll introduce you!"

He dragged her over to one of the stalls where a strong-looking girl tended to a horse, black as night.

"How's he doing today?" said Eli, addressing her.

"Oh, he's fine," she said, jumping to her feet to greet him. "Glad to be back, I think! He needed a good scrub. I've just finished up." She smirked at him and then glared at Arianna, not even bothering to introduce herself. "A drink later, if you're free?"

"You know you're welcome at the tavern anytime," he said, too nonchalantly to be sincere.

The girl giggled, and the sound made Arianna cringe.

Just then, an older woman began shouting for her to tend to a highlife's livestock.

Thank the gods.

Arianna hoped she never seemed that idiotic in front of Liam when she'd been fawning after him.

If I did, no wonder he wasn't interested.

"That'll be my master. I must be off," she said, grabbing a bucket and scurrying out of the pen. "See you soon, Eli!"

He waved goodbye and then led Arianna farther into the pen to get a better look at the animal. As she gazed upon the horse that Eli favored, her breath caught in her throat and she was sure all the color had rushed from her face.

"This here is Phantom," said Eli—Arianna had already guessed as much. "Best friend I ever had in the world."

The horse whinnied politely.

"Phantom?" she whispered, staring into its eyes with nothing short of shock.

"Yeah, that's his name all right," said Eli, proudly patting the side of his head. "Go on. He won't bite."

He took Arianna's wrist and lifted her hand up to Phantom's face; the horse pressed his head into her palm, seemingly happy at her presence.

"That's quite strange!" said Eli, standing back to give them space.

"What's strange?" said Arianna, trying to wrap her head around what this reunion meant.

"Well, he usually *does* bite."

Eli let out a howl of laughter, and Arianna recoiled at the sound—not that it was a particularly sinister laugh, but she realized in this instant that it belonged to a voice she had most definitely heard before.

"Eli," she said, trying to sound casual as she continued to stroke Phantom's muzzle. "That short for anything? Seems… *short.*"

"Three letters," he said, matter-of-factly.

He moved to Arianna's side and placed her hands gently in his, making them into a cupped shape.

"You're right. That is short! Stay *just* like this."

He smiled down at her, pouring some oats into her hands for Phantom to enjoy; Arianna prayed he hadn't noticed how badly they were shaking.

"My given name is Elijah Neve," he said after a moment. "But it's too proper for my taste. That's what they called me as a regulator-in-training, and that's what I use when I'm regulating. 'Eli' is more my flair, though." He cocked his head to the side. "More carefree, don't you think?"

He lugged over a large bucket of water, urging Phantom to drink after he'd finished off the oats in Arianna's palms; she let her hands drop back to her sides, mind reeling and feeling utterly nauseous.

"What about you, Pippa? That short, too?"

He came around and plucked a piece of straw from her tangled hair, not seeming to take notice of her change in behavior.

"Nope. Not short for anything," she stuttered.

Suddenly, she felt the urge to run.

"I think I better be going back now! My friends will be waiting."

"Well, wait a minute!" called Eli as she made for the exit. "There's no rush. I can walk you back. I swear, I'm a gentleman. Let me just finish watering Phantom, and we'll be on our way."

"No really, you've done enough," said Arianna, already halfway out of the pen. "Thanks for showing me around!"

She waved him off, practically running out of the Stables,

spooking some of the other animals as she went.

The city passed her by in waves. The only thing Arianna could see was a blurred face in her final memories of the forest, *Eli's* face—protecting her or hunting her, she still didn't know.

But what she did know now was that he was most definitely real and he'd seen her face, now barely obscured behind a bad haircut and change of clothes. She also knew that he was a 'sometimes' regulator. And whatever that meant in this strange new world, it couldn't mean good things for her.

As she dashed back toward the tavern, her mind darted from one possible horrific ending to the next. She just couldn't process this bizarre place where people laughed and smiled throughout their chores. It reminded her slightly of what she'd once imagined to be the City of Saindora *before* King Devlindor had stolen the crown, though something seemed off... something stinking beneath the surface, waiting to be uncovered—she just couldn't quite put her finger on it, not just yet.

But, for certain, their fun playing pretend had come to an abrupt end in South Luose; they needed to quit this game of chance and leave immediately or find Ferlon Ragaric, whichever happened to come first by fate's hand.

As she stumbled up the next pathway, she found herself in a crowded market, people pushing food and goods in her face. She couldn't take a single step without someone looking her in the eye, trying to get her to stop. And, to her horror, every few feet, she saw her 'Wanted' portrait tacked to a post or littered on the ground—the fear that someone may notice her was suddenly overwhelming, paranoia taking hold of her heart, as if the world was closing in on her.

The thought that people stared at her, piecing the puzzle together right then and there, was nearly incapacitating—she struggled to breathe, shoving through the blurring sea of faces until she felt herself collide with a frail body.

They both tumbled to the ground.

"My apologies!" she squeaked, shaking out of her stupor to help an older woman back to her feet.

She was dressed in all white cloaks, silver and blue chains hanging from her neck. And long, gray locks of hair were braided with brightly colored tinsel—there was a Solomon-like air about her that Arianna couldn't ignore.

"It's quite all right, dear," said the woman in a steady voice, brushing herself off. "I'm not ready for the After Ward yet! I still have a few good bumps in me left."

The woman held her head high, standing a good foot shorter than Arianna; she stared up at her with such poise—Arianna became lost in her pale blue eyes, so deep they seemed to go.

"Not all right!" growled a man, pushing through the crowded alleyway and heading straight for them.

People instantly parted until he arrived at the scene. He was a tall, stocky fellow with a nasty scowl for a face; Arianna assumed him to be the woman's personal protector the way he hovered so defensively. Then two city regulators moved to flank the woman, all with their swords now pointed at Arianna—she was still holding the woman upright by her arm.

Letting go, she instinctively fell to her knees in a low bow, her district instincts kicking in.

"Please accept my apologies, ma'am," said Arianna, hand slowly reaching for the dagger at her thigh.

She felt an animalistic reaction surface, planning to use this fragile woman as hostage if they tried anything—anything at all. In this moment, as she contemplated threatening the innocent elder's life in order to save her own, she knew there was nothing she wouldn't do to survive.

"Put those away, fellas! They're not toys," said the woman. "It's a beautiful day, so I'm *told*, and I'm in no mood for bloodshed. If a little tumble will be my downfall, let it be. But I'm blind, not brittle."

She turned to face them, expression sharp.

"And I'm certainly not broken."

She barked at them in a stronger voice than Arianna would have ever expected to come out of such a small person. There was something very rough about her, very strong, and she found herself wondering if she would actually be able to best her in a fight—people were continuously surprising her in life after the Jar.

The regulators backed down obediently; it was evident that she was *their* master, of a sort.

"Get to your feet, girl. I won't let them hurt you."

Arianna cautiously stood up, and the woman reached out and took her hands in her own. She flinched at the unexpected touch, her skin leathery and soft. Yet, the old woman's grip was decidedly firm.

As she held on tight, Arianna saw her face go from relaxed to rigid in a split second. Then, she let go, seeming flustered at the interaction. She gestured to her personal protector to guide her onward, leaving Arianna behind without any explanation.

"Watch where you're going next time," spat the personal protector. "Or there won't *be* a next time."

Arianna bowed again, frozen in place as she watched the old woman walk down the street, her guards trailing behind.

As the woman turned the corner, Arianna caught her eye one last time, the clouded blue seeming to stare straight through her.

Strange, how she looks without seeing.

"There you are!"

Arianna glanced back to find Eli right on her tail.

"I saw what happened. That was a close call," he said as the gossiping crowd around her dispersed. "You don't want to get on her bad side in your first weeks. Or ever, actually."

"Why is she so important? She's just an old woman," whispered Arianna, letting out a long exhale she hadn't even realized she was holding. "And without eyesight at that."

"An old woman who's managed a seat on the South Luose

City Council in her first decade of citizenship. That's no small feat!" he said. "Besides, anyone who manages to reach old age and stay there for long is someone to be respected... and *feared*. Ophelia, she's ruthless. She'll do whatever it takes to keep the city in order and herself in a comfy position, just like all the rest of the elders here. She may be blind, but that seems to be somehow working in her favor, I'd say. She's currently Head of the Council."

"I see," said Arianna, though she certainly didn't understand that logic.

"I knew you'd get lost out here," he added, a bit accusatory. "It takes time to figure out this maze. Just follow me, and I'll take you back and get you fed. Besides, my tour isn't over. Mya would *kill* me if I only showed you the Stables and the Garden. What a terrible host I'd be!"

Arianna had no choice but to fall in line behind Eli, trying her best to become engaged in his lectures about city life and how it ticked. Everything he said seemed to twist out in a positive fashion, his gaiety unnerving as he shied away from discussing any of the less shiny parts. But Arianna knew they were there. There was an undertone, something truly sinister about it all.

As they walked back toward the tavern, she again laid eyes on the giant statue in the Garden, and it clicked.

This city is one ruled by King Devlindor, the same man who created the Four Corners.

Eli didn't talk much of the punishments or of citizens who didn't live up to their potential; he only spoke of how *not* to get punished, leading her through welcoming streets and charming alleyways. Men and woman stayed hard at work, creating the city pulse without need of being whipped into submission, and Arianna even thought the melted snow on the ground was made warmer by the cheerful atmosphere of it all.

Still, none of it could sugarcoat the reality she knew to be true. *This is the King's land.*

"Here we are," said Eli.

He held open the door to the tavern.

"Welcome back!" sang Demetrius, waving a chicken leg at her.

All three of her friends sat at a table in the empty space, a dusty light shining down on them.

"How was it?" asked Jeom as she went to join them.

"Magnificent," said Arianna, dryly.

She could feel Eli's eyes on her back as he sauntered over to Mya behind the bar; she was preparing for another busy night to come.

"We need to leave," whispered Arianna as soon as he was out of earshot. "And soon."

"Godfrey sent word he'd return in the morning," said Demetrius. "Can't we wait till then? What's happened?"

"We're not going anywhere. Not until we find Ferlon," said Jeom, ready to put up a fight.

"Fine, we can wait one more morning," said Arianna, not wanting to make a scene. "But just trust me on this."

She lowered her voice even more.

"Something's… *off.* I just have a bad feeling about this place now. If Godfrey doesn't pull through by tomorrow, we're going."

"What's spooked you so much?" said Lessa, raising an eyebrow at her as she plucked at some bread. "This is definitely a change of tune…"

"I'll tell you later," said Arianna, glancing over her shoulder. "Not here."

Everyone was giving her funny looks—clearly her friends had had a much different experience during their first day in the city.

"It's all going to work out right," said Demetrius. "Just relax. You've been gone all day. Have some food."

"You don't understand. I learned—"

"Hey, Pippa," interrupted Eli, "come over here. I want you to try this new brew we've just finished. You're going to *love* it."

He motioned for her to join them at the bar.

"A perfect end to the tour! It wasn't that long ago that I was a new citizen. Best few weeks of my life, figuring out what this all actually means."

"It means beer?" she called back, swiveling around in her seat.

"It *means* as many pints as you want, if you know the right people!"

Eli playfully elbowed Mya in the side—she giggled, shooing him off.

"Tempting," said Arianna, still hardly able to believe he was the mystery man in the forest.

How does he not recognize me?

"Come on, a toast is well deserved."

He waved her over, sloshing his drink on the counter before taking a long swing.

"I think he likes you," whispered Demetrius, nudging her forward. "Go on. He's not *too* bad on the eyes, is he?"

The others laughed; everyone, Arianna included, knew very well that he was strikingly attractive.

She looked over at him as he filled another glass.

"I wouldn't bet on it," she said, thinking he was probably just cozying up to her for a better chance at cutting her head off in her sleep.

"Well, don't be rude," said Jeom, smirking. "We've all had some. It's really quite good." He held up his cup, almost empty now, and slammed it down on the table. "More, please!" He got up from the table and crossed the divide to the bar.

"It'll cure your temper." Lessa laughed, following him.

With Demetrius pushing her along, Arianna reluctantly joined everyone at the bar; Mya filled a cup to the brim with a bubbling ale the color of corn.

"Go on. This will be the best decision you ever made," said Eli, pushing the cup into her hands with a smile.

He leaned closer to her so that only she could hear, and

Arianna couldn't help the way her skin prickled delightfully as he whispered in her ear.

"I'm sorry if I was too eager earlier," he said. "It's not every day I meet a girl as fascinating as you."

He held her gaze, his eyes that dazzling green—and his next words were unexpected.

"You can trust me, you know. I understand that's a hard thing to do in this world, but I'm not going to hurt you. I *promise*. You have my word."

Arianna felt her face grow hot as she studied the cup, his statement haunting her.

Does he recognize me... or is he just being thoughtful?

As much as it scared her, something inside of her really wanted to trust him.

Is that what my instincts are telling me to do?

Her thoughts were so jumbled after today that she couldn't be certain, but with her friends happy and safe by her side and Eli smiling down at her, Arianna felt her guard come tumbling down. She said a silent prayer that this seemingly kindhearted man had not been trying to hunt her to her death that dreadful night in the forest. That maybe he really *was* just trying to save her, and maybe he would never come to realize who she was.

Finding the will to be optimistic, as her friends had seemed to have fully achieved after only the gods knew how many drinks so far, Arianna held up her cup with a smile.

"Cheers," she said. "To new friends."

"To new friends!" said Mya, topping off everyone's ale.

Eli beamed, a truly genuine smile, and clinked his cup to hers, the sound signifying a new start.

Godfrey will pull through. Tomorrow, we will meet Ferlon Ragaric, and our lives can finally begin.

Arianna took a big sip of the ale, and it slid smoothly down her throat, cooling her from the inside out. From there, the rest of the night passed by in a blur, filled with song, laughter, and lots and lots of dance. They danced the night away, Eli setting the tone with his enchanting melodies until there was nothing left to do but forget everything but this moment.

THE CITY KEEPER

"WHAT HAVE YOU DONE?" Arianna's eyes flew open as Eli's shouts traveled up to their room. "How could you do this to them? How can you live with yourself, Myrisa?"

"I was just following orders," she heard Mya say. "I didn't have a choice. I don't even know who they are!"

Arianna pulled herself out from a dream-like state.

"They drugged us," she muttered, forcing herself to sit up in the bed—a fog wore off like a veil lifted from her face.

Her throat was sore, and her whole body felt heavy, as if it had been infused with iron, as she willed her muscles awake.

"Something's wrong. I think… they drugged us."

The events from the day before seemed covered in a haze, another night wiped from memory.

"No, no, please!" Mya's voice came loud from down below as the numbness Arianna felt began to fade. Her scream echoed like thunder throughout the building—the sound of someone who knew this would be their final moment of life.

When her cries for mercy finally faded, Eli's panicked voice came again.

"Run, Arianna. Get out of here!" he said.

His words carried up through the stairwell, certainly coming from the tavern.

Wait, did he just say my name? My real name?

Arianna was racked with confusion, but at least one thing was made perfectly clear…

"We need to go. Lessa, wake up," she shouted, planting her feet on the floor. "Get up, now!"

Lessa woke with a start, visibly disoriented.

"Grab your things and let's go!" Arianna said again, placing Solza in her rucksack.

Fear plain on her face, Lessa began flying around the room without question, gathering her things. She called to Sano, grabbed her bow and arrows, and met Arianna at the door.

When they stepped into the hall, Jeom and Demetrius were already there. Black circles had formed under their eyes, and they looked just as afraid as she felt.

Jeom bowed his head. "Ara, you were right. We should've listened—"

Before he had even finished his sentence, both he and Demetrius fell to their knees, eyes rolling back in their heads before toppling sideways to the ground. Whether they were dead or unconscious, Arianna couldn't be sure, but she wouldn't leave this spot without fighting back on their behalf—she withdrew both swords from the sheath at her back.

A small scream escaped Lessa, but she recovered quickly, a steady hand reaching for an arrow and her bow to stand alongside Arianna.

Regulators cornered them on all sides, blocking the stairwell and their only way out; these warriors seemed stronger, fiercer, than the ones she had encountered in the districts—they looked excited for a fight. And with Jeom and Demetrius taken out, Arianna didn't like their chances.

"Drop your weapons or your friends here won't live to see tomorrow," said a regulator as two others held their blades to the throats of the Kane brothers.

Thank the gods, they're not dead... yet.

She glanced to Lessa, who was already lowering her bow.

"Yield," hissed Arianna, without thinking twice—the word never lost its sour taste on her tongue.

She let her swords drop to the ground, wincing at the unbearable sound of surrendered steel. But she refused to be the cause of her friends being harmed any further. As long as they were alive, they stood a chance... however slight.

The regulators stripped them of all their possessions. Then, they dragged them, hands tied behind their backs, into a barred, horse-drawn carriage waiting outside the tavern. The night had barely ended, but the sun was already peeking its head high above the clouds. It sprinkled rays of light on the now quiet city.

Such a deceitful city. Arianna spat on the ground.

She was familiar with this kind of trickery. The beauty and intrigue had worn off now, and she saw South Luose for what it truly was—just a prison with wider walls. They were trapped again, another battle for freedom to be fought.

We should've just stayed in the forest for the rest of our days, surviving off the land.

She wished she hadn't been so eager to belong to some superficial society.

Arianna pressed her face against the steel bars, letting the wind caress her skin through the wide gaps; she had a sinking feeling it might be a while before she felt that wind again. She stared straight into the deadened eyes of Myrisa Lang.

Regulators surrounded the body of their deceased host, their boot prints stained with her blood as they inspected the area. She gripped the bars of her cage tighter.

Traitor.

Eli, though, was nowhere to be found.

AFTER A LONG AND BUMPY RIDE up the winding city streets and through a tunnel of trees where the Nicora Forest broke back in, the carriage came to a halt. The doors were flung open to reveal the palace which overlooked South Luose.

Arianna might've tried to make a run for it, if not for the arrows pointed directly at her and her friends' throats.

"Take them inside," ordered the lead regulator.

They came for Arianna and Lessa first. Their hands were still tied behind their backs, so the regulators had to help them out of the carriage, before forcing them to march forward to the palace. Arianna glanced back over her shoulder to check on the boys and was relieved to find they'd awoken; in fact, they seemed to be in perfect health as they struggled against their restraints.

The Palace of South Luose expanded out in front of them like an open mouth waiting to feed, several tall towers creating the teeth, and each decorated with glass-paned windows reminiscent of the surrounding forest. Statues of stern-looking soldiers lined the walls at the bottoms, and intricate patterns were carved into every surface of the palace façade, depicting a story Arianna couldn't piece together with just a quick look. Finely dressed regulators stood on guard, scattered across the palace grounds and positioned protectively in front of a grand, gated door.

Arianna felt the dull end of a weapon press into her back as the regulators guided her and her friends around to the other side of the palace. They came upon a wooden door with nothing glamorous about it; iron bolts creaked as it swung open, revealing a bare hallway with low ceilings.

"This way," growled a regulator, shoving them all inside.

The door closed, locking out the now early-morning sun and washing them in a dim light, provided only by the torches on the walls. Then, a regulator behind Arianna pulled a sack over her eyes.

The darkness startled her at first, but she was quickly becoming used to it, to the unknown. She took a deep breath and did her best to remain calm. Although, as her friends protested against their blindfolds, it was hard not to share in their fear. *I must stay strong for them. I'm a warrior.*

Arianna paid close attention to her surroundings as they were paraded around the palace for several minutes. Another door creaked open, and the sound of their boots clicked now on tile instead of stone. They were told to stop in this room, the regulators whispering something intelligible.

"Bring them to me!" echoed a deep voice, silencing them.

The words made Arianna's skin crawl, as if General Ivo were breathing down her neck.

"Get moving," said the regulator at her back, shoving her forward—her sack was suddenly ripped off, and her hair fell down around her face in messy tangles.

She squinted, needing a moment to adjust to the light. And when she finally could see clearly, for a moment, she forgot her predicament in the face of such splendor.

They stood in a huge hall with iron and glass chandeliers hanging low all across the space. Vast windows reached from the floor to the ceiling, but the curtains were drawn, letting in hardly anything of the sun. Instead, the flickering candles in the chandeliers gave the room a hauntingly warm glow, with more than enough light to see.

Ornate benches with high backs lined the walls, functional seats, not meant for comfort, and fireplaces were roaring in each corner of the room, keeping the space warm in the frigid morning. In the center of the chamber, steps led up to a throne draped in furs and silks. And positioned directly behind that throne was the largest portrait of King Devlindor Arianna had ever seen.

It was dark—everything about it—from his eyes and his robes to the animal at his feet. It made her instantly cold, any feeling of hope fleeting and distant now.

"Kneel!" barked a regulator before she even had time to set eyes upon the man seated upon the throne. "Hail to the King."

The four were forced to their knees in unison, their fists submissively resting at their chests.

"Hail to Lord Devlindor," they said through gritted teeth and bowed heads.

"You may rise," said the man on the throne.

Arianna lifted her eyes to meet his, and she recognized him straightaway from a portrait during their stay at the well center— the Keeper of South Luose.

"As you command, Keeper Kassime," said Arianna, nodding to the others to follow suit.

The adrenaline she felt in this moment didn't give her much room for fear; she clung to defiance. This would *not* be their end, not at the hands of a royal puppet. *Just survive.*

"Leave us now," he said, gesturing to his guards. "They won't try to run. They've nowhere to go."

Keeper Kassime stared down at his captives, daring them to show any signs of resistance as the regulators filed out of a wide double door; with one glance around, Arianna realized it was the only way in or out of the chamber. She didn't care for his arrogance, and she wanted nothing more than to test it, but he was right—there was nowhere to run. Regulators would have their ears pressed to the door, and they were weaponless with their hands still tied at their backs.

"And send in Godfrey!" he bellowed after them.

Arianna fought the urge to scream, knowing surely now that he'd played a big part in their capture.

Traitors. All traitors!

"Yes, Keeper," said the last regulator in the room before she exited.

They were alone with him now.

"Godfrey has brought me some interesting news," said Kassime, turning his attention to them.

He waited for an answer; when no one spoke, he got to his feet, hands clasped behind his back as he studied them from his pedestal.

"He says there are four *slaves* in our midst, those who have not yet earned their freedom. Those the world is tirelessly searching for."

Arianna took a step forward, her eyes locked on his, so sharply that if they'd been swords, he would've been dead on impact.

"With all due respect, *Keeper*, we're no longer slaves to anyone."

A fire burned in her heart, demanding revenge, calling for blood. *I'm a warrior!*

Arianna could see Lessa in her peripheral vision, clearly panicking at her brazenness and probably trying to figure out if she had some sort of escape plan to go with it—she didn't.

He scowled at her.

"You're slaves to this world until the world says otherwise," said Kassime. "And in this city, everyone is a slave to *me*." Straightening his shining sapphire robes, he glided down the steps to stand before them. "And we're all slaves to the one true King, so you will certainly not be shedding that label in this lifetime."

He pointed to the wall behind him, and Arianna felt her blood boil as King Devlindor's portrait leered down at her with mocking eyes.

"Now, the next words you speak may very well be your last. Best choose them wisely, girl." He leaned forward, hand on the hilt of his sword. "Who are you?"

His lips twitched up in a smile; he knew very well who she was. He stood so close to Arianna now that she could feel his hot breath on her skin and could see soft lines crinkling his smooth, copper face.

"Don't tell him a thing!" growled Jeom.

The city keeper held her gaze.

"There's no point in hiding any longer," she said, unblinking. "The truth has already come out."

The city keeper nodded, his smirk twisting with an emotion Arianna couldn't quite peg—anticipation? Anger? Disbelief? Fear?

"Ara, no," whispered Demetrius. "If we don't say anything… we might still have a chance."

She ignored their pleas, holding her head high to accept her fate. They were cornered, and lies were no longer protection enough—Godfrey, Eli, and Mya were all proof of that. If she were to die now, she'd do so with dignity, with a fight, and as none other than Arianna Belvedor.

Solomon would have supported the decision, too, standing with her in this moment; warriors didn't die begging for their lives on their knees. They owned their endings, looked Death straight in the eye, when it was time.

She cleared her throat. "My name is Arianna Belvedor… of Warrior's District."

Keeper Kassime looked a bit taken aback, as if actually hearing it out loud made it real. He glanced at the others.

"And your peers?"

Lessa was shaking her head, trying to get Arianna's attention, but she wouldn't, *couldn't*, look away from the keeper.

"We're all from the City of the Four Corners."

"I see," he said, a strange gleam in his eye. "Please present documentation of placement." He held out his hand, as if Arianna might suddenly reach within her robes and pull out the elusive papers of freedom.

"We have no such documentation," she said, flatly.

"In the name of the King, so it's true, then?" he said with a gasp. "The infamous escapees are more than just a well drawn-out rumor." He laughed. "I *must* be dreaming."

His voice shook with nerves, and she noticed something more reminiscent of curiosity rather than disapproval flicker across his face. He wasn't focused anymore, his hand sliding away from his hilt, excited by the information.

"What on earth am I going to do with you?" he said, more to himself.

Arianna took this moment to strike.

"This is no illusion!" she said, butting him in the head and sending a hard kick to his stomach.

Keeper Kassime fell to the floor with a thud, a trickle of blood dripping from his hairline and his silver crown flying from his head. He gently touched the wound with a stunned expression. But seeing the blood on his fingers shook him from shocked to enraged.

"Guards," he roared. "Hurry, they've escaped!"

Arianna felt the pull of magic from the pit of her belly—unbidden, uncontrollable, *delicious.* The energy pooled at her wrists in a strange, tingly sensation. Then, the ropes binding her fell to ashes, freeing her hands.

"I knew you had something up your sleeve!" said Demetrius, a smile in his voice.

No, just a little luck at the right time.

She turned to her friends, controlling her magic before it slipped away; they too became free from their binds.

"Guards!" Kassime yelled again, though a bit more frantic—had he seen the magic?

Arianna didn't care, and she didn't waste a second to attack. "Don't let them take you easy."

Her friends all let out voracious warrior cries of their own, preparing to fight, and Arianna lunged for the keeper as he scraped across the floor on his back, eyes wide.

She caught the end of his robe with the edge of her boot and straddled him where he lay before he could reach for his sword. The keeper kicked his legs furiously under her weight, struggling for air as she clasped both her hands tightly around his neck; he wasn't much stronger than she was.

She squeezed, as hard as she could.

Alas, before Arianna could finish the job and before her friends could do anything to help, the regulators poured back into the chamber—at least twenty of them, their weapons held high. It was such chaos that she couldn't concentrate enough to call on any more magic, and she was certain Lessa would be having the same trouble.

"We're surrounded," said Jeom. "Arianna, move!"

There were hands on her, pulling her off the keeper by the time she'd registered the warning.

Everything passed by in a blur—Arianna could barely see a thing save for the incessant flurry of fists and feet pummeling her into the ground. But she saw enough to know that her friends hadn't made it to the door, every one enduring their own struggle against the regulators.

When the beatings finally stopped, Arianna was shaking, dizzy. Slowly, she unfurled herself from a ball on the floor, coughing up blood onto the shining tile.

"Stand her up." Keeper Kassime's words came slow, sharp, unforgiving—regulators lifted her to her feet, holding her in place and forcing her to face him.

"*Look* at me," he said.

Arianna managed to raise her head, tears welling in her eyes and blurring her vision; she tried to blink them away, but even warriors felt pain. She tried to seem as composed as she could upon finding Keeper Kassime's gaze—he seemed excited… a beast awakened from a slumber, ready to feast.

"Take them to the dungeons," he ordered without remorse, his voice hoarse and throat bruised—*at least I managed to injure him*, she thought. "They die at the Altar at dawn."

Arianna's heart skipped a beat at her fate, and Jeom, Lessa, and Demetrius all stopped struggling.

Keeper Kassime picked up his crown, smoothed out his robes, and walked back to his throne, perching under the watch of King Devlindor—it was over.

Barely a week living as outlaws was all the freedom they would experience in this lifetime.

We die at dawn...

Without ceremony, without privilege, and still suffocating from the chains of the Olleb's oppression.

It was then that Godfrey paced into the hall, holding his head high and not even bothering to glance their way. He walked right to the edge of the steps to the throne, bent to his knee (with the support of his cane), and gave the mandatory salute to Keeper Kassime on behalf of the King.

"You're... a traitor," said Arianna through clipped breaths, licking the blood from her bruised lips.

Godfrey smirked at her from over his shoulder and then got to his feet, keeping his back to them.

"I will kill you!" Somehow Arianna found the energy to scream, her own voice echoing into the confines of her soul for how quiet the room was in this moment.

"Bring this man his gold," said Kassime, halfheartedly. He gestured to an attendant as a caretaker began treating his wounds. "And get this filth out of my sight. I have such a bad headache now." He pressed his hand into his temple.

"No, please!" said Lessa, resisting again as the regulators began to drag them all toward their destinies.

Their hands were again bound.

"You can't do this," said Demetrius, trying to twist out of their grip. He looked to Jeom with pleading eyes.

"It's going to be okay, brother," said Jeom as a regulator led him forward, a sword to the small of his back—but even Arianna knew he didn't believe his own words.

We die at dawn.

"Ara, what do we do now?" Lessa craned her neck to look back at her.

Nothing. It's over.

"Don't struggle," said Arianna in the most reassuring voice she could muster. "Remember, we're in this together." She tried to smile for her friend, but the click of Godfrey's cane on the tile made it impossible.

He paused in front of her, a large bag slung over his back, jingling with the sound of an unjustly large amount of coin.

"Yes, don't struggle," he hissed. "This is where you belong." He touched eyes with them all, such indifference in his own. "You didn't earn this world, *slaves*."

He slipped a balled-up parchment from his robes and dropped it at Arianna's feet; it was one of the Wanted portraits. Then, he slithered out the door—like the snake he was—a sinister laugh trailing him all the while.

Arianna snapped, overcome with a rage that roared out of her in such a sound she thought she'd turned into a monster. With her wrists again bound at her back, she nearly broke them in the effort it took to lunge for the back of his throat; she'd give anything to end Godfrey's life for stealing the promise of theirs, but the regulators kept her at a distance.

"By *gods*, sedate them if they're going to keep fighting," called Keeper Kassime over Arianna's cries for revenge. "This has gotten out of hand."

We die at dawn.

A cloud of blue powder suddenly enveloped her, and she couldn't help but inhale it; the room spun, fading to black as stars danced in her vision. The others were forced to breathe in the concoction, too. Then, they all sank to the floor, together, a heap of deadweight.

THE DUNGEONS

AGAIN THERE WAS DARKNESS—though, this time, it seemed thicker and wholly more permanent. Arianna's limbs felt like ice as she tried to warm her muscles. She crawled on the cold, wet ground to find her bearings, and her hands met steel bars as thick as her body.

After a few minutes, her sight began to adjust to the black, but she still couldn't make out anything around her; she attempted to use her voice to see if it might come.

"Lessa, where are you?" Her words trembled. "Jeom, Demetrius? Are you there?"

Her bravery from earlier entirely fell away in this moment of pure solitude.

"I'm here. I'm here, Ara, but I can't see a thing."

Arianna let out a long sigh, more relieved than she'd ever felt before at the sound of Lessa's voice.

"I must've passed out," added Lessa, her voice soft… scared.

"They used sleeping powder on us."

The grumbles and moans of what had to be Demetrius and Jeom responded before Arianna could—they were all still alive, at least for the time being.

"Thank the gods everyone is all right," she said.

"*Thank* the gods?" Jeom was clearly irate. "I'll thank the gods when they actually show their hand in this mess! We're dead men, even if we're still breathing."

No one spoke, Jeom's voice echoing throughout the dungeons for an eerily long while.

'They die at the Altar at dawn.'

That was another voice ringing in Arianna's ears.

Her hands still clung to the iron bars, her skin pressed to the cool metal as she willed her sight to come. And as she listened to the others grow more frantic with every passing second, she just stared into the nothingness until she could make out the endless pattern of bulky, gray stones; they carved long tunnels all around them.

Arianna blinked over and over, thinking she saw something move up ahead. Then she gasped, eyes frozen open when she realized what it was—other eyes gazed back at her from their place in the darkness. She couldn't be certain if they belonged to the dead or the living. But she knew they listened, their silence confirming their fate.

"What do we do?" said Lessa. "How do we get out of here?" There were tears in her voice.

"Godfrey sold us out," said Demetrius, sounding so calm among the chaos. "We should've never trusted him to help us. I'm so sorry I pushed it. We should have never trusted anyone but ourselves."

"No, *Arianna* sold us out!" said Jeom.

His words were like a punch to the stomach.

Arianna shrank back, knowing him to be in the cell across from hers by the direction of his voice. Looking ahead, she could see the shine of his eyes, glaring, and his knuckles shone white in the dark for how tightly he was clutching the bars to his prison.

"I don't know what came over me," she mumbled.

Hearing his accusation, Arianna almost wished she'd stayed quiet when questioned by Keeper Kassime. But it wouldn't have mattered; he'd already known the truth and silence wouldn't have delayed their sentencing long.

"How about insanity!" said Jeom, spitting the words at her. "This is all your fault. We're *supposed* to decide things unanimously, and you didn't even give us a chance."

"What other chance could we have had but to fight?" snapped Arianna, feeling the heat rise in her face. "Don't be foolish, Jeom. They already knew who we were! The keeper was just toying with us."

She stood, letting out a small shriek as the pain from her wounds caught up to her.

"No… you should've stayed quiet," he said, sounding as if he were more trying to convince himself. "Now, because of you, we will all surely die together, just as promised. No doubt about that."

He let go of the bars, the darkness swallowing him as he moved to the back of his cell.

"That's enough, Jeom!" said Lessa—she was definitely in the cell adjacent to Arianna, and she was fired up. "The truth was going to come out either way. At least Arianna was brave enough to own up to it in that moment. The rest of us just cowered there, doing *nothing*. This is nobody's fault, but if you want to start pointing fingers, take a look in the mirror! We all had a part in getting ourselves into this mess, and we'll all have a part in getting us out. Or you're right, Jeom, we *will* die together."

"Wasn't that always the plan?" said Demetrius in almost a lighthearted tone; his voice came from the cell next to Jeom's. "Let's everyone just take a *deep* breath now. Shouting at each other isn't doing any of us any good."

He took one of his own—a long, deep inhale, and a long, drawn-out exhale; Arianna found herself breathing right along with him.

"We're not going to die down here, wherever 'here' is. There's still hope as long as we're alive," he said.

Arianna wanted to believe that, but she wasn't sure she did.

"Well, we're not getting out without help," said Jeom, a little calmer now. "They've got all our weapons. What do you suggest, brother?"

Arianna silently agreed with Jeom, looking again toward the faceless eyes that watched their every move—prisoners just the same. *We're definitely not getting out of here without help.*

"Oh, Sano, he's gone!" cried Lessa, startling everyone.

Arianna heard her rummaging around in her cell, as if the little monkey might be hiding there somewhere, but they'd been separated from their avatars since the tavern.

"Solza, too," she whispered, feeling guilty for the cub's fate—Arianna had just begun to grow fond of her, barely given a chance at their relationship.

Lessa let out a heart-wrenching moan.

"Shh… it's going to be all right," said Jeom—he, Demetrius, and Arianna all walked back to the bars of their cells, trying to show their support, however futile.

"No, it's not! Ferlon Ragaric was our one chance at… at, I don't even know what, and we *blew* it," she said, her voice muffled with tears. "Who will help us now?"

Jeom tried to calm her. "But you just said—"

"I don't care what I said!" Lessa had cracked. "I… I…" She let out a small whimper. "Oh, poor Sano. What if they've hurt him?"

"Ragaric, the enigma," said Demetrius. Arianna felt his eyes shift her way. "I wish your master had been a little more descriptive."

Arianna's stomach twisted in knots at the thought of

Solomon—he'd help them, if he were alive.

If...

"Godfrey! I'll kill him if I ever lay eyes on that coward again," growled Jeom. "He really screwed us over. I don't see a way out of this." He no longer sounded so accusatory, only somber.

"You never know," said Demetrius. "The last time I was rotting away in a dark room, Lady Luck stretched out her hand and saved me." He sounded far away in his thoughts. "I'll never forget when you all came tumbling through that door. I'll try my luck twice. Stay hopeful, brother."

Arianna nearly jumped in the air with excitement as his words landed.

"Demetrius, you're brilliant!" she said.

"I like to think so, but why do you say—"

"That wasn't luck. That was *magic!*" Arianna recalled the enchanting green light she and Lessa had conjured in the Vanishing Tunnels, one that had ultimately guided them to Demetrius' rescue. "Les, we can use our magic to get out of here. We're not out of ideas yet."

"Yes!" said Jeom, a little confidence back in his voice. "It worked on the ropes earlier, Ara."

He began sputtering ideas.

"You can try to cast another spell together, like you did that day in the tunnels... a call for help this time, maybe?"

Arianna heard Lessa sniffle, collecting herself.

"I see you're starting to trust in magic more," she said to Jeom, a hint of hope behind her words. "You're perfectly right... there *must* be a spell we can use to help us break out of here."

"No," said Arianna, an idea sparking in her mind. "We need better chances than depending on our shaky magic, but I know exactly what we can do."

She crossed her fingers and said a silent prayer to every god she could think of.

"Jeom, this one's up to you now. Still have that axe of yours?"

She wasn't sure if the regulators had stripped him of the tube.

"No," he said, sounding so defeated—it was like a punch to the stomach. "They took it from me. Otherwise maybe we could've won that fight."

"Try calling for it," said Lessa, a glimmer of hope in her voice. "You know how. It belongs to you and you alone."

Everyone held their breath as the guttural sounds of his Golden Age kin echoed through the dungeons.

With a sparkling *pop*, the tube appeared in Jeom's hand. It glowed a deep red, as if it had just burned a hole in someone's pocket to escape back to its master.

Demetrius howled in happiness. "Brilliant, *just* brilliant."

"Lessa, I could *kiss* you right now!" sang Jeom. "I can't believe that worked."

She laughed with relief.

"When will you stop doubting yourself?" she said. "And don't thank me. It was Arianna's idea."

The tube stopped glowing.

"I…" Jeom became serious. "Ara, I'm sorry for everything I said before. I didn't mean it. I was just—"

"Please, *spare* me," she said, trying to brush off how much relief his words gave her; she was so grateful he couldn't see her blush. "We can duel over it later. Just get us out of here, and then you can grovel all you want."

"Yes, ma'am!"

"Again I say, thank the gods," said Arianna—with even more conviction than before.

"Do you know how to open the tube?" said Demetrius.

"Thanks to Lessa, I'm confident I do now," said Jeom.

The unmistakable tones of the dwarf language rolled off his tongue again, the low sound enveloping them in something like a warm embrace…

"*Reveliantom!*"

The tube lifted into the air, sparks of bright magenta and gold shooting all around it.

Arianna could see her friends plainly now, the light from the magic chasing away the darkness in the vicinity. She saw others, too—prisoners a long way down, watching in awe.

The tube stretched and grew in length until it was again the shining, gilded axe Jeom had rightfully earned in the Vanishing Tunnels. And as the magic died away, the gleam of the mighty weapon still kept some of the darkness at bay.

"Go on," said Lessa, barely able to contain her excitement. She wiped the tears from her eyes. "Give it a go."

"You can do this," said Arianna, again gripping the bars of her cage; though, this time, with anticipation.

It only took one strike.

A loud bang reverberated throughout the dungeons as the axe—magical metal on iron—cut straight through the thick lock and bars.

"It worked!" Jeom pushed over the heavy door of his cell; it slammed to the floor with incredible force and a thunderous noise, shaking the ground at their feet.

"I'll get you next," he said to Demetrius.

"Stop where you are," came a voice from out of the darkness; it belonged to a man, but Arianna saw no one.

Lessa gasped, and the chamber instantly grew quiet.

"Who's there?" said Jeom, going stiff as he peered out of his cell, trying to see down the dark passageway. "Stay back! I'm armed."

"Be careful," whispered Lessa, watching his every move.

Jeom held tight to his weapon, slowly stepping over the broken door. "Where'd that voice come from?"

He turned in circles.

Suddenly, Arianna spotted a pair of eyes growing nearer, until they were right behind Jeom. "Behind you!"

There was a thud, Jeom cried out, and the axe fell from his hands as he toppled to the floor.

"No, Jeom!" screamed Demetrius—it was the first time Arianna had heard him truly panic, an unnerving sound. "Get up!"

A whoosh of air blew through the tunnels, and with it came a blast of light so bright that Arianna was forced to shield her eyes and look away. A moment later, the shocking brightness faded and the dungeons were left softly illuminated by what appeared to be hundreds of glass spheres dangling on invisible strings from the ceiling—flames flickered in all of them. Still, nobody was there.

Arianna didn't know what to make of it at first, but she could see clearly now; Jeom was sprawled out on the ground, unconscious, his axe just out of reach.

She glanced to Demetrius and Lessa, both on their knees, stretching their arms through the bars of their cells in a futile effort to help him. Then, her attention was drawn back to the ceiling—the flames there flickered in and out of a pinkish-purple, *unnatural* color.

I know this fire.

She looked back and forth for any sign of the culprit, the never-ending dungeons unwinding before her. Cell upon cell lined walls that kept going until their ends were again swallowed by blackness. And the moans of others crept into their lonely section now, echoing throughout the dungeons. It seemed as if the keeper's prisoners—the ghosts of those already gone as well as those still hanging on—were disturbed by the light, awoken from comatose states.

"Who's there?" Arianna cried.

A cloaked figure suddenly appeared out of a dark corner, stepping into the light.

Demetrius and Lessa stood, scurrying to the backs of their cells. But Arianna still clung to the bars, not letting go of the little hope she'd found down here. And if she were to die now, she refused to die without dignity...

Warriors look Death in the eyes.

The figure kneeled next to Jeom; Arianna *still* couldn't see a face, but something told her it was more than just a man.

"Stay away from him!" she said. "Who *are* you?"

"Who am I?" The figure stood, lowering its hood.

Arianna fell to her knees—she had been, somewhat, right. To her, he was more monster than man—the keeper, their killer.

"It's you…" she said, head hung low.

There was no more hope.

"*You*," he scoffed, walking up to her cell. "You have no idea the words you speak."

Arianna found the will to look into his eyes.

I'm a warrior, and I will die like one.

"To many, I am Honorable Helix Kassime, Keeper of South Luose." He pointed to the thin crown atop his head. "*This* is my identity."

Arianna wouldn't blink for fear her life would end and she might miss it.

He knelt down so that they were exactly eye level, his voice low. "Though to few, I'm known as Ferlon Ragaric. A sorcerer of Olleb-Yelfra and a guardian of the forgotten Golden Age."

Arianna swore she saw a flash of silver streak across his stone-cold glare; her mouth fell open.

Did I hear that correctly?

Arianna couldn't speak, afraid she might've imagined this strange statement as the city keeper, a ruler of the Olleb and one of King Devlindor's very trusted followers, lingered in her presence.

Sorcerer… and a guardian of the Golden Age? What does this mean?

Her gaze again found the ceiling, and she couldn't deny the truth burning bright before her eyes. A glow settled within her heart as she looked upon the flickering pink fires—she knew this magic, had used it before.

"Master Bell, he said that—"

"If Solomon sent you here, he must be dead or dying!" said Kassime. "To trust this alias with anyone outside of the guardians… and with *children*, no less." He scowled. "Where is he hiding? Why has he sent you? Tell me straight, or you'll find yourself dead by morning."

He looked nothing if not sincere.

Arianna was more than taken aback, hardly able to comprehend the situation.

"He's dead," she said after a moment. The words felt hollow. "I saw him last alive barely two weeks ago now. He had sent me here to find Ferlon Rag… well, *you*, I guess." She averted her eyes. "But now I've learned that he's dead."

Keeper Kassime stood, turning away from her. "So the great wolf has fallen?"

He grew silent, the unnerving whimpers of the other prisoners again filling the space. He swiveled back around to face her, and Arianna realized he was expecting a response—she nodded.

"I see," he said, lifting his chin high and narrowing his eyes as he stared down at her—he was clearly deliberating something.

Arianna just hoped that, whatever it was, it meant she and her friends could keep their heads.

There was another long, awkward silence. "Come then," he said, "we have much to discuss."

With the flick of his hand, there was a resounding *click* and their gates swung open. And with the snap of Keeper Kassime's fingers, Jeom and the axe rose into the air, eerily floating behind him as he began to walk back in the direction he'd appeared from.

Magic! Strong magic… Solomon sent us to find another sorcerer?

This turn of events was too bewildering for Arianna to feel anything other than uncertain. But she didn't hesitate to leave her cell, and neither did her friends. She, Demetrius, and Lessa all locked eyes, so many more questions unfolding before them. Saying nothing, they followed Keeper Kassime through a hidden door that led to a winding staircase—as the door closed behind them, Arianna could still hear the haunting moans of those rotting away, left to darkness or death.

The image of the ghost in the well center Gallery flitted across her mind; she wondered what actions could've led these people to such a terrible fate as a permanent stay in the Luose Dungeon. It was much like the Tunnel of Tombs in the mountains, only the bodies rotting here were still alive… for the most part.

They reached the top of the staircase, and Keeper Kassime led them through a dark corridor until they came to another door.

"*Operium undrio*," he said, hands on the handle.

It swung open, revealing a large, domed chamber in the shape of a pentagon with five doors to choose from. But before Arianna had time to really look around the impressive space, the keeper hurried them all through one of the doors and then stopped to address them.

"This is the attic above the north tower," he explained—Arianna was sure they all looked dumbfounded. "I come here to practice, and no one else but me knows this place exists. It's been cloaked with a spell. From the outside, it's visible, another beautiful part of the South Luose palace, but from the inside there's nothing to find. You will sleep here for tonight… until I figure out what to do with you."

The three stepped farther inside, cautious, but were pleasantly surprised to find their belongings awaiting them.

"Sano!" screeched Lessa as he flew into her arms.

Solza was there, too, and she didn't hesitate to run to Arianna, weaving in and out of her legs at the reunion—the knot in Arianna's chest began to unravel, and she closed her eyes a moment.

Thank you, Solomon.

Keeper Kassime let his magic fall away from Jeom without any finesse—he landed on a rug with a thud and woke with a start, rubbing at the back of his head and definitely confused.

Arianna caught his eye and put a finger to her lips.

Keeper Kassime had his hand on his hip, taking them all in. "I trust you know well of magic, then? Of the Golden Age?" he said. "If Solomon sent you to find me, to find *Ferlon*, then you must."

"Yes, sir, we do," stuttered Lessa, shifting back and forth on her feet.

Keeper Kassime narrowed his eyes at her with a curt nod. He picked up Arianna's dagger from the pile of their things and began turning it over in his hands, examining it; she noticed he wore a ring, the same one from his portrait, the stones most certainly Aura and Ora.

He glanced at the avatars, Sano and Solza, clinging to their masters, and set the dagger back down, mumbling something to himself that Arianna couldn't quite make out.

"From here on forward, you'll address me *only* as Keeper Helix Kassime. Forget you ever heard the name Ferlon Ragaric at all," he ordered—the four remained speechless, wary.

Arianna's eyes flicked to the door that led to the dungeons, and Keeper Kassime didn't miss the motion.

"You are permitted to explore the attic, just don't touch anything that doesn't belong to you." He marched right up to Arianna, glaring down at her. "And don't even *think* about trying to leave. None of you will be leaving here until I've decided what's to be done with you. Let tomorrow decide your fates. Until then, good night."

He left the room abruptly, leaving the door to this room wide open. But what had to be the sound of a lock being sealed with magic reached their ears loud and clear from the direction of the stairwell.

Arianna looked up, finding the moon splashing down on them through a glass-topped ceiling which covered the expanse of the area.

How long has it been? She guessed a full day had already passed since their capture.

She kept her eyes up, at such a beautiful sight, surreal considering all they'd just been through. It was as if the sky adjoined the room, blanketing them in infinite protection. Arianna became lost in its scope, feeling closer to the stars than ever before; wisped clouds wove in and out of their diamond-like maze, and the moon shone bright, keeping close watch on her all the while.

"What is this place?" said Jeom, breaking the silence. "What are all these strange instruments for? Why did the city *keeper* bring us here? Is he going to kill us?" His hand flew to his forehead. "*Ah,* my head."

"Be still," said Lessa, coming over to check on him. "You took a nasty hit and missed… quite a bit." She gently pushed him to lie back down and then looked around. "I think this is an alchemy room."

"Alchemy?" said Demetrius.

"It's another word for magic… potions, like what Talis was training me to do." Lessa shook her head, eyes wide. "But this is on a whole different level."

"Potions? But why would the city keeper have anything to do with potions?" said Jeom.

"Because he's also Ferlon Ragaric," said Demetrius, matter-of-factly. "And a sorcerer… *and,* apparently, a guardian of the Golden Age, if I heard that right?"

"What!" Jeom tried to sit up again, but Lessa kept her hand on his chest, shaking her head.

"Maybe Keeper Kassime is a master healer. A *magical* healer, like Talis," said Lessa, ignoring him. "Ara?"

"Maybe…" she said, unable to form a steady thought—she was still staring at the sky.

I almost thought we'd never see it again.

"What did he mean by 'anyone outside of the guardians'?" said Demetrius, inspecting their new surroundings. "Never heard that one before."

Lessa just shrugged. "I have no idea."

Arianna couldn't engage; the weight of her exhaustion was too much. She lowered herself onto the rug, and Solza came to join her, nuzzling into her lap; it was in this moment that all her emotions flooded to the surface, the shock wearing off and leaving space to feel. Silent tears rolled down her cheeks as she internally thanked Solomon again for rescuing them, one last time. Solza never left her side, her fur catching every teardrop, but her friends gave her the space she needed to properly grieve, each finding the isolation they needed in this vast attic of the palace to unravel and rest... and to prepare for whatever the morning might bring.

13

FINDING FREEDOM

MORNING CAME, DROWNING ARIANNA in warm and welcome sunlight, the glass ceilings expanding high over her head. It felt as if the sun had fused her into the soft rug, and she couldn't bring herself to move even a finger for how comfortable she was. There wasn't a sore muscle in her body; she assumed Lessa must've snuck back to work her magic on her while she slept, making it seem as if yesterday's beating had never even happened.

Solza was still snuggled beside her, soaking in the light as if they shared a single mind.

Unwilling to let go of such a peaceful moment, Arianna welcomed this new wave of hope, thinking over the tumultuous days since they'd fled the districts. She and her friends had faced peril, treachery, and deceit from every angle, yet here they were, safe and sound—and in the Palace of South Luose, no less.

The night before, she had been sentenced to death. Now, she basked in sunrays that fell down on her from the most beautifully decorated windows. As if the morning light had triggered the glass to somehow morph from crystal clear, now stunning splashes of blues, reds, yellows, greens, and indigos made a rainbow of light dance about her vision. And if she looked closely at the detail, the outlines of what appeared to be kings and queens, gorgeously preserved landscapes, and even a soaring dragon or two were made quite visible.

So much wonder, hidden in plain sight...

Much like what they'd discovered down in the City of Undor, there was no mistaking what these depictions embodied; there had only been one Golden Age in the legends of history, and here it was, etched in the windowpanes above.

It was truly a magical sanctuary of sorts—the makings of a brand new utopia, if they were permitted to stay.

"Come on, Solza, let's go and find our friends," said Arianna with a sigh. "We can't stay here forever."

She tore her eyes away from the enchanting glass sky and nudged Solza to join her; the avatar gave a gentle snap at her fingers but otherwise ignored her.

"You lazy beast," she said, poking her again. Solza gave a warning growl that Arianna didn't want to test, so she left her to rest while she explored alone.

Since she hadn't had the mental capacity to really register where she was last night, Arianna now took a moment to explore the alchemy room in more detail. She slid her hand across a long table topped with several steel and glass instruments; they were similar to the ones she'd seen Lessa use many times, though these were on a much greater scale. There were also jars filled with strange substances that she wouldn't know the first thing to do with, but one in particular caught her eye, its contents a dark red liquid. Dipping her finger in, she decided to taste it. She stuck out her tongue at the rancid flavor. *Prillyberries, of course.*

With a hint of magic, she thought.

Where is our healer?

There was nothing else here of interest to Arianna without Lessa there to explain, so she left the alchemy room in search of her friends—there was only one door to choose from, the one Keeper Kassime had escorted them through last night, so she opened it and stepped back into the main, pentagon-shaped chamber.

Of the five doors this room featured, she knew the one behind her led to the alchemy room and the one across from her led to the secret stairwell in the dungeons; from Keeper Kassime's warning, that one would certainly be locked, but Arianna wasn't in the least bit tempted to step foot into the dungeons again. She considered the other doors.

Where do you lead?

Her friends must've found a place to sleep through one of these, and she was eager to explore, the mystery nearly as tantalizing as when they'd opened door after door in the Vanishing Tunnels, never knowing what magical surprise lay on the other side. But Arianna took a moment to appreciate where she was first; the pentagon chamber seemed engineered as only a 'passing through place,' but it was remarkable, nonetheless.

Where she didn't find lush carpets, wooden slabs with a rose-colored shine lined the floors, sparkling as the sunlight filtered through a perimeter of windows at the top. Sophisticated chairs with cushions patterned in fine threads were spaced evenly about the room, and two opposite walls were overtaken by grand mirrors with ornate, gold frames, making it seem as if the chamber stretched on forever.

The room's elegance was breathtaking in its simplicity, every detail carefully chosen so that one particular aspect didn't overcome the other.

Arianna paced around the chamber, admiring the portraits hung above each one of the doors; they depicted regal-looking men or women that Arianna recalled no mention of from the Learning Center.

The first she came upon was a painting captioned 'Queen Ivanna of the City of Belgradia'—the woman had sharp green eyes and long hair of a deep red, and Arianna was left to ponder the world in which she had once reigned. She certainly had a seductive authority about her, no king by her side. And she proudly wore a crown atop her head, jewels covering her neck.

The next portrait that caught her eye was of a portly, older man with a gentle face, his eyes a striking golden brown and his smile so inviting. The crown he wore matched the bright gold thread of his cape, and his jeweled hand clutched the shoulder of a young man who boasted the same eyes and kind smile; it was captioned 'King Damas and Prince Neas of the City of Saindora.'

Arianna had to reread the caption again and again, until she could no longer deny what she was looking at—these were the last rulers of the Golden Age before King Devlindor had taken the throne. Remembering the sad story painted in *Olleb-Yelfra the Fallen*, Arianna took a moment to mourn their fates... the loss of a budding young prince and the decay of his grieving father.

There would be no successor to this royal bloodline. No other rightful king or queen would come to claim the throne and continue the peaceful existence King Damas and his son had controlled—King Devlindor had stolen that future away from the Olleb and created his own.

She grimaced. *Never forget.*

Not wanting to let the darkness slide back in, Arianna tried the door closest to her and entered another room. Inside, she found Jeom snoring rather loudly in a corner, clinging to the Axe of Crissy; it looked as if Lessa had gotten to him too.

She stifled a laugh and took in the new setting; the space was vast, undecorated, and much darker than the last, not nearly as many windows to let the light in. Instead, torches were arranged along the walls, lit with what appeared to be permanent, magical flames.

No wonder Jeom slept here, she thought. *It's reminiscent of the Inventor's Zone.*

The floor was tiled in smooth, splotched marble, and large candlesticks stood tall in every corner of the wide, empty space. Arianna walked to the far wall, finding a display case with full-body armor, shields, chainmail, and the like—she was used to seeing regulators in armor, though not in anything quite as brilliant as these.

An array of fine weaponry was set up next to it, covering the expanse of the back of the room. Arianna gaped, a wide smile stretching across her face—there were arrows with tips fashioned from vibrant metals, throwing stars and flails, a silver longbow subtly ornamented with gems, and a vast collection of daggers (although not one nearly as splendid as Aurora). There were also swords, axes, and spears, of all different types and each one beautifully crafted—it was truly a warrior's dream.

Arianna studied each one carefully, even recognizing some of the precious stones that could be found in Undor fused into the creations.

"What is this place?" she whispered to herself, running her hand across a red and gold shield.

Then she noticed the barrel of wooden swords in the corner and knew exactly where she was.

A sparring room!

Though this one was more fit for a noble than what she was accustomed to in the districts.

She wanted to wake Jeom up to test out any one of these weapons, but she refrained, tiptoeing out of the room to let him sleep. Selecting another door to explore, Arianna discovered Demetrius wide awake and studying in the next chamber, one crammed from the base to the ceiling with nature.

Almost every inch of the place, save for the wood floor, was made from glass, so the sun enveloped her in light once again. She felt as if she'd stepped right back into the forest, although this was more what she might expect of a jungle—it was warm, *almost* uncomfortably, and trees and strange plant life climbed the walls, searching for a way out; even a colorful bird or two had a home here, flittering about the canopies of vines dangling overhead.

Demetrius barely acknowledged Arianna as he navigated around the greenery, looking as good as new. Clearly entranced by his findings, he poked at potted plants. And flowers of many colors, some with spiked stems and others with glossy bulbs, had his full attention. She knew this was probably a haven to him, so much different to the Jar, a new nature-filled world to explore.

Arianna was entranced, too, as she observed from the doorway—there was just something oddly *different* about this nature; she thought everything swayed unusually with a bit of life. And although she was no agrarian, she was quite sure some of these plants didn't have a place in their world.

Not wanting to draw Demetrius away from his thoughts, Arianna went back to the pentagon chamber and entered through the final door—she spotted Lessa immediately, a book in hand and curled up on a large sofa. There was an empty vial on the table, so she assumed she had just finished healing her own injuries. Sano was with her too, of course, and a mess of scrolls was piled near her feet.

This room had two such seating areas, one on either side. Light tapestries were strung up over tall windows, the sunlight softly filtering through, and shelves upon shelves, stacked with more books and scrolls than even the Learning Center held, created three of the walls in this chamber.

Arianna's eyes were drawn to a large portrait hung up above a fireplace, the centerpiece of the room.

"Is that…?" She gasped.

Without a doubt, Arianna recognized the faces of a young Solomon Bell and Talis Churry in the painting. Their arms were strewn across each other, as if the best of friends; she walked farther into the room to get a better look, too intrigued to even bother speaking to Lessa yet.

Several other people joined their young masters in the portrait, painted happily alongside them. Arianna had to look twice when she recognized a much younger Keeper Kassime there, too—he stood front and center, with a head of thick, brown hair, his ring proudly showing, and that familiar scowl on his face.

For a moment, Arianna even thought she recognized a scrawny Cyn among them but decided her eyes must be deceiving her now; there were, though, about ten others in the portrait for whom she had no names. She found Solomon's face again, so many questions on her lips.

What do you want me to do here?

As she took in the rest of the room, a massive jade sculpture atop a podium drew her away from the portrait, reminding her so much of her utopia. It was intricate in every detail, mixed with traces of gold.

Reading the description, Arianna was stunned to find it a replica of the City of Saindora, practically the only place outside of the Warrior's District that she had any knowledge of. For slaves, only the High City had ever been of any importance, and…

"'The rest of the world, you'll just have to wait and see. If you can survive. *Hail* to the King!'" said Arianna in a mocking voice, recalling her lectures. "Well, I sure see now."

Lessa looked up, startled out of her reading frenzy, eyes puffy and red from what looked to be a full night awake.

"Oh, Ara, it's just you," she said, letting out a sigh of relief. "You *scared* me." She sat up, waving her over to the couch. "Come here, you won't believe what I've found out."

Arianna shooed Sano off the sofa so that she had room to sit, careful not to step on any of the scrolls scattered on the floor. "What did you find?"

"This place…" Lessa gazed around in awe. "This is where we belong. Solomon, he was right to send us here. These are all the answers we've been seeking." She stretched her arms out wide. "It's *full* of magic!"

Arianna remembered when Talis had forced her to study the scrolls from his own little collection, enough to even fit in their rucksacks. And yet, the information they'd learned from that 'little collection' had been immense, life-changing.

She took in the bookshelves around her now, stacked with more material than she thought she could ever go through in a lifetime; but if each book and scroll had even *anything* to do with magic or the Golden Age, then she could only imagine what they might learn—a vast hoard of explanations probably lay on these shelves, answers that they had been eagerly seeking for the last several weeks.

"Just think," she whispered, almost afraid at what they might find.

Just then, Solza strolled into the room, obviously looking for Sano.

Arianna beamed. "Maybe we can learn something of the avatars as well!"

Lessa bit her lip, clapping excitedly. "I know. There has to be something—"

"Arianna Belvedor, is it?" Keeper Kassime loomed in the doorway; only the gods knew how long he'd been watching them.

The girls jumped to their feet, greeting the man who had almost thrown them to their deaths with as much politeness as they could muster. But from his expression, Arianna thought he wouldn't soon be forgetting that she'd tried to choke the life out of him just yesterday.

"Yes, Keeper Kassime," she said with the slight bow of her head, silently thanking herself for strapping Aurora back to her thigh—though he'd rescued her and her friends from the dungeons, he still hadn't made it clear whether or not he would prove friend or foe.

"And you are?" he said, looking to Lessa.

He appeared much as he had upon their first meeting—wearing the thin, silver crown atop his neatly combed hair, a decorated vest, and a very fine sword at his waist.

"My name is Lessa Thur," she said in a small voice. "I… Talis Churry, he was my master in the Healer's District." She glanced at the portrait.

Keeper Kassime recoiled at her words, the shock plain on his face as his eyes flicked to the painting as well. But he quickly recovered his normal nonchalant state.

"Very well," he said, walking into the room. "And your male companions?"

"They're half-brothers, actually," said Arianna. "Jeom and Demetrius Kane. From the Creator's and the Agrarian's Districts."

"From all four districts?" His voice pitched. Then he turned away, staring again at the painting. "How intriguing," he said, though to himself.

Before he could utter another question, Arianna's curiosity beat him to it. "Who are you, *really?* What is this place?"

He turned to face her, studying her intently.

"In time," he said after a moment. "Go and fetch your friends. We have important things to discuss."

He moved well clear of the girls and sat himself on the other couch at the opposite end of the library.

"And this is *not* a play area," he added with the loud snap of his fingers—a playful Solza and Sano immediately slunk back to their masters, responding to what had to be a magical command. And by the look on Lessa's face, they were both wondering the same thing.

"Stay here with the avatars," whispered Arianna to Lessa, not trusting the keeper one bit. "I'll go get the boys."

She left to retrieve Jeom and Demetrius from their solitudes. And when everyone was gathered in the library, Keeper Kassime invited them all to sit together on the other sofa.

"So, it has begun," he said, considering them all with a perplexed expression.

"What has?" asked Demetrius, a lightness in his voice—he
was covered from head to toe in dirt.

"The prophecy is in motion," said Kassime, nodding to himself, "and we must all do our part to make sure it sees through to
the end, no matter what may come."

"You know about *the* prophecy?" gasped Lessa, leaning forward with wide eyes. "What does it mean?"

The keeper eyed the open scrolls on the floor and settled on
Olleb-Yelfra the Fallen—Lessa must've been referencing it earlier. He closed his eyes and spoke softly in verse:

*Light is light and dark is dark, but never shall they
live apart. One shall seek what the other denies. If
it is found, thus follows the demise. When one
eclipses over the other, life shall end for he and his
brother.*

"The Golden Rule," said Arianna, placing a hand on her
heart; she recalled the moment she'd plucked that parchment
from General Indra's skeleton in the City of Undor, and again
when they'd seen it inked on *Olleb-Yelfra the Fallen* in, presum-
ably, a seer's blood.

Keeper Kassime closed his eyes a moment.

"This prophecy is what the Guardians of Gold was founded
upon," he explained, garnering their full attention. "A hope that
balance can be returned to the world." He opened his eyes, his
gaze fixed on Arianna. "A hope that begins with you."

"I don't understand," she said, shaking her head. "How has
this *prophecy* been set into motion? And what does any of it have
to do with us?"

"What are the Guardians of Gold again?" said Jeom, hugging
his axe to his chest.

"All in time," said Kassime, raising his hand for quiet before anyone else could speak. "And there's much *you* must tell, but let's start at the present."

His tone grew a bit gentler, though he wasn't exactly warm. He waved his hand toward them, so indifferently, as if what he said next wasn't life-altering at all...

"I'll need to grant you your freedom. You can't very well stay cooped up here the rest of your lives, now can you?"

His eyes filled with that bit of excitement again, as they had when Arianna told him they were, in fact, the escaped slaves the King was hunting.

"Freedom?" stuttered Demetrius.

Lessa squealed in delight. "You can truly do that for us?"

Jeom scoffed. "What of the guards and the regulators? And the people in the city who saw us being taken here?" he said, rightfully skeptical. "We can never be free now that you've declared our identities."

"He's right," said Arianna, not allowing herself to be baited. "We're supposed to be dead already, by *your* orders. And Godfrey... you've even paid him for turning us in." She felt her anger rising.

How dare he play with our emotions like this!

Keeper Kassime just gave a flick of his hand, as if all of this were of no consequence to him.

"My guards don't know what it is they've seen," he said with a smirk. "They never do, mindless bunch they are. Besides, they didn't hear me question you. And the city people, *please.*" He rolled his eyes. "I sentence citizens to their deaths every single week." He leaned back in the sofa. "Godfrey, on the other hand, has already been dealt with."

"Dealt with like... dead?" said Arianna, hopeful.

"A prominent citizen like that?" Keeper Kassime snickered. "You know nothing of politics, do you? *No,* I mean like magic," he said. "Godfrey doesn't remember a thing and his pockets are full of gold. He won't have anything to complain about. In any case, four people from the dungeons have already taken your place this morning at the Altar. It's like you never even existed inside these city walls."

"Taken our place?" said Demetrius, raising an eyebrow. "What do you mean, exactly? What happens at the Altar?"

"Today at dawn, four citizens were beheaded. In *your* place," said Kassime—again, much too casually. "The Altar is where we publicly hold any punishment or 'passing' ceremonies in South Luose. Citizens are forced on to the next life, if they can't hold their own in this one."

He put a fist to his chest.

"Hail to the King," he said, dryly.

"Beheaded?" whimpered Lessa. "But that's just... wrong!" She squeezed Sano tight in her arms.

Keeper Kassime seemed uncomfortable with her reaction, but Arianna and her friends were all uncomfortable with his.

"They were sentenced to die regardless. Your arrival just moved up their timelines, and we needed the space in the dungeons anyway." He cocked his head to the side, dismissing Lessa's disgust. "Don't worry so much. You'll get used to it, as you did in the Jar."

Arianna pursed her lips, calculating their situation—they were suddenly in the favor of someone who reminded her so much of General Ivo, someone with a cruel power and who wasn't afraid to use it. And yet, right now, they *needed* someone like him to lend a helping hand.

"So, now what?" she asked, remaining cautious. "How do you intend to grant our freedom?" She lifted her chin high, holding his gaze.

She hoped she seemed as nonchalant as him, but inside she was panicking, praying, *dying* for this freedom he dangled in front of her eyes—she wanted to care that others had died in their place, but right now she couldn't find the space in her heart. It was a cruel world they lived in, and right now, all she wanted was freedom for herself and her friends.

Just survive.

"Now, we have to get you brand new identities," he said after a moment. "I've thought it through, and, really, there's no other way. There's nowhere in this world you can hide as well... *you.*" Keeper Kassime got to his feet and began to rummage around one of the bookshelves.

The four locked eyes with each other but didn't dare even whisper, knowing he would hear. Moments later, he had selected a single scroll from the shelf and brought it over to Arianna; they all leaned in to read.

"An identity concealment spell?" said Lessa, reading the parchment quicker than anyone else. She looked up at him.

"A potion," said Kassime, nodding. "No one will ever recognize you this way."

"You mean, you want to literally change us? Is that even possible?" said Jeom, scratching the hair on his chin.

Keeper Kassime crossed his legs at his knees. "What do you think?"

"So... we won't *really* receive citizenship documentation then, will we?" said Arianna, unable to help the glimmer of gloom in her voice.

"If I understand this right, we won't even exist," said Demetrius.

Keeper Kassime let out a barking laugh that startled them all; the hairs on the back of Arianna's neck stood up.

"I can only imagine Bell putting up with such naivety! How did you survive him?" He shook his head, and Arianna felt the sting of his words. "I can't just grant you, Arianna Belvedor, the most sought person in all of the Olleb, her freedom. Not when it's the King who is after your head." He looked her in the eyes. "Do you even really understand your predicament? Next to him, you're the most famed person to walk this land at present. Excuse me, *infamous*. Thus, if you want to truly live without fear, you'll need to become different people completely… and forever."

"Do whatever you have to do," said Jeom.

Arianna didn't respond, internally fuming, and trying to focus on not leaping after the keeper's neck again.

How dare he speak to me like that.

He was right, of course, but still…

Keeper Kassime addressed Lessa, ignoring the obvious hesitation from everyone other than Jeom.

"You'll be helping me," he said—it wasn't a question. "If you were truly Talis' apprentice, you must be terribly gifted. He wouldn't waste his time otherwise. You know about alchemy, I suppose?"

"Well… I only really learned to mix remedies that could *heal*," she said, fiddling with a loose string on her robes. "Talis taught me some tricks to make them more effective, like just saying simple words when creating brews that all the healer-slaves were taught in the Jar. Potions, I suppose, but utterly normal ones." She shrugged.

Keeper Kassime smiled.

"Well, the *simple* words you learned make your remedies more powerful than any other healer you've ever trained with," he said, matter-of-factly. "You've been taught to transform matter of the Olleb into something else entirely, whether you realize it or not. When magic touches these 'remedies,' as you call them, you alter their chemistry altogether. This is alchemy, and Talis Churry was the best alchemist I've ever known."

He leaned forward.

"I'm going to teach you some new combinations. Potions that do *more* than just heal. Would you like that?"

A glow of excitement spread across her face. "I'm in!" she said, throwing up her hands.

"*Lessa*," hissed Arianna, glaring at her with wide eyes.

"Oh, come off it, Ara," said Demetrius with a smirk. "Only

one option has been laid out, and you *know* we're going to take it. What other choices do we have?"

"Ain't that the truth, brother!" said Jeom, slapping him on the back—evidently more than ready to throw his name away for someone else's, if it meant no more running.

Lessa just shrugged, chewing on her lip with a guilty smile.

Arianna ignored them, facing Keeper Kassime.

"How do *you* know all of this?" she said, arms crossed at her chest. "We need more of an explanation first before we can just carelessly trust you with something like this." She gestured to the scroll.

Kassime laughed again, though more subtly this time, considering her with such curiosity.

"I learned the same way your masters did," he snapped, taking her aback. "We trained together, for many years. We call ourselves the Guardians of Gold, the ones who protect the remnants of the Golden Age and the ones who still resist." His voice became sharp. "The guardians have passed down our memories, carefully, for centuries as Devlindor continues to destroy all the magic and all the history that came before him."

He got to his feet, hand on the hilt of his sword as he stared down at them, challenging them.

"I wasn't the first guardian, and I *won't* be the last." He gazed around the library, seeming to disappear in his memories. "We alone hold the knowledge of the former world, and we alone can bring it back. But it's taken time, and it'll continue to take time." He bowed his head low. "There have been... many setbacks."

He walked to the center of the room, beckoning the group to stand with him—they did so without question, Arianna in the lead.

"Whatever your past and however you came to be here, you're a part of this now, whether you like it or not," said Kassime, eyes locked on Arianna and Lessa. "So out of respect for your masters, my friends, I'll *consider* teaching you what I know and the secrets of the guardians. But on this day, the only promise I make to you now is your freedom. I'll do that for Solomon and Talis, at the very least. Am I quite clear?"

They all looked back and forth at one another, fear and anticipation plain in their expressions.

As Demetrius had said, what other choice did they have? And even if they *had* been faced with a clear choice to walk away, Arianna wouldn't want to turn her back on a chance at learning more about the enchanted side of the world—not when magic continued to save her life and that of her friends over and over again.

"Before we continue, if you think you can accept this responsibility… of knowing all that you do and all I may teach you, I ask you to repeat after me." Keeper Kassime held his fist to his chest, but this time, he didn't hail to the King. "Hail to the World. Hail to Olleb-Yelfra!"

His statement was resounding.

No one hesitated to follow the request, their voices ringing out together in a harmony throughout the room.

Arianna knew it in her heart, right then and there, that she'd made a binding pledge to herself and to the Olleb. And with such a promise, she vowed to become worthy of the knowledge that had been bestowed on her by Solomon, Talis, and, hopefully one day soon, the keeper; her eyes never left the portrait as she spoke the words, Solomon smiling down at her all the while—this was, at least, one decision she was certain was right.

When their voices fell away, Keeper Kassime let out a sigh, something that Arianna hoped was relief but also could've been more like dread…

"In just a few short hours, you'll be made new again," he said. "From there, we'll begin planning your lives. I'll be watching your every move from here on out, and if I find you reliable enough, formal training will soon begin. But one foot out of line and you'll regret it." He took a deep breath, taking them all in. "No doubt you all have the potential to become gifted Guardians of Gold. Certainly so, if Solomon sent you my way."

He beckoned for Lessa to follow him into the alchemy room.

AS THE HOURS PASSED, Arianna, Jeom, and Demetrius waited patiently in the library, sitting in silence as they tried to comprehend the exciting future that lay ahead—the freedom that would soon be theirs and the secrets that they may come to learn. Strange smoke traveled to their noses from the alchemy room as Keeper Kassime and Lessa worked tirelessly to prepare the concoction. And soon, everyone was called to meet in the pentagon chamber.

Lessa, covered in slime and her forehead dotted in sweat, carried four jars filled with a cloudy liquid that stirred of its own volition, swirling about like a tiny, jarred twister.

"How does it work?" said Jeom, eyeballing it warily; she passed him a jar.

"It'll act almost as a shield that you carry within you," said Kassime. "Its properties create a sort of illusion from the inside out. To the naked eye, you'll look completely different. And to the unaided ear, you'll sound of a new voice."

Demetrius laughed, a dumbfounded expression on his face. "How is that even feasible?"

"The illusion manifests based off of dormant traits you already possess at your core," said Lessa, looking to Kassime for confirmation; she handed Demetrius a jar.

Keeper Kassime nodded, seemingly impressed. "A person you could've been if your genes had aligned differently at the moment of conception," he added. "We're all capable of being someone else, and this magic is a reflection of that."

"No one will recognize us… at all?" said Arianna, growing more comfortable with the idea—she thought of her portrait papered everywhere in the city and imagined what it might be like not to care.

"No one," said Kassime.

Arianna took a jar.

"Your eyes will be the *only* true piece of you that remains visible to the outside world." He tapped his temple. "Eyes never lie."

He paced about the group, everyone with a jar in hand.

"Now, let me be perfectly clear." He seemed nervous. "The only way I can provide you documentation, your *true* freedom, is to provide it to people that never actually existed. No one will notice or question you this way. You can have whatever life you want."

He stopped in front of Arianna.

"Isn't that why Solomon sent you here?" He didn't wait for a response. "I believe very deeply that it is. We were all taught this magic together, long ago."

Arianna didn't know what to say, to think—*had* these been Solomon's intentions when he'd sent her to find Ferlon Ragaric? To let go of her identity in order to gain some semblance of freedom?

Is this why he died for me?

Keeper Kassime just smiled—it wasn't exactly reassuring, but Arianna could tell he was trying to be.

"Drink up," he said. "And then everyone must grasp hands so that the magic doesn't affect our own perceptions."

Arianna didn't wait to contemplate this task a second longer, driving herself mad with trying to decipher right from wrong; she drank the potion down in one big gulp, the others doing the same. When their glasses were emptied and back on the tray, Keeper Kassime ordered them to grab hands, and they all formed a circle.

As the liquid settled in Arianna's belly, it began to warm her from the inside out. Then she felt it land, a spark of energy engulfing her from head to toe and shooting from one hand to the next, connecting them all in an extraordinary sensation.

Alas, the warm tingle quickly turned to pain—an *extraordinary* pain, one that Keeper Kassime had not warned them about.

I shouldn't have trusted him!

Arianna cried out, clutching her stomach as the liquid burned there for what seemed like an eternity; she couldn't help but think that they'd been poisoned, a cruel trick for the keeper's enjoyment to slowly watch them die.

The others seemed to be experiencing the same agony from what she could faintly tell, and quickly the circle was broken.

Keeper Kassime just stood idly by, waiting.

Finally, a clarity and calm came over Arianna. She opened her eyes, and everything seemed... ordinary (though she knew deep down that all had somehow changed).

The room was quiet again as the others, too, appeared to regain their control. Keeper Kassime appraised them all.

"It's done," he said with a delighted clap.

"What... what's done? What even happened?" said Lessa, wrapping her arms around herself.

"Seems nothing at all," growled Jeom, looking himself over.

"That was *quite* unpleasant," said Demetrius, wiping the sweat from his brow.

They all observed one another, searching for the changes Keeper Kassime had promised, but they all appeared to look and sound exactly the same.

"Oh, you are a skeptical bunch!" said Kassime, his mood much lighter. "Come. You shall see."

He ushered them over to a mirror mounted on one of the walls.

As Arianna and her friends assembled before it, their mouths fell open. Four strangers stared back at them through the glass, frantically searching for something recognizable—they found nothing.

Arianna stroked her own face, and the stranger in the mirror did the same; she looked into the chestnut eyes of a sad, tired face. *Is this me?*

The girl had thick, straight hair hanging neatly to her waist. It was black as night, the beautiful brown curls she'd always treasured completely wiped away. Her face was plumper too, set in light skin with a deep blush pattering her dimpled cheeks and tinting puckered lips. Undeniably, this girl was beautiful—in a different, *darker* sort of way than Arianna had ever thought herself. And though it didn't seem to resemble her at all, she could somehow make a slight connection. Or pretend to anyway.

The one thing she did know for certain…

Those are my eyes.

Unchanged and electric.

Arianna studied the other three strangers by her side through the mirror; Lessa still boasted her striking blue eyes she would recognize anywhere, but they were now set in a sun-kissed and freckled face. Bright red, almost orange, hair cascaded down her shoulders in delightful waves that Lessa had never been able to achieve as a blond. And she was stacked with more of a warrior's build; she'd left her dainty qualities behind, emulating more physical strength than ever before.

I hope my new body can still hold a sword. Arianna flexed her hand and was relieved to find that she felt the same, no more or less vigor than normal.

Demetrius had gone drastically lighter, his green eyes standing out even more against pale skin and silvery blond hair that hung long past his shoulders. He'd gained several inches in height, clearing that of even Jeom in his normal body, and he was much leaner, with sharp cheek bones and jaw lines that made his normally relaxed face seem perpetually stern.

But unlike the rest, Jeom had taken the strangest turn of all, shrinking a full foot in size.

His skin remained just as dark as before, but he'd adopted an extremely burly guise, with none of the natural charm he was used to leaning on; his hair grew wild with a long beard to match, and his brown eyes glared menacingly back at the others through the bush on his face.

"Damn it!" he shrieked, gawking at the others who had all been endowed with better looks. "What in the *gods'* name is this? Some kind of joke?"

Arianna couldn't help it and burst out laughing; and through the mirror, she saw her friends' new identities do the same—all except Jeom, who was irate.

"A mirror will *always* show you only what's on the outside. For that, they're easy to deceive," said Kassime, seeming satisfied at the outcome. "As is the rest of the world."

Arianna looked away from the mirror, studying all her friends again through her unaided eyes; she was overwhelmingly relieved that they all still appeared to be the people she knew. "So, anyone who looks at us will see the faces in the mirror, but we'll continue to see each other truly?"

Keeper Kassime nodded. "*Precisely.* Now, are you ready to say goodbye to who you once were?"

"Truly… forever?" said Arianna.

She couldn't help the quiver in her voice.

"Are you sure we can't change back someday?"

Keeper Kassime shook his head.

"All you can do is remember and remember well. Just like with the old Olleb," he said, sincerely. "One day, it will end and another will begin again in its place, a new Golden Age. But I'm afraid that now we can only protect the past with our memories and a well-kept library of the history that once was."

He looked them all up and down.

"The same goes for your true identities. There's no going back, if you want to live a normal life."

Arianna gave a resigned nod. "Can you at least tell us what the prophecy has to do with—"

Keeper Kassime laid a hand on her shoulder, squeezing hard and making her squirm.

"I've honored Solomon's obvious wishes. But, as I said before, I'll only grant you more knowledge of the Golden Age, of what I know, should I find you worthy. Until then, I won't say any more."

"Did you learn your riddles from Master Churry?" said Lessa, rolling her eyes.

That drew a genuine chuckle from Keeper Kassime.

"Think of it this way," he said, gathering up the empty potion jars, "you could become great guardians of knowledge someday, and that's a *valuable* gift to have. So, let's see how you fare in these new skins before I give away all my worth."

He clasped his hands behind his back, staring up at the portrait of King Damas and Prince Neas.

"I just need to see first what Solomon and Talis surely saw in you. And I need to understand what strengths have aided you all so far in your journey. Then I can make my assessment. Shall we begin?"

He handed Arianna a scroll tied with a red ribbon.

It was stamped with a brilliant gold and black emblem—the Warrior's Crest—and it displayed a date nearly five years prior.

She unfurled it with shaking hands to read the declaration:

Her friends received their own documentation slips as well, each declaring their freedom. But, for some reason, this moment seemed a lot less celebratory than Arianna had pictured it. The paper that supposedly granted her citizenship was weightless, wrinkling in her fingers as she read, over and over, the name written in smudged ink.

Aridyn Lareigh, a citizen of Olleb-Yelfra.

"I'm free?" She gaped down at the paper she'd waited her entire life to hold in her hands.

"You're free," said Kassime.

PART TWO

14

A CURSED SOUL

"SIR VLADAMOR WILL TAKE HIS LEAVE NOW," said Kassime, entering the attic library. Arianna looked up to find Jeom and Demetrius following at his heels; they were both sweaty, so Arianna presumed they had been sparring in the other room.

"The necromancer's finally leaving?" said Demetrius, catching his breath.

"He should be riding out at any moment," said Kassime, an abnormal glow on his face. "I've already seen him off."

"Finally!" said Lessa, pulling her nose out of a book and startling a snoozing Sano awake. "Let's hope we don't see him around these parts ever again."

"This is fantastic news," said Arianna, patting Solza on the head. "Hear that, girl? We're finally getting out of here!"

Keeper Kassime had locked them away in the attic above the dungeons for three weeks now, his promises of a better life indefinitely stalled by the necromancer's untimely arrival; the appearance of Sir Vladamor at the gates of South Luose had always been expected—he was the King's most trusted advisor and Princess Elisa had sent word of his imminent visit just days after Arianna's escape from the districts—but he'd shown up before the keeper could make proper arrangements for the group. And even with the protection of new identities, he didn't think it wise that the necromancer be the first test.

Arianna and her friends were more than happy to stay unseen for a short while, not wanting anything to do with such a man… *monster.* Stories of him were prevalent in the Warrior's District, of the King's Right Hand, and after hearing the secrets Keeper Kassime had to share about him, there was not a single reason Arianna would ever wish to cross his path. It had been a peaceful few weeks in the attic, at least, as they waited for his departure day. But they *were* getting restless up there.

Arianna ran to a window that faced the front common grounds to try to spot Sir Vladamor's brigade take leave, anything to distract her from her boredom. She spotted the gold mask first, knowing it to be his signature detail.

He was positioned atop a decorated horse at the front of a procession of regulators, clutching its reins with black leather gloves. And he dressed as such, as a regulator, but she knew with just one glance, even from a distance, that he was much more than that; Sir Vladamor would tirelessly hunt her until the end of his days on the King's behalf—and he had more than enough influence to do so.

She homed in on her reflection in the windowpane and a pale-faced beauty stared back.

He would never succeed…

Thanks to Keeper Kassime's magic, Arianna Belvedor was nowhere to be found.

"I just don't understand how someone could choose such a life as a necromancer," she muttered, thinking of his story.

"Easy," said Jeom, peeking out of the window beside her.

"For power." He plopped down next to Demetrius who fiddled with a small potted plant now (slowly the nature from the greenery room had begun to find its way into every corner of the attic).

In the districts, elders and regulators referred to Sir Vladamor by many names—the King's Shadow, the King's Right Hand, Head of the King's Guard; he was more heavily titled than Master Bell. But the Guardians of Gold recognized him with another name that Arianna wouldn't soon forget…

A necromancer, with a soul as black as night.

From what Keeper Kassime had described of him, if King Devlindor was considered the most powerful person in all the Olleb, then Sir Vladamor would be a close second. He was a dark remnant from the Golden Age, created—not born—unnaturally over time.

And with his help alone, the King had been able to take over the free world, unstoppable for centuries.

"He's really not… human?" said Arianna, trying to see through his mask and clothes for any hint of something unnatural, for he did *look* like just a man, on the outside.

Keeper Kassime came to stand next to her, staring down toward his peer.

"Everyone is born as an equal creation in this world, a balance of both dark and light, but one's choices and life experiences over time can tilt the scale," he said. "And some lean to one side much more than others."

He set his gaze on Arianna.

"As I've somewhat explained before, a necromancer is *not* human, not a naturally born creature of the Olleb… though the shell they walk in used to be. Sir Vladamor was born into a bloodline rich in magic, but he eventually gave in to the darkest parts of his soul completely—"

"Thus, forfeiting the natural balance," said Lessa, reiterating what she'd learned from the library's multitude of manuscripts.

Keeper Kassime nodded, his look distant.

"As a consequence, his soul was chipped away so much that he lost touch with his humanity." He shook his head. "It takes just one spell combined with the ultimate sacrifice of death to complete such a transition."

"A *spell* made him this way?" said Demetrius—all eyes were on the keeper now; they hadn't yet heard him speak about this part of the necromancer's origin story.

Jeom whistled. "Magic scares the pants off me," he said, arm draped over the back of the sofa as he let Sano hop around him.

"Good," said Kassime, his lips pressed in a thin line.

"So he had to murder someone for these… dark powers?" said Arianna, still not fully understanding what he was and how he'd come to be; she considered the handful of people she'd already sent to the afterlife and shuddered, wondering which way her own soul might lean.

"No, not at all," said Kassime, shaking his head. "*He* himself had to die."

"Didn't you finish reading the scroll?" said Lessa in a re-proachful tone—she rolled her eyes when Arianna, Demetrius, and Jeom didn't respond.

Keeper Kassime saw he had their full attention with this topic.

"Yes, he had to die first to even have a chance at such a trans-formation. The magic then chooses what happens next. And once Death latches onto a life, there's only one spell that can tether a soul back to the world of the living—*Onasyuda*." Arianna froze. "Likewise, it takes someone with extreme power and skill to per-form such strong magic."

Arianna's heart seemed to constrict at his statement, as if someone held it in their fist and squeezed just enough for her to recall her mortality. She knew the magic he spoke of well, had experienced it personally on her first encounter with Talis. Her hand came to rest on her stomach where she still had the faint scar from the failed Warrior's Challenge with Grinda—she was no stranger to Death.

In fact, as Talis had explained to her, the *Onasyuda* spell was her very first experience with magic.

"Then what happens?" said Lessa, coming to the window next to Arianna, as if reading her mind. "How could a soul turn so… evil, from only a word?"

"Then it's up to fate," said Kassime with a shrug. "Magic is and always will be a mystery. But one thing's for certain, it takes a strong will to cross the planes between life and death, and so stronger the survivor would naturally return. Sir Vladamor succumbed to the darkness, to necromancy, on his journey to the afterlife, and now that he's back, he's able to wield some of the blackest power nature has ever relinquished: control over the dead."

"I have trouble wrapping my head around that one," said Demetrius, shooing Solza away from his plant; she kept pawing at the leaves.

"Well said, brother. I say, let the dead rest," said Jeom, eyes wide. "I want absolutely nothing to do with that."

"Most would agree with you," said Kassime. "It's a lot to risk in exchange for power or for second chances. The majority who attempt it aren't able to complete the transition after death. They simply just cease to exist. In order to survive, both the subject and the magic *must* agree on a chosen path." He held up his hands, moving them up and down. "To follow the light or to be consumed by the shadows. The odds are in no one's favor, and there's no telling what a 'successful' summoning back to life might even return." He sighed. "Magic is so fickle like that."

Arianna listened intently, a question burning on her lips, but she wouldn't permit it to be spoken.

If one does survive the spell, is there no other option but a second life doomed to darkness?

She tried to piece together the fragments of her memory around her own death—vividly, she recalled a pool of blackness that had threatened to swallow her whole, how easy it would've been to just stop fighting and give in.

But I didn't give in. I followed the light… didn't I?

She could feel Lessa's eyes hot on her back as the conversation continued; Arianna was sure that the mention of the *Onasyuda* magic hadn't gone unnoticed to her either.

Why didn't Talis or Solomon speak of this before?

"Can a necromancer be stopped?" said Demetrius, coming to the window as well. "It seems unnatural… for one person, or whatever he is, to hold that kind of power."

Keeper Kassime laughed, his voice a heavy sound.

"It's the most unnatural thing that exists in this world! His soul has been *cursed*, drenched in dark magic. But everyone and everything has a weakness, no matter how strong and powerful they appear. Nothing can last forever. Not even if the King decrees it so." He straightened his crown.

"Right, nothing lasts forever," said Arianna—the keeper's words sank in, but they didn't feel right.

Again, she focused on the face of Aridyn in the glass, wondering if her reflection would always remain so distorted.

"Now pack your things," snapped Kassime, grimacing as he glanced around the messy library. "I'll be back in an hour to show you to your new quarters. I can't *stand* the lot of you wreaking havoc up here. It's sinful."

Arianna was overcome with excitement, forgetting her blackening thoughts.

"And clean this mess up," he growled, making to leave. "This is a palace, *not* a pigsty." He slammed the door on his way out, but she knew he was excited, too.

Everyone remained silent a moment, the air filled with such anticipation that it was almost tangible.

Arianna was the first to speak, turning away from the window. "Did we hear him correctly? Just an hour… and we're out of here?" She wanted to jump up and down.

"I think so," sang Demetrius, a cautious smile stretching across his face.

"We've done it," said Lessa as Jeom pumped his fists in the air. "We're about to get everything we ever dreamed of!"

Their joy was no longer containable—Lessa and Jeom flew into a dance about the room, Demetrius swung Sano in circles in the air, and Arianna knelt down to hug Solza, thinking of all the possibilities.

We're safe. We're free.

Though more sinister thoughts kept pressing into her mind, Arianna easily shoved them away; three weeks safe and sound in an attic full of magical mysteries had fully revitalized her spirit, and she wasn't ready to let that feeling go.

They were to officially take up residence in the Palace of South Luose under the charge of the city keeper himself. And there was no better position to have in the world than a palace placement—prosperous futures as highlifes awaited them; she couldn't possibly have imagined a more joyful conclusion to such a harrowing journey.

Amidst the celebrations, Arianna was drawn back to spying on the necromancer; with Keeper Kassime's words ringing in her head, it was easy to spot the magic-riddled monster behind the mask now… he wore the King's Crest proudly. She realized only then that Sir Vladamor might've even been close to Solomon once upon a time—surely their pasts in the King's favor had intertwined their lives.

The thought of Solomon pained her still, and she pictured it was him riding away instead of the necromancer; she placed her hand against the windowpane, ready to leave her friend in the past as she prepared to take hold of the life he'd laid out for her.

Arianna froze, her hand pressed upon the window still, just as the necromancer snapped his head around and lifted his mask, glaring in her direction. His face was hardly a face at all, but his eyes were dark and searching.

Not possible. He can't see me.

Arianna tried to shake off the cold feeling wrapping around her body, like a tightening rope.

No, it's not possible.

She knew the tower had been cloaked with strong magic, and so he certainly saw nothing but beautifully stained glass windows, as Keeper Kassime had assured them so many times. And if he, for some reason, *could* see a face so high up, it wouldn't be hers.

As the necromancer gazed toward the north tower, Arianna had to look away.

Averting her gaze, she made a silent wish that Sir Vladamor would leave and never return as she considered his creation and the extent of his powers. But even with her eyes closed, she could see the details of his monstrous face, already burned into her memory—skin so pale it showed the blood circling beneath his cheeks and pulsing in his veins, and lips paper thin from the way he pursed them. And his eyes… filled with nothing but hate.

Arianna thought him a skeleton of sorts, walking about in a costume of flesh.

Her curiosity overcame her, and she looked again to see if he still searched; he was already riding off, his procession of regulators in tow.

Arianna watched until the city swallowed them. Then she ran across the library to another window that faced toward the land outside of the city walls. Sir Vladamor and his regulators were racing at full speed across an open meadow, headed in the opposite direction to where she and her friends had entered the city.

"Thank the gods, they're gone," breathed Lessa, appearing beside her. She was holding the scroll she'd referenced earlier; it belonged to the guardians' library and detailed Sir Vladamor's disturbing history, entitled *A Cursed Soul.*

"I thought you might want to have another look at this, considering what the keeper said today…" She cleared her throat. "The part he mentions, it's just the last few pages."

Arianna knew she was referring to the *Onasyuda* magic.

"Thanks," she said, feeling her cheeks grow hot; she took it from her. "Maybe I'll finish it later."

At Keeper Kassime's insistence, they had studied every day about the Golden Age while he took his time to assess their abilities and prepare them a life outside of the attic. Arianna had naturally wanted to know more about the man leading the hunt for her head, the necromancer, but she wasn't a fast reader and had only made it about halfway through that history lesson. Even so, she had no trouble imagining his beginnings, especially with the keeper's added color to it.

As her friends began to pack their things, readying for their futures, Arianna stayed by the window, picturing Sir Vladamor and the life he had once lived… before meeting his dark destiny.

"MASTER LETHANDER, PLEASE DON'T DO THIS. Please don't make me go," pleaded Vladamor. *He bent at one knee, unable to lift his eyes to meet his prosecutors.*

"Quiet!" spat Master Lethander.

Finding an ounce of courage, Vladamor reluctantly lifted his gaze to meet the revered elf's—the leader of the Nicora Elven Clan. He watched him closely, the way he moved with such elegance and authority as he addressed the tribe.

You have no right to do this to me! Vladamor would have screamed the words out loud… if he had truly believed them.

Long silver and gold chains adorned Master Lethander's neck, each one signifying great achievements in his lifetime. They sparkled against his skin, mocking Vladamor with every layer; jealousy gripped him then, as if the chains of such unattainable, honorable triumphs were being tied around his own bare neck, squeezing the life from him.

"Vladamor…" said Master Lethander, his voice ringing across the open field where they gathered, tall grasses whipping softly at their knees.

Vladamor's heart pounded fiercely, hardening against the vicious verdict to come—he'd chosen his path, and now he would pay the price. "You cannot do this…" His voice was barely audible.

Master Lethander puffed out his bare chest, the sun beating down on it as if to offer him its blessing, his long hair glistening like silk beneath its rays. "You've attempted to trade ancient Nicora secrets to those outside our realm, and in doing, you have disgraced yourself and disgraced us all."

There were hundreds of elves there today—everyone from the tribe, he thought—to watch his demise and revel in his torture. Banded together, they looked like a sea of white fish out of water, their pale skin glimmering against the backdrop of the giant, silvery trees.

Master Lethander dragged Vladamor to his feet. "Because of you, our sister is now dead!"

The crowd began to whisper, angry and sorrowful sounds, as they recounted her demise, one of the most beloved in the family.

"Her throat was slit! You monster," yelled one of his sisters, stepping forward. She didn't let any tears fall, but her cheeks burned red hot, hands shaking at her sides. Vladamor thought she might send an arrow flying toward him at any moment, her fingers itching for her bow. "Like she was trash to be tossed aside. Because of your selfishness, your greed, your needless appetite for more, our Delira is dead."

"She wasn't supposed to be there," retorted Vladamor, his voice coming in a whisper.

He tried to meet his accuser's eyes, but the sun beat too brightly.

"You can't even look at me… you coward," she said, melting

back in with the crowd.

"I loved her! You knew that," growled one of his brothers, now taking the stand. "I would've taken care of her for the rest of our days. But Delira loved you… for what reason, I can't possibly fathom." He pointed his finger toward him. "And you just threw her to the wolves. Murdered by humans, no less! How you've shamed us."

The elf spat at his feet, and others had to pull him back to avoid a fight.

"You're a monster, and we'll not grieve your fate to come," yelled another.

There were murmurs of agreement from all around. Vladamor couldn't hold back his emotions any longer, letting out a terrible cry as his fear rose to the surface for all to judge.

"Do you deny these accusations?" hissed Master Lethander, gripping his wooden staff, as if he meant to pummel him with it—no amount of tears could reason with him.

"You don't think I loved her, too?" Vladamor screamed toward the sky, spit flying from his mouth. He paraded within the tight circle now formed around him, arms tied behind his back. "She wasn't supposed to be there! She didn't have to try and save me. She was always trying to save me. I cannot be saved!"

His breath came heavy as the words poured out, sweat beading on his forehead and dripping down his cheeks; he desperately wanted to push the long hair from his eyes, the weight of it clinging to his skin. He just stared on, helpless and wild.

Another of his sisters stepped forth from the crowd, just as beautiful as the one he'd lost. Her words came soft but utterly filled with grief—each one piercing, as if an arrow to his heart.

"You were always ignorant to the love Delira had for you, Vladamor," her voice shook, eyes rimmed red with tears, "that we have all tried to have for you. And, in this, you are also wrong…"

The elf moved closer to him, grasping his chin in her hand and forcing him to listen, to look her in the eyes.

"Delira didn't risk her life to only save your own, my fallen brother," she whispered, silent tears streaking her cheeks now. "She was trying to save us all."

She waved her arm out wide, gesturing to everyone in the tribe. And when he looked, considering them all, he found nothing but his own shame reflected in their expressions. Then, she placed her hand on his chest, and Vladamor's heart beat even faster, as if it were trying to leap out of his body and into her palm.

"You've betrayed your brethren, and for this, Delira has unjustly paid the ultimate price. Now, it's your time to face judgment," she said, glowering up at him. "You've brought this upon yourself, Vladamor."

It was then that he lost all control—even knowing there was no undoing his fate, Vladamor tried to assuage his guilt, to explain away his disgrace.

"It was just supposed to be me," he said, panicked. "I confessed to her that the humans promised us riches beyond our wildest dreams, in exchange for just a small bit of our knowledge." He felt as if every muscle bulged from his body for how strongly he was trying to force them to listen. "It was nothing! They weren't sorcerers. Our magic would be useless to them. I just wanted us to run away and be free to live our own lives, by our own rules."

He searched for any pity from his peers, trying to convince them of his story; they all remained silent.

"I couldn't have known they'd kill for curiosity, the ignorant bastards!" he said. "I couldn't have known Delira would follow." He let out a roar of frustration. "It's not my fault. She wasn't supposed to come! And they never even got what I promised them, because of her interference in the meeting."

His head drooped, hair hanging over his face.

"It was... nothing. I didn't—"

"Delira gave her life to save you and our clan's future," said

Master Lethander, demanding his attention—the elven guards suddenly surrounded Vladamor, pointing their swords at him from all sides. "Her sacrifice protected your life and kept our clan's legacy from falling into the wrong hands. That's hardly nothing."

"I only meant well," said Vladamor, shaking his head. "You must believe me!"

Master Lethander walked up to him in the center of the circle; his eyes said more than his words ever could—livid, unforgiving.

"I don't," he uttered, so that only Vladamor could hear. "You have only ever wanted to help yourself. You've disobeyed one of our most steadfast rules, divulging our sacred secrets to the human race. Something your ancestors have died to protect!" He pursed his lips. "What a young fool you've proven to be. Such traitorous tendencies."

Master Lethander took a deep breath, squaring his shoulders.

"I should've never trusted you to go to the City of South Luose alone. In this, I do take the blame I am owed."

The world seemed to grow quiet then, waiting for the verdict… just the sound of the wind rustling through the trees to be heard, their maroon leaves raining to the ground in piles at their feet.

"Nicora Elves, I speak to you now," said Master Lethander, raising his arms high and walking around the inside of the circle that had now squeezed even tighter about Vladamor. "Sister Delira is dead. She gave her life to protect the secrets that this traitor sought to sell."

He upturned a satchel full of gold coins.

"For human gold! For metal."

He dumped the gold on the ground, and it shone brightly atop the muddied field.

"No," said Vladamor—all the conviction had fled from his voice.

Master Lethander ignored him, his only focus on the crowd.

"Our brother—" he spoke the word like it was acid on his tongue "—has made more than one mistake in his lifetime, but this is by far the foulest. What say you, my brothers and sisters? What say you?"

Not a second later, Vladamor heard the words he was most dreading to hear—they landed without mercy, like venom to his soul.

"No… please! I beg of you," he said, sinking to his knees, their judgment weighing him down.

Master Lethander loomed over him, his staff raised in the air as he quieted the crowd.

"Your brethren have spoken," he said. "Vladamor of the Nicora Elven Clan, I hereby banish you from our tribe and strip you of your birthrights. You're no longer privileged to this realm! You are no longer our brother now."

The crowd cheered, their voices like a haunting choir to his ears as the guards pushed him, facedown, to the grass.

An elderly elf walked up to him, striking him clean across the cheek; Vladamor wanted to melt into the earth as he looked upon his very own mother.

He could barely speak through his tears.

"Mother, I'm sor—"

She took shears to his hair—one of the signatures of his tribe—before he could even finish his sentence.

Vladamor felt the weight of it fall away, silver locks covering the ground at his feet. Then, she snipped away the rope binding his hands. And without even a word of goodbye or one glimpse of a tear, she ran back into the arms of the jeering crowd.

"Wait…" Vladamor reached a hand toward her, but Master Lethander stepped into his path.

He was holding Vladamor's sword, a precious possession gifted to him as a young elf from their supply of priceless dwarf-made weapons, as was part of his birthright; he'd trained with it for many years.

With just a few magic-laced words and the aid of the mighty staff, Master Lethander melted the sword right before him—nothing remained of its existence, save for a couple of red rubies that refused to die.

Vladamor gazed, unseeing, into the distance, the taunting voices and furious faces bleeding together in a blur. He was dizzy, his head too heavy to hold up, as he heard the words only ever spoken before in whispers, rumors even, resounding in his ears.

The voices of his former brethren fused together in unison now, all chanting as they locked hands; and the silver tattoos of the Nicora Clan—wrapped around every elf's wrist and etched on the backs of their hands—seemed to connect them all in this moment, bright magic passing from one to the next until the entire circle was glowing—all except for Vladamor.

"No, please stop! You cannot do this," he said as his own marking began to burn.

He looked down to his hand and saw the silver ink had begun to blacken, as if rotting beneath his skin.

"Spare me this final torture, I beg you!"

"We bind your powers, until your final hour," they sang. "We bind your powers, until your final hour."

The words came like blades slicing into his skin, over and over, forcing him open so that his power seeped out into the world; Vladamor tried to hold on with every ounce of energy he had left, but it was a futile effort.

"We bind your powers, until your final hour."

He felt like his head might explode, and he madly pulled at the little hair he had left.

"We bind your powers, until your final hour!"

It felt as if all the air had been forced from his body in one fell swoop. Then, the chanting ceased.

Vladamor looked up into the pitiless face of Master Lethander.

"Leave here and never return," he commanded. "If you dare

to step foot in our realm again, you'll be slain on sight."

He kicked at the coins littering the dirt.

"And don't forget your precious gold. You'll be needing this in the human world. Although, I doubt you'll find that your sacrifice will pay off for very long."

With tears streaking his face, Vladamor collected every single coin he could find, and the remaining rubies from his sword; he shoved them into his pockets with shaking hands. The guards and procession of elves marched him to the edge of the Nicora Forest, driving him toward a sea of black desert that bordered the woodland. There, he saw only two options—cross the desert or circle back to the City of South Luose, a place where he feared he may again meet the humans who had murdered Delira.

Taking a deep breath, he stepped out into the desert, wanting to run as far away as possible from the memory of his lost life; the Nicora Elves watched as he began his journey across the sand, but he only heard one voice now—that of Master Lethander, chanting a new phrase that would eternally haunt him...

Vladamor looked back one last time, hoping to memorize the faces of his family, praying that someone would call out for him to return. But when he did, the forest had vanished entirely—in his soul, he knew it was gone to him forever, cloaked with magic he could now never hope to attain.

He glanced again to the marking on his hand; it was void of magic, too, just faded black ink on his skin and a permanent reminder of what he'd lost.

In the years after Vladamor's banishment, he wandered as far away from the Nicora Forest as he possibly could, to the edge of the world, it seemed. He murdered an isolated citizen in order to assume a human identity and eventually settled in the south, on the outskirts of the City of Saindora. Learning to blend in with the humans, he survived on scraps and peddled stories of the elusive elves whenever he could manage.

Of course, no one believed his tales of this concealed, magical *part of their world. No human had ever been privileged to know the secrets of any elven clan in Olleb-Yelfra, and that was all he was to them now—human.*

ARIANNA'S EYES STAYED GLUED to Sir Vladamor's back until all that was left of him was a cloud of dust billowing in his wake. She looked down at the crumpled scroll in her hands and unfurled it one last time to try to discredit even the slightest connection between her story and his.

From the detail itself, it was evident that the first half of the parchment had been penned by one of Sir Vladamor's own kin at the time of his banishment, yet the second part of the scroll appeared a mystery, added in a good time later by an anonymous author from the looks of it; the ink was brighter, almost like new, and the handwriting was different. And while it didn't paint a pretty picture, it did prove to be one of the last surviving documents detailing the end of the Golden Age.

Arianna skipped down to the part Lessa had suggested, reading about Sir Vladamor's end—or rather, his bloodcurdling beginning—with a new perspective.

> *It would be many years before Vladamor's life would drastically change once again. However, this time, the ripple effect from his decision would prove catastrophic to the entire world.*
>
> *It all started when he'd learned news of Master Lethander's alliance with King Damas of the City of Saindora; such a union had been created to foster learning and to break down the longstanding*

barriers between the elf and human races—and in agreeing to train human nobles in sacred elven practices, Master Lethander and the Nicora Elven Clan had willingly dismantled the very law which Vladamor had been exiled for betraying so long ago.

For this, Vladamor's desire for retribution was all consuming, but he would never get the chance at revenge against his former leader. Not even a year later, the Olleb was reeling from the news that Master Lethander had murdered the son of the king and was, consequently, executed by a palace lord.

As shocking as such a story was, Vladamor knew it to be just that, a story… a masterful lie—the honorable Lethander was no murderer, and for him to be bested by a young human in a fair fight was inconceivable.

Alas, when word spread of King Damas' wish to eliminate the Nicora Elves in response to the 'treasonous' attack by Master Lethander, Vladamor saw an opportunity to satiate his desire for revenge; he waited for weeks to gain an audience in the palace and to assist the efforts. But when his day finally came to speak with King Damas, Vladamor was instead greeted by a young lord, Kyrone Devlindor, who would lead the charge on the king's behalf (His Majesty was, after all, in such a sickly state).

Lord Devlindor grew intrigued with Vladamor's

elaborate tale and offered him one chance to prove his worth, to locate the tribe. And to Vladamor's utter surprise, with Master Lethander dead, the location-cloaking magic had been lifted; he was easily able to lead the king's army across the Black Sand Desert in an ambush against his former home in the Nicora Forest.

Thus, on one fateful night for the Olleb, the Nicora Elven bloodline was eliminated before sunrise, slaughtered in their sleep. King Damas, conveniently, passed away soon after the conquest, and the young Lord Devlindor was crowned king; Vladamor never left his side, quickly becoming his right hand in rule.
In the early stages of their pursuit to hoard magic and to eradicate whole species of enchanted beings, the pair discovered a powerful spell. For fear it should fall into the wrong hands again, I shall not name it here; however, it held the potential to access a great power they both very much coveted—and they were both willing to take the risk it posed to acquire it.

King Devlindor recited the ancient verse while driving his own staff through Vladamor's heart, effectively killing him… just as the spell necessitated. And as they'd hoped, with the elven clan gone, Vladamor's dormant powers awakened at that very moment, his magic merging with the spell and grasping tightly around his already blackened soul (with such magic, only death could allow his mind to completely accept the darkness, a curse he willingly invited in). Then, the King's

Though the spell which had apparently been the catalyst to the Olleb's suffering wasn't written down anywhere that Arianna had ever seen, not even penned in ink on this parchment, Keeper Kassime had confirmed what her heart had been trying to tell her all along since the day she came to know of Sir Vladamor's *true* story—his was more like her own than she could've ever fathomed.

Sometimes, when she closed her eyes at night, she could almost taste the word on her tongue. *Onasyuda.*

This ancient magic was a living, breathing part of her now, literally pulsing through her veins since the day Talis had brought her back to life; she wondered how long it had taken for it to fully turn Sir Vladamor into a monster…

Could he have stopped it, if he'd wanted?

Arianna sensed the power within her, boiling at the surface and vibrating in her bones. Though she wished, with all her soul, that this feeling was only a figment of her imagination, she just couldn't deny the facts.

Sir Vladamor lives and breathes by the same magic as me.

And with this realization, Arianna regretted ever meeting Talis Churry at all.

Keeper Kassime helped them now, but what might he do if he assumed her prone to such darkness as Sir Vladamor—to necromancy? What if he were to find out the lengths Talis had gone to just to keep her alive?

I can handle this. I can hide this.

Arianna would try to keep the bad Talis had instilled in her buried deep down, keep her darkest thoughts under lock and key until she found out more; they were smothered now, subdued and resting to make room for the hope Keeper Kassime had granted them. But with every difficult choice placed in their path, a destructive, hate-filled energy inside of her became harder to ignore.

Arianna found her reflection again in the window, expecting to see the face of her fake identity, of Aridyn—but, this time, her own face stared back through the glass, a nightmarish version of herself, eyes burning silver and a deadly sneer.

With a gasp, Arianna clasped her eyes shut, willing this dark reflection to go away.

I shouldn't have to choose between death or darkness!

She hoped, with everything, that her second chance at life wasn't already a shackled slave to the dark.

15

BEGIN AGAIN

THE HOUR CAME AND WENT, and as promised, the city keeper promptly returned. "Come with me," he said, looking past them to the now spotless space. He tried to hide the smile that flickered across his face, but Arianna didn't miss it.

She glanced around the attic, too, and felt a sort of sadness; much had changed for her in just the few short weeks they'd been sheltered there.

With nothing to do but explore the guardian treasure trove of knowledge that was the palace attic, the four had been permitted to read to their hearts' content about the Golden Age, obtaining more knowledge than they even knew what to do with; they further bonded with the avatars (although Arianna still didn't know what Solza's magical aptitude might be); they sparred with each other, testing out Jeom's axe against mere common weapons to see what it could really do; and they practiced the little magic they knew, until Keeper Kassime assessed whether or not he was willing to teach them more.

Most importantly, the four had grown more comfortable with their new identities each day. Now, it was time to put them to the test in the real world; Keeper Kassime had prepared them with strict instruction on how to conduct themselves as high-lifes… their back stories and their expected behavior now so ingrained that they all almost believed each other when they practiced—though, no one spent much time in front of the mirrors.

With Keeper Kassime in the lead, they left the attic the same way they'd entered, traveling down the steps and back into the dungeons—this time with all their belongings and the avatars in tow. The staircase seemed to lead downward forever, Arianna's ears popping from the sudden altitude change, and a damp smell seemed to engulf the air all at once when they reached the bottom.

Jeom let out a shriek as they passed the cells of their short-lived prison; there were new inhabitants now. Their arms reached toward them through the bars, agony in their eyes and pleas on their tongues.

"Ignore them," said Kassime with indifference, shining the lantern away from their eyes. "They'll be rotting here for much time to come and had better get used to it."

"What could they have done to deserve this?" said Lessa, clearly forgetting herself in the city keeper's presence.

"Do not pity them," he snapped. "Those men were caught taking a woman without her consent. Every citizen is entitled to a *choice* with their body! It's a basic right."

He made sure his voice was heard loud and clear before they moved on, and the resounding moans of the prisoners confirmed that he had been.

"Such behavior is not condoned in the Olleb, whether or not someone is paired for a partnership. Per the King's decree, it's a weakness to be so controlled by lust or desire. And weakness has no place in his world."

"Well, that's one law the King and I can actually agree on," said Jeom. "Monsters deserve to be caged."

"Me too," mumbled Lessa, not looking back—Jeom wrapped his arm around her shoulders.

Arianna considered the keeper's words, her thoughts settling on Mya and the partnership she'd had with her Gabriel, before her untimely passing. She wondered who in the city had the power to determine such unions, that a man and a woman might be compatible to bear a child or to share the same household, all for the Olleb's endurance. It seemed a difficult thing to control, especially when people seemed to love of their own accord, without rules or regulations—and yet, somehow King Devlindor found a way.

The thought of being forced into a partnership with a stranger, to surrender an innocent child to this unyielding world made Arianna sick to her stomach; and she couldn't help but wonder if whoever had given birth to her had ever once felt the same.

"Do people ever get out of the dungeons alive?" asked Demetrius in a troubled voice.

"Hardly." Keeper Kassime chuckled. "If you mess up badly enough to be sent here in the first place, then this world isn't fit for you."

Demetrius frowned. "But… they're treated like animals."

"Worse than that. Animals we put out of their misery. And at least their skins and meat are of value. These people are just wasted space, until their rot sprouts new life from the soil or I need someone to make an example of."

The air around them grew eerily quiet, only the keeper's words bouncing off the stone walls—Arianna's nerves spiked every time she was reminded of the fact that their lives lay in the hands of a man who had bent so fully to the King's cruel will. But she knew that he'd been playing two lives for decades now, and the city keeper was just one of two faces…

As Arianna was still alive today, it was evident he could still be a good and merciful man.

Leaving the worst of the Luose Dungeon behind, Arianna felt the ground slant upward with every step, as if they climbed a slight hill. A hefty iron door came into view not long after, and Keeper Kassime knocked upon it using the giant brass ring at its center; the ring itself was in the form of a snake. As the brass met the iron, a sound much like the annoying hum of the Warrior's District bell sounded throughout the tunnels.

Arianna was certain everyone in the palace would've heard. She pressed her lips together, trying to fight away her fears.

Arianna Belvedor is gone.… I am Aridyn Lareigh.

She sucked a deep breath in through her nose just as the door creaked open, sliding across the ground with a noise like nails on stone. It took the strength of two palace guards to pull the door fully open from the other side, and Arianna was anything but patient—a bright light suddenly spilled into the passageway, and they all stepped into a beautiful hall of the palace, the decay of the dungeons wiped away.

"Keeper," said one of the guards, bowing slightly before pushing all his weight against the door, sealing it like a vault. "Who… where did these people come from?"

His brow wrinkled as he assessed Arianna and her friends, instinctively reaching for the handle of his sword.

Arianna held her breath, knowing that these guards must think it odd that their city keeper had found four well-kept people on his most recent trip to the dungeons.

"Quiet," said Kassime, holding up his hand before the brazen guard could speak again.

He glanced from left to right, finding the hall empty. Then, he cocked his head to the side, a smirk on his lips and the guards in his sight as he began to speak in a tongue unknown to Arianna.

Her mouth fell open as the guards' eyes began to cloud over. "What's happening—"

Keeper Kassime's voice grew louder, not allowing her to interrupt. And when it looked as if the men were both fully void of life, only then did he stop.

"Take these words to your soul," he said softly, unblinking, holding the guards' veiled stares. He gestured to Arianna and her friends. "These are citizens with palace positions. They have permission to enter or exit the dungeons at their leisure and will never be questioned as to their motives again. They are nobles in advanced training, and their command will be followed without difficulty. And if you are *ever* questioned about them, you will say the very same."

As if puppets, the guards repeated his words in a mindless fashion. Keeper Kassime gave a curt nod of approval and snapped his fingers; with the sharp sound, the men seemed to jolt awake, their eyes filling again with life.

Arianna reddened as the more inquisitive guard considered her for a second time, considered Aridyn—the guards bowed low, no further questions, and took their places again by the door.

"Come," said Kassime, ushering them down a hall; there was a hint of a smile in his voice.

Lessa, Demetrius, and Jeom had been stunned into silence, but Arianna was full of questions. "What kind of magic was *that?*"

"Yeah, and how do I get it?" joked Demetrius, pretending to wipe the sweat from his brow.

Arianna glanced back at the guards, unnerved that they still appeared as if nothing at all had happened.

"Solomon was a master warrior and sorcerer, using his swords as his strength," said Kassime. "Talis is both a healer and potions master, and I'm a master at *mind* magic." He lifted his chin a little. "Among other things."

Arianna almost jumped into the air as yet another enchanted piece of this world unfurled before their eyes. "*Now* I see how no one will remember Godfrey's accusations about us," she said, looking back to the others as they walked.

"It's also how I've been able to stay safe as Helix Kassime… city keeper *and* Guardian of Gold," he said, a shadow crossing his face—he had yet to confide in the group his own backstory.

Lessa fell in step with him. "So, with magic you've convinced the world of a new identity, too? Of Helix?"

"Yes," he said, curtly, never looking at her. "I had to leave Ferlon behind, to help pave the way for something good. So trust me… I know how you may feel."

Arianna wanted to pry more, to learn the story behind his own identity shift, but she thought now not the time to ask. She wondered though… if the keeper did change his name and erase some past life, had he drunk the same potion and changed his appearance as well?

Who is the real Helix Kassime… and why did Ferlon Ragaric have to go?

"What's going on?" said Demetrius, craning his neck to try to see—as soon as they'd rounded the next corner, the palace had sprung to life, a bustle of noise coming from somewhere up ahead.

Arianna could practically feel her friends' giddiness, all so eager to explore and test out their new faces; she remained cautious, quietly assessing the best way back to the attic should the keeper's magic somehow fail them.

Keeper Kassime picked up the pace, guiding them in a different direction. "You'll see soon enough," he said, hurrying them down a long hallway.

He wouldn't even stop to let them give the palace the full admiration it deserved, but Arianna drank in as much as possible without a pause in her step—there were certainly rough edges to it, surely built long ago, but the worn rugs and smoothed walls arching high above their heads made it seem inviting, warm even, brought to life through vast murals with soft shades and subtle details that, when woven together, gave the hall such grandeur.

"Solomon would've loved this," she said, marveling at the

intricate artwork decorating the ceiling.

"He did love it," said Kassime, twisting his ring about his finger. "He spent much time within these halls."

He nodded to a portrait on the adjacent wall, and Arianna almost lost her breath.

There he stood, Master Solomon Bell, dressed just like she remembered him from the first day they'd met. Nothing less than elegant, regal, and sophisticated, he was pictured at the left hand of King Devlindor himself.

"I've never seen him… portrayed this way," she said.

"What? At the side of the King?" Kassime chuckled. "This was before your time, I suppose. But Solomon Bell has always been in the King's favor. His Great Wolf of the East, as they say."

"*Hmm.*" Arianna knew the history but didn't much care to be reminded of it. Besides, this wasn't indicative of Solomon's true character.

He died for us. He betrayed King Devlindor.

Her attention settled on another in the painting, and she recoiled—Sir Vladamor stood to the right-hand side of the King, gloves, gilded mask, and all. But one detail Arianna hadn't noticed on the real-life version of him was the chain that he wore, an exquisite red ruby at its center.

"Come," said Kassime, not letting her linger. He placed his hand on the middle of her back and escorted her away. "I want to show you all to your rooms now. I think you'll be rather pleased."

Arianna tore her eyes from the portrait to continue down the hall. Then, one by one, her friends disappeared behind closed doors until she was the only one left.

"Your room is just over here," said Kassime after they'd dropped Lessa off at her new quarters.

Reluctantly, Arianna followed him, but she didn't feel good about separating from the others—she glanced back to Lessa's door and found her waving back at her in encouragement, waiting to see which room she would claim with a huge smile on her face.

Keeper Kassime stopped just a few paces down and pulled on the gold-plated handles of the double doors before him. Just the entry alone had Arianna overwhelmed. *What could possibly be inside a room such as this... for me alone?*

She clung to her hopes—to the keeper's reassurances and Solomon's sacrifice—that this was it. This was the last stop on their seemingly never-ending quest for freedom.

She glanced again to Lessa who mouthed, "Be brave." Then she disappeared into her own room, Sano following diligently behind.

Arianna chewed on her lip as Keeper Kassime entered.

"Here we go," she whispered to Solza, who was uncomfortably stuffed into her rucksack—a tactic that wouldn't work for much longer, seeing how fast she was growing.

She stepped through the doors.

Arianna might have fainted if she weren't so strong-hearted, but the room really almost brought her to her knees.

Everything was washed in a warm sunlight that filtered in through tall, skinny windows from across the back wall. Curtains gently fluttered in the wind where a couple of the windows stood open, making it seem as if the room had been tickled with magic, and a four-poster bed was the centerpiece of the space, a rich mahogany draped in sheer hangings and fur blankets.

A beautiful armoire, five times the size of her, stood open to display colorful garments and robes all ready for use, all fit for a highlife. And a vast rug with intricate, gold stitching covered the expanse of the ground—Arianna vividly recalled each morning in the Jar, pressing her toes against the cold floor before racing to her boots...

"I can't even fathom this," she whispered.

And with elegant seating areas and more surfaces to set her belongings on than she actually had belongings, there was truly nothing to be desired.

A standing oval mirror near the armoire caught her eye last, its crystal and gold frame so hypnotizing that Arianna almost forgot where she was and what she was doing. Of all the furnishings, this was the most beguiling. That it could have anything to do with her, much less *belong* to her, was absurd; she thought she might burst into flames if she looked into it, for it was surely only meant for the reflection of a noble… not a runaway slave.

I'm a warrior.

She took a deep breath, taking it all in.

Besides the elegance of it all, the thing that surprised her most was that the room was also red, bright red, *everywhere*.

It sprinkled the décor as if in theme.

Not so much that it was overpowering or distracting from anything else, but enough that it reminded her of the Warrior's District everywhere she looked, so much of home. And though the home she had grown up to know was far less than kind, it was familiar still—for the first time in her life, she was so very glad for all the red.

Arianna could all but imagine her Warrior's District friends, her foundation—Liam, Noah, Pippa, Solomon, Cyn—standing right there with her. Their sacrifices and risks had finally paid off, and she silently but profusely thanked them for their part in it.

"I don't know… what to say," said Arianna after a long while. Tears welled in her eyes but she blinked them away before they were, hopefully, noticeable.

She turned to look at Keeper Kassime; he'd been watching her all the while.

"I can't thank you enough, truly."

He nodded, once again hiding the remnants of a smile—one that made Arianna really *want* to trust him.

"Are the others' dwellings also so… familiar?"

She had a hunch this shocking representation of her district was not a coincidence.

"All of the palaces across the Olleb pay similar homage to the City of the Four Corners, King Devlindor's most prized accomplishment," said Keeper Kassime, matter-of-factly. "We've all called the districts 'home' at one point or another." He made this statement so surely that Arianna wondered if his mastery of mind magic also allowed him to read people's thoughts.

She widened the distance between them, her guard shooting right back up.

"Though, I hope the remembrance doesn't strike you at odds," he said. "In time, you'll see the Four Corners not as the living nightmare you were raised to know and fear but as a symbol of strength and unison, of *brave* people fighting to survive."

He lowered his voice, as if someone might overhear.

"Don't let King Devlindor destroy what it means to be a warrior and a survivor of the Jar. If you're able to rise above and embrace your past, you'll be stronger for it." He laid a hand on her shoulder, and Arianna squirmed a bit; it wasn't a gesture he normally offered. "This, I can assure you."

Arianna bowed her head from the weight of her relief.

"We're *already* stronger for it," she said, thinking of her friends and the arduous journey they'd suffered to get here.

Keeper Kassime cleared his throat.

"All right, better rest up before dinner," he said. "Someone will be along in a few hours to collect you."

Arianna's eyes widened. Suddenly, she didn't feel so confident in the magic trick meant to fool the world. Right now, she'd much rather never meet anyone again and just live out the rest of her days in sweet comfort here in this room. "Dinner? With who? But I'm not—"

Keeper Kassime clutched her shoulders again, trying to show compassion in his own, awkward way.

"This is your home now," he said. "This is your home now, and you're safe here."

Arianna stared blankly up at his copper face, unable to make sense of this silver-lined future. Then he let go, leaving her in the center of the room.

"You don't have anything to fear now," he added from the doorway. "You don't have to run anymore. This is your *home…* get used to it."

He said the word 'home' with such fire, as if to break through whatever wall he knew she'd built up in her head; it didn't quite budge, but she felt its foundation crumbling, wavering in the face of his conviction and even the promise of one night's sleep in that bed.

When the door shut and she was alone, Arianna let her breath escape her in a heavy sigh.

"Come on, Solza," she said, letting her down to explore the room by her side. "We needed some quality time."

Trying to slow her racing mind, Arianna ran her fingers across the silk tapestries, Solza already fraying the edges as she chewed at them. She kicked off her boots and let her toes revel in the soft carpets beneath her feet—and that's when the tears finally came.

Again, she wept for Solomon's death and Liam's uncertain future. She mourned for the loss of her own identity and that of her friends. And she cried over the fear that the necromancer had instilled so deep inside of her.

There was, however, a breaking point when the tears turned to that of joy—Arianna reveled in the happiness of discovering Solza, now that she'd accepted her fully, and for the keeper's protection when Solomon could no longer bear that burden. And maybe most importantly, she cried over the privilege that she could do so alone, with no one to bear witness to this moment's explosion of emotion.

When there was no sound left in her throat and no tears left to fall, the next thing Arianna did without hesitation was add Solomon's cloak to the beautiful armoire; the white velvet was dirtied now from so much wear, and the rubicund silk lining had worn. The Warrior's Crest, however, still shone brightly on the back in stitches of gold, never to be dulled.

She laid her hand at the breast of the cloak and pictured the ones she'd left behind in the districts, blood-red with the number twenty-two stitched at the heart in silver.

My name is Arianna Belvedor, and I'm finally free.

As she observed the cloak now, on its hanger, it looked as if nothing more than an option among the rest, blending in effortlessly with the other colorful garments and lost in an abyss of furs and fancy fabrics.

INTRODUCING ARIDYN

SHE WOKE TO A RAP ON THE DOOR. She hadn't meant to fall asleep, but such a drastic change of scenery was exhausting to comprehend. Her heart throbbed ferociously in her chest, as if throwing itself against the barriers of an iron cage.

It happened again. Arianna had seen the girl with eyes that shone like silver coins and who struck her dead each night that passed, each time she closed her eyes to dream. Though she couldn't speak the words aloud, she now knew why these nightmares occurred and what spurred them to take hold in her most vulnerable hours. It was an innate darkness inside of her, trying to break free and take over.

Whether the darkness had been born the day she died or if it had always been stirring at her core, there was no denying its threat any longer.

What might she become if she gave in?

After all, she now understood the dangerous lure of dark

magic. She had learned the story of Sir Vladamor.

Willing her body to move from the comfortable bed and shake off the terrible nightmare, Arianna threw a blanket over Solza so that she blended in with the furs, pulled on a silk robe and tiptoed across the room to the door.

Holding her breath, she cracked it open.

"Apprentice Aridyn?" squeaked a girl with a curly afro and friendly face. "I've come to fetch you for the feast."

Arianna flinched, trying to hide herself behind the door, but the girl pushed her way in.

"Oh, my," she said, looking her up and down with her hands on her hips. "You haven't even combed your hair! Here, please, let me help you dress."

Arianna bit down on her tongue, waiting for the girl to have some kind of recognition and shout out her suspicions for the entire palace to hear. She expected, though, that she could best the girl before she had time to even open her mouth. But no— that wouldn't be right.

That's not something I would do… is it?

Arianna had the sudden urge to escape.

The girl came toward her, staring her straight in the eyes. She was young, possibly a newly freed slave from the Healer's District.

Agrarian's maybe?

She had a gentle, bird-like air about her, and Arianna wondered how on earth she could've survived this long in such a brutal world.

"Please sit," she said, kindly, gesturing to a settee in front of the mirror.

Arianna obeyed, though every muscle in her body had tensed. She glanced to where her swords lay across a table.

The girl stood behind her so that Arianna could see them both reflected in the mirror; she watched her every move as she began to fix her hair into two long braids, tendrils falling about her shoulders—Arianna began to relax.

The girl wasn't working with the lush, brown curls she was used to but rather Aridyn's long, black locks she hadn't yet gotten to know. In fact, she didn't see Arianna at all. As confirmed by her reflection, only a pink-cheeked, delicate-featured highlife sat before the mirror, not a fugitive of the Olleb.

"If you'll permit me, I have to get you presentable for the banquet, *quickly*. It's going to be quite the affair," said the girl, seeming a bit flustered.

She pinned Arianna's hair fancily about her head, the braids hanging long down her back—it was such a style that Arianna had never seen before on any elder or highlife, and she didn't much like it.

"My new master taught me this trick. I'm sorry if it's not what you're used to. I could try something else."

Arianna realized she was frowning and quickly flashed a fake smile.

"I'm only just learning how to be an attendant."

"No, it's… quite all right," said Arianna, trying out her new voice. "An attendant?" She didn't know much about this job placement, only that they seemed to come hand in hand with a highlife position.

"Yes, miss. I tend to the needs of those living in the palace. Whatever the master attendant asks of me."

She cocked her head to the side, putting the final touches on this hairdo—Arianna was stunned at how fast she'd managed to get Aridyn's hair under control. Her real hair would've put up a much bigger fight.

"Don't you have attendants where you're from?"

"Oh, why yes!" said Arianna, her voice cracking. "I just meant… so you've only just earned your citizenship, then?"

The girl giggled.

"Yes, miss, we've only *just* finished the citizen celebrations, but I'm finally starting to settle in. It's a dream come true, isn't it? To earn citizenship! And I couldn't have asked for a better placement. I never dreamed that I'd work in a palace one day."

"I know what you mean," whispered Arianna.

The girl smiled. "I'm told that I'll be your personal attendant during your extended stay," she said. "And I promise to take *good* care of you, on the keeper's orders. Now stand up, I need to get you dressed."

Arianna did as she was told, and her attendant slid off her robe so that she was embarrassingly naked; she wouldn't look in the mirror at Aridyn now... it felt wrong.

Flicking through the wardrobe, the girl placed a hand on Solomon's cloak—Arianna froze, but she quickly moved past it, instead pulling out a dress.

It appeared simple on the hanger, though when her attendant helped her into it, the cloud-like fabric laid across her ever so gently, nothing like she'd ever felt touch her skin before. The dress flowed effortlessly from black to silver in beautiful patterns, and finished with a stunning bottom that rolled slightly out in a train of delicate white waves.

Arianna squirmed in the foreign fabric, resisting the urge to rip it off her body; it was somehow too comfortable and too tight all at the same time, and certainly not suitable for any kind of fight.

"My, how lovely," said the attendant with a clap of her hands. "Fit for the Princess, even."

"What did you say?" snapped Arianna, trying to process this new version of herself.

It was all starting to seem like some grand joke—only a few weeks ago, she was a fugitive running on barely any water or sleep. And now she was Highlife Aridyn Lareigh, smelling of perfume and donning fancy clothes.

"My apologies!" gasped the attendant, bowing her head low. "Have I offended you?"

Arianna's eyes widened. "Do *not* bow at me!"

The words just slipped out.

The attendant froze, looking as frightened as Arianna felt.

"Please, I'm so sorry," she said, throwing her hands up. "I… I spoke out of turn. *Please* don't report this to my master. I'll be whipped at the Altar!" Her entire body trembled like a spooked animal. "I only meant that you're very beautiful." She shook her head. "I shouldn't have said that. I know that Princess Elisa is the one and only princess. I just meant—"

"It's all right. Just… forget it," said Arianna, turning away.

Get a grip! This is your one opportunity to move on.

The attendant made to bow again but stopped midway.

"Thank you," she mumbled. She ushered Arianna to stand again in front of the mirror while she made the finishing touches to her look. "There! All done."

The attendant didn't offer another compliment, but Arianna could tell by her expression that she wanted to. And when she finally lifted her eyes to her reflection, she was also stunned by who she saw, a young woman so pleasing to the eyes, and irrefutably a highlife.

"Whenever you're ready, miss," said the attendant, holding out a pair of sparkling slippers.

"Please… call me Aridyn," said Arianna, quietly, stepping into them.

The word sounded strange as it rolled off her lips, but she would have to get used to it sooner rather than later.

"Certainly, Miss Aridyn. Right this way."

The attendant offered a cautious smile as she opened the door for her to pass, clearly still shaken by Arianna's outburst.

I'll have to apologize to her later, should I make it through this dinner alive.

"Thank you," she said, trying to sound as kind as possible— the attendant visibly seemed to relax.

Arianna struggled to move in the fitted fabric, but she eventually got the hang of it. She stepped into the hallway, searching for her friends.

"Everyone will already be waiting for you," said the attendant, laying a light cloak over her bare shoulders. "We're already late as it is! Please, follow me."

The attendant walked at a brisk pace, and Arianna had trouble keeping up, hardly noticing anything around her as she focused on not tripping over her dress. Taking turn after turn, the one thing that she did recognize was how truly massive the place was; they passed several chambers for lounging or entertaining guests and more statues than Arianna thought there were actual people who lived here. And although it was *nothing* compared to the vastness that had been the underground City of Undor, the palace did hold its own allure; she speculated if, like in Saindora, magic had once run through these halls, if sorcerers or enchanted creatures had also resided here.

Eventually, the attendant slowed as they came upon an open area surrounded by tall columns. The ceiling here was high, passing through several floors, and Arianna realized it to be another tower. At its very peak, there was a mural depicting what looked to be the end of a battle.

She assumed it to be one of the earlier civil wars King Devlindor had *valiantly* put to rest; in the Learning Center it was taught that not long after his crowning, many small wars had come to pass. Greedy people wanted power, the educators had said. They tried to dethrone him and uproot all the order he'd 'blessed' upon the world.

A successful revolution never came to pass, not even close—those wars were spoken of as great victories for the King and for Olleb-Yelfra, after which peace was finally had and 'war' was never heard of again.

Arianna looked away, disgusted by the portrayal. *Lies!*

King Devlindor had waged war against the last people who remembered, against a resistance who bravely battled to keep the freedom of their memories, of a life filled with magic and of family.

Never forget.

The attendant led her down a new passageway and, suddenly, the scent of flowers filled her nose and stars winked down at them—here there were several wooden benches, a large bubbling fountain, and a sizeable garden, its vines wrapping around everything.

Arianna took a deep breath, letting the fresh air cleanse her mind of its worry.

"This is it," said the attendant as they came upon a wide door at the other end of the small courtyard. "Everyone is waiting to welcome you and your friends. Have a wonderful time!"

The girl smiled and removed Arianna's cloak from her shoulders, hanging it on a rack filled with others much more magnificent than her own.

"I'll stop by your quarters in the morning with a bit of breakfast," she said. "Hopefully soon you'll feel comfortable enough to call the Palace of South Luose your home."

She pulled the handle.

"Wait…" said Arianna, putting her hand out to stop her. She still felt so guilty about earlier. "What can I call you?"

The girl blushed. "Miss, I'm below your station. Please just call me 'attendant,'" she said with a slight bow, opening the door.

Arianna's insides twisted together; this girl who was experiencing the beginning of her eighteenth year—just like her—had survived the festivals and rid herself of her defining number. Yet, she still couldn't claim her own name.

What kind of freedom was that?

Then, Arianna remembered the first chilling lesson about freedom from Keeper Kassime…

We're all slaves to the King.

Arianna squared her shoulders and faced her destination; inside, she found fully armored palace guards lining the room. They looked as sharp as ever, the tips of their swords firmly pressed into the floor, both hands on the hilts.

Everyone stood as she entered the room, including Keeper Kassime—he was seated at the front of a long, decorated table adorned with a plump roasted pig and more dishes than Arianna could count. Her mouth watered.

"Come, come," he said, waving her forward.

She straightened her back and walked, slowly, toward the table, trying to appear confident in the eyes of about eight finely dressed elders watching her every move.

Keeper Kassime gestured for her to come around to his side where she was greeted by three familiar faces—seeing Lessa dressed in a magnificent purple dress, Jeom donning sophisticated robes of orange, and Demetrius in those of a deep charcoal… she could hardly believe it.

They all stood at one side of the keeper at the table, one seat left open just for her; she squeezed in between Keeper Kassime and Demetrius.

"Good evening," she said.

Now, more than ever, Arianna wished for the guidance of Solomon. But all she could do was remember his teachings—she'd been trained by the hands of someone revered in Olleb-Yelfra, and if he'd taught her anything at all, it was a highlife's etiquette. She smiled now, bowing slightly as Solomon's memory alone gave her confidence.

The dinner crowd bowed back, and then they all took their seats.

"Well, as you all know," began Kassime, addressing the people that Arianna did not recognize, "I've gathered you all here tonight to help me welcome some *very* special guests to South Luose." Arianna turned red as he listed their fake names, pointing to them one by one. "It's my pleasure to introduce you to our newest palace apprentices. Lilith, Jaxin, Darrios, and Aridyn."

She forced a smile as her new name left his lips.

"They've come a long way from the City of Kampaulo and were the best in their crafts, receiving much praise from their city keeper. She's sent them here to hone their skills, in hopes that they may one day prove worthy enough for a presentation to the King."

There were murmurs of interest from around the dinner table as they assessed the new palace additions.

"Well, Helix, it's about time we had some *real* talent around here," said one woman at the end of the table. "Every year I'm less impressed with the turnout from the Free Falls."

Her skin was fair, and she had dark hair and hooded eyes.

"My sentiments exactly," he said, nodding. "I'll work with them from time to time, but they'll, undoubtedly, assume apprenticeships under some of you."

One burly man Arianna realized to be the same master creator who had branded the arms of his students during Transition Week. Her eyes flicked to Jeom, wondering if that would be his new trainer, too.

"They've shown great promise," continued the keeper. "And we must show our respect to them now as highlifes of South Luose. They'll do great things here. I'm sure of it."

Keeper Kassime raised his glass and everyone else followed suit, welcoming the four into their world of riches. Then, the table fell into animated conversation as Arianna and her friends, clumsily, tried to find their place among it.

Arianna took a sip of her drink and let the sugary, sparkling liquid tickle her tongue and her senses.

Just what I needed. A bit of wine to loosen up.

She listened intently and spoke as little as possible.

A voice at the end of the table caught her ears, and she found the unmistakable eyes of an elder she'd met before—the old councilwoman she had knocked to the ground after running from the Stables.

For a split second, Arianna feared the woman might recognize her, but again, she remembered she was no longer in Arianna's skin. What's more, the woman was clearly *blind*.

"So," said Ophelia before she took a big sip of wine, her other hand fumbling about the table in search of her utensil. Papery skin hung off her bones and she looked fragile, as if she might break at any moment under the weight of her jewels. She stared straight ahead and addressed no one in particular as she drank. "You've been chosen for an apprenticeship in the Palace of South Luose. How marvelous you must feel."

She waved her empty glass in the air, and a server promptly refilled it.

"Yes, it's quite marvelous," said Arianna, feeling inclined to respond—no one else around the table seemed to pay her any mind as they dug into their pork and potatoes, sipping happily on their drinks and prying into each other's lives.

"It's not often ones so young are appointed such an honor," said Ophelia, her tone inquisitive. "Say, what might you have done to deserve such a gesture from your masters in Kampaulo? I would love to hear this tale."

The words slid sharply off her tongue, the compassion she'd shown to Arianna before on the city streets in no way apparent tonight; it was easy now to see the strength within this old woman that Eli had claimed to be so impressive.

"Ophelia, *please*, go easy on the wine," said Kassime with a guffaw. "Don't worry your pretty head! These children are no threat to your seat as Head of Council. No one's outranked you yet. They've a *long* way to go to do that."

He seemed embarrassed on her behalf.

"Rest easy," he added. "You still hold the title of the youngest person in the Olleb to ever be offered a governing position. But it's not so uncommon anymore for the young and skilled to rise quickly as highlifes. It's beautiful to see the world's progression in this way."

Others across the table agreed, but Ophelia scoffed, digging into her food.

"*Children*," she muttered through a mouthful.

"Just five years out of the Jar… that's *too* young, if you ask me," barked an overweight and drunk man seated at the middle of the table. He raised his glass, spilling it all over his shirt.

Arianna just smiled politely, thinking it incredible they saw a woman five years her senior sitting before them—she'd barely been a citizen five minutes.

Magic is such a wonder.

"Master Jon Tayshin is of the Warrior's District," whispered Keeper Kassime so that only she could hear. "He will be your trainer."

Arianna considered him with disgust, doubting anyone so sloppy could be master of anything. "Lovely," she said through gritted teeth.

Keeper Kassime pointed out some of the others.

"The master creator goes by the name of Gansevurt, and the agrarian is Mistress Serina." Arianna lingered on her.

Where have I heard that name before?

"And Ophelia, she's been part of the South Luose City Council practically all of her citizen-life, if you'll believe! She earned a highlife position in her first year out of the Jar and has been climbing the ranks ever since."

He pointed toward the opposite end of the table.

"The others here are some of the councilwomen and -men under Ophelia, helping me to keep the city in order."

"Do they all reside here in the palace?" said Arianna.

"We have a Master's Wing that you'll see soon enough," said Kassime. "Master trainers come and go with their crafts, never staying too long, but they're always welcome here when they want. They've earned their right to a highlife."

He nodded to Ophelia.

"She sometimes resides here as well, but typically the council members have quarters elsewhere in the city. This house is mostly for entertaining noble or other highlife guests, like Sir Vladamor and his guards. And, occasionally, we also foster *exceptional* apprentices." He winked at her, and Arianna returned a weak smile.

"And who will my apprenticeship take place with?" interrupted Lessa, her curiosity plain as she peered down the table. "Are any of you healers?" She was met with abrupt laughter.

"Are you dim, child?" snapped Ophelia, smacking her lips as she waved her finger about. "Our city keeper is the best healer these parts have ever seen! I daresay he'll be taking you on. From the sound of it, you've got a lot to learn."

Lessa was utterly embarrassed, shrinking in her seat, as Keeper Kassime engaged her in conversation over the healer's art. Arianna left them to chat about their future lessons and turned her attention to Demetrius; Jeom had left him alone, already engaged in talks with Master Gansevurt.

"Whatever's the matter with you?" said Arianna.

He appeared paler than normal and he had barely spoken a word the entire night.

"That's my trainer," he said, nodding to Mistress Serina at the other end of the table.

Arianna raised an eyebrow. "I don't understand... we've all met our trainers tonight. I'm not much pleased by my assignment either, but it's better than our last option. *So,* what about her?"

Demetrius took a deep breath and tossed back his drink.

"No," he said, locking eyes with her. "That's my former *master...* from the Agrarian's District."

Arianna's mouth formed an 'O', realization hitting her.

She had never seen such hate in Demetrius' eyes before, but she knew it was warranted.

"She's every memory I despise about my life in the Jar," he said. He squeezed his eyes shut. "I just want to forget."

"Don't do anything rash," whispered Arianna, eyeing the knife clenched in his fist. "You're not a slave any longer, you're... Darrios. We'll help you through this."

He nodded, opting to use the knife on his food instead.

Arianna gave a small sigh of relief, the cogs churning in her head as she struggled with that unexpected twist.

"How do you do it?" she heard Master Tayshin say, talking loudly over everyone as he vied for Ophelia's attention.

He rudely waved a hand in her face, and Ophelia seemed to smirk right back at him—Arianna wondered if she couldn't *really* see through those clouded eyes.

"If I gave away my secret to success, someone might very well use it against me," said Ophelia, eyes drifting in Arianna's direction. "We wouldn't want that, now would we?"

Arianna shrank back in her seat, feeling like a lamb up for the slaughter surrounded by all of these drunken elders. She picked up her own drink and chugged it; both she and Demetrius were ready for another round.

From then on, the night passed by in a bit of a blur, and Arianna grew much less nervous to add to the conversation. Though, after long, this group was much more concerned with drinking and stuffing their mouths full rather than too much chatter. As the night wound to an end, Keeper Kassime finally excused them, and they made to leave.

As Arianna bid the elders farewell, Master Tayshin suddenly grabbed her wrist from across the table, knocking his glass clean over—wine grew quickly into a dark red stain atop the white tablecloth.

"Your training begins tomorrow," he said with a slur, the first he'd spoken to her all night. He let go of her wrist, holding his hand out for another glass of wine. "Try not to disappoint me."

DAY ONE

ARIANNA PULLED BACK THE CURTAIN of the carriage window to find the sky a rosy pink as the sun began to rise. The city passed her by in strings as they moved deeper down the streets, citizens beginning to trickle out of their quarters for the start of another day. The wind tickled her skin, biting her cheeks as the horses sped through the empty cobblestone streets of the now quiet city. *My city.*

She found herself wishing for the comfort of her Warrior's District robe, of the heavy fabric to ensure some warmth, even on the coldest of days; she tugged at the beautiful cloth enveloping her now, so thin and with little functionality.

At least there's not a number on it.

Sighing deeply, Arianna found comfort instead in the way the air moved slowly through her lungs, calming her from the inside out as she contemplated this new chapter.

South Luose proved to be a creator's haven, the infrastructure ever-expanding with the forest for supply at its edges. Arianna imagined that this must be how the Creator's District always smelled, smoke filling her nostrils and rising to the sky as the flames of creation burned endlessly on; her thoughts wandered to Jeom and his passionate new trainer, Master Gansevurt. She hoped he'd find some peace here finally—that they all would.

The clatter of hooves came to a stop, her attention drawn to the road as the horses veered off the paved paths and into a large, open meadow. It would stretch boundlessly on, if not for the high city walls encasing it. Here, the sounds of South Luose disappeared altogether, as if a barrier separated the city from this grassy, unkempt zone, the bustling metropolitan washed away with the simplicity of soft winds and long, swaying grass.

How peaceful.

She closed her eyes and relished the sudden serenity.

The field stretched all the way to the tip of the forest; the grass grew long and wild, and as the horses plunged forward across a somewhat marked trail, a crisp scent floated to the air, replacing the thick city odor.

Arianna found herself lured toward the forest as her carriage neared the edge of the field. It was as if the trees towered tall over the stone walls, trying to break in… calling to her. The want to explore was all consuming, and she found herself missing the wildness that the Four Corners had once offered, the surprises and challenges she could always count on. *Now I've truly gone mad.*

Arianna craved adventure, *always*, and now that it was apparent that her quest for freedom had truly come to an abrupt yet well-deserved end, she was having trouble relaxing into the arms of her comfortable present. Her mind lingered on past excitements, reliving the exhilarating battles, the puzzles solved, and the countless magical mysteries unveiled.

She stuck her head out of the window to reel in her wandering mind; the city grew smaller in the distance, the palace watching them closely from atop the high hill. South Luose was home now, and this marked day one of her new life as not only a citizen of the Olleb but a respected palace highlife with an apprenticeship to match.

This is my home.

Arianna's focus strayed again toward the silver trees—she just couldn't help but imagine where she and her friends might've ended up, had they taken a different path after leaving the Village of Draminet.

Probably dead.

"We're here, Apprentice Aridyn," called the carriage driver, slowing to a stop. "This is the edge of the Nicora Forest, miss, where I'm told you'll have your lessons with Master Tayshin for the time being."

Before he could come around to the door to assist, Arianna had slid out, refusing such gestures. She gazed up at the maroon leaves decorating the canopies and dusting the wall.

The Nicora Forest...

The very place in which Sir Vladamor had once lived his life as an elf of the prominent Nicora Clan, a life before exile.

Arianna peered back across the meadow and pondered if that monster had ever walked this path as a young elf, possibly happy and free. Before surrendering his soul to King Devlindor and destroying all of the good in the world, had the necromancer stood where she stood now?

Looking down at her feet, Arianna saw her boots were already covered in mud.

"Let's go, Solza," she said—Keeper Kassime had grudgingly granted Arianna's request to bring her avatar along to trainings, hoping that her alleged 'gifts' might quickly develop with the freedom to roam. Though animal companions were strictly against the law, who could punish her if not him?

She had promised to keep a low profile, not allowing Solza to be seen by too many city folk. And if anyone *should* raise questions, Keeper Kassime would erase the thought from their minds.

Arianna was quickly learning that the hierarchy here received special privileges that common citizens did not... privileges which appeared accessible to anyone, should one work hard enough to prove themselves of such worth. It was a compelling force, this fruit being dangled just out of reach. And now she clearly understood just how King Devlindor had been able to sustain such control over the Olleb—citizens saw no other option but to accept and respect those with the power to give them more. Worst of all, it kept people hopeful for a future that most would never attain.

An endless fight for more. Never satisfied, this world.

Then again, it seemed that neither was she.

Solza jumped out of the carriage at her command and sat on her haunches by her feet. Her eyes were hyper-focused on something in the trees, but she didn't dare to stray.

"What do you see, girl?" said Arianna, patting her head.

Arianna followed her line of sight and knew Solza must miss the woodland, the freedom. In fact, she *sensed* that she did... it had once been her home.

"I'll be back before sunset," said the carriage driver, tipping his hat to her before speeding off.

Arianna ran forward. "But wait! Where do I—"

The horses were already kicking up dirt as the carriage raced back across the meadow.

She sighed, watching him go. "Well... I suppose we better get this over with, then."

Arianna slipped her dagger from the sheath at her thigh, its black blade glistening in the sun as she gripped the handle tightly; there was no palace large enough, no noble life sweet enough that would ever let her trust the unknown—not after her first seventeen years of life.

Though her cloak labeled her as a highlife, Arianna took

solace in the familiar stretch of the leather pants Cyn had gifted her long ago, and her broken-in boots that kept her completely grounded in this new world of fancy robes and jewelries of useless decoration. And most importantly, her twin swords were crossed at her back, giving her all the confidence she needed—just like they always had been and always would be as long as her heart continued to beat.

She smiled widely, feeling the freedom in that, her heart beating strong within her chest.

My name is Arianna Belvedor.

Even if nobody else really knew.

She spotted a tiny shed leaning up against the wall. It swayed with even the slightest breeze and appeared to be the only structure around for miles, almost camouflaged as the forest tried to take it over. Other than that, the field was quite empty, just another spread of grass and mud.

"You wait here," said Arianna to Solza; she trekked over to it and pushed the door open.

"Hello? Master Tayshin?"

The sun bounced off several shiny objects—the shed was filled with weapons.

Cautiously, Arianna stepped inside to look around. Rusted axes and swords dangled from the walls and ceiling, chiming as they softly knocked into one another.

"Never let your guard down," came a voice from behind.

Arianna shrieked and tripped over a barrel of weapons in her hurry to see who it was; her dagger fell from her hand.

When she looked up from the ground, Master Tayshin was hovering over her with a disapproving expression. He picked up Aurora, studying it closely.

Arianna got to her feet, dusting herself off.

"Clearly, your first lesson should be on awareness. Your head will be rolling across the floor before you even realize you're being attacked," said Master Tayshin, handing Aurora back to her.

Arianna had barely gotten to her feet when she registered the glint of metal swinging toward her, the sharp side of a sword now just an inch from her neck.

She sucked a breath in through her teeth, holding it in her chest. If she moved at all, she would surely end up in the Well Center before the sun was even fully in the sky.

Master Tayshin snickered, lowering his weapon. "This is who they send me?" His voice was low, but Arianna heard every word.

She scoffed. "You startled me! I was told to meet you for training, not to expect an attack before a proper greeting," snapped Arianna, feeling her cheeks run hot.

"A *proper* greeting?" said Master Tayshin with a glower. "And do your enemies normally give you a proper greeting before they attack?"

He didn't wait for her to respond—he grabbed Arianna by the hook of her elbow and pulled her out of the shed, back into the open air.

Arianna didn't resist, but the touch of his calloused fingers around her skin made her want to break his hand. After their first introduction last night and seeing him now, her opinion of Master Tayshin was already formed—she thought him truly a belligerent fellow, with none of the finesse that Solomon had carried.

It took all of her patience not to whip out of his hold, but he was her so-called 'master trainer' now, and she would need to respect him as such if she didn't want any trouble; there was a formal etiquette to be had between master and apprentice, as Solomon had impressed upon her, and she would try her best to obey it now—this was, after all, her second chance.

Master Tayshin let go of her arm, turning to face her.

"Never address me so lightly again, Apprentice Aridyn."

She cringed at the way he spoke her new name.

"You may be in the keeper's favor, but you're not at all in mine. That privilege is earned."

She glared at him in response, unable to make her face

pretend anything different than what she actually felt. He had no idea of her accomplishments.

I've already earned enough in this lifetime.

Master Tayshin held her gaze, challenging her to defy him and evidently enjoying her reaction.

"You'll refer to me from this point forward as 'Master,'" he said, brusquely.

Arianna gritted her teeth, forcing a smile.

"Yes, Master Tayshin." She bowed her head, although slightly. "I offer my apologies for my disrespect." She couldn't help the bite in her tone.

Master Tayshin let out a startling howl of laughter, tossing his head back. "You're a stubborn one, aren't you? I'll enjoy breaking that. Let's remind you of your place, shall we?"

Every muscle in Arianna's body clenched to hold her lips together.

Curse you, Kassime!

Why did she get stuck with this arrogant man for a trainer? How was she expected to endure this for years to come?

I hope the others have better luck than me.

She let out a long exhale through her nose, accepting the inevitable—their new identities had come at a price, and now it was time to pay up. Assuming the role of Aridyn and leaving Arianna behind meant proving herself as an apprentice puppet to Master Tayshin and to many other prying eyes; she couldn't ever let anyone question what she had done to deserve her noble station.

Thus, for a life as South Luose Palace residents, Arianna and her friends would now need to earn their keep and become worthy of what they had so eagerly taken.

"And what's this odd-looking creature?" said Master Tayshin, setting eyes on Solza—he reached out to touch her.

"Are we saving him for lunch?"

Solza snapped at his fingers, and he chuckled, stepping back to a safe distance.

"*She* is nobody's lunch," said Arianna as Solza slunk between her legs.

She felt the skin on her calves warm instantly as the avatar pressed against them. Then the warmth shifted into an energy that seemed to flow through every vein; Arianna thought she might take off in flight at any second with all of it simmering at the surface, as if Solza's touch had ignited her own magic.

"Hmm... I see," he said, considering them with a raised eyebrow—she couldn't even remember why she loathed him in this moment, feeling nothing but complete. "And I suppose the keeper knows you've tried to domesticate a wild beast?"

This drew Arianna back to reality. "I... er, we agreed I could try and train her to hunt for an experimental period, to see if she proves useful to humans." That was, more or less, what Keeper Kassime had told her to say.

"Very well then," said Master Tayshin. "What do I care, as long as it doesn't get in our way."

"Solza," whispered Arianna, kneeling down and smoothing out her raised fur, "why don't you go and explore? Go find yourself something to eat... practice hunting."

Solza gave her one love-filled look and then sped off into the tall grass toward the trees.

"Bring us back something juicy!" howled Master Tayshin.

Arianna gazed after her avatar; it had only been about a month since their first encounter, but their bond was growing quicker than her mind could ever fathom—when she spoke, Solza listened and, *somehow*, understood.

Deep down, Arianna knew that this inexplicable bond would only grow stronger with the passing of time, just as Lessa had promised. She'd felt averse to the companionship at first, but now it excited her like nothing else.

And while Solza still held a tight lid on many untapped secrets, Arianna was beginning to grow certain that she had figured one of them out—Solza's *literal* closeness seemed to give her a boost of strength, especially at times when she could use it the most.

At first, she thought it was all in her head. But, looking back, she was starting to see things from a new perspective. Even now, the farther Solza ran, the less she could feel her warmth, until eventually the strange energy completely dissipated, leaving Arianna feeling more alone than ever.

"Finished daydreaming, or shall we get started?" barked Master Tayshin, drawing her back to the present. "We need all the time we can get. It's no doubt your skill needs work."

Arianna doubted that *very* much.

She doubted he could even lift his sword in time to best her without her back turned, as it was before.

"Certainly, Master." She turned in circles to try to spot a clearing. "Where's the dueling area?"

"This is it." Master Tayshin spread his arms out wide, nothing but fields and trees to his back.

"What do you mean?" Even in the Warrior's District Arianna had had access to a proper sparring room or battled in the fully equipped Dueling Arena. She couldn't be expected to train in a muddied field... not as a highlife.

As she took in Master Tayshin and her future apprenticeship under him as Aridyn, the emptiness that Solomon had left in his wake began to stretch a little wider—how could this man ever compare to the greatest master, warrior, and friend that was Solomon Bell?

"Is there a problem?" said Master Tayshin, cocking his head to the side.

"No, it's just that you—"

His grip on his sword tightened.

"—I mean, *Master*, you have such high honors. Why would you choose to duel outdoors and not in a suitable sparring room?"

Master Tayshin frowned and marched farther into the meadow, where the carriage hadn't passed before; Arianna followed at his heels. When they stopped, the grass was up to her knees, the ground too soft underfoot. And from this angle, she saw a hefty horse was tied to the back of the shed.

"A master warrior is not one who waits for suitable and comfortable conditions to fight. You must learn to be adaptable to anything that comes your way," he said. "You never know when or where you'll be when your life depends on it. It could be in a beautifully arranged sparring room, or in the middle of a damp meadow."

He tapped his foot on the ground. Then, he lunged at her with his sword.

Arianna didn't even have the time to withdraw one of her own. She dived out of the way, twisting her ankle slightly on the landing, for the ground was extremely uneven.

"I haven't even got my weapons out! You don't fight fair," she said, wiping the mud off her hands. "And won't we be using wooden swords for practice?"

"Ha! Is that how they had you training in Kampaulo? I have a feeling you'll be another disappointment yet," he said, thrusting his blade again.

With a grumble, Arianna swiftly pulled out a sword and parried the attack. But the annoyance this man drew out of her was quickly building up to anger; Master Tayshin didn't have the slightest idea of who she was or what she was capable of. *I'll show you!*

The chance to possibly shut him up with the sharp end of her blade excited her. She had so much pent-up energy just waiting to be released after being cooped up in the attic and would more than enjoy taking it out on him.

Master Tayshin smirked at her, and Arianna realized she was playing right into his hands… she realized it and could do nothing to stop it. He was provoking her, coaxing her to reveal her true colors—the overly passionate and impulsive fighter that Solomon had *always* scolded her for being.

Even with such awareness, Arianna couldn't stop herself from losing focus and letting go of her emotions; it was like a breath of fresh air to release control, to let herself run wild with the wind, no thoughts or promises of reining herself in.

Thrust, parry, step back, step forward. Thrust again.

A dance she knew like the back of her hand.

Alas, without focus, it was sloppy and ineffective; Solomon would've died twice over if he could see her now.

But something else seemed off… something other than her spinning temper—Arianna felt weighted down by this new body, and her sword just didn't seem to fit as well in Aridyn's hand as she'd at first thought when practicing for fun with her friends in the attic.

She wondered what Master Tayshin saw when he looked at her, too, observing her stance and her swing. Could he see the strong, spirited warrior she had worked so hard to become? Or did he only see the pink-cheeked, soft-skinned woman who she'd traded places with?

Stop, it's all in your head.

Nothing felt different; the sword didn't *actually* weigh heavier in her arms or move oddly when she swung. It was only her self-confidence as Aridyn that had wavered.

It wasn't long before Arianna was on the ground, watching Master Tayshin's round belly bouncing up and down with laughter at her embarrassing failure—she wished the mud would envelop her completely.

"Back to your feet," he said, catching his breath. Then, he drew a second sword, clearly more comfortable with two. "And save yourself the trouble of trying to muscle through this duel. Evidently, that's not your forte."

She stood up, and he gave her a few pointers about her form that went in one ear and out the other. *How dare he try to correct the form that Solomon taught me.* Although, she really *wasn't* embodying her late master's teachings right now, and she couldn't help but notice subtle similarities in their styles.

Arianna had learned to favor twin swords from Solomon early on and could hear his voice lecturing her now.

'It's always double the challenge and double the lesson when watching two weapons at once.'

She drew her other sword as well, matching his stance, and the battle continued.

After a while, the sun had risen high in the sky and Master Tayshin called it quits.

Arianna was drenched in sweat, her hair long since piled atop her head and her cloak discarded on the ground. Her breath came so hard that her chest hurt, and she could already feel her muscles aching from lack of exercise after being cooped up for so many weeks.

"How depressing you turned out to be," said Master Tayshin, wiping the sweat from his brow. He sheathed his swords across his back. "Five years of freedom, you say? Could've fooled me." He began to walk back toward the shed.

"Wait, we're not done here!" Arianna struggled to pull herself out of the mud he'd left her in.

He didn't even turn around. After untying his horse and situating himself in the saddle, he rode back to where Arianna was waiting, still catching her breath.

"We'll go again tomorrow. Same time," he said, not even bothering to hide his disappointment.

"But, Master, I… was told trainings were to be just every other day?"

"Well, I was told you were a warrior," he spat. "We're both leaving dissatisfied today, now aren't we?"

He whipped the reins and the horse galloped off toward the city, kicking up mud in her face.

Arianna screamed out after him in anger and threw her swords to the side. Then, she lay back down in the mud, staring up at a cloud-speckled sky. Her thoughts were too messy to form into something comprehensible. She was just glad she had survived her first lesson… that her Aridyn mask was, at least, still fitted on.

Solza came back to find her not long after, licking the mud from her cheeks. Her eyes glowed bright, as they sometimes did, and Arianna instantly felt a wave of calm come over her; with it, she realized how utterly foolish she'd acted today. *You have to do better! Don't waste this opportunity.*

She peeled herself out of the mud, fruitlessly trying to clean herself off as they waited for the carriage to return. About an hour later, as the sun began its descent, it arrived.

"Enjoy your lesson?" asked the carriage driver from his seat at the front.

"*Tremendously,*" said Arianna.

She climbed in after Solza, arms crossed at her chest as she pouted out the window.

"Don't be put off," he said, coming around to shut the door. "Master Tayshin is hard on all his apprentices. Everyone's let him down so far, and he takes it to heart each and every time. After so many years… it wears on him, I think."

"What do you mean 'let him down'?" said Arianna, giving him her full attention.

"I guess, not so much 'let him down' but rather *died,*" he said, tipping his hat, as if in remorse.

"Died? But how?" Her curiosity was piqued. "And how many have passed?"

"I don't know how many. We've lost count by now after all this time, but you're the first apprentice he's had in ages, miss," he said, matter-of-factly. "There's a rumor in the wind that anyone who trains with Master Tayshin is cursed to die young, so many promising warriors stay away and opt for lesser acclaimed masters."

Arianna was incredulous. "But he's supposed to be one of the greatest trainers of the last century! And a rumor has kept people away, a *curse?* That's ridiculous." She waved her hand to disregard it. "I can think of a lot of other reasons to stay away from that man, but a rumor would never stop me from an opportunity to train with the best."

Her own words made her heart sink. *I have to do better.*

The driver put his fingers to his lips, seeming a bit anxious—Arianna wondered what the punishment was for talking ill about one highlife to another.

"You can speak freely with me," she said, making sure he couldn't find doubt in her expression. "But I don't believe a word of that."

"Of course, miss." He shrugged his shoulders. "It's just a rumor I've heard. There's no such thing as a… curse."

The word left his tongue in barely a whisper this time, as if he feared there might be regulators hiding in the field to pass judgment.

"Just a rumor is all." He smiled.

"Right," said Arianna—a chill ran up her spine as she thought of all the curses she knew to be true. "Best we leave that kind of talk to the wind."

The driver tipped his hat again and shut the door.

Arianna's imagination ran wild then with the reality of *dark* magic, of monstrously magical creations like Sir Vladamor and the probability of countless other terrible 'curses' plaguing the land.

No thanks to the King.

And for the entire ride home, she was left to ponder whether or not the rumors about dead apprentices surrounding her new master could bear any truth. *Home…*

As they reentered the city, eventually, Arianna's thoughts drifted back to something more familiar and cold; *home* had once been the slave barracks, filled to the brim with other girls who dreamed of their own pictures of freedom; it was the label of a place where she could never truly feel safe, fighting all the time to keep her heart pumping, to live to see the sun rise one more time over the cusp of the Blancoren Mountains.

Survive the bitter and endless winters, *fight* to keep her head on in duels, *hope* for the elusive 'freedom'… that was Arianna's old definition of 'home.' And, thankfully, none of those were apparent in this comfortable present.

Though, for all its terrible memories, growing up in the Warrior's District had given Arianna one thing—a furious ambition to ceaselessly reach for her goals, *always*. And it was with this thought that she recognized what had really been gnawing at her mind today…

She no longer had a purpose in life, except to become someone else entirely to try to fool the world.

Arianna had fought, killed, and nearly died ten times over to earn her citizenship, one way or another, and now she finally had it in hand. *What comes next?*

She couldn't help but think 'now what?'—even knowing how selfish and ungrateful it seemed. Alas, after all the wishing and wanting, moving so fast for so long, it was extremely difficult to stop and be still in the moment.

This feeling will pass. Just… try and be happy now, be in the present.

Still, Arianna couldn't help the surprising direction her mind wandered in, eager for the next exciting trial of strength, for something new to fight for. And though she didn't think that Master Tayshin could hold even a candle to Solomon, at least, for now, he proved to be something of a new challenge.

18

BLOOD FOR BLOOD

THE CARRIAGE DROVE BACK through the city, winding up toward the palace; Arianna noticed the streets seemed strangely quiet, nothing like what she'd experienced before around this time of day, when she had toured with Eli.

Where could everyone be?

Rounding the next corner onto a main path, her driver had to slow—a riot was funneling into the city center, crowds pushing and shoving all toward the same direction.

"What's happening?" she called to the carriage driver over the shouts of excitement.

"Take caution, miss," he said, loudly, his voice carrying above the noise of the gathering crowd. "Looks like they're out for a hanging tonight."

"That can't be good," Arianna whispered to herself.

She gently pushed Solza to the floor so that she wouldn't be seen by any prying eyes.

The carriage had to crawl now, the driver doing everything in his power to keep the horses calm as a heavy throng of riled people enveloped them; they were forced to travel in the same direction, and Arianna knew immediately where they were headed as a pristine and landscaped area opened onto their path—the Garden.

The only area here where people hadn't taken over was the space between the statue of the King and the main platform; two staircases there led to a high balcony held up by impressive columns. And the architecture of the stage itself was exquisite; it had an uncanny resemblance to what dominated the Square in the Warrior's District—a huge emblem covered the back wall, glaring under the falling sun.

Instead of the Warrior's Crest, like Arianna had grown up staring at each morning, the golden gleam of a coiled snake—the mighty symbol of King Devlindor—glared down at her; much like the snake, the Garden coiled into a wide circle in front of the stage, his statue in the middle.

So many bodies stormed the area that Arianna couldn't even make out the colorful symbol of the Four Corners beneath their feet. Alongside well-tended flowers and trees, a stream lazily weaved in and out of the area, dividing the symbol into its major sections until it disappeared somewhere back behind the stage; she supposed if she followed it through to the end, it might lead her straight back to the Nicora Forest.

It would all be very lovely, if not for the second, smaller balcony standing at the edge of the Garden, one bloodstained to its very foundation. It loomed quietly on the outskirts, waiting for someone else to feed it.

The Altar. Even in her thoughts, it sounded foreboding.

She gulped, unable to look away.

The sun began to drop down over the horizon now, washing the area in a low light. As lanterns lit up through the crowd, it seemed with the veiling of night something more sinister would come. Everyone was squeezed in, shoulder to shoulder, their eyes flicking between the Altar and the main stage.

Arianna looked on, the Garden feeling foreign to her. Although she had stood there earlier for the morning verse, the view she had now was quite a new perspective. Only hours ago, before she had trained with Master Tayshin, her feet had been planted on that very balcony all eyes observed now, the King's Crest chiseled in gold directly behind her back.

She had peered nervously down at the faces of the city—commoners she may, or may not, one day come to know. The surrealness of it all had been almost incapacitating, but, at Keeper Kassime's insistence to 'get used to it,' she'd lifted her fist to her chest alongside him, her friends, and the City Council, choking out those familiar, dry words—*Hail to the King. Hail to Lord Devlindor.*

The thousands of people below had repeated after her, after the nobles of the city. The force of their combined voices together had almost knocked her backward, and Arianna imagined it was exactly how General Ivo must've felt each day in the Square, leading the King's salute.

There was a control in it—a true power over the people.

And now, as she stared out of the window of her carriage, she knew the entire city would remember Aridyn's face and know her by name after the keeper's introduction.

The people quieted and made a small path for her as the carriage, one trimmed with delicate silver patterns, inched toward the front. So many eyes gazed at her, memorizing every false feature. Grimaces formed on their faces as they tried to get a good look at Aridyn; it was the same expression she'd so often worn when a regulator or elder passed her in the Warrior's District— they loathed her, yet drank her in.

But they don't know me… not really.

She could feel the burn of eyes on her skin, and knowing that Aridyn's pale face would show every hue of her embarrassment made it so much worse as they committed every detail to memory. But to Arianna, they became just a blurred sea of faces.

Then, she spotted a face she most certainly knew—they were being restrained by regulators.

"Stop!" she called to the driver.

The horses immediately came to a halt, the jeering crowd growing louder.

Her voice came in a whisper then. "Eli?"

He struggled as several city regulators forced him up the stairs to the Altar. People shouted at him, throwing trash and rotten food at his feet as an army of guards hurried to hold back the crowd.

"Control yourselves!" Kassime had now appeared on the main balcony, assessing the situation.

Everything about him today was dark; he dressed in a sophisticated, black vest with a sword at his hip, much like his uniformed regulators.

The crowd instantly quieted at his command.

"He's a murderer!" screamed one man over the silence.

Arianna recognized him as Harrin, the brawny patron from Mya's tavern on her first night out in South Luose—a time in her life that now seemed distant and misplaced.

"Anyone who speaks out of turn again shall lose their tongue," said Kassime, his eyes finding Harrin, too. His voice didn't even rise above the normal octave. "I must be in a fair mood, if I'm offering you a choice."

Harrin's head hung low as he disappeared back into the crowd. In the next moment, the regulators had turned their sights on Arianna, flanking the carriage, swords and shields at the ready. Her driver opened the door with a bow.

"Apprentice Aridyn," he said in a shaky voice.

She would never get used to being so honorably titled.

"Our keeper has summoned you."

He held out his hand for Arianna to take, and this time she

didn't refuse, with so many people watching.

She followed the regulators through the swarm, eyes cast down, imagining what they must be whispering about her— *what's her part in our city's hierarchy, this messy girl with mud on her boots?*

Arianna understood now the sheer hatred that sometimes came packaged with respect. And as she climbed the podium stairs toward Keeper Kassime, embracing her new position as a highlife, just like she'd done this morning and would do every morning in her foreseeable future, she caught Eli's eye.

For a split second, she froze, haunted by the pain in his expression. Though, when he looked away (in what could only be described as revulsion), Arianna had no choice but to continue to her place next to the keeper and the other highlifes on the stage, feeling the sting of her status.

Just three weeks ago, Eli had tried to save her and her friends, shouting out for them to run when Godfrey had sent the regulators to ambush the tavern; he'd *known* who Arianna really was all along, calling her by name—she'd been over it countless times in her head… wondering his fate, wondering why he hadn't said anything, wondering why he'd even tried to save them at all.

Arianna's disguise as Pippa had never fooled him, and she desperately wanted to know how he'd discovered their secret and for what reason he never turned them in, as Godfrey surely had. There was so much she wanted to ask.

But, as far as he knew, Arianna Belvedor was dead.

Though it troubled her still that Eli was, undoubtedly, the one who'd handed her the drugged drink in the first place, she'd decided that he must not have known any better—he just seemed so *good.*

She couldn't believe that he'd meant them any harm. After all, he'd tried to save her twice now… *Hadn't he?*

Whatever the truth, to see him in this way, on the Altar, made Arianna's stomach twist in knots and a lump form in her throat.

His fate was out of her hands. All she could do for him now was ask the gods for mercy.

"What's going on?" she whispered to Keeper Kassime who was busy surveying the crowd.

"There's been a crime," he said, matter-of-factly. "The City Council is deliberating the evidence now. They've already questioned the offender. For *most* crimes, citizens are given a trial to decide the best course of action."

"What crime did he commit?"

Keeper Kassime ignored her and marched toward where six representatives of the City Council sat behind a table facing the Altar. Dressed in robes of white with gold collar trims, they were huddled together in whispers.

Ophelia was there, too, at the center. She stood, slowly, chains dangling from her neck and her long, braided hair hanging over her shoulders. She gave a signal to the keeper that Arianna knew couldn't mean anything good for Eli.

He turned to address the crowd. "It is time!"

The Garden fell silent.

Keeper Kassime gestured to the City Council table, giving them the floor.

"We've come to a verdict," said Ophelia, blankly gazing off into the distance. "We find Elijah Neve guilty of the murder of Myrisa Lang."

The city shouted its approval, and Eli screamed out in defiance.

Arianna's breath caught in her throat, shocked that his trial had anything to do with the night they were captured.

He was the one who murdered Mya?

She remembered her last look at their timid host, lying in a pool of her own blood with an axe to the head. And though she wouldn't have wished Mya dead, Arianna knew in her gut that she'd been working alongside Godfrey—betrayal came at a cost in this world, and the poor girl had paid dearly.

Keeper Kassime stepped forward, the crowd electrified.

"Elijah Neve, you're hereby stripped of your citizenship. You're no longer worthy of our Olleb!" There wasn't a lick of remorse in his voice.

Nobody in this world is safe… ever.

"We don't tolerate murder for personal gain, *slave*. And from someone who has been fully trained to carry out the laws on behalf of the King…" He spat on the ground, and there were more shouts of protest from the crowd. "Your sentence is a public whipping. You're to endure twenty-three lashes in tribute to Myrisa, who had barely begun her twenty-third year of life." Keeper Kassime put his attention back on the people. "We will observe a moment of silence for our sister citizen," he said, closing his eyes.

A hush fell over the crowd instantly, as if such a thing were some kind of ritual. Everyone's reaction seemed so instinctive, so desensitized to Eli's fate that Arianna didn't doubt such occasions happened regularly in South Luose—the moment of silence seemed to stretch on forever before the keeper spoke again; Eli was still screaming.

Keeper Kassime took a deep breath, holding his head high. "Regulators, take your positions!"

A burst of applause sounded from below as they uncoiled their whips, and Eli went quiet.

Arianna barely had the heart to look at his face. But when she did, he appeared so resigned, surely knowing that further struggle would only make things worse.

The regulators forced him to his knees, his hands tied with ropes to two parallel poles. Then, they ripped off his tattered shirt, and Arianna saw his bare chest was covered in the same exquisite tattoos she'd glimpsed before on his arms; the markings inched all across his stomach and spread across his back in swirls of black, a striking contrast to his tan skin.

Before Arianna could even react to the sinister scene, one of the regulators had lifted his hand and brought down his whip hard on his back.

Eli let out a scream of pain that Arianna had had the horror of hearing only once before in her lifetime—the memories of Pippa's cries reverberated through her mind, yanking her back to that dreadful past. Another lash came down, and she saw dark red blood bead on his skin, dripping to his heels. He threw his head back with a second howl of agony.

"Stop!" said Arianna, tugging at Keeper Kassime's robes as he came back to stand beside her, not seeming the least bit perturbed by the gruesome scene. "He won't survive this. No one could survive this!"

He looked down at Arianna with cold eyes, shrugging her off. "That's the point, *Aridyn.*"

She recoiled at his words.

"This is the price you pay for your identity. This is what you wanted all along, and we all have a part to play now," he said. "So, *get* used to it."

A troubled look flashed across his eyes before his stone mask settled back on and he returned his focus to the Altar.

"I see," said Arianna, her voice cracking as the fifth lash ripped across Eli's skin.

She watched as he found the will to look at his condemners, raising his eyes toward the balcony... toward her. Sweat dripped down his forehead, his face twisted in torment—but his eyes couldn't have been more full of hate.

Arianna kept his gaze for as long as she could, trying to show him a kindness, trying to show him that she wasn't a part of this merciless system. Alas, with the tenth lash, she had to look away, ashamed to be perceived as one of his punishers. *This is the price we pay.*

Solomon had warned her...

'The land beyond here, which you call freedom, is no kinder place than this children's nightmare you're locked in. It will

demand the skill of both your body and mind if you're to survive its battles.'*

Arianna kept learning this lesson, over and over. And as the regulators brought their whips down again, Eli's aching voice piercing her heart, she learned it again.

Just like the Jar, Olleb-Yelfra was ruled by an evil king, and his wrath would be felt across all the land as long as he lived. She had been a child to wish for such a freedom as this.

I'm a child no longer.

Her fists balled at her sides, her breath coming heavy.

"Do what you must," she said, firmly, "but I'll not stand here and watch this torture. I *refuse.* I've seen enough bloodshed to last me a lifetime, and this just isn't right. How can you be so cruel?"

There was nothing anyone could do for Eli now, but, at the very least, Arianna thought she might be able to live with herself if she walked away.

She made to leave, but Keeper Kassime caught her by the elbow, yanking her back to his side.

"*Cementas cuerpal,*" he whispered in her ear.

Arianna's body went rigid, as if iron had been pumped down her throat and solidified.

"What did you do to me?" she said, barely able to twitch her lips, eyes remaining fixed on the Altar.

"You'll stand here until we're finished," he said. "No one, *especially* not a highlife, will walk away during a public punishment ceremony. It's the law, to be obeyed by all, including us. Even your friends are down there now."

Arianna shifted her eyes around as much as she could, following Keeper Kassime's line of sight; sure enough, she spotted the terrified faces of Lessa, Jeom, and Demetrius in the midst of the chaotic crowd. They must have been too far away to make it to the stage in time, but they were close enough that Eli's blood probably splattered their clothes.

"You'll stay for as long as I deem it necessary."

Time stood still then, frozen, just like her, as Eli's ghostly screams echoed all around the Garden. Arianna tried to remember his voice from the first time she'd laid eyes on him in the tavern, humming along to his guitar. But, before long, that sensual sound, that playful and confident man, had dissolved away into nothing.

Twenty-two strikes. It was almost done.

With the twenty-third stroke of the whip, Eli hunched over in his shackles, hanging like deadweight. His bloodied back had seemingly melted off him, his beautiful tattoos almost unrecognizable. One of the regulators took a cloth and wiped his whip clean, blood literally sopping off the weapon to add to the already red-stained platform.

"The punishment is complete, Keeper," called the other regulator. "Twenty-three lashes for twenty-three years taken too soon. Blood for blood."

He bowed his head and the keeper bowed back.

"Now clean this mess up," Keeper Kassime ordered. "Everyone is free to go." He dismissed the crowd with barely more than a flick of his hand.

Nothing further need be stated after such a shocking show; everyone would remember this message for a long time to come.

The crowd gave one last round of applause and then slowly began to disperse, leaving the Garden to go back to their duties, as if nothing out of the ordinary had happened.

Keeper Kassime turned toward Arianna so that no one else could see, waving his hand in front of her face. She stumbled forward into his arms as her limbs regained feeling, released from the spell.

"Don't ever take away my free will again!"

Her hands shook uncontrollably as she shoved off him, wanting so badly to pummel him in the face.

"What do you mean?" said Keeper Kassime with a scowl as

he considered her. "You did that all on your own."

Arianna gave him one sharp look that she hoped would haunt his nightmares forever and then hurried to the front of the balcony to get a better view of the Altar—she almost lost her stomach at the people below praising the finale, Eli's dead body the victorious ending.

"It's time to go, Aridyn," said Keeper Kassime.

Arianna stumbled back to his side, in a daze, seeing nothing but Eli's lifeless face in her vision. She let him guide her down the steps to the carriage with the other highlifes, and she almost made it… then, she recognized a voice that made her hair stand on end.

"*Godfrey*," she growled, instinctively reaching for the hilt of her sword. He was in conversation with a member of the City Council not far from where she stood.

"Just keep walking," whispered Keeper Kassime, again moving much faster than she would've given him credit for—he had a good grip on her arm, his fingers burrowing deep into her skin so that she couldn't make for her weapons. "That battle has already been fought. You're the winner, even if you can't see that right now."

There was a warrior's cry deep in Arianna's chest dying to come out as the keeper escorted her past Godfrey, but her voice caught in her throat—the last person she wanted to deal with right now was the traitor who had indirectly sent Eli to his grave.

He had a huge smile on his face, greeting every noble that walked by, and Arianna was now in his sights; he caught her free hand just as they passed.

"Apprentice Aridyn, of the City of Kampaulo," he said in his slimy voice. "I'm quite pleased to finally meet you. And at such a memorable event, no less. Welcome to South Luose. I'm Godfrey and always at your service, miss." He bowed, as far as he was able with his cane to help his balance.

Keeper Kassime pressed into her again, a silent threat.

Arianna snatched her hand away from Godfrey before she

broke his fingers right off.

"Pleasure," she said through clenched teeth, hurrying ahead to the carriage.

"Godfrey," said Kassime with a nod, not sparing him another word.

Godfrey smiled again as they walked away. He watched them closely until they got into her carriage—but Arianna watched him, too, wondering all the while if a part of him knew at all that this 'Aridyn' he saw and greeted so devotedly would be the hand that ultimately ended his life.

She was sure he knew nothing, probably planning his next payday. And she was sure that she'd kill him. One way or another, Godfrey would die by her hand.

Kassime let out a long sigh once in the carriage. "Time to go home."

"Yes… let's go home." Arianna pulled the curtain to the window closed and hugged Solza to her chest, thinking of Lessa and the boys.

I have to keep my family close. A single tear escaped her control, her silent goodbye to Elijah Neve.

19

EXPOSED

"WHERE WILL THEY TAKE HIM?" Arianna couldn't tear her eyes away as the regulators dragged Eli's body back behind the palace and out of sight after the procession had ended.

The driver opened the door for her and Keeper Kassime, helping them out of the carriage and gesturing for the guards to ready the main entrance.

I can't bear this right now.

She kept her eyes averted to Solza, who walked at her side; everyone they passed—the gardeners and cooks, the maids and the messengers—slightly bowed to them as they entered. Just a nod of the head it was, but it demonstrated her place at the top of this ruthless food chain.

Arianna felt as if she'd betrayed those at the bottom to get here, those that had sincerely earned their keep.

I'm so sorry, Eli.

"He'll be discarded with the others," said Kassime. "This is the punishment for murder."

Arianna glared at him as they entered the palace. "And how is murder defined in a world built upon death? Haven't we all *murdered* to stand where we stand? I mean, the Free Falls in and of itself demands blood on everyone's hands."

She folded her arms across her chest, falling out of step with him as he walked ahead—he hadn't dismissed her back to her quarters yet, so she followed him still.

"That's not murder," said Kassime. "That's survival of the fittest and survival of valuable and strong people proving that they're worthy of citizenship."

He pulled off his cloak and held it out for a nearby attendant to put away without a pause in his step, so comfortable in this world, it seemed.

As Arianna observed him from behind, eyes glued to the silver crown glinting on top of his dark hair, she found him quite hard to decipher. This city keeper, though appointed by the King himself, secretly opposed his leader with knowledge and practice of magic as a Guardian of Gold.

Though a traitor to his core, for some *bewildering* reason, he still defended and justly upheld King Devlindor's laws—ones he ultimately vowed to help overthrow.

"How is that any different at all?" huffed Arianna. "Where do you draw the line?"

She slipped out of her cloak as well and handed it to the attendant, feeling sorry for the way he cowered around them before scuttling away.

"Thank you," she mouthed.

She waited for Keeper Kassime's inevitable explosion—Arianna's temper was nothing compared to his, and she could sense him growing more frustrated with each question she dared to ask; he had no patience with her at all, much less than with the rest of her friends, and she couldn't understand why.

In fact, he hadn't shared *anything* about himself or his

motives so far… just that he was helping them as a favor to a late friend.

"You think Elijah Neve deserved his life?" he spat, whipping around on her. "He killed a woman, a hard worker, who paid her dues always on time and had nothing but a bright future ahead. She ran a business, had a successful partnership, and as such, was a valuable addition to South Luose." He pointed a finger at Arianna. "That woman *earned* her citizenship. She earned a life here, and that scum snatched it away. A drifter, someone who existed only for himself and who was more trouble than he was worth! You tell me you sympathize with that?"

He sucked a deep breath in through his nose and marched ahead toward the doorway of his quarters; they were located in the lavish west wing of the palace, devoted solely to his privacy, and in quite the opposite direction to where he'd put her and her friends.

"How can you be so certain of that truth?" said Arianna, racing after him. "How can you judge his worth so surely, when you didn't even know him?"

At this, Arianna felt the strike of his hand sting across her cheek before she even saw it coming. The force knocked her clean off her feet, her hands catching her before her face could collide with the tiled floor; Solza leaped back, frightened by his sudden outburst.

"Because we found this in his pocket and the axe in his hand at the scene of the crime!"

Keeper Kassime tossed something to the floor.

Arianna lifted her eyes to find the jagged coin from the City of Undor, gleaming bright… save for the dried blood staining the side where the gilded axe would normally shine.

"Elijah awaited judgment for weeks while I dealt with you all, and now was the time to publicly show justice for our slain resident. The offense couldn't go unpunished with how visible Mya's station was, but this—" he pointed to the coin "—should not

have been entrusted to *anyone* other than a guardian, you inso-
lent child. Do you know how many people I had to track down
to erase this from their memories?" He was practically seething.
"How do you know so little about this world yet have already
seen so much?"

With a shaking hand, Arianna picked the coin up from the
floor, contemplating the keeper's words. Then, she wiped the
blood from her lips onto the back of her sleeve. She was in utter
disbelief at what had just happened and couldn't find the words
to defend herself.

"Familiar, is it?" He shook his head, lifting her off the floor
by the collar of her shirt. "I know this was your doing. Don't even
think about trying to lie." He narrowed his eyes.

Arianna felt all his power then. Magic radiating off him,
barely hidden behind a cool mask of perfection.

"*Well?*"

Arianna averted her gaze, finding Solza's instead; a growl
rumbled in her throat, but she held her ground.'

"It's... the coinage from the City of Undor, the lost home of
the dwarves," she mumbled.

"Correct," he snapped. "And do you realize what could have
happened if this had fallen into the wrong hands, gotten back to
the *King?* We're not the only ones who remember, you know!
There are many dark practitioners alive today who protect the
King's secrets faithfully, just as Sir Vladamor does."

"I'm sorry," she said, flinching under his grasp; there was no
magic trick up her sleeve that could best such a practiced sorcerer.
He had all the control. "We didn't know anything about the
guardians. We didn't think... we just gave it to Mya as payment
for her hospitality, for a few nights' sleep—"

He scoffed, eyes bulging in anger.

"Say no more of your excuses! This part of the world you've
found is not a game to be toyed with. It's been buried deep by
the greatest power ever known to this earth, and to uncover it and

share it so carelessly not only endangers everything the guardians have sacrificed but also any possibility the Olleb has at regaining her future."

He let her go and she stumbled backward.

"Solomon may have been my friend, a brother, even, long ago, but times have changed," said Kassime. "I'll not have my position compromised, and I'll not have all that the guardians have worked to preserve be upended by some rash children! We're waning already, and one wrong move could end us forever." He snatched the coin from her hand. "Now get out of my sight."

"I—"

Keeper Kassime slammed the door to his chambers in her face before she could find her voice.

Arianna understood in that moment why King Devlindor had entrusted him to rule over South Luose—traitor to the crown or not, he scared her to her core.

Although Keeper Kassime's words would not soon be forgotten, neither would the young man who had first showed her kindness in this new world. No matter what the keeper thought, Eli had not deserved to be slain in such a gruesome fashion and probably buried somewhere behind the palace without ceremony.

"It was Mya who slipped the drug in our cups," she whispered at the keeper's door.

She headed back to her quarters to try to forget the terrible day, having to ask for directions several times on the way. When she entered her room, she left Solza to her own devices and went straight to her bathing area; a hot bath was waiting for her, steam fogging the room.

Thank the gods for that girl.

Her attendant must have anticipated her arrival and had prepared the washroom fully. Incense smoked in the windows, immersing Arianna in a honeyed fragrance, and candles on every surface chased away the darkness that had begun to settle around the palace.

Arianna didn't waste a second. She stepped out of her dirtied clothes and walked up the marble steps, then dipped her toes into the bath water. The heat frightened her skin at first, but in a moment's time she was lowering her entire body into its depths, letting it soothe the aches of her body and soul.

She closed her eyes, and her mind instantly transported her back to her utopia. She imagined swimming all around the warm waters with the waterfall crashing down behind her and the firebugs illuminating the shadows—but this was not a utopia at all.

Her eyes flew open, and she stared upon a mirrored ceiling, Aridyn Lareigh gazing back. She searched anywhere for herself in this beautiful stranger, but she just couldn't see.

Arianna blinked, finding the mirror again, except this time the face of her new reflection was joined with another. She shrieked, jumping to her feet, water sloshing over the sides of the tub as she gaped up at the malevolent version of herself. "Go away!"

Arianna pulled at her hair, squeezing her eyes shut to try to will this ghost gone. But when she looked again, the girl was still there, hiding in the glass, a hand on Aridyn's shoulder and a leer on her face.

The girl from the mirror began to laugh, violently, and with Aridyn by her side, the real Arianna was nowhere to be found, forced out of the picture.

"I said, *go* away!"

She picked up a stone soap dish and chucked it at the ceiling; the mirrors cracked with the collision, instantly raining down in sharp shards over her head.

Arianna realized her mistake too late, holding up her hands to try to protect her face, but her eyes remained wide open in shock as the glass suddenly froze in midair, Aridyn's face multiplied all around her.

Did I do that?

Arianna looked at her hands, mouth agape—she was so

stunned by her unintended charm that she didn't have enough time to move herself out of harm's way before the magic wore off. The glass unfroze, slicing at her exposed skin in a wave.

Then, the soap dish came crashing back down, smacking her right in the forehead. Arianna fell into the bath, the waters splashing wildly around her until they settled with her lying still at the bottom.

"THERE YOU GO. EASY DOES IT," said Lessa, helping her into a robe and over to the bed. Sano was glued to her shoulders. "Don't you ever get tired of all these near-death experiences?"

Arianna pulled the covers to her chin and brought her hand to her head.

"I just slipped," she said without much conviction.

"I gathered," said Lessa as she dabbed an ointment on her bruised lip and forehead. "Thankfully, I was in my room when your attendant started screaming for help! You really gave her a fright. She found you floating in a pool of your own blood."

Arianna groaned.

"Don't worry, I sent her off to fetch some supplies," said Lessa. "But can you please try and be more careful? We only just got our lives back."

Arianna took the prillyberry juice Lessa handed to her and drank it down in one gulp.

"This is starting to feel like a bad routine," said Lessa, taking the empty cup from her.

Arianna sighed. "I know. It's just this new identity. It's been a... hard adjustment."

She considered telling Lessa about what had really sparked the incident, about the other girl in the mirror.

"Believe me, I fully understand. Pretending to be Lilith isn't my favorite part of this new life."

Lessa's eyes flicked to the mirror near the bed; a girl with red hair and freckled cheeks looked back.

"We'll get used to it though," she said. "We have to."

"It's not just that, Les," said Arianna, chewing on her lip. "I don't *only* see Aridyn in the mirrors. There's something else… watching me." Lessa raised an eyebrow, and Arianna drooped her head. "I can't really explain it, but I feel like I'm going mad."

"Well try!" said Lessa, losing her temper. Sano screeched, jumping to the floor to find Solza. "Because this can't happen again. If there's something going on with you, be candid. I can't always be here to save you from your reflection."

She stormed away from the bed and began busying herself with cleaning up the trail of water Arianna had left from walking across the room.

"We have to be careful now more than ever," she said, on her hands and knees with a towel. "This is our one chance to get it right."

Arianna let her head fall back on the pillow, staring up at the beautiful canopy draping her bed; a stitch of guilt formed in her stomach—if she was feeling so out of sorts, how might Lessa be taking things?

"It's the dreams again," she said after a moment; she owed it to Lessa to be honest with her. "I guess they never really went away." With each word, Arianna felt a pressure lifting off her chest.

Lessa stopped cleaning, her shoulders slumped.

"Can't you just… ignore them?" she said, her tone gentler. "Ignore them until they go away."

"I can't ignore my dreams," said Arianna without thought; it was as if Solomon had taken over her voice. "I've tried that, and it just doesn't work."

"Well, what do you suppose they mean, then?"

"I have some theories," said Arianna, aware of Lessa's waning patience. She didn't want to push her too far. "In the dreams, I'm normally killed by some masked monster or an insidious version of myself."

She cast her eyes down, tugging at a loose thread on her sheets as she remembered the time in the forest when she felt as if she might *actually* drown.

"I'm starting to see this evil in every mirror I pass, every reflection, and I wonder if… if maybe it's a reflection of what I carry inside." Arianna choked out the confession. "Maybe I'm *supposed* to die." She shrugged. "It's the better of the options at least."

"And what's the other option?" said Lessa, sitting on the side of the bed.

Arianna felt her skin grow hot as she struggled to keep her next thought to herself. It was a fruitless effort.

"To become like Vladamor!" It was a huge relief to admit her fears out loud, but she wasn't fully pacified. "Don't you get it? After all the selfish choices I've made, maybe my soul is blackened now. Maybe this is as far as my destiny goes…"

Her mind wandered again to the necromancer and all of the similarities that connected them.

"I'd rather die a thousand deaths than become anything like that soulless monster."

"Don't be so foolish," said Lessa. "We haven't come all this way for you to think like that. Death will come for us all, as Death surely does, but not before we've finished living and *not* because you're meant to die."

She tilted her head to the side.

"Am I really going to be the one to remind *you* that destiny is what you make of it? Haven't we proved that time and time again?"

Arianna just shook her head, not knowing what to believe anymore.

Lessa laid a hand on her hand.

"You were born as a number, meant to be nothing more than that, and then you grew into a warrior. Then that warrior became a witch in a world without magic, and now that witch lives in a palace." Lessa grinned, gazing around the room with an awed expression. "Our destinies are bright and they've barely begun!"

Arianna felt the hope Lessa carried in her heart, much stronger than her own.

"You just don't understand," she said, shrugging her off. "You read of Vladamor's history. You heard what Kassime said. I was reborn by the same spell as a necromancer! A *necromancer*, Lessa. What are my options if not death or darkness? I *can't* become like him, but I feel like I'm on my way."

She looked Lessa in the eyes, truly wanting answers.

"Tell me, what other options do you see?"

"I knew we should've addressed this sooner," said Lessa, the smile fading from her face. "Ara, I don't care what those texts say. You're not some evil spawn of the *Onasyuda* spell. You're as good as it gets, if ever there was a definition of the word. You saved me countless times, not to mention Jeom and Demetrius. And you led us to freedom and uncovered the magic in the world, even if our little group is the only one who knows it."

Her eyes bored into Arianna's, as if to embed what she was saying in her brain.

"It's human nature to make mistakes, and this world is a testimony to that. All you can do is learn from them. I'm *telling* you, you're not fated to darkness."

"But you don't know that," said Arianna in a whisper. "What if I am transforming into something wicked? You can't deny that my magic is stronger than yours, and I've had such terrible… thoughts."

"Ha, you wish you were stronger than me!" said Lessa with a laugh, putting her arm around her shoulders.

Arianna returned a faint smile.

"Listen to me," said Lessa, hugging her close. "You think I haven't daydreamed of King Devlindor dying in more ways than one? Or been racked with guilt for the way we left our friends back in the districts?"

She sucked in a deep breath, a shadow crossing her eyes.

"We've been through a lot. But Talis wouldn't have just willingly conjured up another necromancer to add to this world of horrors. He's the smartest person I know, so there's got to be a different explanation, and we'll figure that out sooner or later. Just no more talk of this, okay? We all do what we have to in order to survive. It's as simple as that. You can't punish yourself for taking your life into your own hands. Our choices have been messy and complicated, but they're *not* wrong."

Arianna nodded, though she still wasn't fully convinced enough to let go of her worries. She needed to know more about the spell Talis had used to bring her back to life. Until then, she had no intention of telling anyone else, not even Jeom or Demetrius, of her fears—and by Lessa's reaction, she was certain that, even in the magical world, imagining such evils wasn't exactly normal.

"Not a word of this to the boys, all right?" said Arianna. "And especially not to Kassime."

"Of course," said Lessa with a comforting smile. "Your secret is safe with me. Now, if all that necromancer talk is done, I *think* we could use something to take the edge off."

She walked over to one of Arianna's cabinets where a silver carafe sat waiting. "Wine?" said Arianna, perking up.

Lessa beamed.

"I thought earlier that it would be nice to celebrate our first day as highlifes together," she said. "Although, that was before you tried to off yourself with a soap dish."

Arianna stuck her tongue out, and Lessa laughed.

"It's amazing, though, Ara! Just the snap of our fingers and we can have anything we want."

She gathered up two crystal glasses, and Arianna pulled herself out of the bed to join her, already feeling much better with the prillyberry working away her headache.

They sat on the floor, playing with their avatars and recounting their 'first day' stories as citizens of South Luose.

"How were your lessons with Master Tayshin?" said Lessa, taking a swig of her drink. "He seemed… nice."

Arianna rolled her eyes.

"Dreadful," she said, watching Solza tear one of her decorative pillows to shreds. Her spotted fur stood on edge as she attacked the cushion. "Yours?"

"It was okay," said Lessa with a sigh. "But the master in Kassime is just as harsh as the keeper."

"I can only imagine," said Arianna. "I guess I'll count myself lucky, then."

She took a drink from her cup and nearly spat it out.

"Ugh, what in the King's name is this?"

"I've no idea," said Lessa, her nose wrinkling up as she tried another small sip. "I just asked for the finest."

"This would've never even made it to Mya's tavern," said Arianna with a laugh, but it was abruptly snuffed out. "I saw you in the crowd today… at the Garden."

Lessa cast her eyes to the floor, forcing down another sip. "It seems that public punishments demand the presence of the *entire* city. It was just awful, wasn't it?"

Arianna nodded.

They hadn't spoken much about Eli or Mya since the night of their capture, no one wanting to relive the horrible memories. But now with the full picture, Arianna decided it was time for one last confession.

"He saved me, you know? Eli was the one who found me in the forest, the man I spoke about before, in the well center. I *didn't* imagine him. I know it was him who saved my life back there, before you all had arrived."

She stroked Solza's fur, and the gesture calmed her as she re-called that frightful day.

"And for whatever reason, I think he kept our secret. He knew who we were all along."

Lessa didn't look as shocked as she imagined she might be; Arianna supposed that after everything, it would be hard to surprise any of them anymore.

"I'm sorry I didn't believe you the first time," she said, solemnly. "Whatever it's worth, he didn't deserve to die like that. Nobody does."

Arianna thought of the lost souls in the Vanishing Tunnels who might never move on from their improper burials or unfulfilled ambitions; she hoped with all her heart that Eli would not stay among them, that his soul could find peace wherever his body might lie now.

"To Eli," she said, raising her glass. Lessa joined her, and they drank together in his name, the flavor of the wine beginning to grow on them both.

Tomorrow, Arianna resolved to return to the Stables and make a trade for Phantom in exchange for one of her carriage horses so that she could repay his sacrifice in some small way.

"Thank you for listening… about everything."

"That's what I'm here for," said Lessa. "I can't battle by your side in your mind, but I'll help you figure out what's going on in any way I can. But you're a warrior, Ara. If there's anyone who can win a fight, it's you."

Arianna took a deep breath, silently accepting that challenge, even though she knew Lessa couldn't really understand the danger she felt she was in—the next time the girl in the mirror showed up, she would stand up and face her.

20

A LEGACY

"SO, TELL ME," SAID KASSIME as he escorted the four through the dungeons and up to the attic. "You've flourished with your new identities in the real world for just a little while now. How do you feel?"

He unlocked the familiar door at the top of the stairs using just the palm of his hand.

"It's going quite well, sir," said Lessa as they entered the pentagon room.

Arianna stopped for a moment, finding the mirror where they had first laid eyes on their new identities. Now when she looked, she didn't see the reflection of four perfect strangers but the faces of people she'd begun to know well.

Keeper Kassime led them to the library and directed them to sit around a large, bricked fireplace.

"*Solza ven immito.*"

He waved his hand, and pink flames suddenly grew where

before there'd been nothing, licking at the wood and spreading a warm glow about the room.

The library was filled with a world of secrets, and Arianna could barely concentrate as all of its wonders began to grab her attention once more—they hadn't been permitted back here since the day Sir Vladamor left.

The painting of the young guardians above the mantel, the picturesque jade carving of Saindora, and the hundreds of manuscripts with countless stories to be told called to her, as if in whispers. Even in the three weeks cooped up in this haven with nothing but time, Arianna had barely begun to understand all the wisdom left behind from the Golden Age available here. She was overjoyed to be returning so soon.

But, mostly, she was eager to spend some quality time with her friends; it seemed like she hadn't seen them in ages, though it had only been the better part of a week. Her schedule with Master Tayshin kept her far busier than the others—she barely had time for supper these days. She had so many questions she wanted to ask, but Keeper Kassime hadn't beckoned them here for chatting—there was something important to be said.

Arianna turned her attention to him after she and her friends had made quick greetings; he was seated on a couch that looked toward the fireplace, taking them all in.

"I'm glad to hear things are going good. I hope Lessa's sentiments are the same for everyone." They nodded, and his lips twitched up in a small smile. "Palace life does you well. You all are glowing."

His eyes wandered over to Arianna, and she glared back with contempt, still remembering the sting across her cheek from when he slapped her not long ago.

"Your masters would be proud of you," he said before turning to the boys. "And how is the training coming along?"

"Master Gansevurt is phenomenal," said Jeom, clearly thrilled to discuss his apprenticeship with the others.

"Yes, he's rather… *enthusiastic*, isn't he?" said Kassime, folding his hands across his lap. "He's got a true appetite for his craft."

"Rather brilliant that is!" said Jeom, jumping to his feet with devotion in his eyes. "I've never seen a creator more skilled. I feel so inferior now that I know the possibilities. And just think what I could do once I learn how to wield the power of the Crissy Axe. Just *think*."

Jeom rolled up the sleeve of his robe to reveal a red and raw stamp on his shoulder—the Creator's Crest, a snake coiled around a mallet, was carved right into his flesh.

"How about that beauty?" said Jeom, flexing his muscles.

Lessa gasped, and Arianna's mouth fell open.

The mark was terribly inflamed, seeming to bubble and ooze with every contraction, obviously infected.

"Brother, you've been branded!" said Demetrius, standing up to inspect it.

"I was offered a permanent position as a lead apprentice in my group," said Jeom with a prideful expression. "Master Gansevurt sees great things for me. Besides, I only branded my fake identity. I only branded Jaxin."

He nodded to himself, smiling all the while.

The room was silent a moment and then Arianna burst out laughing; it felt so good. She hadn't laughed in a while.

"What a fool you are!" said Lessa. She covered her mouth with her hand to try to stave off her own giggles. "Here, let me have a look at that nasty thing."

Jeom puffed out his chest, lowering himself back to the floor next to her; she fished in her robe pocket for something and then sprinkled what looked to be some kind of powder on his arm. Almost instantly, the swelling started to decrease.

Demetrius took deep, slow breaths, appearing as if he might fall over in a fit of laughs, too, at any moment. "Jeom… you know… that's not how it works."

"What do you mean?" said Jeom, hissing through his teeth

from the sting of Lessa's remedy.

"It means that scar is *permanent*, genius," said Arianna. "New identity or not."

Demetrius lost all control then, the joyful sound of his laughter filling every space in the library.

"She's only joking, right?" said Jeom, shoving Demetrius so that he fell over to the side.

He looked to Keeper Kassime for confirmation.

"I'm afraid not," said Kassime with a snicker; he didn't appear surprised at all. "Welcome to the Creator's Club."

Then, he lifted his sleeve to show off the same mark on his own copper skin. Although, instead of a blotchy red wound, it was now a raised scar.

"I come from the Creator's District as well."

He cleared his throat.

"Well, Ferlon Ragaric does," he said. "Once upon a time, Master Gansevurt was also my trainer. I only found my calling in healing after I had the pleasure of meeting Talis."

He glanced toward Lessa with a slight nod.

"I still know my fair share of creation, though. When the time is right, maybe we can see what kind of magic that axe of yours can stir up?"

"Thank you, sir," breathed Jeom; he fingered the tube at his belt concealing his axe. "I'd like that *very* much."

Arianna was a bit taken aback, too—so far, the keeper hadn't permitted them to use any magic around the palace.

What's he got up his sleeve now?

Keeper Kassime turned to Demetrius. "And you, how have you taken to Mistress Serina… in Darrios' identity?"

It was no secret to anyone in this room that Demetrius had been in no hurry to adopt this new life once he'd learned of his renewed apprenticeship with his district master.

"We have it easy," whispered Lessa.

Arianna nodded, feeling a little ashamed that she had any

complaints about Master Tayshin at all, knowing Demetrius' tortured past in the Agrarian's District under that woman.

Though, as Demetrius began to detail his experience as a highlife apprentice, somehow he found only kind words to say about Mistress Serina; Arianna couldn't fathom his source of positivity, forced to work with someone who had berated and discouraged him at every turn for so many years.

"I've spent a lot of time with her in the palace greeneries and reading about the wildlife of the Olleb," he said. "There's just so much more for me to learn! And now that I'm a respected citizen, Mistress Serina isn't as… difficult to work with. I've given her a second chance, and she's well lived up to it."

"In her eyes, you're no longer a slave," said Kassime. "You're Darrios, and you've earned your right to respect, even from your elders."

Arianna supposed he was right. Still, she counted her blessings that she'd ended up with a trainer like Solomon in the Jar.

"I won't even ask if you feel you're doing well," said Keeper Kassime, turning his gaze on Lessa.

"But I—"

He smirked. "You are."

"Oh, thank you, sir," she said, her cheeks turning pink. "I do feel like Master Churry left me in a good position for advanced training under you. He taught me well in many things…"

She glanced toward the window, and Arianna knew she worried over her former master and friend.

"I do wish I could make time to practice again with my bow." Her shoulders slumped. "I've barely touched it since we got here."

"She's got warrior potential," said Demetrius, patting Lessa on the back. "I've seen it for myself."

"I don't doubt it," said Keeper Kassime with a nod of approval—it was plain that he was growing fond of her. Somehow, she'd managed to break through his hardened shell.

"We'll carve out some time for all of you to practice those

skills further. Don't you worry." He stood. "Speaking of which…"

He abruptly left the room and came back a few moments later with the sleek longbow Arianna had first noticed on her walk through the sparring room. He beckoned to Lessa, and she floated to her feet as the others gawked.

"I know Talis would've wanted you to have this," said Keeper Kassime. "It used to be his."

"This was… my master's?" Lessa glowed. "I don't know what to say," she breathed, accepting the extraordinary gift with shaking hands.

She gently turned it over, eyes glittering as she admired the silver and blue designs; her old bow paled in comparison. Then she tugged on the bow string to get a feel for it, and Arianna was glad to see that her form was still steady.

"It's quite remarkable," she said, running her hand across the handle. "And so lightweight. What's it made of?"

"It's elf-made," said Keeper Kassime.

There was a collective gasp around the room.

"Incredible," said Demetrius.

"Quite," said Kassime. "Elves were well-known masters in forging weaponry. And as they mainly inhabited woodlands, naturally, the bow was a common tool in the various tribes around the Olleb… should they need to defend themselves in high territory, you see."

"They really created this?" said Jeom, studying the fine craftsmanship for himself. "But I thought that dwarves—"

"Dwarves were *not* the only creators of the Golden Age," said Kassime. "Elves were masters of many things, holding tight to secrets that even in that era weren't known by the rest of the world."

He studied Jeom's reaction, the light of the fire glinting off his crown. "I haven't any arrows to give," he said. "However, you should be able to help Lessa with that, correct? Consider it part of your advanced training. I'm sure Master Gansevurt won't mind. And if he does, send him to me." He looked down to the weapon in his hands. "She'll need something sturdy and worthy of this bow."

"I'd be honored!" Jeom was grinning from ear to ear as he handed it back to Lessa.

She gave him a big hug and then sat back down, laying the longbow across her lap, examining it all the while.

"And what of you?" said Kassime, leaving Arianna for last.

"My lessons are going quite well, thank you," she lied. "Master Tayshin is different… but talented, I suppose."

She kept her gaze on the bow, hoping he wouldn't notice how she really felt; she didn't want to be seen as weak or whining next to everyone else's encouraging experiences.

"He's no Master Bell, though." *Damn, why did I have to say that?*

"Jon Tayshin is an *esteemed* warrior," said Kassime, taking a serious tone with her. "If he finds you worthy, then you have an opportunity to exceed with greatness. Do not waste it. Now is not the time to pine for the past. He can teach you much more than you probably give him credit for, and certainly more than your memories of Solomon can."

I doubt that very much.

Arianna pressed her lips in a tight line to keep from saying anything else rash; she tried to picture this 'greatness' in her new master that everyone claimed was there, but after a week of being tortured through trainings with him, she still didn't see it.

"Keeper," said Lessa in an unsteady voice, "if you feel we can safely sustain this ruse, I think I can speak for all of us in saying that we'd like to remain with you for as long as possible. Your hospitality has been more than we could've possibly dreamed of when we escaped the Jar." She glanced to the others for confirmation. "I don't know what we would've done had we not found you."

Jeom and Demetrius were nodding along emphatically, but Arianna felt as if the walls were closing in on her—thinking of staying here like this, under Master Tayshin and under Keeper Kassime's exacting watch. Didn't they feel as if something was missing? She needed something… more.

"I intended nothing less," said Keeper Kassime, smiling down at her. "Things have been going smoothly, so I see no reason why you shouldn't stay. It's the least I can do—"

"We don't *want* your least," said Arianna, the words flying out with no control.

All eyes turned on her, shocked and confused.

"Excuse me?" said the keeper through gritted teeth; the memory of his slap stung her again in this moment.

"Err… apologies, sir. That came out completely wrong," said Arianna, feeling her face redden. She got to her feet, positioned directly beneath the portrait of the young guardians as she faced him—they were uncomfortably close. "What I meant, and I think I too speak for everyone, was that we would like to be officially inducted to the… resistance. To start our *real* training now."

Jeom's mouth formed an 'O', and Demetrius cocked his head in interest. Lessa's eyes were peeled open, probably waiting to see whether Keeper Kassime would push her straight into the fireplace or not; his expression was unreadable.

Arianna tensed but stood her ground as he scrutinized her—she'd thought a lot about what he had said to her on the night of Eli's death, and his words steered her now.

"A world which we know very little about is a part of us in ways we don't truthfully understand," she said, gesturing to Solza and Sano. "We owe it to ourselves to learn more about these connections. It's all well and good to be highlifes, to go about training and our futures like we're normal. But we're *not*, and I don't want to waste this opportunity. I want to continue the legacy of the guardians, as you, Solomon, and Talis have vowed." She touched eyes with all her friends. "And I'm sure they do too."

Keeper Kassime lifted his chin, remaining silent as his eyes narrowed in the direction of the others, clearly trying to gauge their reactions.

Lessa set her bow aside and came to stand next to Arianna. "We've come so far already," she said, filling the uneasy silence and drawing the keeper's attention to her. "I know we won't disappoint you if you just give us a chance."

"Yeah, you can trust us with this," said Demetrius, hopping to his feet. "We owe you everything! We stand by what you made us swear on the first day."

"Agreed," said Jeom. "It's a part of who we are now. Part of our make." He ran his thumb along the healed ridges of his new mark.

Arianna let out a sigh of relief, knowing that no matter how much time they'd spent apart or what their new names might be, they were still family and they were still on the same page. She squared her shoulders.

"Whether we chose this life or not, it's our duty to uphold the true legacy of our world and *your* duty to teach us," said Arianna. "Like you said, we shouldn't pine in the past. This is our present and our future." She kept his gaze a moment, not allowing his hardened expression to unnerve her. Then, she and Lessa sat back down with the boys to await judgment.

Keeper Kassime circled the room. And with the crackling fire, his shadow loomed eerily over them all.

"So, you think you have what it takes to be guardians?" he said after a moment, his gaze glued to the portrait. "Let's see, shall we?"

He faced them, head cocked to the side.

"First, we have Jeom, the boy who, supposedly, shares a royal bloodline with a fallen dwarf race." He chuckled. "Then there's your… half-brother, you say? Well, he has yet to show signs of being linked to the magical world in *any* way." His gaze rested on

Demetrius. "Unless unbendable compassion and an unnaturally talented way with the earth counts for power."

"Who says it doesn't?" snapped Jeom.

Demetrius touched his arm, seemingly not insulted.

"Could be," said Kassime with a shrug; he ranted on, unaffected by the outburst.

"And there's you, of course." He turned to Lessa. "The girl with the magical healing touch, a knack for potions, and as bright as they come. We've no idea what you're capable of yet. Though, I imagine much, much more than what I've seen so far." There was a compliment in there… somewhere, though it was overshadowed by how unimpressed he appeared to be.

She slumped, everyone looking somewhat defeated as Keeper Kassime continued to point out their shortcomings; what they *did* know and what they *could* do didn't really seem to matter to him at all.

What else must we prove to be taken seriously?

He came to stand in front of Arianna, peering down at her with judgment in his eyes.

"And finally, there's Miss Belvedor. A slave turned warrior and sorceress," he said. "Clearly the leader of this misfit group. There's a resilient power in you yet… though one that lacks *much* control." He clicked his tongue on his teeth, shaking his head.

Arianna felt naked under his scrutiny, wondering if he could read minds as well as manipulate them.

Can he sense the darkness within me?

She prayed not, because despite what Lessa thought, Arianna was still quite certain it was there.

"Patience and respect are significant qualities which I haven't seen present in you," said Keeper Kassime—the accusation stung, mostly because such qualities *weren't* present in her and she knew it.

She opened her mouth to retort, but he held his hand up.

"My point exactly," he said with an incredulous laugh. She

pressed her lips shut, and resisted the urge to thump Demetrius for snickering. "Loyalty, though, is another. And in this, you excel more than most."

He looked toward where Sano and Solza lay sleeping.

"You also declare there to be avatars in our midst, yet it's unclear yet if the cub shows any hint of developing magical aptitudes as Sano has. That would make her... just a *cub*."

Arianna let out a long exhale. "So, what is it that you're saying?" she said, feeling her temper rise; she didn't care that she was proving him right. "What, we're not good enough for you, then? We were good enough for Solomon and Talis!"

"No, you're not good enough!" he yelled, the fire reflecting in his eyes as he challenged her.

He straightened his back and found again the portrait.

"But I daresay you will be. With some fine-tuning, of course." He nodded to himself. "Solomon and Talis wouldn't have put their trust in you lightly, and now that I know a little more about you, it's clear they were grooming you for this all along."

Lessa and Arianna began to whisper excitedly, thinking of their past trainings with their masters in a brand new light.

"And as far as the boys... well, that's a welcome bonus."

"So... you'll teach us, then?" said Lessa, chewing on her lip; Arianna held her breath.

She wasn't even fully clear on what a guardian was, but she knew in her heart that she yearned for it.

"I will."

They all sat up straighter, and Arianna found it within her to show some respect in this moment—she wanted to be worthy of whatever Solomon was preparing her for, she felt the significance of it... even if she didn't particularly like, or even yet trust, Keeper Kassime.

"In addition to your mandated advanced trainings, you'll meet me here in the attic on a regular schedule for individual and group lessons. It's evident you each have your own gifts, but there's a lot of other knowledge to impart on you, too."

Arianna clung to every word.

"Being a Guardian of Gold is more than just mastering your inherited skills or reading scrolls of history. It's about sharing knowledge *and* respecting it. Be each other's teachers and diversify your strengths. No longer divided like the Four Corners, as King Devlindor would have it, guardians shall forever stand *together.*"

"We'll really be guardians?" said Arianna, feeling the responsibility weigh on her in an amazingly satisfying way.

"That's my hope," said Kassime.

Demetrius did a few fist bumps to the air, and they all grew giddy with happiness.

Solomon, we did it! This must be the path you meant for us. Wherever you are, thank you…

She would finally be able to focus on something worth her energy, on something indescribably good.

"*And* for your first official lesson," said Kassime, quieting them, "I think it's about time you understood a little bit more about me and my beginnings. Let this be your commencement as apprentices of the Guardians of Gold."

He put a fist to his chest and the four friends promptly stood to follow his lead.

"Hail to the World. Hail to Olleb-Yelfra!" they sang in unison.

Then, by the light of the fire and with all eyes on him, Keeper Kassime began an enthralling tale dating back to a time when he was not much younger than they were now.

FERLON RAGARIC

THE WORLD WAS DIFFERENT than he'd expected as he stepped out of the Vanishing Tunnels, leaving the Four Corners behind. He followed the group in a daze, one foot in front of the other and never looking back. The Blancoren Mountains receded, getting farther and farther away as he moved closer to his new future.

The next few nights were spent in the Village of Draminet, celebrating with his peers and his trainers after having completed the 205th Free Falls Festivals.

Staring at the paper that signified him a citizen, stamped with the crest of the King, he saw his name written out in elegant ink—*Ferlon Ragaric.*

No longer would he be referred to by 'two-forty-eight', as the silver number stitched on his purple robes had always labeled him.

He had earned the rights to his name without contest.

It had been unlucky, though, for the slave who'd been put up against him in the festivals. Ferlon had always been one of the best in the Creator's District, his fingers working a sort of magic.

He couldn't stop going over it in his head.

The test to be passed before being welcomed into their eighteenth year was one they had all regularly trained for in this part of the Jar: forging weapons. And the task had been simple—all seventeenth years were grouped in pairs of two and allotted the week to construct one flawless weapon in the district Inventor's Zone to be judged for multiple criteria. There could be only one winner per pair, and after all winners were selected, the weapons were ranked to inform placement.

For those less talented and with the district's limited supplies, a week wasn't a lot of time to create anything notable. But for him, it had been plenty; Ferlon purposefully chose to craft something small where the detail would be seen, opting to weld an iron throwing star with four points. There wasn't much of a focus on creating these types of weapons during his years of training, for they weren't widely used by warriors (aside for show on a belt). But he knew the general had a fondness for them and he wanted to gain all the points he could get.

The bell was rung, signaling the start of their timer; the seventeenth years worked, unsupervised, from dusk until dawn, day after day, making either their last weapon or the first of hopefully many to come.

Ferlon had such finesse at the task; his fingers cramped and bled, and he missed nearly every meal, but when all was said and done, there was no doubt that he'd crafted one of the finest weapons yet. The detail was exquisitely intricate, the thin lines of an abstract design shining in the barely cooled metal as he held it up to the light of a lantern.

At the end of the festival, the losers in each pair were to be killed, using their own failed weapons.

Ferlon had always been a composed, emotionless sort of boy. It left him with little in the way of friends and more time than most to master the crafts that came with being a creator-slave—but just because he kept to himself didn't mean he was comfortable with killing someone.

He shuddered thinking about it now, on his way to freedom.

He'd had to pull on his leather gloves to even grip the weapon created by his opponent so as not to get splinters from the poorly polished handle; a mallet was such a simple, inelegant weapon to begin with that Ferlon never would've selected it with such high stakes at risk. Even still, the detail of this particular weapon was downright sloppy, its head lopsided and corrupted from overhandling. And it was still hot to the touch, scalding iron just pulled from the furnace, visibly rushed craftmanship.

With such a creation, his peer hadn't stood a chance at winning his freedom… against *anyone* with the slightest idea of how a proper blacksmith worked.

Alas, Ferlon also wasn't surprised at this outcome—though he didn't know this boy personally, he'd seen him around the district, always focusing on building and neglecting the welding portion of his trainings; being a creator-slave was a well-rounded responsibility, and, regrettably for him, the Free Falls Festivals test hadn't leaned in his favor.

The regulators tied his opponent with ropes and nailed them to the ground. Then, Ferlon heard the bell ring again, demanding he carry out the boy's death sentence; that sound would forever resonate through his memories, along with his peer's agonizing screams.

That night was the first time he'd ever taken someone's life, but he hadn't doubted the necessity of his action. If he had failed, his life would've been taken just the same.

It's the way of the world.

Still, it became a haunting memory—it had been impossible for him to kill quickly with such a poorly made tool, and thus his opponent hadn't died right away. Ferlon had had to swing the mallet at least five times before the boy stopped making sounds.

And even then, he wasn't quite certain he had died immediately.

When it was all over, there had been this heavy quiet, just an instant of silence between the boy's life being taken and before the crowd cheering to bring out the next pair.

But in that moment, Ferlon looked down at the body, the boy's skin sickly white with blood dripping all across it, his face unrecognizable.

"Rest in peace, Helix Kassime."

He knew he wouldn't, his soul fated to a restless existence in the Tunnel of Tombs; never would he earn the chance to see a world outside of the frigid Jar of Stone, not in life or even in death. But Ferlon hoped, at least, that maybe he might hear someone use his name before he went.

Ferlon pocketed his throwing star and walked away toward the winners, careful not to disturb the other mutilated bodies, the discarded weapons left lodged in their corpses.

A loud fellow from another district offering him a drink snapped him back to the present, and Ferlon hoped not to drift back into his thoughts again; he was at the local tavern in Dra-minet, awaiting escort to his new life.

"Don't know why you're sitting here alone. I hear you were best in your year?" said the boy. "Solomon Bell, pleased to meet you." His red cloak was strewn across the floor, and his muscles bulged through his shirt.

He held out his hand, and Ferlon shook it.

"I was, too," he added, puffing up his chest.

"Cheers…" said Ferlon, not really sure how to act—he wasn't used to small talk with anyone.

Solomon flashed him a disarming smile, his strength and cheerfulness exposed in every way. "Cheers!"

Ferlon pitied those who had surely lost against him in the Warrior's District. He'd heard rumors of the bloodshed that went on there, but he didn't ask any questions; every new citizen in this tavern had lived through a similar experience. It was a rite of passage to kill in this world. So tonight, and probably for many nights to come, was the time to do their best to forget what they'd done to get here.

"This here's Cyn," said Solomon, wrapping his arms around a curvy woman with big, bouncy curls and pink-flushed skin. He pulled her over to the bar to join them.

"Hi there," she said, giggling at Solomon. "Are you excited for the new-citizen celebrations? It's irritating that they only waited until now to tell us about such a thing, but I'm so looking forward to having some fun finally!"

"You bet," said Ferlon. "Been waiting my whole life for this moment."

"Haven't we all," said Solomon, taking a long drink. "Transition Week, they call it."

"It wasn't the most pleasurable experience... the festivals, huh?" said Cyn, twirling a long curl around her finger.

Solomon laid a hand on her shoulder.

"It's all over now. There's nothing but happiness ahead. Another round, please," he said, leaning over the bar.

"Of course," said the bartender with a wink. "Anything you lads want. We always serve new blood for free. Besides, I hear you earned your keep tonight."

"That we did!" Solomon graciously took three beers and passed them around.

"To freedom," he said, Ferlon and Cyn joining in.

"Anyone want an apple?" interrupted a drunken, stocky boy dressed in green. "Lifted them from the Dining Hall before my festivals."

He patted the bulging pockets of his robes.

"I thought, one last hoorah if I'm gonna die or live. Know what I mean?"

The boy smiled and took a bite of a juicy red one.

"So sweet and *so* worth it."

Cyn gasped, wagging her finger at him. "It wouldn't have

been worth your life if you were caught." Then, she smiled, tossing back her hair. "*But* we wouldn't want them to go to waste, now would we?"

The boy laughed, tossing her a fruit. "Now you're a culprit, too."

She bit her lip in mock fright, cleaning off the apple on her robes.

"Hopefully, we'll find you a better treat now that we're free," she said. "I hear there's loads of delicious meals available to us now."

"There's nothing that can replace the value of this to me," he said without thought.

"And why's that?" said Cyn.

His brow wrinkled for a moment as he considered the question, like he'd never thought of it before. "I suppose, it's the first thing I ever took for myself."

A shadow crossed his face.

"Those bastards don't control everything," he added, laughing wildly.

Ferlon couldn't help but smile at his brazenness. "I'll... take one, too," he said, excited at the idea of friends—if there was ever a time to remake himself into someone less lonely, it was now. Finally, he could focus on something other than winning his freedom. Now he could really begin to live.

The boy passed out the rest of his apples, and Solomon ordered him an ale.

"Are you an agrarian then?" said Ferlon, forcing himself to be part of the conversation.

"I sure am," he said. "Placed in South Luose's culinary apprenticeship. And in the palace, no less! Can you believe it? I've always loved learning about agriculture, but *cooking*? I never really saw myself as that. I guess they see potential." He took another bite, speaking with a mouthful. "My name's Nico. What about you all? Where are your placements?"

"I'm a little embarrassed to say… but I've actually been placed as an apprentice caretaker at the South Luose Well Center," said Cyn. She gulped down her drink.

"Don't be embarrassed. You're going to do great!" said Solomon. "Who knows. Maybe that's your calling, if that's what was chosen for you."

"I suppose the Warrior's District caretakers recommended me as such," she said with a shrug. "I had it coming. I spent more time tending to this one than dueling."

She nudged Solomon playfully in the ribs, and he feigned being wounded.

"And I was always so good at caring for myself," she said. "They would've been fools not to notice."

"They do see everything," said Ferlon, taking another sip of his drink—it almost immediately made him light-headed.

"Stop your worrying," said Solomon. "It happens sometimes. We're not locked into the professions stemming from our districts. Some people will grow into different vocations than others. That's what's so great about freedom. We can really be anything!"

Ferlon thought him a natural leader; his ambition made him truly forget Helix Kassime for a moment and want to *be* anything. But just for a moment…

"Oh, I suppose," she said.

"Just stick with me," he said, squeezing her to his chest. "We'll be fine. Besides, you should be proud that you can call yourself a warrior and soon a healer. Now who here can say that?"

She averted her eyes, but Ferlon didn't miss her blush.

"I have an advanced apprenticeship in South Luose as well," said Solomon. "I'm hoping to become a personal protector." He looked to Ferlon. "What about you?"

"Well, looks like we're all headed down the same path, then," he said, wondering where it might lead them. "My advanced training is with a Master Gansevurt. He's supposed to be one of the best master creators residing there."

"That means we'll all be traveling together," said Cyn with a clap of her hands.

"Seems so," said Ferlon, pondering this sudden change from loner to what he supposed could be the start of real friendships—he hoped that he'd make a good friend someday. After all, he hadn't any practice.

"How wonderful!" She raised her glass, and they clanked again to cheers, all so thrilled to even be able to have a reason to do such a gesture in the first place, one they'd only ever seen the elders make.

Suddenly, Cyn grabbed for Ferlon's hand and tried to pull him up from his seat. "Treat a lady to a dance?" she asked as a band started up in the corner.

"I… I'll come along after uh… I finish my drink," he said, all his nerves abruptly rushing to the surface.

Cyn pouted and looked to Solomon—she didn't even have to ask him; he had her swirling around the tavern in seconds.

Ferlon watched them with envy in his eyes, envy for Solomon's confidence and Cyn's carefreeness. They were just a whirl of red robes, laughing and jumping along to the music with no cares in the world.

"You know something…" said Nico, who still sat with him at the bar. "It's like we *literally* killed for this drink."

He was staring solemnly down at his mug. Then, he chugged it in one gulp.

"Almost worth it." He pushed his empty cup away and ordered another.

Ferlon gazed back to the dance floor, studying all the smiling faces and trying to absorb the shouts of laughter, such a strange melody to his ears. The different cloaks of the Four Corners blended together now in a spectrum of spectacular color through dance and celebration—the reds, greens, blues, and purples all mixing into one as the former slaves swirled about in each other's arms, embracing their first breaths of freedom.

Again, his eyes found Solomon and Cyn; he stayed with them for a while until, inevitably, his mind flashed back to the terrible scene from just nights before. He wondered if Helix Kassime would have made a good friend, too, and if he might've fared well on that dance floor.

He threw back his drink and shook the image from his mind. *If Helix Kassime had to die for me to live, then that's what I'm going to do!*

"Come on, Nico," he said, firmly.

He didn't wait for an answer, dragging him onto the dance floor. Then, he walked right up to Solomon and Cyn, stopping the pair's dizzying duet.

"May I cut in?" said Ferlon, holding his hand out to Cyn— he held his breath, hoping she wouldn't notice that his hand was shaking.

She smiled, shoving Solomon away with a laugh. They began in a glorious spin about the floor, Solomon and Nico dancing alongside them.

"WE MET JUST ON THE EDGE of our district prisons, starting our new lives together. And I won't lie—" Kassime chuckled, fidgeting with the four-pointed throwing star at his belt. "I latched on to that Bell. He had such a charisma about him. We couldn't have been more different in that way, but we grew to be great friends in the end."

His eyes flicked to the portrait where Solomon smiled down at them.

"He'll be greatly missed."

Arianna swallowed the lump growing in her throat as the others began bombarding him with question after question.

"And what of Master Churry?" said Lessa. "I see him there in the painting. I know he's a guardian, too."

"Talis' story starts long before Solomon and I came into the picture, and I won't be the one to tell it," said Kassime. "We'll see him again soon, I hope."

"If Ferlon was your given name," said Jeom, "you must've drunk the same identity potion, too. I just knew it!" He slapped his knee.

"I can't be so sure…" said Demetrius, scrutinizing the keeper. "So, do we see you now as Helix or Ferlon?"

They were all dying to know more, wanting all the details of Keeper Kassime's life and the guardian's history in a single second.

"Jeom is right," he said, curtly.

Jeom gave a silent cheer, but Keeper Kassime did not appear amused; his face held a grave expression, a darkness in his eyes.

"I was forced to change my identity. Who you see now is not who I am. Just like you, I've been playing a part…" He cleared his throat, "… for decades."

He got to his feet, a passion in his voice.

"I'm a Guardian of Gold with the first given name of Ferlon Ragaric, and I'm playing an important role so that one day the 'Kassimes' of the world can have a future. Helix is my constant reminder that I'm *good*."

Arianna's heart constricted with his words; they sounded so rehearsed, like he'd been telling himself the same story for years. *How can he be so sure he's good? How can any of us?*

"After such a long time, it's very easy to forget," he said.

For the first time since their meeting, Arianna felt empathy for the keeper. He was cruel at times, unpredictable at others, but she understood now that he had to be, for the sake of the guardians; he'd given his entire life to protect a cause he believed in, constantly struggling with living two opposite existences… for the greater good.

And whether he was truly good or not, she had to give him his due respect.

"But why did you change your identity in the first place?" said Demetrius, running a hand through his hair. "What's the reason you hide?"

"Another time maybe," said Kassime, gazing out the window. "That story is far too long for one night."

He stepped away from the couch and waved his hand in front of the portrait—Arianna watched in awe at the display of magic.

The young group in the painting began to move, slowly, as if someone had captured a real moment in time. She saw Solomon's head toss back in his booming laughter and Cyn smoothing out the wrinkles in her robe. She even found Talis with his arm around her master, none of them a care in the world.

"Why didn't Cyn just lead us to you from the very beginning?" said Arianna, absorbing the image of her caretaker in her most glorious youth. "We told her we searched for you, for *Ferlon*, and instead she led us to Godfrey."

"Ah beloved Cyn," said Keeper Kassime. "She was inducted to the guardians by Solomon's insistence, and she's always faithfully kept our secret. She knew me as Ferlon long ago." He sighed. "But I've since erased her memory of me and of anything to do with the Guardians of Gold."

He tapped his temple. *Mind magic.*

"She doesn't remember she's ever even met me, or that she's a guardian at all. And she knows nothing now of magic," he said with a soft smile. "Though, I'm glad to see that she's always finding her way back to this world. Once magic touches your heart, it can never *truly* be undone. That's why people like us even exist."

Arianna was sure that Keeper Kassime could see all the questions she had on the tip of her tongue by just one look.

He paced around the library, fingers grazing the shelves.

"There was a time where we once flourished," he said, clearly lost in his past. "We held frequent gatherings here, but those times are no more. You might not understand it yet, but I erased Cyn's memory for her own safety."

He ran his fingers across the portrait, a solemn look settling on his face.

"It was a necessary step that we all agreed on, and I've been isolated since then. Solomon was the only person whose memories I spared, because he never returned to South Luose after…" He shook his head. "I thought he'd given up, but I'm glad to know that I was wrong."

He took them all in for a long moment, and then gestured again to the portrait.

"You never know what the future may bring," he said, "and it's not always what you plan for. There are only a few of us left from what you see here, and it's time to rebuild. Hopefully, others survive us in different parts of the land, but for the last seventy years, the Guardians of Gold have effectively disappeared."

"Rebuild for what, exactly?" said Lessa, scooping Sano into her arms as he gently stirred awake.

Arianna leaned in closer, not wanting the story to end; Solza came to snuggle against her as soon as she was separated from Sano.

"To ensure the prophecy comes to pass," said Kassime. "Until then, our responsibility is to protect the knowledge we possess. If there comes a day when there's no one left to share it, how could the Golden Age ever be restored?" He began to walk toward the door. "I think that's enough for tonight. I trust you can see yourselves out now? Supper will be served soon. We can discuss more in the days to come."

"Wait, please!" said Arianna, running after him. "Please, just help us understand a little bit better before you go. Tell us about the prophecy."

He glanced to the others, each one of them with pleading expressions as they still huddled by the fireplace.

"Ah, *very* well," said Kassime, resigned to one last query. He lowered himself back on the couch, crossing his legs. "As I believe you already know, the King created the Four Corners in the hope of keeping a prophecy from coming to pass, a foretelling of his demise."

"The Golden Rule," whispered Lessa.

He nodded.

"The Golden Rule is actually an ancient truth that was formed long before Devlindor walked this earth and which will hold true long after. It tells of a natural balance to the world. If the table shifts in favor of good or evil, life or death, then it could cause extreme devastation to either side in order to restore balance."

He clapped his hands together, and Arianna jumped.

"It's like magnets, always trying to find each other, destroying everything in their path until they meet again."

He waved his hand over some sort of orb instrument on a table near the couch, and bright smoke began to swirl violently inside until a black cloud consumed it.

"In this illustration, magic is the magnet… and the dark is winning."

"But what does this have to do with us?" said Arianna, pulling out one of a thousand questions running through her mind.

"Yeah, you said that the prophecy had been 'set in motion' practically the first moment you laid eyes on us," said Jeom.

" *Well*, it could have nothing to do with you whatsoever." His eyes bored into hers. "Or it could have everything to do with you, which is my hope. Only time will tell." He snapped his fingers and the orb went back to being stationary. "Magical maturity is reached at the age of eighteen," he explained. "Thus, if four children of different aptitudes met before maturity, this could certainly cause a major shift in power." He leaned forward. "And, children, what's the number one law of the Four Corners?"

"No slave may have contact with another outside of their

district," they said in unison.

Arianna and Lessa shared a glance, both surely remembering the day they'd broken that rule to pieces.

"Exactly!" said Kassime, growing excited. "Magic in its purest form is divided into four elements—Earth, Air, Water, and Fire, like the justly named gods that grace us. When channeled through intelligent conduits and linked together, those elements are at their strongest. And if those conduits joined and tapped into the elements *before* maturity, their power would be that much greater."

He pointed to a small table where Lessa had safely stored the scroll *Olleb-Yelfra the Fallen.*

"The King knew this and used the slave districts to try and isolate these elements so that new power couldn't grow while he hoarded the rest. No person, good or bad, should be able to control such magic. It's meant to be distributed equally across the world. And in order to contain it, he's gone and destroyed every enchanted civilization… dwarves, elves, and everything in between, until all that remained left were humans, because—"

"Because he still needed someone to rule," said Lessa, a grave expression on her face—she was clearly one step ahead while Arianna and the boys struggled to keep up.

"*Precisely*," said Kassime.

Lessa shimmied her shoulders a bit at the validation, and Arianna rolled her eyes. *Show off.*

"But not all people have magical capabilities, I thought," mumbled Demetrius—he seemed a bit downtrodden, and Arianna realized the keeper's earlier comment must've weighed on him more than she'd thought.

"This is true… to an extent," said Kassime. "Think of it this way. Some people just never manifest in their powers, *but* everyone and everything in this world leans toward one element or another. It's part of our natural make. Innocent children, with nothing to corrupt their minds, understand this connection on instinct. It's a gross misuse of power, but the King has managed to manipulate this ancient magic for centuries—"

"By controlling the children!" exclaimed Lessa, jumping to her feet as the answers all fell into place for her.

"I still don't understand," said Jeom, scratching his head.

Arianna was also trying to wrap her head around all this, how it connected to the prophecy, to them.

"In the Opalls, before you're even sent to your districts, the Opall Mothers, unknowingly, are using some of the oldest magic ever identified to decide your fates. They're forcing children to reveal their elements," said Kassime, twisting his ring around his finger. "Letting their natural instincts guide them—Water, Earth, Air, or Fire… healer, agrarian, creator, or warrior."

Blue, green, purple, or red.

Arianna tried to picture herself as a baby crawling toward a red-colored cloth, her choice made before she even knew what a choice was.

"So, you're saying that because we escaped the Four Corners, met before our eighteenth year, *and* are each from a different district—"

Keeper Kassime held up his finger. "More accurately, different magical elements."

"Right… elements," said Arianna, unable to stop her face from wrinkling with skepticism. "But what you're saying is that you think we're nature's way of fighting back?"

"This is crazy!" said Jeom. "I can believe in all of this around me." He threw his arms out wide. "But some fated, magnetic pull bringing us together? That's really absurd."

Arianna fell into a fit of giggles, and she clasped her hands over her mouth at her rudeness.

"I'm sorry, but he's right," she said, trying to hold the laughter behind her teeth. "This *is* crazy. We're not the start of anything. We're just four people who—"

"Who escaped an inescapable system that was put in place

three centuries ago by one of the strongest sorcerers on this earth in order to avoid just this very thing?" said Kassime without a trace of insincerity.

Her laughing stopped abruptly.

"What's *crazy* is that the four of you met at all! It's both unfathomable and much too coincidental not to have Fate's magical hand in it."

The four began to murmur their doubts.

"Now, I'm not suggesting that you'll be the fall of Devlindor's Kingdom," said Kassime, uncrossing his legs. "But I daresay you *could* be the beginning of the end."

"How can you be so certain?" said Lessa, frowning. "I've seen the Golden Rule written in that scroll, and I've seen it again in the City of Undor being protected by the dwarves. Why in the world would King Devlindor let such a secret slip, and how has it spread so widely?"

"The Golden Rule may have been foretold to him by his seer, but it's also part of ancient philosophy thought up well before the King's time," said Kassime, "as I mentioned."

He pointed to an inscription carved into the far wall, the Golden Rule bared yet again; Arianna was staggered that they hadn't noticed this before, but now that she had, she was enthralled by the riddle once more.

"The King's seer may have told it to him in the comfort of his own palace, but what she failed to mention was that this prophecy is not his alone. It's just the way it *is*."

He held up his hands, shifting them up and down.

"There must always be a balance, and when something disturbs that balance, it must eventually be restored," he said. "Out of fear and ignorance, the King created the City of the Four Corners to stop what he determined his 'prophecy.' And one day, even if it's centuries from now and we're well in our graves, with that decision alone, he's ensured his own downfall. The guardians have been waiting, patiently, for that day to come ever since we procured this knowledge…" He nodded toward the scroll.

Arianna had an 'aha' moment as everything clicked together, thinking of the day Talis had passed *Olleb-Yelfra the Fallen* to her and Lessa.

He'd *wanted* them to find the prophecy.

Keeper Kassime sat back with a long exhale.

"I think you all are the spark to a magical ripple effect that *will* eventually kill the King. And I'm certain that if Solomon and Talis knew you girls had linked up with two others from the remaining districts, they would think the very same." He was slowly shaking his head, staring down at them with an incredulous expression. "I just pray I live to see it."

Arianna felt a wave of sadness settle over her then, turning her attention to the young faces of those guardians that were now certainly gone from this world.

"What happened to them all? How did so many… die?" Her voice came in barely a whisper.

Keeper Kassime waved his hand again and the painting froze, back to normal.

"You all have many hard lessons ahead, but why don't you start with this…?" He touched eyes with all of them. "Trust in each other, and you'll survive this as I have. But understand that magic can be just as dangerous as it is fascinating." His words landed with gravity. "You'll do well to remember that."

He made to leave again, whispering a string of foreign words as he went; Arianna couldn't help but commit them to memory, for they sounded so beautiful and kind. Then, she felt something burning on the palm of her hand.

She sucked a breath in through her teeth, grabbing at her wrist to try to relieve the sudden pain, but it was gone before she had a chance to even cry out. When she turned her palm upward to see what had caused it, Arianna found the outline of a golden dragon had etched itself onto her skin; her friends watched the same magic play out across their hands as well.

The symbols shimmered there for a moment and then vanished from sight.

Everyone but Jeom was speechless. "What the—"

"This is the mark of the guardians, your key to this realm," said Kassime, gesturing at the attic. "And the Golden Rule is the foundation of our fight. This is your legacy now, and you must protect it."

With that, Keeper Kassime left the library, leaving them to their thoughts.

THE TRANSITION

SHE TASTED MUD as she lay facedown in the grass—cold, earthy, and wet. It was a taste beginning to grow almost as familiar as blood on her lips. The only comfort she took in this position during a duel was the way the mud soaked her bruised skin, cooling the heated blood underneath and bringing a bit of relief to the constant pain coursing through her body. She lay perfectly still for just a moment before she was yanked back to her feet by Master Tayshin.

"I haven't the slightest clue why they've sent you to me," he said, staring at her with a sort of pity in his eyes.

Arianna didn't even see a hint of sarcasm in his expression, and why would she? After another full week of nonstop training, she had been pummeled into finally respecting and accepting his undeniable skill. He was valued here, and she was wasting his time.

"I'm just... lacking a bit of motivation is all," she said,

exhausted as she lay down her weapons—it was the truth. In the Jar, her life had always been on the line and now it wasn't. So what was she killing herself for?

An attendant provided fresh sheets every morning when, for her entire life, she'd been accustomed to the same smelly blanket. A cook prepared her anything she liked, anytime she liked, when before a simple apple would've been the highlight of her day.

A carriage brought her wherever she deemed necessary, and she couldn't even recall the last time she'd had to open a door herself; in the Warrior's District, she'd walked miles and miles a day—to and from her quarters, the Square, the Dueling Arena, and the Dining Hall—relying only on her body for support.

Now that life of struggle was gone.

As Arianna studied the new blisters forming on her hands, she knew she'd gone soft. She'd always assumed the callouses from constant, vigilant work would be permanent fixtures on her palms, but with the nightly hot baths and fragranced lotions she lathered herself in, they'd all but melted away—Arianna was losing her momentum as a warrior, her muscles weakening by the day, but she'd gained momentum as a new Guardian of Gold.

Her thoughts wandered to her lessons with Keeper Kassime, wishing for this practice duel to end so she could go back to trying to master her magic.

She had hoped the motivation her new guardian lessons had given her would carry over to her lessons with Master Tayshin, for he was losing his temper with her, but even that left nothing in the way of an immediate threat; poring over enchanted histories and practicing magic gave her nothing but joy and happiness.

The only threats Arianna really faced in the present were her own vivid nightmares—and that she'd deal with in time.

"You know what your problem is?" said Master Tayshin as he tiptoed around her, sword raised.

Arianna didn't answer, focused on trying to scrape the dried mud from her face. From the corner of her eye, she saw Solza watching them intently; her avatar was growing by the day, her juvenile features strengthening while Arianna seemed to wither away.

"Your problem is that you've been pampered too damn long," he spat. "Helix should've listened to me about letting you lot live in the palace. Right damn waste you're turning into!"

Arianna tossed her arms to the air.

"You're absolutely *right*," she said, genuinely. "What's the reason for dueling each day when I'm no longer scraping toward my freedom? My home is the safest in the city, and we train in chainmail and armor most of the time."

She scratched at the glittering metals across her chest.

"I guess… I just don't see the point to keep fighting now that I have what I want."

That was one of the first truthful things she'd ever said thus far to Master Tayshin. She'd finally come to accept that she was safe under the guise of Aridyn Lareigh, and with that added comfort, any sense of danger had melted away.

She closed her eyes, tilting her head back as a soft breeze tickled her face, swaying the grasses of the field around her. The sunlight warmed her cheeks and birds chirped in the trees—Arianna savored the peaceful moment.

A sharp pain suddenly pierced her arm, and she let out a howl, her voice chasing the scattering birds; she'd seen too late her master thrusting his sword at her unprotected flesh.

She grabbed her arm, blood staining her hands.

How familiar.

"This is part of your lesson," growled Master Tayshin, staring her down. "I don't know how you've so easily forgotten the world you belong to, but *this* is it."

He swiftly grabbed her injured arm and dug his finger so deep into her wound she thought she might faint.

"This is Olleb-Yelfra. You come from a city of slaves, and you live in a world built upon that base. Every soul around you for the rest of your lazy life will want what you have. Every single person who has frozen in the Jar, who has killed for their exit, who has bled for their life, will always want *more*. It's the way of the world, human instinct."

He let go of her, blood smearing his hand, and she fell to her knees back into the mud.

"We are never satisfied!" he screamed to the wind, arms stretched out wide.

Arianna gritted her teeth through the pain as she held her injured arm, unable to hold back the tears that had pooled in her eyes.

"What are you saying?" she said through clipped breaths; her fingers itched toward her dagger, the adrenaline she felt now unlike anything she'd felt in a long while.

"I'm saying that you're *never* safe."

He laughed in almost a manic fashion.

"No matter your station, there'll always be someone who wants what you have or wants to keep you in your place. If you let your most valuable skills slip, you're of no more use to this world, and this world will just as soon spit you out."

The moment Eli had been stripped bare of his citizenship and rights before being publicly whipped to death flashed across her eyes.

"You're young," said Master Tayshin, nodding to her swords discarded on the ground. "Just a few free years under your belt, Apprentice Aridyn, and you've earned your way to the very top. That's a *long* way down to fall. Best try to find your drive again before you end up like me."

He patted his belly. Then, with one of the quickest moves she'd ever seen, a slovenly old man or not, he had his sword at the ready.

"I think you're a lot more dangerous than you look," said Arianna with a smirk, getting used to his unpredictable mannerisms.

She picked herself up off the ground and reached for a sword with her good arm.

Master Tayshin grinned, signaling for her to begin.

It was in this moment that Arianna finally wanted his approval, for he'd fully proven himself to her by reminding her of who *she* really was—and it was easy to forget in this pampered body.

Master Tayshin was not only a good trainer but a great master to have on her side. He emulated Solomon in almost every way, now that she cared to notice; he knew exactly how to grab her attention, harsh tactics or not. And, clearly, she needed someone extravagant like him to keep her on her toes lest she might actually forget her real name.

As Arianna stood to face him, blood dripping down her arm, she didn't feel any more pain. She only felt the drive to become better and stronger for whatever fight may, or may not, one day come. She'd needed his painful reminder that anything could happen—even when all seemed safe.

Never forget. It was a lesson she wouldn't soon take for granted. She had everything she had ever wanted now, and she'd fight to keep it that way for as long as possible.

Arianna carefully measured every footfall and every swing as Master Tayshin lunged with attack after attack, feeling like her old self again. And when they were finished, she bowed low.

"Thank you for a wonderful lesson today, Master," she said with sincerity. "I won't disappoint you again. This I promise."

He bowed back and then hopped on his horse to be off.

"Better not if you want to keep all your limbs!" he said, taking a swig from a flask in the saddle. "Don't forget what you fight for, Aridyn. Freedom earned is not freedom kept in our Olleb."

Arianna took that to heart. In all its glory, South Luose had proven to be just a fancier replica of the Four Corners, as Mya had once deemed it.

A thought flickered through her mind then that King Devlindor must've felt like that too... once. Arianna was sure it had all started with the 'want,' but it took something else, something darker, to keep him clambering forward.

That won't be me.

"From now on, lessons will be every other day," said Master Tayshin. "I need a break from you."

Arianna beamed, for she knew that meant he at least didn't hate her anymore.

"And get yourself to the well center," he said, whipping the reins of his horse.

"Yes, Master!" she called after him as he sped off into the sunset. "Hear that, Solza? I think I'm growing on him."

Solza gave a lazy grumble in response, rolling around in the tall grass and soaking in the sun.

The carriage driver came soon after to collect them. "We better hurry, miss. Looks like you're in need of a healer, and I suspect it might rain soon. We don't want to get caught in a storm out in these fields."

Arianna and Solza climbed in, and they rode back to the city, the horses galloping at a faster than normal speed to try to beat the storm he claimed was rolling in. As they left the fields and the edge of the forest behind, returning to city life, Arianna got a glimpse of Mya's tavern. It looked different during the day, and she noticed a man was now busying about inside, serving the onslaught of guests.

She supposed the Luose people would still need a place to go after their hard day's work, even following Mya's abrupt passing. Curious to lay eyes on it again, Arianna decided that when she returned from the well center, she'd ask if the others might join her there for a drink; she was sure they'd be curious, too. And they still hadn't been able to spend much time together outside of trainings, already nearing the end of week two parading about the city in their new identities.

The city well center loomed in front of her like the mountain it was, and Arianna realized it was the first time she'd ever really gotten a good look at it since they'd snuck away in the night. Her lessons with Master Tayshin began early and ended late afternoon, the sun still high in the sky, readying for its descent, so the city was still in full swing with the well center at the core; people dashed in and out of the doors—caretakers, regulators, and citizens alike.

"Hang in there," called the driver. "Almost there."

Arianna wiped her cheek as she felt a light sprinkle of rain through the open window. "I'm all right."

She had to be strong to get back to her normal self, and warriors didn't need to be coddled; Master Tayshin had reminded her of that.

The carriage came to a stop, and the door flew open.

Her driver gasped. "You're not all right," he said. "You're bleeding all over the place! Let's get you treated."

Arianna looked down, finding her shirt soaked in red.

He helped her out, guiding her through the front doors of the well center.

The wounded and sick sat all together in a large room along wooden benches, waiting for their names to be called before they could be assigned a well room and caretaker. Strange injuries and conditions ailed each one of the soon-to-be patients—one man seemed to be coughing up blood, and there was a woman whose right arm was covered in an outbreak of nasty boils. A group of young girls all had their fingers stained purple, looking sick to their stomachs, and an older man seemed to be on his last breath.

"Wait here. I have to announce you," said the driver.

"Announce me?" Arianna was left leaning up against a doorway, overwhelmed by the commotion. She pressed her hand to her forehead. "I need to sit down."

In the Warrior's District Well Center, there was only the dying or dead, nothing in between. But here, it was a melting pot of unfortunate afflictions.

Her attention was drawn to a woman being dragged in by

two regulators. She was barely alive from the looks of it, and she stunk so badly that Arianna felt a wave of nausea come over her as she passed; her eyelids hung heavy, and the skin sagged off her bones, clothes ragged and ripped. There was such a shocking paleness about her, as if she'd lived years without sunlight.

Arianna watched a city caretaker-in-training help the regulators put the woman onto a cart.

"From the Luose Dungeon?" he said in a shy voice.

The regulators confirmed.

"Her sentence has been served," one replied.

The young caretaker checked under her eyelids and looked for a pulse.

"Oh lucky for her! She still has a heartbeat," he said.

The regulators tossed furtive glances at each other. Then, the one in the lead smiled, slipping what looked to be a shining dagger from underneath her robes.

"Not for long," said the regulator, sticking the woman in the side with her blade.

Arianna gazed on in horror, along with the young apprentice.

A senior healer came to the young man's side, greeting the regulators as if they hadn't just publicly murdered someone in a hospital.

"Relax, take a deep breath," he said. "She goes to the Study. She'll be more valuable to the Olleb this way after all the trouble she's caused. This is how it works."

The young apprentice nodded, and with shaking hands, he pushed the woman away down the hall, a trail of blood staining the floor in small droplets behind them—Arianna knew exactly the direction he'd be going in.

"Apprentice Aridyn Lareigh is checking in!"

Arianna cringed, hearing her carriage driver's voice loud and clear over the commotion of the waiting room.

"She's been injured in a practice duel with Master Jon Tayshin. Please tend to her with immediacy."

The room quieted, all heads turning to look her way; Arianna's cheeks burned, and she cursed this new wretched face that turned the brightest red one could imagine.

"Of course this is his doing," said a kind voice. "Right this way, Miss Aridyn."

Arianna lowered the hood of her cloak and was staggered to be staring right into the smiling eyes of Cyn. So much had already happened since their last meeting that she couldn't help but give her a big hug on sight.

"Oh, my," said Cyn with a nervous laugh. She patted her on the back, and the onlookers began to gossip immediately. "You must've hit your head pretty hard. Follow me and let's have a look, shall we?"

"I… *yes*," said Arianna, feeling awkward in her new skin.

All she wanted was to tell Cyn that they were all all right, that Solomon's sacrifice was not in vain. She hoped, with the keeper's permission, that maybe one day they could lift the memory spell on her sweet-hearted caretaker and remind her of the magic in this world.

"Looks like you've taken quite the beating today," said Cyn as they entered a well room. "I take it Jon hasn't been going easy on you? It's a miracle you haven't been in here sooner. Have a seat on the bed."

Arianna hopped up, and Cyn began to tend to her arm.

"Yes, but I suppose I let myself get a bit out of shape these last couple of… weeks."

Arianna couldn't believe how the time had passed her by in this new body—more than a month had already come and gone since the keeper had first led them from the dungeons and changed their lives forever.

"But I have a healer friend at the palace," said Arianna, wanting to keep the conversation going. "She keeps me out of here for the most part."

Cyn laughed her bubbly laugh as she daubed some blue gunk

on her open wound. It sizzled, but it didn't hurt, and Arianna could see the remedy already working, and without magic—Lessa had a long way to go in her training, both guardian and not.

"I haven't known Jon to go easy on anyone, though he's a lovely man," said Cyn. "That is, when he's not dueling. Or *drinking*. He was an esteemed trainer in the districts when I was just a slave myself."

"You knew him?" said Arianna, raising an eyebrow.

"Quite well, dear," she said. "How times have changed."

Arianna winced as Cyn's hands slightly shook, suddenly a little less gentle.

"So," said Arianna, curiosity overcoming her as she remembered the keeper's tale, "you must've been a slave in the Warrior's District then, to have known Master Tayshin. He was a trainer there for a time, I suppose?"

Arianna couldn't hide the skepticism clear on her face, unable to picture Cyn as anything other than a gentle healer. Yet, here she was, confirming Keeper Kassime's story.

"That I was," she said, nodding. "Though, I was terrible at the craft. It's a wonder I even passed the festivals there. I was never meant to be a warrior."

"Then, how did you? *Pass*, I mean?" said Arianna, completely fascinated by this side of Cyn she'd never known.

"Same way as we all did, dear. Kill or be killed."

She let out a deep sigh, a soft smile on her lips.

"If it wasn't for that Bell, though, I would've been done for. No doubt about it."

"Solomon Bell?" said Arianna, trying to seem nonchalant yet desperately wishing for her to say more about their pasts. "You mean, *the* Solomon Bell, the Great Wolf of the East?"

She hoped she played the part of Aridyn well.

"Yes, that'd be him," said Cyn with a chuckle and the shake of her head. "You children, so young still. It was different back then. Not so many games. It was less about the show and all about survival. There was no scoring system to see how clean you left the battlefield or any of that." She dabbed more of the remedy on her skin. "If you left at all, you were lucky *and* citizen-worthy."

"Sounds the same to me," muttered Arianna, biting her lip as Cyn opted to stitch the wound shut as it healed.

"That may be so, but back then was surely a simpler time," she said, nostalgic. "Nevertheless, a time I wasn't meant to survive, if not for Solomon. I couldn't even hold my own with a sword, and I had never taken a life. I always hated the idea of killing anyone." She shuddered.

"May I ask what happened?" said Arianna, playing on Cyn's talkative nature; she knew her too well not to try.

And right on cue, her beloved caretaker began to pour out her personal story to a stranger.

Arianna refrained from laughing—Cyn really hadn't changed a bit over the years, and it was comforting to hear her ramble on for old time's sake.

"At my Free Falls, we had all been divided up into groups of five. Each group was paired off with another and only people from the same side could survive."

She held up her hand, counting her fingers.

"That meant five, or *less*, out of ten would gain freedom," said Cyn. "I was fortunate enough to be in Solomon's group. I think, somehow, he'd pulled a favor to arrange it that way." She stared off into space. "I don't think I even got a drop of blood on my robes! When I made it to South Luose the first time around, I had an apprenticeship here at the well center. I was a natural, and I've been a caretaker ever since." She shrugged.

"Wait..." said Arianna. "Do you mean to say that you've never *killed* anyone?"

This was truly a shock.

"How could you—"

"I know," said Cyn, lowering her voice. "It's a rule I may very well have broken. But I was meant to be a healer and everyone knew it. It happens sometimes, people placed in the wrong districts."

She seemed to gaze back into her past, and Arianna wondered what she saw there.

"Solomon never let me out of his sight," she said. "We were the only two to survive our round, the only two from our group. He killed every one of those kids on the other team. Every last one of them."

Her voice cracked then.

"He made it look like it was my swing that killed the last boy standing. It happened so quickly…" she said. "My hands were holding the sword that ended his life, but I didn't kill him. I just *couldn't.*" She squeezed her eyes shut. "My eyes were closed the entire time."

Cyn let out a sob, and Arianna gave her hand a reassuring squeeze—it was then that Cyn remembered herself, looking at Arianna with nothing less than fear in her eyes.

"I'm sorry, I shouldn't have said all that." She stumbled back from the bed. "I don't know what came over me. Please don't—"

"No one will hear of this from me," said Arianna, offering a kind smile. "You have my word. Thank you for your healing today."

She ran out of the well room then, before Cyn could say anything else and before she might say something to give up her own secrets.

"Where to now, miss?" asked the driver as she climbed back into the carriage.

Solza was curled on the seat, basking in the last rays of falling sun, rain clouds now almost fully overtaking the sky.

"Let's go back to the palace, please," said Arianna, wiping a stray tear from her eyes.

He tipped his hat to her and began to walk to the front.

"And stop calling me 'miss.' We're going to be spending a lot of time together from now on," she said, firmly. "Please, just call me Aridyn."

"As you wish, Aridyn," he said, beaming. "And you can call me Tobias. I *mean*, if that pleases you." If his skin weren't so dark, Arianna would've sworn she saw him blush.

"Tobias," she said, trying out his name. "It's lovely. Thank you for sharing it with me." She knew by now that most who served highlifes kept their names to themselves.

He offered a friendly nod and then hopped into the driver's seat, snapping the reins of the horses with Phantom at the lead.

AS SOON AS ARIANNA ARRIVED at the palace, she found Lessa lounging in the inside garden area near the fountain, Sano playfully chasing at the scattered raindrops at her feet. Solza darted after him, and Arianna came to sit on the bench alongside her friend; they began to whisper about their days. And after a time, they requested an attendant fetch Demetrius and Jeom to join them.

The four sat in the courtyard, taking a moment to just listen to the relaxing sound of thunder as the clouds rumbled and groaned above them. The rain came in large droplets but very little quantity, as if the sky held tight to every last bit before inevitably breaking.

As Arianna stared up at the darkening clouds, watching the storm unfold, she broke the silence.

"We have a lot to catch up on. How about a regroup tonight?" She shifted in her seat. "I thought to venture out of the palace, maybe to Mya's tavern…"

"That sounds like a *great* idea!" said Jeom, cracking his knuckles—he was clearly excited at the thought of returning to the start of their Luose adventures.

Demetrius gave the thumbs up just as Solza pounced on his lap, licking at his face, and Lessa smiled in agreement, her eyes glued to the sky.

"We better get out of here now," she said. "The sky's about to collapse down on us."

Moments later, a blast of thunder rocked the palace and the clouds split open, the sound of rain pounding the towers.

Arianna looked up as the raindrops aimed like arrows straight for them—she held up her hand to shield her face, and the water froze.

"You're really getting the hang of that!" said Demetrius.

Arianna laughed, looking to Solza who had stilled on Demetrius' lap, eyes glowing bright.

"I can't take all the credit," she said with a wink to her avatar. "I'm still not quite sure how I do that."

"Someone's coming!" said Lessa. "Quick, let it go."

With the fear of being caught, Arianna lost concentration— the rain unfroze and soaked them in the same second.

"Nice work!" snickered Jeom, shoving Arianna, playfully. "Let's go dry off and meet down here in an hour."

They all agreed, racing toward their wing of the palace and leaving a trail of water behind them in their eagerness.

Something was changing in the air, a contentment settling around them as they all adjusted to their new lives; Arianna was beginning to accept that their story might just have a happy ending after all.

Though, she couldn't help but think that for a split second, as the rain had stayed frozen above her head, that the monstrous version of herself had again been reflected all around her—just like when the glass ceiling had broken.

23

BACK TO BLACK

ARIANNA PUSHED OPEN THE DOOR to Mya's tavern with her friends right behind; it felt as if she had stepped back through time. The tavern stilled, everyone checking to see who entered as an energetic band continued to play in the corner.

No one came to greet them this time, and Godfrey was, thankfully, not their guide. But the looks they received differed from before, as if they didn't quite belong once they lowered their hoods and showed their known faces among the commoners—Arianna felt the blood rush to her cheeks as she led the group across the room to the empty seats at the bar.

"If you're ordering food, I can ready a table," said the soft voice of the man behind the counter; Arianna recognized him from her earlier ride through town.

"Thank you kindly, but no need," said Demetrius. "We're comfortable here." He flashed a smile, and the barkeep flinched—Arianna knew his Darrios identity didn't have the friendliest face, always appearing so stoic.

"Can we just start with a few brews for now, please?" said Arianna.

"Of course," he stuttered.

He wiped down four glasses and filled them to the top; Arianna didn't dare let her eyes leave his hands as he poured their drinks, recalling the terrible night they were poisoned.

"Thank you," she said.

"So what brings you to this part of town?"

"We knew Mya, actually," said Lessa, forcing a smile. "We thought we… owed it to her to have another drink."

"Is that so?" The barkeep perked up at the mention. "Well, then these drinks are on the house." He poured himself a glass, too, raising it to them. "Cheers." He drank his beer in one gulp, a solemn look settling on his face.

Arianna looked him over. He had chubby cheeks, wavy brown locks, and kind eyes.

"I'm Gabriel," he said, wiping his mouth on the back of his hand. "It's a pleasure."

"Pleased to meet you," said Arianna. "I'm—"

"Oh, I know who you are." He grinned. "All of you."

She laughed nervously. *Not likely.*

"Gabriel, huh? I remember that name," said Lessa. "Mya had mentioned you before."

"Did she now?"

His lips curled into a soft smile.

"We hadn't known each other that long," he said. "We were paired solely for our child-bearing potential, and we fully endeavored to fulfill that duty to the Olleb. Though, she wasn't *really* my type, if you know what I mean." He winked at Jeom, but he was too busy with his drink that he missed the gesture.

The others snickered, knowing full well that Gabriel wasn't *his* type.

"I admired her for the work she put into this place, though."

He looked around, nodding to himself. "Sad to see the ways of this world took her from me so young. She was a grand partner to have in life. Didn't deserve her ending."

"We're sorry," whispered Arianna.

The words were forced, her thoughts conflicted over the girl who had so badly wronged them.

"Means a lot," said Gabriel with a sigh. "Excuse me a moment. Duty calls."

He left to tend to other customers, and Arianna's thoughts drifted away—dwelling over Godfrey's unjust existence, Mya's death, and Eli… his energetic presence was surely missing from this place, his ghost probably on his way to haunt the tavern.

Arianna followed Gabriel as he busied about, still lost in her mind as the others fell into conversation.

"What can I get you?" he asked a man at the end of the bar who was waving him down—something about him seemed so familiar.

He sat alone, his hair hanging long over his face, and he was surrounded by empty glasses. Gabriel poured him another drink, whiskey she thought, the strong, earthy smell wafting into the air.

"Do you know that man over there?" she said to Gabriel once he walked back her way. "Is he all right?"

There's just something about him…

But she couldn't put her finger on it.

"Oh, him? He's harmless. I think the festivals got to him pretty bad, though. Been in here every night since he arrived, drinking himself stupid. If he keeps it up much longer, he'll probably be discarded. New citizens are given a bit more… time, though, to integrate." He chuckled, shaking his head. "Well, of course, you know that. You probably had no trouble getting comfortable here by the looks of it!"

Arianna just smiled, nodding awkwardly until he went away.

She turned to Lessa, reaching for her hand for support. "I think that's Liam!"

She felt as if all the wind had been knocked out of her.

"What? What are you talking…?" said Lessa, swiveling on the stool to face her. "Are you all right?"

Arianna shook her head, so much nervous energy coursing through her all of a sudden. "Over there, that man at the end of the bar. I think that's Liam."

Lessa leaned across the bar to have a look for herself, the music drowning out their whispers.

"I guess that *could* be him?" she said, obviously not convinced. "He looks to be in bad shape, though. Are you sure?"

"Positive," said Arianna in a stunned voice. "I have to go and speak to him."

"Okay…" said Lessa. "But, if that really is him, don't tell him who we are. Not here and not when he's in such a state."

Arianna nodded and took a deep breath, smoothing down her hair—she'd never been so nervous to speak to her best friend before, but she had to try. She couldn't just ignore the opportunity to reconnect after all they'd been through together in the Jar, but he wouldn't recognize her in this skin. Knowing him, he'd probably see her as a threat because of her station.

"Is this seat taken?" she said, walking over to the stool closest to him.

Thankfully, he'd been sitting at the farthest corner of the bar, near to the band and away from prying eyes in case things went sideways.

The man turned toward her, and Arianna couldn't help but gasp as she finally saw him properly—it was Liam all right, but the right half of his face had been burned so badly that it was almost unrecognizable, as if he were two different people altogether; there was Liam Black, the handsome and ambitious boy from the districts that she knew well. And there was this broken version of that strong warrior, someone who had very clearly survived to his freedom by the skin of his teeth.

"Hi… my name is Aridyn," she stuttered with a gulp.

"Aridyn Lareigh. Pleased to meet you." She held out her hand.

His eyes were glassy, the alcohol taking full effect over his mind as he looked her up and down.

"What do you want?" he snapped. She dropped her hand back to her side. "Can't you see I'm busy here?"

His voice slurred, but Arianna still recognized the soothing tones that had always calmed her before a duel or talked her down when her emotions sprang too high. He raised his hand, trying to wave Gabriel over for another drink.

"Here," said Arianna, settling in next to him. "Why don't you have this instead?"

She pushed a glass of water in front of him, but he shrugged it off.

"I'm sorry," she said, not sure the best way to go about this. "I don't mean to intrude on your…" She cleared her throat. "It just looked like you could use a friend."

He glared at her. "I have a friend!"

His words came loud over the band, pulling the attention of those nearby. He brought his head to his hands, covering his face.

"*Had.*"

Arianna's back straightened; she could feel Lessa's eyes on her, warning her not to say something she'd regret, but she wanted nothing more than to reach out and tell Liam that his friend *was* here, right by his side and always would be.

He'd obviously been drinking himself into a stupor all of these days to try to repress his anger. And no matter what words had passed between them so many weeks ago, she wanted nothing more than to take his hand in hers and tell him that it'd all be all right. Alas, she couldn't jeopardize their identities by telling a belligerent and broken Liam that she was really Arianna Belvedor—he would think she was mad.

Besides, from what they'd learned back in Draminet, she knew Liam probably remembered nothing of magic, of Sano healing him, or what he'd witnessed of her own power when she defeated Grinda. It had all been wiped from his mind by the King. *He'll never believe a word I say.*

She resigned to remain Aridyn.

"Everything will work out," she said, not even sure if he heard. "Just drink this, okay?" She smiled in reassurance as he glanced up at her, seeming so defeated.

He chugged the water, slamming the empty cup down.

"The name's Liam," he said after a moment, holding out his hand.

Arianna took it without hesitation, feeling the familiar calloused palm in her own; she wanted to rest there forever and draw him in closer, to confess all her secrets, as she normally would to Liam. But she resisted—Arianna Belvedor couldn't be there for him right now.

He eyed her with suspicion as he pulled his hand away. Then he threw his cloak over his shoulders and drew the hood over his head, attempting to cover the scarred side of his face. Tossing a silver coin on the bar for Gabriel, he got to his feet.

"See you," he said to Arianna, wobbling toward the door.

"See you…" she whispered; her heart wrenched as she watched him go.

Heading back to her friends, Arianna saw they had moved away from the bar and were sitting now at a table, picking at what looked to be some sort of cake. Demetrius waved her over, and she came to sit down.

"What was that all about?" he asked with his mouth full.

"Just an old friend," said Arianna. "I'm sure I've mentioned to you about Liam before." He nodded, and she sighed. "Well, like everyone else, he surely thinks I'm dead."

Demetrius hugged her around the shoulders.

"Better he thinks it than you actually be it," said Jeom, about to shove another piece into his mouth. "You can't ever tell him. You know that, right?"

"I know!" said Arianna, slapping the cake from his hand.

"There's nothing we can do?" said Demetrius—Arianna wagered that he'd received one hundred percent of the sensitive gene and Jeom zero, if it worked like that between siblings.

She perked up. "Maybe… *if* we had a plan."

Her thoughts took a new direction, trying to see if there was any way to bring Liam into the fold, to show him the light before he fully drowned in his own darkness.

Jeom shook his head in disagreement.

"We can trust him," implored Arianna—Jeom would have to be won over for any such plan to work; they were in this together. "He was my best friend in the districts, and he saw me use magic. Sano even healed him! We can trust him. We just need him to remember."

She glanced to Lessa for support, who shifted uncomfortably in her seat.

"You should've seen his face, Les," said Arianna. "He's wounded inside *and* out. There has to be a way we can help."

Arianna started in on the dessert, the flavors exploding her taste buds as she pondered Liam's shattered spirit.

"We could at least give him a chance," said Lessa, turning to Jeom; the healer in her had been easily persuaded. "He's obviously in need of care. After all, he did support us when we fled during the Free Falls. He was on our side."

She peered up at Jeom with her big blue eyes, not letting him look away. And before he could protest, she shoved another piece of cake into his mouth.

Demetrius almost spat out his drink in laughter for how taken aback Jeom was.

"We'll have to think it through, carefully," said Lessa. "After how you said Kassime reacted to us giving away just a coin from the Golden Age, he'll not take lightly to us involving another person with our secrets. He's going to need some convincing."

"What do you propose?" said Arianna, leaning in and internally thanking Lessa for her support. "Not to mention, we'd have to convince Liam, too, and he's not exactly in the *convincing* mood right now, I'd say."

"Well, let's see… I think we'd need to get him to the palace for our best shot at persuading him in one go," said Lessa, musing over the options. "He *has* to believe the moment we tell him everything. We can't risk him leaving the palace and running his mouth."

"We could try at the Gathering Ball!" said Demetrius. He rocked back and forth in his seat, giddy from the drink. "I've heard people speaking about it in the city. It's supposed to be a huge masquerade event held annually at the palace."

"That's a brilliant idea!" said Lessa. "My attendant was going on and on about how amazing it was last year."

"Gathering Ball?" said Arianna, out of the loop.

Lessa nodded. "It's the one event where everyone comes together to celebrate in unity, not divided as the districts. The masks are meant to symbolize this, but everyone is supposed to wear their district colors to represent how our backgrounds helped strengthen the Olleb…" She shrugged. "Something like that, but it's a big deal. Preparations have already ensued."

"How in the heck is a crowded ball going to be a good time for this?" said Jeom, gawking. "I don't think *any* time is a good time. It's a bad idea."

Demetrius bobbed along to the music, trying to shake Jeom into a happier mood.

"Oh, loosen up, will you? What's the harm in *trying?* Everyone is required to be in attendance, and that includes her friend," said Demetrius. "It's the perfect time to sneak him up to the attic for some good old-fashioned persuasion tactics. If he's anything like you, he'll need a real show!"

Jeom rolled his eyes and Demetrius began cackling.

"I think you've had enough," said Jeom, sliding his brother's mug away—though he glanced to Arianna with a softer expression that told her he was, reluctantly, on board.

"Well, when is it?" said Arianna, eagerly. "When does this ball occur?"

"It's nearly a year away, during the same time as the Free Falls Festivals," said Demetrius. "It's perfect really. It gives us all, *including* your Liam friend, a chance to get used to our new lives before we cause any more disorder."

He waved his hands in the air to mimic catastrophe, nearly toppling out of his chair.

"A whole year?" said Arianna, frowning. "But that's so far away."

"He's right though, Ara," said Lessa, pushing a drink into her hands. "We all need some time to adapt. A couple of weeks is nothing. It won't do anyone any good to face another change so soon. Besides, we'll need time to strategize."

Jeom had a scrunched look on his face, as if he were thinking too hard.

"Say I go along with this," he said. "What do we do about Kassime? He's the one I'm really worried about. Like Lessa said, he'd never be okay with this, and he's our ticket to freedom here. We can't screw this up."

"Just leave him to me," said Lessa, grinning.

Arianna already knew she had him wrapped around her finger, just as Talis had been.

"And then I'll leave it to you all to show Liam the truth."

"Challenge accepted!" said Arianna, thinking of the bond she and Liam had once shared—if she could just have the chance to show him that she was still around and get him to the attic to remind him of magic, then he'd have no other choice but to believe.

The thought was placating; she would count the days until the Gathering Ball.

As the four sat in the tavern, retelling their stories about training and gossiping about the new world around them, Arianna felt at peace with almost everything in her life. They talked about the old days and looked forward to the new until the hour was late. And with the waning music, they paid their dues with the overflowing gold from their pockets, wished Gabriel a good night, and promised to return soon.

Walking to where the carriage awaited them, they found Tobias asleep in the driver's seat. Arianna went around to the front, gently waking him.

"Sorry to keep you up so late!" she said. "Next time you must join us."

"Oh, don't mind me, miss," he said with a sleepy smile.

Soon they were off, trotting at a snail's pace toward the palace in the dead of night.

Arianna pulled back the curtain of the window slightly, peeking out. The stars twinkled down, like firebugs flickering in the night, and all seemed to be in perfect order; the earlier storm clouds were nowhere in sight, the horses trotting through the leftover puddles on the street.

But as the carriage wheels splashed up a rather enormous bout of water, a woman shrieked. "Damn horse!" she shouted after them, fist shaking in the air.

Arianna recognized that voice—she pulled back the curtain further for a better look; all she saw was the back of her head, but the ghost-white hair and voice of Ophelia would've been hard to mistake. She was hidden away in the dark corner of an alleyway near the City Council quarters and speaking to someone hiding in the shadows.

Arianna kept her eyes glued to Ophelia. Then the person in the shadows moved in a way that his face was momentarily washed in light.

She sucked a breath in through her teeth, clenching the curtains when she saw who it was. "Godfrey…"

He caught her eye, smiling with a broken-toothed grin, as if they were the best of friends. Arianna sat back in her seat, seething, clenching and unclenching her fists.

You will pay for what you did! Never forget. She couldn't help the darkness trickling back into her mind.

"What do you mean? Where?" said Jeom, going stiff.

"He was speaking with Ophelia just now," said Arianna, unblinking as she tried to rein in her anger.

"At this hour?" said Lessa. "How odd... I wonder what that was all about?"

"Nothing good, I assume," said Demetrius, sobering up. "Nothing good."

They rode the rest of the way in silence, their wonderful night darkened by the ominous thoughts that came with the mention of Godfrey's name.

The feeling was haunting—Ophelia, as head of the respected City Council, was surely doing something wrong mingling with the likes of him. As Demetrius had said, nothing good could come of it.

Arianna hardly crossed paths with her, except for the daily commendation to the King, but whatever their business, she prayed it never came her way; everything and everyone that Godfrey touched seemed to crumble into dust, and she wanted to keep Aridyn in one piece.

As the carriage neared the palace, Arianna gazed out of the window again, just as its wheels passed over one of her very own 'Most Wanted' posters. It was in the mud, her face and the number twenty-two painted on the crumbling parchment; the wheels tore it straight in half, and the remnants of the parchment became drenched in a pool of black water.

It dawned on her only then that the focus of gossip in the tavern had not been on escaped slaves. There was no discussion about a treasonous Arianna Belvedor or her accomplices... Come to think of it, she'd spent now two weeks exploring the city, training with Master Tayshin, and having conversations with other Luose locals. Though her name had crept up in a few conversations here and there, it was in no way the amount she would've expected from the uproar she'd witnessed in Draminet; the excitement over catching her for the highlife reward seemed to have fled right alongside Sir Vladamor—most likely stirring a fuss in the cities beyond these borders.

Arianna hoped then that Sir Vladamor would search far and wide for her, chasing her to the ends of the earth and away from the edges of the Blancoren Mountains while she stayed safely in South Luose. No one here suspected them anymore, not even Godfrey. And with magic on their side, she started to believe they never would.

SOLZA AND SANO

ARIANNA FELL INTO THE COMFORT ZONE of being Apprentice Aridyn of South Luose, soon replacing one routine with another, one life with another. Months flew by, and just as she used to be Arianna of the Warrior's District, living one day like the next, so did Aridyn—the only difference was that this life was worth living.

The darkness she knew she carried inside her, planted there by the *Onasyuda* spell, dissipated a little each day; and she slipped away, too, burying herself deeper beneath this new skin so that it wouldn't return.

Arianna embraced her noble identity and the rich city life that came with Aridyn's face. She embraced Solza, the avatar that she had at first shunned, and she embraced the magical side of her that was now growing every day as an apprentice guardian.

Her friends were still her friends, just as before. Though, as danger had first bonded them, it was now the promise of a happy, healthy life that brought them closer together. Alongside their advanced trainings, they practiced under Keeper Kassime's instruction several times a week in the attic, growing more knowledgeable of the magical world with each passing sun; and Arianna felt herself becoming stronger, too, not only physically but in her magical mind as well.

Lessa had also grown comfortable in her new skin as Lilith. In guardian trainings, her powers had grown exceptionally, and in this, she took the lead; unlike Arianna, she was a natural at sorcery. Her magic never let her down when she called to it, and the execution of her spells was flawless—the ghost girl just had so much control over her magic, always one step ahead in her practice.

It seemed to take Arianna a few more tries to get things right; she always felt her magic bubbling at the surface but only with intense emotion or pressure did it spill over into something tangible. No matter how much she tried to concentrate or coax it to come, she could never release her magic the way she wanted—though, when it did finally happen, it was *always* an impressive and powerful show.

'*Magic can be just as dangerous as it is fascinating,*' the keeper would warn; this was the most important aspect of training he wished to impart as he guided the girls through spells and incantations of every kind.

Arianna could feel her magic's dangerous potential.

There was such an explosive energy inside her that sometimes she even feared it herself. But Keeper Kassime's lessons had taught her that each person's bond with magic was unique—no sorcerer the same as the next. With practice, anyone could be made stronger and wiser within the frame of their own talents. It was fruitless to try to draw comparisons.

She found truth in this lesson as the months drew on, could see herself growing into a talented young sorceress. It would just take her a little more time to gain full control—and now time they most certainly had.

On this particular day, as Arianna raced toward the attic with Solza at her heels, she had prepared to perform the levitating spell that the keeper favored; she and Lessa had finally completed their mandatory readings on the subject and were ready to put them to the test.

Arianna opened the door to the sparring room, which had long since been turned into their magic dueling grounds—Lessa was already there waiting, eyes glowing silver with a spell on her tongue. "*Levantis bora!*"

Arianna's body flew into the air, as if suddenly she was the weight of a feather. She was too shocked to even scream, her heart lurching right into her stomach.

"No fair!" she called down after catching her breath. "I didn't have time to shield."

Arianna was so high up now that she could see the intricate detail of the dark-patterned ceiling.

"It's beautiful up here," she said, reaching out to trace the pattern. "Les, this is amazing! You're doing great." She kicked her legs and waved her arms, trying to gain some momentum in this gravity-less state.

"Hush," hissed Lessa. "I'm trying to concentrate."

Arianna felt the weight of herself come tenfold then, heavy and solid; her body began hurling downward. She couldn't help the shriek that came out of her as the ground seemed to rush toward her face. But just as she was about to collide with the stone floor, her body froze midair before gently lowering down.

"Keep your concentration!" said Kassime—he'd been watching from the doorway. "There will always be an outside distraction, but you mustn't lose focus… unless, of course, the intention is to kill the person in the air."

"Thank you, sir," they both said with a bow.

He walked away, the door slamming behind him with just the flick of his hand.

Arianna turned to Lessa, narrowing her eyes. "You better thank the gods he was there. I would've been splattered all over this room!"

Lessa had an impish grin on her face as she scratched the back of her head. "Sorry," she said, the magic rushing from her eyes. "Think we better pull out the mats." She chuckled.

"That was *not* funny!" Arianna threw a kick to her side.

Lessa was quick to block—they'd practiced such moves already many times.

"One more time," said Lessa with a smirk, beckoning her forward. "Come on."

Arianna laughed, jumping at her again; they were both more than willing to let out some energy the traditional way for a change.

Under Master Tayshin's apprenticeship, Arianna had already learned many new dueling techniques, both with a weapon and without. She felt more equipped now than ever before to enter a battle. And although Lessa had also grown into quite the nimble warrior herself, she still had a lot of catching up to do before she'd be able to best Arianna without her bow and arrows for help.

Within minutes, she had Lessa pinned to the floor.

"You're getting better," said Arianna, holding out her hand to help her up.

Lessa took it, hopping to her feet.

"I have a good teacher," she said through heavy breaths. "Want to add the swords?"

Weapons training was also a mandatory part of being a guardian, so Arianna had spent ample time sharing her talents as a warrior with her friends, each slowly on their way to earning the title, too.

"Do you even have to ask?" Arianna tossed her a blade from a barrel, and then she grabbed her jeweled ones from the corner of the sparring room. "Just one round. I'm still pretty sore from beating Jeom earlier."

Lessa rolled her eyes.

"Shields or no shields?" said Arianna with a grin.

With a howl, Lessa thrust her weapon, putting all her strength behind it; Arianna blocked the attack, twin swords crossed at her chest, knee bent for support. She shoved off the impact, and Lessa slid back a few feet.

"I guess no shields then," said Arianna, laughing. "Works for me. It's all just added weight anyhow."

With that, they ran forward again, the sweet sound of metal resounding across the room.

Arianna still outranked all her friends with every weapon—except for, of course, the bow; Lessa's aim had only gotten sharper. She had impressed even Master Tayshin with her skill, accompanying Arianna to her lessons with him on occasion, to practice shooting targets in the field.

Still, she had almost made a proper swordswoman out of Lessa, and Jeom took weapons with thick blades in his stride.

Demetrius, on the other hand, had taken a vow to spare lives, so Jeom transformed his old scythe into a shining new staff. He swore with that weapon in hand, he'd never again take a life. Thus, with Keeper Kassime's blessing, Arianna trained him in more passive methods of battle.

"Yield," said Lessa as the tip of Arianna's sword nudged her back.

"Good work," said Arianna, sheathing her weapons. "That wasn't easy for me. You've really grown."

"Thanks!" she said, reaching for her flask of water and then chugging. "The keeper's been giving me a few pointers on that side, too. Just wait until you see some of the new tricks I can do with my bow."

"Of course he has," said Arianna, dabbing the sweat from her brow with a cloth. "You're his favorite."

Lessa scowled. "I'm not his favorite. We just spend every waking moment together since he's my guardian *and* advanced training master. I see him more than even you or the boys these days!"

"I was only joking. I understand," said Arianna, though she was sure Lessa didn't believe her.

Arianna appreciated every lesson the keeper gave her and had since put away grievances about his harsh tactics at times, but they had never quite warmed to each other following their first meeting in the palace throne room.

"Oh, you're bleeding…" said Lessa. Arianna glanced down to find a small cut on her shoulder. "Ha!"

Lessa clapped her hands, jumping up and down.

"I *am* getting better. Here, try some of this."

She handed Arianna a tiny jar from her pants pocket.

"What is it?" she asked, twisting open the lid to find a strange green gel.

"It's something new Demetrius and I made together, actually. It works like a charm. Just remember to use the healing words I taught you to give our remedies a nice boost. Go on, try it."

Arianna dipped a pinky in and rubbed the gel across her shoulder, in the same place where Solza's mark still shone brightly. "*Helthra saludis emencia.*"

A spark of magic stitched the cut back together without even making her flinch, a more enjoyable healing experience than most of her times spent in the well center; and with Lessa's growing skills, she found herself needing a trip there rarely these days—unless she just wanted an excuse to see Cyn.

"It's amazing, isn't it?" said Lessa. "Demetrius has the healer's touch! It's really incredible all we've learned from each other."

Arianna fervently agreed, reflecting over their advancements in so many areas—Jeom and Demetrius didn't have powers like Arianna or Lessa. Keeper Kassime had since determined they weren't of sorcerer bloodlines, so spells and incantations didn't work for them in the same way. But, as the keeper would often remind them, '*magic flows through everything*'…

And the boys certainly had unique talents of their own, gifts that Keeper Kassime helped them to hone.

Jeom, assumed to be from a dwarf bloodline, was not just a natural creator—he was a *magical* one, and his control over the Axe of Crissy made that plain.

He learned more about the dwarves, the earliest creators, than any of them could have imagined to be true on their first quests through the City of Undor; and Keeper Kassime gave him special instruction in incorporating the charmed dwarf touch into all of his creations.

He also discovered more about the extraordinary properties of his axe and why it had been so heavily guarded—it was able to conjure up powerful protection spells at the owner's will, and to use it in anything other than defense could corrupt the wielder to darkness, something Jeom would not soon test.

He became one with the axe, its magic giving him bouts of luck in every move that he made; and Arianna enjoyed teaching him how to handle it properly. Soon, they were well-matched opponents in both magic and metal, Jeom repaying the favor by teaching her the fundamentals of creation. And with the addition of his lessons with Master Gansevurt, he quickly lived up to the part of the ambitious creator apprentice that the city knew well as Jaxin.

Though Demetrius still had yet to show any definable connection to a magical lineage, the keeper deemed his talents in enchanting nature as magic just the same. He was one with the earth, one of nature's purest forms of magic, and thus worked hard to learn the unique offerings of the natural world and its magical significance.

With patience and care, Demetrius could make anything grow in any environment. And he seemed to be a glossary for the nature of the Olleb. He became a recluse in the attic greenery and learned as much as he possibly could through his agrarian apprenticeship with Mistress Serina—completely surrendering his hostility toward her as he accepted the future that the identity of Darrios afforded him.

Lessa also spent much time teaching him to mix healer remedies, together their knowledge combining to the result of bewitching concoctions that even the South Luose Well Center would've been lucky to get their hands on.

From one mind to the next, the four had become linked in more ways than one. And with Keeper Kassime as their guardian guide, they continued to challenge each other, to discover what they didn't yet understand and to excel greatly in what they did.

"All right now," said Arianna, stretching her arms out as she examined the perfectly healed skin. "Stop stalling. It's your turn to do some flying."

Just clear your mind. Concentrate.

She called to the levitation spell, and with all the built-up adrenaline from their duel, a surge of energy coursed through her body on command—her control *was* getting better. All the time they were allotted in the attic, all the hours spent flexing their minds and their muscles was beginning to pay off. "*Levantis bora!*"

And even without Solza's undeniable energizing edge, the power was a stunning force.

"Wait, I'm not rea—" Lessa's voice was lost to a scream as her body launched into the air.

There was an echo of silence.

"Wow, you're right," said Lessa after a moment. "It is beautiful up here!" Her voice was muffled, her cheeks pressed up against the ceiling.

Arianna giggled. With a wave of her hand, she gently flicked Lessa about the room.

Her power waned not long after, so she lowered her back to the ground, feeling every muscle constrict as she concentrated. When Lessa was safely on her feet, Arianna collapsed to the floor.

"That was superb!" said Lessa, running to her. "You're really getting the hang of it, but you have to learn not to exert so much of yourself each time. It's always all or nothing with you."

"I know, I know," said Arianna, batting her away as she gasped for breath.

Lessa passed her a small bag. "Time for a break. Here, have some nuts."

Arianna took them gratefully, knowing well by now that nourishment was the second-best way to boost her energy levels back up—Solza was the first.

Keeper Kassime had taught them so much about the ways of magic that Arianna was finally beginning to understand this large piece of herself that had been for so long suppressed; living felt so full now, her mind constantly soaring with new information. And each day, the terrible memories of her former life seemed to fade farther and farther into the background.

"Hey, everyone!" Jeom's voice bellowed out from the library, sounding panicked. "I think I've found something. Come here, quick."

Lessa and Arianna dropped what they were doing and ran through the pentagon room, knocking into Demetrius on the way—he had stumbled out of the alchemy chamber with a frilly, orange root in hand.

"What's all the fuss?" he said, annoyed at the disruption.

"Oh, I'm sure your plants can do without you for one minute," said Arianna, wiping a smudge of dirt off his shirt.

Demetrius huffed, combing his hand through his hair with a sheepish grin. "You know... it's hard, being constantly sought after all the time."

Arianna pretended to gag, and Lessa slapped him on the arm. "Oh, just go on!" she said with a laugh, pushing him through the library door.

They found Jeom sprawled out on one of the rugs, his shirt thrown aside as he sunbathed under the window with Solza and Sano curled up nearby. His axe was propped up against the window ledge, catching the light and sending flecks of gold dancing all around the room. He lay on his stomach and had a large scroll unfurled before him; he was studying it intently.

"Jeom Kane, *reading*? Without someone looking over his shoulder?" Lessa feigned a gasp. "Now I've seen everything!"

They all laughed, joining him on the floor; he barely noticed, so enthralled by the words he'd discovered.

"What've you got there, brother?" said Demetrius as Sano bounded into his lap.

Solza barely bothered to move an inch, paralyzed by the sun, so Arianna gently laid her head across her avatar's long body, resting there—it was incredible how large the animal had grown over the course of only about a year. When Arianna had first discovered her, she could easily hold her in her arms. Now, even Jeom struggled to do it at her current size.

"It's the avatars," he said. "I think I've finally found something!"

"You're kidding?" said Lessa, snatching the scroll from under his nose and skimming it. "Oh… you're *not* kidding." She kissed him on the top of his head. "You brilliant boy!"

"What is it?" said Arianna, shooting back up. "What does it say?"

"Well, I wanted to do some further study on the Axe of Crissy," said Jeom, his hands moving in the air excitedly. "To see if I could learn anything more about it. So, I started searching in the section about magical creatures. If you remember, the axe is, *supposedly*, fused with the teeth of a dragon defeated by King Undoriamus—"

The section on magical creatures was one part of the library the girls admittedly hadn't made time for yet. Preoccupied with memorizing new incantations and mastering their magic, Arianna and Lessa had put the fruitless hunt for records about avatars on hold.

Keeper Kassime hadn't known much about them either,

other than that they were supposed to have their own magical abilities and that they were extremely rare. Just like Solomon and Talis, he'd left them only with riddles—and soon the girls realized that no one actually had any answers at all.

The keeper had given it his best effort to try to find out more about Solza and Sano. But the histories taught to him as a guardian hardly mentioned the subject. He did believe, however, that their powers *could* develop with training, just like Arianna's and Lessa's. And over time, that theory was certainly proven.

Sano was quite a good healer and unnaturally speedy as he bounded through the air, almost as if he could fly. And even more incredible was that Lessa actually had the power to heal, too—she could channel his ability.

It had accidentally happened once when she'd been wounded from dueling with Demetrius. Her reflex was to immediately put pressure on the cut; when she removed her hand, the cut had been replaced with a slit of silver for a scar. Sano had been nearby at the time, and Demetrius said that both of their eyes had glowed bright silver, just as they normally did when they used magic; it had been a momentous breakthrough in the treasure hunt for knowledge on avatars, and Keeper Kassime noted it down and added it to the shelves with the other magical histories.

Solza's mystery was unraveling, too. Arianna had already detected that when her avatar was near, her own energy became heightened. She was a stronger, more powerful person—magical or otherwise—and that was not a capability Sano possessed; it was Solza's own peculiar magic.

Alas, neither of the girls knew how to control this magic, or if they even could. Was this power to use solely at their avatars' discretion? Or did their uncanny bonds affect it somehow? So while Lessa and Arianna had made notable advancements, they still had more questions than answers about their loyal, enchanted animal companions.

"—I didn't get too far into the scroll before she snatched it out of my hands," said Jeom, glaring at Lessa who still greedily read over the text, "but I did find out that all dragons had some kind of connection to avatars."

"Right, right," said Lessa as her finger flitted across the parchment. "My, it *does* seem that dragons are connected to avatars in a special way… there's only a short description of them here, but it's definitely a world more than we've known until now!"

"What does it say?" Demetrius tried to peer over Lessa's shoulders, but her nose was practically in the scroll.

"Just baffling," she muttered.

"Tell us!" said Arianna, tugging at her own hair.

She was two seconds away from ripping the parchment out of her hands.

Lessa cleared her throat. "Well, one thing's for certain, these avatars basically share our lifeblood, Ara." She looked up, her finger holding her place in the text. "If we should die for any reason, it seems Solza and Sano would soon follow. However, it also says that if the avatar should die, we'd have a second chance at life…"

Just as Arianna and Lessa had naturally suspected, this bond was not to be broken without a serious sacrifice.

"Unbelievable," said Kassime as he snuck up behind them. "Truly unbelievable, what you've found here. And all this time, right under our noses."

"There's no way anyone could ever read everything in here," said Demetrius with a kind smile.

"Imagine if there were," said Kassime. "May I?" He held out his hand to Lessa, and she obediently handed it over.

"Here you are, sir," she said.

"It's supposed to be a history of dragons," added Jeom, unabashedly delighted at his findings. "But *I* saw that it mentioned the avatars in there, too."

Kassime glanced down at him from over the parchment. "Good work," he said—Jeom beamed.

Arianna got up on her knees, dying to know what it said.

"Will you please read it?"

Keeper Kassime nodded, bringing the parchment closer to his face. His words came softly as he read aloud the first description any of them had ever heard of an avatar:

There's no way to locate an animal with the soul of an avatar inside, though many a fool have tried. Furthermore, an avatar cannot become such until bonded with that of a worthy human.

Only the pull of the universe can bring man and avatar together, blessing them both with extraordinary gifts. Once this bond is complete, the avatar then has the ability to control the natural elements of the world, alongside its own unique magic. However, avatars cannot move through the elements alone—they need the help of their masters to do so. The connection between man and avatar is such that if death should come to the master, the avatar's soul would soon follow to the afterlife. Conversely, should the avatar die, the master would experience a second chance at the world of the living.

Though most avatars on record have only transformed across two or three elements in their lifetimes, their first and foundational form is the element in which the avatar was found. Should an avatar grow to control the elements of water, air, and earth, this remarkable being then has the capacity to master the final element, thus transforming into one of the strongest magical creatures ever known in the existence of Olleb-Yelfra—a dragon.

Dragons embody all of the natural elements, up to and including fire. The first avatars to complete a full transformation, through to the fourth cycle, reproduced in this form and populated the Olleb with many of its species. The mighty dragon thus became the natural protector of Olleb-Yelfra, master of all elements; with the exception of an avatar dragon, who are obedient only to their masters, dragons have no loyalty to humans or any other species surviving in the Olleb.

Be warned, their only allegiance is to Olleb-Yelfra herself. They are born ingrained with the drive to protect her at any cost. If and when a dragon feels its marked territory has become threatened, they will fight back and, in turn, may cause incredible destruction.

The Three-Headed Dragon of Crissy is one such history to be told, named for the Great Crissy Wars: a bloody battle fought between man and elf. During this dark time, the dragon's territory in the northern part of the Nicora Forest was threatened and much of it destroyed by destructive magic. In retaliation, the dragon laid waste to the City of Crissy, effectively ending its ruler's selfish pursuit of elven secrets—the Nicora Elven Clan claimed this a victory.

Leaving only ashes in its wake, the Three-Headed Dragon of Crissy was, consequently, uprooted from its home and is said to have found shelter in the Vanishing Tunnels, threatening the thriving dwarf population of the great City of Undor.

Keeper Kassime carefully rolled up the parchment, placing it back on the shelf.

"What a vision," he breathed. "We've always known the extinct dragons to have been the natural protectors of the Olleb. That's why they're the symbol of the Guardians of Gold…"

He held up his right hand, showing off the faint shimmer of the golden dragon symbol, just as they each had imprinted on their own palms—barely visible to the naked eye.

"But to know even a fraction of what it means to bond with an avatar is some of the most valuable knowledge we've yet to uncover from the Golden Age! Even then such creatures were known to be rare," he said. "It's a miracle the King didn't destroy this piece of text in his purge. The detail… now we know what a bond with an avatar could *actually* mean."

He gazed down at Lessa and Arianna, Solza and Sano close by their sides.

"You both had an extraordinary blessing granted to you. And now, you can begin to truly explore it."

"What do you mean?" said Arianna, glancing to Solza—she was fast asleep, completely unaware of this pivotal moment between them. "How?"

"It means that your avatars are only in the first stages of their powers, much like you," said Kassime, an excited gleam in his eyes.

"Keeper…" said Lessa, curling a strand of hair around her finger, "what do you think the text is suggesting by 'move through the elements'? It seems to suggest that… that they could physically *transform*."

She tickled Sano behind the ear, an incredulous expression on her face that surely matched Arianna's.

"Don't you dare say you don't believe it!" barked Kassime. "I think not only can they transform, but they must be able to control the natural elements. Just think about it. It all makes sense now."

He scooped Sano into his arms, the little monkey happy for the attention.

"Putting his unique healing abilities aside, in all your training with Sano, he's become quick as lightning the way he moves. He's a *flier*, cushioning off the air. That's his element!"

As if to prove his theory, Sano flew out of his arms, bounding about the tall bookshelves in such a way that it was hard not to believe him.

"So Sano is… a master of the air?" said Demetrius, gaping at his own conclusion. "And his unique magic is obviously his healing powers, then."

Keeper Kassime was nodding, all eyes still on Sano.

But Solza had Arianna's attention. "I found her in the forest," she mused.

"Yes," said Kassime, a profoundness in his tone, "a creature of the earth, most energized and familiar when she's running through fields with the grass on her paws."

"But does she have any powers yet?" said Jeom.

"I've already told you," snapped Arianna, affronted. "She's got the ability to boost my magic, healing me from the inside out. I think, healing my mind even…"

"Yeah, Jeom, just because you can't feel it, doesn't mean it's

not true," said Demetrius, prodding him playfully in the ribs—
Jeom shooed him away.

"But she's never *controlled* any earthly element that I know
of," said Arianna, tapping her finger to her lips. "Not like Sano
does with the air."

She watched Sano flit about the room, doubting if she even
believed he was using abilities outside of a monkey's normal capacity.

She looked between Keeper Kassime and Lessa. "So, you're
saying that you think Solza could change into something *else?*"

"That's how I interpreted it," said Lessa with a shrug.

"Could be," said Kassime. "We won't know until it happens.
If it ever happens…"

He knelt down to stroke Solza, and her eyes popped open—
so much electricity there.

So much magic. That was one thing Arianna didn't doubt in
the least.

"From the sound of it, most avatars don't shift at all without
proper training. And Solza doesn't have a hope of gaining control
over her powers until you do," said Kassime.

Arianna folded her arms across her chest, and he laughed,
glancing over to the portrait of the guardians.

"Imagine if you both could help your avatars move through
the other elements. You could have a chance to do more than just
sit on all this knowledge and wait," he said. "You'd have the
power to lead us into the next revolution."

"The next revolution?" said Jeom, looking perplexed.

"Is that what happened to the others?" said Demetrius, his
voice pitching with surprise. "Did you try and fight back?"

"There's nothing to tell now," said the keeper, abruptly. "We
tried to fight back before we were ready, and we failed. Now almost everyone in that picture is dead."

He bowed his head, letting out a heavy sigh.

"I hoped to see the day this kingdom could go free, but that's not my goal anymore. What I wish is to keep my vow as a guardian and do all I can to protect the old knowledge. We've got a lot of work to do to make sure we learn as much as we possibly can and grow as much as we are able. That way, those that come after us will have ten times our strength and experience to defeat the King and fulfill the prophecy. We're in the service of the Olleb."

"But if our avatars *did* grow," said Lessa. "If they could master all of the elements?"

"If we had dragons on our side…"

He smiled, a strange look crossing his face.

"Now that would be a whole different story."

PART THREE

25

THE GATHERING

TOBIAS OFFERED HIS HAND. "Apprentice Aridyn," he said. Arianna responded instinctively now, holding out her own as she stepped down from the horse-drawn carriage. She planted her feet on a red velvet carpet lined with finely dressed palace guards on either side.

"Thank you, Tobias," she said with a smile. "Have the attendants bring my bags to my chambers, please. I think I selected the perfect outfit for tonight."

She discreetly planted a gold piece in his palm, and he thanked her profusely.

"Cutting it a bit close, are we?" he said.

"Dress shopping was never my forte," said Arianna.

"The costumes are the best part of the ball!" said Tobias, shaking his head. "You're a funny one, miss. Try and have some fun tonight, will you?"

She smiled as he began to guide the horses and carriage to the usual space behind the palace.

"I'll see you on the dance floor!"

Arianna laughed and waved him off. "Oh, I'll try. See you tonight!"

The palace sprawled out in front of her, magnificent as usual yet more alive than ever before. She had left the premises just long enough not to be missed while the staff prepared for the event that the entire city had been waiting for all year long. Carriages with carefully groomed horses began to line up along the curled pathway in front of the palace by the tens. And hundreds of magnificently dressed people on foot filed inside, knocking each other about in their excitement.

I'm running so behind!

As the sun began to settle behind the clouds, Arianna shivered as an uncomfortable wind wrapped around her skin. By now, the warmer seasons were already long gone. So, every time the sky darkened with the falling sun, familiar chills blew down from the Blancoren Mountains—always a sharp reminder of the lie she lived.

She could easily shake the feeling off now, though, perfectly comfortable as Aridyn Lareigh of South Luose.

It had been nearly a year since Keeper Kassime officially announced them as his guests to the palace and city. Their eighteenth year had come and gone in what seemed like an instant. And tonight, at the brink of just their nineteenth year, the four would be honored attendees at Luose's annual Gathering Ball.

Hosted at the end of each year before Transition Week in all of the Olleb's capitals, the Gathering celebrated equality in citizenship and signified an important reminder to the people of Olleb-Yelfra that no matter their social status, they had all—each and every one of them—earned a place in the free world.

Arianna dreaded the night filled with mingling, dancing, and all the other things Aridyn could do well yet Arianna liked little. Although she had fully adopted Aridyn's persona, the charade was exhausting at times. She missed being herself once in a while, missed being Arianna Belvedor.

It was as if she repeatedly took a test, always carefully measuring each answer and never allowed a single mistake. Over and over, she'd taken this test, answering questions about her training in the districts, her time after freedom, or how she ended up a highlife so young—and she continued to pass flawlessly with well-learned lies.

Two regulators flanked her, parting the crowds as she walked through the double doors of the palace and toward her chambers. The curiosity of passersby and their whispers about the well-kept resident of the city keeper used to make her uneasy, but now Arianna could easily block them out. She had practiced well not to make herself too much of a statement and therefore kept mostly to the palace grounds with the others; the only exceptions were the many nights she'd slipped off to visit Liam at Mya's tavern.

Her thoughts and nerves focused on him this night—the possibility to welcome the new year as Arianna Belvedor alongside Liam Black, her closest friend since childhood, was all but consuming. She couldn't wait to finally share her secret with him.

After a lot of persistence, Liam had finally let Aridyn in. And now almost a year since she'd found him scarred, broken, and drowning himself in whiskey, he would finally be inducted again into the world of magic; she had waited long enough for him to emotionally heal and long enough for her and her friends to find stability in their new identities—now was the time.

Tonight, Liam would get the chance to become a guardian-in-training, just like the rest of them.

After dancing and dinner, they'd sneak away with him to the attic where Keeper Kassime had agreed to observe and pass a final judgment as to Liam's future—magical memory wipe or a Guardian of Gold? Arianna hoped with all her heart that Liam could hold his head on long enough to react with a willingness to understand. Though he would surely need some convincing, her biggest worry was that the keeper had to *also* agree that knowledge of the Golden Age was worth risking on Liam Black.

Arianna dismissed her guards and headed toward her room. As she walked through the maze of halls, she deliberately took the longer route to avoid the hordes of people who'd arrived too early to the party. Attempting to shift her thoughts away from worries of her future with Liam, she focused on each footfall, the echo of her polished boots a welcome sound in these secluded parts of the palace.

The smell of sweet pastries and pies settled in her chest as she cut through the large kitchens, sucking in as much of the aroma as she could. The palace cooks barely even lifted their eyes from their work as she passed, utterly consumed with tonight's robust feast for the city.

Leaving the kitchens, Arianna danced around the decorators busying about one of her favorite lounging chambers. She ducked under garlands of silk and jumped over piles of ribbons to avoid disrupting the workers as they readied the magnificent room for an onslaught of guests.

A spool of bright red ribbon caught her eye.

That would go perfect!

She swiped it and slipped out of the room, heading deeper into the palace and leaving the noise of the oncoming festivities behind.

Arianna slowed as she passed the wide stone door leading to the dungeons. The regulators on guard tonight nodded to her, and she flashed them a disarming smile, as was routine.

Almost daily now she'd entered through that door, the smell of rotting flesh stinging her nose anew as she hurried through to the attic stairwell; she could unlock the entrance to the attic using only the palm of her hand—the golden guardian tattoo the key to the cloaking spell Keeper Kassime had used to hide it from everyone else.

"Have a good evening, gentlemen," she said, knowing that

she'd be back soon and hopefully accompanied by Liam.

She left that corridor, traveling up a set of staircases with an overhung balcony at the top.

"There you are!" squealed Lessa, waving down to her from the terrace; Arianna climbed the steps to meet her. "Tonight is going to be just fabulous. Can you believe all this? Can you believe we made it an entire year!"

She took Arianna by the arm and guided her down the hall toward their rooms.

"You know, sometimes I *can't* believe it at all. Sometimes I really feel like I'm living a lie," said Arianna. Her mouth curled up in a smirk.

"Hush now," said Lessa with a giggle, squeezing her closer. "Lie or not, tonight will be *epic*."

"Yes, yes," said Arianna with a sigh, reflecting on the time passed.

"We only have a couple hours before Kassime wants us downstairs," said Lessa. "I'll meet you here soon? The boys are already getting dressed."

Arianna nodded.

"Great! And *maybe* have a glass of wine before you leave." Lessa waved her hands in the air, doing a little dance. "You need to loosen up. It's the party of the year!"

She disappeared into her room, and Arianna could hear her singing from behind the closed door—she wouldn't have fared well in an entertainment placement.

Arianna snickered, pushing open the door to her own room; the packages from her earlier shopping trip were piled neatly in the corner.

Solza immediately greeted her, purring and wrapping her tail around her feet.

"I wish we could trade places for tonight," said Arianna, wrapping her arms around her neck. "You don't have to worry about all the dancing."

Solza snuggled closer.

"Miss Aridyn," called her palace attendant, startling her. "In here, quickly now. We haven't much time to get you ready! I've run you a bath."

Arianna sighed and gave Solza one last squeeze.

"Be back soon," she whispered. "*Levantis bora.*"

With a slight flick of her hand, she levitated the leftover chicken from her lunch plate onto the floor; Solza pounced.

"Coming!" sang Arianna, tossing her cloak aside and stripping down to her knickers before her attendant could reprimand her some more.

She entered the washroom, the steamy lavender scent beckoning to her.

"Please, just call me when you're done," said her attendant with a slight bow.

"Thank you," said Arianna. "My, you look lovely!"

This was the first time she'd ever seen her attendant all fancied up and out of working clothes.

"How *kind* of you," she said, flouncing her robes of green. "I haven't been this excited for something in ages!"

She blushed at the compliment.

"Well, then, I'll make sure to hurry," said Arianna. "I'd hate if I made you late on such a special occasion."

"Oh, don't mind me," she said. "I'm here to serve you. Besides, the night's not going anywhere." She narrowed her eyes, scrutinizing her. "Although, I can't imagine what compelled you to go shopping on your own… and so close to the ball. There's plenty here you could've selected from. Do you want me to have the seamstresses enhance your wardrobe?"

"Oh, no. That won't be necessary, really! I certainly didn't mean to offend anyone," said Arianna, realizing too late that she might very well have. "It's just, for tonight, I wanted something more… me."

She gave a weak smile, and her attendant said no more,

leaving her to bathe. The next couple hours came and went, and Arianna was spun into a magnificent creation.

"You've done a splendid job," she said, studying herself in the mirror, just for a moment, as they readied to leave.

"And still a minute to spare," said her attendant, clapping her hands at a job well done.

Arianna beamed. "Here, I've got something for you," she said, opening up one of the smaller packages from her shopping trip. "Stand here a moment."

"Something for me?" stuttered the attendant. "I don't know—"

Arianna didn't give her a second to protest, turning her to face the mirror. She laid a chain of silver across her neck and clasped it at the back.

"Oh, my!" Her attendant's face went as red as the accents in her room, her hand grazing over a vibrant green jewel at the center of the chain.

"It's an emerald," said Arianna, wondering if it could've been mined long ago from the jewel-lined labyrinths of the City of Undor. *Anything is possible.*

"I can't accept such a gift, Miss Aridyn," she said in a hushed voice. "No, no… this is much too valuable." She squeezed the jewel beneath her palm, eyes glittering.

"You can and you *will,*" said Arianna in the strongest highlife tone she could muster. "Besides, I don't really have much of a need for these types of things."

She waved her arm to the wardrobe filled with jewelries. They sat there collecting dust all year, items she only ever wore once in obedience to the keeper; all were gifts of useless function to her, though extremely beautiful to look at. And she'd seen her attendant gawking at them enough to know her taste.

"You've been an incredible help this year, and you deserve to look extra special tonight. This celebration is for you, too." Arianna smiled, holding out a matching pair of emerald studded

earrings, and her attendant took them eagerly, putting them on—
she stared at her reflection for a long while, twisting and turning
to admire the jewelry. "There! Now your outfit is complete."

"Oh, thank you *so* much, Miss Aridyn!" she said, wrapping
her arms around her. "You're too kind. This is the most amazing
placement I could've ever dreamed of. I'm so happy our paths
crossed."

Arianna laughed, hugging her back.

"So am I," she said, blushing. "Okay, go on now. You don't
want to be late too! You know I'm always running behind. I'll see
you there. I'm supposed to escort Lessa, and I'm sure she'll be
waiting on me."

The attendant thanked her again and scurried out of the
room, wiping her eyes as she went. Arianna followed soon after,
bumping into Lessa in the hall.

"Ready?" said Lessa, her face glowing with a mixture of
makeup and utter delight.

"Just one more thing I almost forgot," said Arianna. "Can
you help me please?" She carried the red ribbon in her hand. "I
thought it would look nice…"

"Ah, the perfect touch," said Lessa, tying it around her waist
in a bow at her back. "There, you look stunning!"

Arianna closed her eyes a moment, sucking in a deep breath.
"Okay, let's get this over with."

She held out her arm for Lessa to take, and they made their
way to the party, headed toward the main gallery.

They walked for a while in happy conversation until they had
no choice but to pass through a dreaded corridor, inescapable
with their destination—a long mirror created the length of an
entire wall in this part of the palace, decorated in jewels and
gilded frames.

They both had to stop and stare, falling silent as they faced
their own reflections; perfectly elegant strangers gazed back at
them through the mirrors at every angle.

Arianna and her friends had indulged very little in looking upon their fake identities. Each time it was as if it were the first, always breathtaking in the worst ways. She normally didn't care to look long, but this corridor forced her to *really* see Aridyn. Thus, she and Lessa took a moment to straighten their fine dress and sparkling jewels, leaning in to the discomfort.

Arianna's eyes froze open as she glimpsed a flicker of her own face in the reflection, the face with the darkness inside. For a year now, Aridyn had helped her to suppress that monster within, and the nightmares had faded over time with meditation practice from her guardian trainings. She'd fought back, just like she swore she would, and she'd earned countless dream-free nights in return.

However, always in the back of her mind, always lurking, there was a lingering sense of danger—and it showed its face now. Despite all her efforts, she knew the darkness was still there, waiting for her to make one wrong move.

Arianna shook her head, the face vanishing.

"Don't forget your mask," she stammered.

She pulled a sparkling red and gold piece over her eyes, hiding Aridyn away as best she could—it wasn't a perfect solution, ignoring her fears, but it was enough for now.

Lessa followed suit, putting on a mask of similar elegance, blue feathers jumping out of a silver frame.

"Ready," she said, fixing it in place. She let out an exasperated sigh, cocking her head to the side as she took herself in. "I just wish this Lilith looked as good in blue as I do. I just can't stand all this red hair!"

Arianna snorted. "You both look too good to be true," she said, turning away from the mirror.

"Come on," said Lessa. "We'll be late."

She pulled Arianna through the corridor, and they promptly left the mirrors behind.

Shoving through the crowds all headed in the same direction, they entered a wide hall filled with statues every few feet. And ivy crawled up the walls, as if the forest had broken its way into the palace. Then they came upon a familiar chamber, their final destination—the very same room Arianna had first laid eyes upon the day Keeper Kassime had sentenced them to death.

But the space felt different than before, less foreboding when being used for a ball rather than a punishment.

Every fireplace had been lit, warm and inviting. The benches rearranged to accommodate as many people as possible, and the curtains drawn back on the windows for a grand view of the city. The iron chandeliers dazzled this evening, every candle lit so that it appeared as if hundreds of stars burned above them, and fine carpets had been laid out. Even the subtle sounds of music floated through the air, reinventing the space into something festive.

What was normally the room where Keeper Kassime decided the fates of misbehaving citizens or welcomed honored guests to the palace had fully been reimagined into the massive Gathering Ball—Arianna was staggered.

Alas, although space was abundant, there was no way the entire city could be accommodated here; many other chambers throughout the palace had also been transformed for the celebrations—the dining hall, the ballroom, countless lounging areas, and, of course, the multiple gardens across the grounds had all been equipped to accommodate the steady flow of citizens. Some would have to wait at the gates for hours before they were let inside. But wait they would, and it'd most definitely be worth it.

Arianna looked around the packed room, everyone hurrying to find a place at long, decorated tables before the celebrations began. Jeom and Demetrius were waving at her and Lessa from the highlife section, various tables united to the keeper's throne and directly under the lifelike portrait of King Devlindor. She pursed her lips, finding the King's eyes.

Hope you're enjoying the hunt.

Then she hiked up her dress and walked to join them.

"Magnificent, isn't it?" said Demetrius, lifting a metallic green mask off his face. His eyes stayed steady on the flow of people filing through the door.

"Wish they'd start already. I'm starved!" said Jeom, showing off a sequined mask of maroon and gold. "Wow! You girls look really… *really* lovely there."

He gaped, hands flying to his cheeks as he looked them up and down.

"When did you get so charming?" said Arianna, pretending to fan off his flattery.

He wasn't wrong, though—she and Lessa were catching many eyes tonight with their striking costumes.

Lessa donned a tight dress of light blue and white, silver embroidery streaking throughout. When she moved, it appeared as if clouds slithered across a blue sky of satin, hugging her curves. Her feathered mask, swirling with silver glitter, made her eyes pop as the focal point of her face—she looked sunny and bright in every way.

Arianna, on the other hand, made quite the opposite attraction. She'd selected a flowing chiffon dress with deep reds. It faded through brilliant spectrums of oranges and yellows until inevitably ending in a train of black, as if the sun were just about ready to settle in for the night.

She had chosen it specifically for the resemblance to the sunstone in the Vanishing Tunnels, all the while marveling at how someone could possibly have the imagination to create such a pattern without ever having laid eyes on it.

And with her golden mask dotted with bright red jewels, she could hardly go unnoticed.

Through her own eyes, the long, dark curls of her true identity draped over her shoulders and chest, having finally grown back out again. And her tan skin complemented the colors in her dress rather nicely, unlike the pale white that Aridyn couldn't seem to leave behind no matter how many hours she spent outside. *If only everyone else could see me this way.*

"Yes, very fitting choices," said Demetrius, pinching the fabric of Arianna's dress. He lowered his voice. "But it's a shame we have the real you all to ourselves. The rest of the world is truly missing out on two very pretty ladies."

He winked, as if reading her mind. Then he and Jeom pulled out chairs for both of them to sit.

"Such gentlemen," said Lessa with a look of approval. "And I'd say the same for the both of you."

"I can't imagine you picked those out yourselves," said Arianna with a chuckle.

She plucked at the outfits the boys wore; Demetrius donned elegant robes of gold and green, and Jeom looked ever so handsome in a fitted vest of deep purple and black.

"You both certainly play the part of a highlife well!" said Lessa. "I'm sure the ladies will be just swooning after you tonight. Save a dance for me?" She teasingly batted her eyelids.

Jeom flashed his signature smile. "I wouldn't dare refuse you, Miss Lilith."

"Why, aren't you all a stunning bunch tonight!" said Kassime—he was in a particularly jolly mood as he came to stand at their sides, observing the crowd swarming the tables below.

The Gathering Ball was meant to show respect to the district from which one came while also celebrating freedom. Keeping in this tradition, the keeper managed to show respect to both Ferlon Ragaric's original creator heritage alongside Keeper Kassime's adopted Healer's District persona. He flaunted long robes of bright silver with clear influences of blue *and* purple. And he was, perhaps, the most finely dressed person in attendance, as the city keeper should be on such an occasion.

"Thank you, sir," said Lessa, giving him a respectful kiss on the cheek. "You look quite handsome yourself."

His cheeks reddened as he cleared his throat and straightened his gleaming crown.

"Go on and take your seats," said Keeper Kassime. "I'm about to begin. And you should make your greetings after my speech." He nodded to the other highlifes in the section, all eyes on them, all eager to gain an audience with the keeper's favorites.

The four grumbled their agreements and settled back into their chairs; Arianna put her attention on the quieting crowd, the people of South Luose—gathered together as they were now, she could almost picture them to be a field of brightly colored wildflowers swaying in a breeze. It was a beautiful sight to see, and one she wished she could see more often.

Keeper Kassime walked back to his throne, higher than every other seat in the room, and called for silence. "Welcome to the 288th Gathering Ball in the City of South Luose!" His voice rang out across the excited sea of citizens.

Arianna's mind flashed back to the moment when General Ivo had announced the 287th Free Falls in her district. "I can't believe it's already been a year since the festivals," she whispered to Lessa. "I wonder how the seventeenth years fared this year…"

Her mind flicked to Noah, but her imagination wasn't very optimistic about his success. Keeper Kassime's speech was, thankfully, the perfect distraction.

"There's much cause for celebration tonight. Each and every one of us here has earned our citizenship. Treated our freedom with respect in the eyes of the law. This is what has kept our Olleb flourishing for almost three centuries now. And on behalf of the King," he gestured to the portrait, "I thank you proudly. I hope to celebrate many more South Luose Gatherings with you as your city keeper, and I look forward to bringing this city into its prime as we finish out this decade."

He lifted a shiny gold goblet into the air.

"But first, let's raise our cups to honor those who have made it possible for us to stand where we stand today. Let us remember why we are here."

Arianna sipped her drink, watching intently as each district was recognized for their unique strengths.

"To the Agrarian's District!" He gestured for them to stand. "Which without we would've never had a foundation to heal the land back from its war-torn state. Those who make it possible for our nourishment and who produce the ingredients necessary for survival and healing, we drink to you."

He took a long sip from his cup as hundreds of people stood up in silence, glistening in all their green glory; Arianna spotted Tobias in the crowd, and she even saw her attendant among them, her emeralds making her stand out.

Demetrius too stood proudly alongside Mistress Serina, gazing down toward his peers from the highlife table; their fellow agrarians seemed to look to them for guidance, and so he raised his goblet high and drank—those standing followed his lead.

"Secondly, I invite the healers of the land to stand," said Kassime as the agrarians took their seats. "The Healer's District may be the most obvious necessity of the Olleb yet. And we commend you for your noble work—"

Arianna watched as the crowd turned a brilliant blue, those from the Healer's District getting to their feet.

She found Cyn almost immediately, bubbly and excited in a royal blue gown—there weren't many souls who remembered her as a warrior, and she didn't appear to acknowledge her beginnings in any way with her costume choice. But Arianna knew her secret and so did Keeper Kassime... even if Cyn didn't think she'd ever met him at all; Arianna thought he spoke directly to her with his next words.

"You've healed our wounds a thousand times over and have made it possible for the Olleb and its people to endure under the harshest of circumstances. Every one of us here today has felt the touch of a healer, the positive ripple effects from a district that nurses us back to health or cares for our youngest during their most vulnerable years. To you, we drink."

They all lifted their goblets to their lips, and Lessa joined them on her feet, smiling brightly all the while.

"Third, I welcome the Creator's District. I honor you with fervor," said Kassime as a throng of people in purple took to their feet to accept their honors, glasses raised high.

Jeom stood too, bumping the table so hard their drinks sloshed everywhere. But he stood proudly, nonetheless, right alongside Master Gansevurt.

"Against all odds, this district has brought finesse into this world, kept our hard-working citizens sheltered, and provided safety in the form of weaponry—without which we couldn't be hunters or warriors. You've helped us develop Olleb-Yelfra in more ways than one, so enjoy tonight as you've well-earned it!"

Jeom gulped down his drink along with the rest of the creators, and Master Gansevurt gave him a joyful slap on the back as he coughed it down.

"Last, but certainly not least, to our fearless warriors. Wear your red proudly forevermore," said Kassime, his tone turning serious.

Arianna was quite surprised to see that when the warriors stood, there was significantly less presence than that of the other districts—including the regulators and palace guards who were allotted this as a moment's lapse in their duties.

She took her golden goblet in hand and slowly rose to her feet.

Tonight, she stood alone at the highlifes' table, wondering if Master Tayshin had drunk himself into a stupor again. All eyes on her, the keeper continued.

"The Warrior's District has always been, and always will be, the most difficult to survive. That much is known," he said. "Their festivals are only won after immense bloodshed, similar to all. However, their district experiences this fight for survival each and *every* day—"

He raised a hand into the air, as if to stop any objections that might arise at such a strong statement.

"Now, don't let me lessen the hardships we've all faced in the other corners of the Jar. But the fact remains that the Warrior's District is the only one where slaves are encouraged to use their weapons against one another persistently... routinely." He walked to stand beside Arianna, and she felt her skin grow hot from all the attention. "This is the most effective training. Every day they're taught the brutal lesson of life and death. Thus, their chances of survival are much less because the Olleb can only spare its resources on the *very* best for us to have a fighting chance."

He laid a hand on her shoulder, his fingers cold against her warm skin.

"These brave souls will always stand by us and protect us from those who stray from the rules of the Olleb and endanger her continuity," he said, firmly. "In the case of unforeseen disasters, we can look to our warriors for guidance and leadership. They're the ones who keep the law of the land in check, from the smallest to the grandest, and who make it possible for all of the other districts, and therefore the *world*, to thrive. No matter what your title now—be it apprentice, regulator, guard, protector, master—we drink to you, my friends."

He raised his glass high. "Thank you all."

The room seemed to grow quieter, if at all possible, and with the keeper's last words Arianna felt again the fury that King Devlindor had instilled inside of her every time she thought of those she'd lost. *I drink to you, Master Bell.*

She lifted the goblet to her lips, and those standing followed her lead; the red liquid slid down her throat, cooling her tongue momentarily before it landed in her stomach with a slight burn.

Setting the goblet back on the table, she wondered what those down below thought of her—a warrior so finely dressed, prim and proper. She showed off their signifying warrior red through sequins and silk, jewels and ribbons, a color she'd always associated with the blood of the dying.

Arianna stayed standing, and the Warrior's District citizens did not immediately sit as she looked out at them. If they were anything like her, they were hardened from their first seventeen years of life. Strong and rough around the edges from their time spent as slaves, and even likely their time as citizens, she was sure they must sometimes still struggle to find the connection between then and now.

Their clothes were clean and wrinkle free, and they sparkled and shone just like her. But their pain and anger echoed in their eyes, suppressed—just as she suppressed her own dark reflection.

The friends they'd lost, the lives they'd stolen, and the blood that had certainly been shed by their hand for them to be standing here were stained on their skins eternally. As survivors of the Warrior's District, their souls would never fully heal, never *really* forget… no matter what they did with their lives thereafter.

Arianna bowed her head then, letting her hands rest on the ruby chain hanging down her bosom. It took all her strength in that moment not to rip the jewels from her neck, to erase Aridyn and throw away all that King Devlindor had forced her to become.

He had expunged Arianna and taken a piece of her soul in the process. Yet here they were, gathered to celebrate him.

Never forget!

Lifting her eyes back to the masked crowd, Arianna held their gaze for a lingering moment. She hoped that in this gesture her fellow warriors could somehow sense that she stood with *them*—not the King and not his botched system of strength—no matter what mask she wore. She finally took her seat, and the Warrior's District survivors followed, blending back into the room to complete a vibrant representation of the Four Corners.

Arianna tore her eyes from the crowd, swallowing the lump in her throat. She glanced down at her golden goblet, a bright red lipstick stain now smudging the shine.

"Wonderful!" said Kassime, clapping his hands to try to shake off the sour ambiance that had settled in the air. He walked back to his throne. "But let's not forget the *most* important commemoration of tonight."

He made a fist and placed it firmly at his chest.

"Hail to the King. Hail to Lord Devlindor!"

The crowd echoed the sentiment, their voices booming off the walls; Arianna wanted to raise her hands to her ears, as she had always wished to do at such times.

Hail to the World. Hail to Olleb-Yelfra.

When the tribute was over, the crowd began to buzz again with excitement.

"All right, all right now," said Kassime with a smirk. "Dig in! You've all certainly earned it. Enjoy the celebrations to your heart's content! The palace is yours tonight."

The room exploded in applause, and then the party began—everyone devoured the piles and piles of food on their plates, passing around trays of delicious cakes and endless bottles of wine or whiskey. Lively music started up and, almost instantly, the crowd became drunk with joy, dancing in the center of the chamber under the brightly lit chandeliers.

People poured in and out of the room, running this way and that, excited to explore the palace and to mingle with their friends, and all certainly trying to bump shoulders with those at Arianna's table.

"Lovely, just lovely," said Kassime, walking back to join Arianna and her friends. "Go on, children. Enjoy yourselves! You deserve it more than most. I'm so pleased with how far you've come in just one year."

He leaned in close so that only Arianna and Lessa could hear his next words.

"And I know your masters would be very proud of you as well. Talis and Solomon would be overjoyed to see all you've accomplished thus far."

He kissed the tops of their heads, and Arianna felt that maybe with another year's time she might make some better competition to Lessa in his eyes. *I think he's warming to me now after all.*

She smiled, and Lessa sniffled, giving him a big hug.

"Now go on and have some fun. I command it! I can't be bothered to entertain you all tonight. There's too many people to see to."

"You got it, Keeper," said Demetrius.

Jeom was nodding along, already with his mouth full.

They began to eat and drink merrily, their goblets refilled over and over again.

"May I have this dance, miss?"

Arianna looked up from her plate to find Liam; he bowed to her and held his hand open across the highlife table. She swallowed whatever food she was chewing and nodded, quickly wiping the crumbs off her dress.

Jeom snickered, and she kicked him under the table, hoping she left a bruise. Then, with her heart aflutter, she took Liam's hand and walked around to his side.

No number of lessons from her attendant had prepared her for this moment. Liam led her to the dance floor, shamelessly wrapping his arms around her waist and swaying with her back and forth to the steps that every highlife *should* know. She couldn't have been more embarrassed if she tried.

"Where did you learn to dance like this?" she said, barely able to meet his eyes for how focused she was on his feet.

He smiled down at her, his long hair falling around his face in bountiful waves.

"I guess I'm just a natural," said Liam, spinning her around in circles.

"You'd fare better dancing with Lilith then," she said, dizzied, pointing to Lessa—she had paired off with Demetrius, making an elegant partner, while Jeom nodded along to his own beat close by.

Many others danced in circles around them, too, but Arianna hardly noticed them now, Liam swaying her slowly to the seducing sounds of a band of string instruments. It was as if time had stopped and the hundreds of people filling the party had all but disappeared while they danced.

"What is it?" said Arianna after the third song, feeling herself flush under his scrutiny—he stared far too long.

"Sorry," he said, shaking out of his daze. "There's just something about you. Ever since you forced yourself into my life it's been on the tip of my tongue… but I can't quite put my finger on it." He tilted his head, still staring.

Arianna chuckled in relief, feeling a little more like herself and so hopeful for their plans for him; Liam was starting to see through Aridyn and into her heart.

"Maybe you will soon," she said, lifting the crimson mask off her face to the top of her head.

Staring straight back at him, she became lost in the twinkle of his familiar hazel eyes; they were forever searching hers.

One side of his face, the scarred side, was covered with a solid glittering black mask. Gently, she laid a hand on it.

"Tonight, at midnight, meet me in the main garden. I have something I want to show you," she said, her voice shaking with nerves.

He let her hand remain on his cheek for only a second before he moved it away; she was glad, though, that he hadn't flinched.

"Oh? And what might that be?"

He pushed a strand of hair behind her ear, before spinning her around once more.

"I pray it's nothing bad," he joked.

Arianna laughed, Aridyn's cheeks probably turning as red as her dress.

"No, no… nothing bad." *I hope.*

He agreed with no more questions, and they continued to get lost in the music. Tobias even took Arianna for a turn around the room before handing her back to Liam. But eventually their blissful moment was interrupted.

"May I present our entertainment for tonight!" called Ophelia from the highlife table, tapping her utensil on her cup—the music screeched to a stop, and she gestured for everyone to return to their seats just as a lanky man appeared in the middle of the emptying dance floor.

"Make room, make room! I handpicked him myself."

He was dressed in a bright suit of all four district colors and wore a ridiculous hat and mask to match.

"All right," said Liam, looking rather disappointed by the interruption. "Until midnight, then."

"And not a minute later," said Arianna, squeezing his hand. "This is *very* important."

"I wouldn't dare take chances with you." He grinned and just as suddenly planted a kiss on her cheek. "And, Aridyn, I'm so very glad we met. You've… done a lot for me this year. More than you know."

He walked to his seat, leaving her alone on the dance floor with a big smile splashed across her face.

"See you soon," she whispered with a slight wave.

Her heart glowed with the anticipation of what was soon to come. She could hardly wait for the hour to pass, for the Gathering to get into full swing and for the niceties to be over so they could all sneak away. *Everything is going perfectly*, she thought as she found her way back to the highlife table, her friends already waiting.

THE JESTER DANCED around the room, putting on quite the show for the guests; Arianna couldn't stop the giggles that came out of her as he bounced around the highlife table, doing tricks just for them. When he turned his attention away from the highlifes, Arianna held up her glass to cheers her friends at the hopeful addition of Liam, the hour speeding by as if in a single second. Their wine was replenished, time and time again, and they all drank merrily to their successes.

She glanced at a large grandfather clock hiding in the corner—it showed nearly midnight.

Then, over the laughter and merriment, she heard the voice of the one person she'd prayed *not* to meet on such a happy occasion. A shiver rolled down her spine.

"Enjoying yourself, are you?" said Godfrey.

Arianna snapped up from her conversation to find the beady eyes of their wrongdoer staring at her through a spikey mask; her breath stalled in her throat, lips pressed into a thin line as the keeper's hand lay across her knee, warning her to remain neutral.

"Quite," she said, forcing the word through her lips.

Kassime leaned around her to address him. "To what do we owe the pleasure?"

Jeom, Demetrius, and Lessa also put their attention on the slippery man who had first shown them through the city streets. Godfrey leaned heavily on his cane, his black skin glistening in contrast to his oversized sea-colored robes.

A healer? Arianna scoffed.

"Just wanted to give my regards, sir," he said with a bow. "The night's just getting started, and I didn't want to miss my chance once the festivities really kick up."

"That's kind of you," said Kassime, though his tone suggested he thought otherwise.

Arianna admired his indifference, wondering if she'd ever be able to master that kind of calm. *Just breathe.*

"It's my pleasure entirely," said Godfrey.

He reached his arm across the table to shake the keeper's extended hand, knocking over a full bottle of wine in the process.

"Godfrey, you weasel!" shouted Ophelia, waving her napkin at him from down the table.

She snapped her fingers and the jester she'd hired hopped over to their table in an instant, carrying with him a tray of new bottles. All eyes focused on their area, following the jester's every movement, everyone falling to hysterics as he jokingly stole more bottles out of people's hands on the way.

"At your service, ma'am," he said, bowing low with the tray of wine held up high over his head.

"My apologies," said Godfrey, stumbling back. "I'm so clumsy with this bum leg."

He plucked a bottle from the tray and set it down directly in front of Arianna as she hurried to clean up the mess.

"It's fine," grumbled Kassime, the jester bounding away to do more tricks for the guests. "You're dismissed."

Arianna looked up just as Godfrey made to leave.

"Take care now," he said, catching her eye.

She didn't even dignify him with a response.

As the party continued on, Arianna kept a close watch on the clock. Ophelia's entertainment wound to an end, and even Kassime had to crack a smile at the finale—the jester slammed his hands down on the highlife table with Arianna in his sights. Then he picked up the wine bottle and pretended to guzzle it; he frowned, dumping it upside down to show the crowd that the bottle was empty.

"Not even a drop left for Clarke the Clown?" he sang, pretending to cry to the sound of more laughter.

Arianna finished the last swig in her goblet with a smirk. Then she stood, clapping for him along with everyone else in the room.

"It's been my sincere pleasure entertaining you all tonight." He gave a deep bow to his audience and cartwheeled out of the gallery.

As Arianna sat back down, a dizzy spell came over her. "Oh my…" she breathed. Her hand flew to her forehead.

She could suddenly hear her heartbeat pounding in her ears,

slow and unsteady. She glanced to her friends for help.

The keeper was still laughing gaily as the party raged on in full stride, pairs dancing in circles around the room to the spellbinding music. Everyone seemed to be having an incredible time. But for Arianna, something had changed.

In her dizziness, she heard the clock begin to chime over the music, merging with the sound of her heartbeat. Time seemed to slow, passing in single seconds and all leading up to what she knew in her soul was about to be a terrible ending.

One. Keeper Kassime tossed his head back in laughter, clapping his hands along to the music. *Two.* Lessa squeezed her hand so tightly she thought her bones might break, her friend's skin so cold against her own. *Three.* A smooth voice filled her ears, swaying her concentration as someone began to sing along to the band. *Four.*

She locked eyes with Godfrey from across the room.

"Goodbye," he mouthed before slithering away through a back entrance.

Five. She clutched at her stomach, feeling as if something eroded there from the inside out. *Six.* She glanced again to the crowd, Ophelia's clouded stare penetrating her from across the room. *Seven.* The anguished moans of her friends pulled her attention, drowning out everything else. *Eight.* Arianna searched for a sign of Liam, but he was nowhere to be found. *Nine.* She found the strength to get to her feet, clutching the table for support.

Ten. The keeper abruptly stopped laughing.

"Ara… something's wrong," said Lessa. Her words slurred as she tried to stand up, clutching at Arianna's dress.

Eleven. Lessa dropped to the floor, tearing off the red ribbon around Arianna's waist in the process; she landed in a heap alongside it, contorting in pain as Jeom and Demetrius seemed to worsen over their plates.

The music screeched to a halt, now no other sound but for

her friends' screaming—then the clock struck midnight with a resounding bang.

Twelve.

"What's going on?" yelled Kassime, jumping up from his chair. "What's the matter with you all? Are you sick?"

He paced in a panic, looking back and forth between the four of them and shouting orders to the palace staff. Other elders and healers crowded around them, all confused by the unnerving display at the highlifes' table.

Arianna could barely speak, her voice stuck in her throat as she tried to steady this terrible feeling stirring within her. She could only stare down at her hands; their grasp on the table was the only thing keeping her upright as she attempted to find a sense of calm.

There was a moment of clarity as her wine goblet came into view, the red staining the gold bottom and the empty bottle next to it—she swiped the bottle off the table and it shattered against the tiled floor with an earsplitting sound.

Everyone in the vicinity jumped back.

"Poison!" she said through gasps. "We must've been poisoned. *Godfrey...* it was him." She found the strength to point to the door, but he was already gone. "He's poisoned us."

The onlookers nearest to them let out stifled shrieks, and soon gossip of poison twisted through the crowd, wine bottles and goblets being thrown to the floor as everyone grew panicked. Many even started to exit the chamber in a hurry.

Keeper Kassime lifted Arianna's goblet and sniffed the residue at the bottom.

"You're right." His eyes seemed to widen in both shock and understanding. "I know what this is. But... how?" he said, a horrified expression on his face. He whipped around to peer down the highlife table. "Ophelia!"

His voice rang out over the panicking guests, but she was already long gone, too.

"This wasn't only Godfrey," he hissed. "This was *her* doing. He must've helped her lace the wine."

Then he dropped his voice low so that only Arianna could hear, but she wasn't prepared to accept the words that came next.

"She knows about you! Ophelia is a seer, part of the Shadow Resistance. The guardians… we thought our magic had fooled her, but *we* are the fools."

In the now dead silence of the room, hundreds of eyes on them, the hazy sound of slow claps reached Arianna's ears. She lifted her gaze toward the main entrance, afraid at what she might find as the crowd parted for someone new in attendance—Master Solomon Bell, flanked by Warrior's District regulators on all sides, made his way down the aisle.

26

THE LAST DANCE

ARIANNA DIDN'T KNOW WHAT TO THINK, watching Solomon Bell march up to her table at a moment where she was barely able to stay on her feet. "You're alive?" she said through gasps, wanting him to catch her in his arms.

She thought she might be hallucinating as the poison worked through her body. But in the background, she could hear Lessa still thrashing on the floor, crying out from the pain that was sure to incapacitate her at any moment.

"As ever," said Solomon. "And you are?"

"I—"

"Solomon! This is quite the… surprise. Pleased to see you again, my friend," said Kassime, clearly taken aback. His voice was unnaturally loud as he attempted to drown out the sobs of Arianna and her friends.

Though many guests had already fled after rumors of poison, a group of worried bystanders still lingered, looking completely

confused at the disturbing display of four young highlife apprentices all fallen ill. They didn't know what to make of it, but they
appeared as if they *knew* something bad was about to happen—
just as Arianna felt it, literally, in her gut.

Keeper Kassime was lost for words, his brow furrowed. "You
must pardon my shock. It's just, we heard a rumor of your—"

"Of my death?" said Solomon, head cocked to the side—his
eyes then scanned the crowd, appearing to search for someone
else. "Whoever relayed that information was *quite* misinformed.
Only hopeful wishes, I'm afraid." He straightened his back. "You
may call me 'General' now."

"Of course," said Kassime with a cautious smile. He gestured
to Arianna as Solomon's gaze settled again on her. "This is Apprentice Aridyn. I'm afraid she's not herself at the moment. Why
don't I have someone make you a plate? You can take my seat
while I help her and the others to their quarters. I think it must've
been something undercooked, you see. We're so glad to have you
join us though!"

Arianna looked away from him, trying to compose herself and
hold back the conflicting tears of pain and joy as the poison ate
away at something inside her—she didn't quite understand what.
And the more time that went by, the harder it was to ignore the
fire burning within, consuming her from the inside out.

Unable to suppress it any longer, she cried out in another gasp
of pain, grasping the table harder for support.

The boys hadn't yet collapsed, like Lessa, but they were on
their way. She was too now… nearly there.

"That won't be necessary, *Ferlon*," said Solomon.

Keeper Kassime froze, gaping at him in disbelief.

"What did you just call me?" he said, his voice shaking.

With Solomon's words, Arianna felt the keeper's hand on her
back—the only thing keeping her from toppling to the floor—
suddenly go rigid.

Something is terribly wrong. Every thought in Arianna's head was scrambled and all her senses had slowed, but this was abundantly clear.

She managed to lift her head and found Cyn staring straight at them, watching the scene play out. She was shaking her head and waving her hands, frantically, as if in warning. But when Arianna blinked, Cyn's face had disappeared within the crowds.

Did that just happen?

Solomon turned his attention again to Arianna; he leaned forward to whisper in her ear. "I want to return something to you."

His voice held none of the kindness that she remembered, and the burning in her stomach began to clutch tighter, her hair standing on edge as his words wrapped all around her like an ice-cold blanket. "Let me go!"

Solomon's regulators dragged someone through the main entrance. And what remained of the curious crowd stirred in whispers, now completely perplexed at the disruption to their celebrations—Arianna watched in horror as Liam Black was pulled through the chamber by his long hair.

"Do you know this boy?" said Solomon, a slight smile on his lips.

"Master Bell, I… I don't," muttered Arianna before letting out a loud howl of pain, again grasping her stomach.

"How about now?" He nodded to one of the regulators who slowly turned their sword at the nape of Liam's neck.

Liam strained to break free of the regulator's hold. "Please," he cried out. "I've done nothing wrong! I've broken no rules."

"Yes, I know him!" said Arianna, breathing heavily as the regulator twisted his sword again.

She pressed her hand to her aching head, trying to see unhindered through the pain; her brain wasn't working fast enough to tie the pieces together as she considered what Keeper Kassime had meant about Ophelia's betrayal and Godfrey's hand in all of this, the poison doing its best to weaken her all the while.

"We met at Mya's tavern," she spat out. "He's new to the city, from the Warrior's District... I believe. We're acquaintances at best."

She looked Solomon in the eyes, trying to read him, trying to understand his point. He couldn't *possibly* know who she was. The magic didn't work like that.

But he said Ferlon's name...

He snapped his fingers, and the regulator dug his sword deeper. "Is that so?" said Solomon over Liam's cries.

This time Arianna couldn't help but lose her patience.

"Stop this, Solomon!" she choked out. "Please, what is it that you want? Why are you doing this to him? What's going on?"

Solomon kept her gaze, but Arianna saw none of the friend that she knew in his eyes—the momentary joy she had felt at finding him alive had gone, replaced with the pains of the poison eating her away. She felt as if she might really die, and she wasn't sure if Lessa and the others weren't already gone.

Solomon turned his back toward her, walking to Liam. He grabbed him by his shimmering red robes, forcing him up to the highlife table. Then Solomon slammed him down in front of her, pressing his head upon her cleared plate.

Liam's eyes were tear-filled and they looked up at her, pleading. But she could barely keep up the strength to stand, let alone save him from this humiliation—all Arianna could muster up the energy to do was lay a hand reassuringly atop his. He grasped it, not daring to let go.

"Tell me how you know this boy!" screamed Solomon, his expression menacing.

Arianna suddenly knew in her soul that Solomon *did* know who she was. He wanted her to confess the truth, but her mind was all but unable to accept that realization.

How could he?

Arianna ripped the mask from her face, its sparkling jewels tinkling to the floor as she turned her eyes on Liam. Taking a deep breath, the burn in her stomach growing stronger, she could barely speak but in a murmur. "He's my best friend." She squeezed his hand tighter.

"Arianna… is that you?" Liam's voice was soft as the realization dawned on him. "By gods," he breathed, "it's been you all along, hasn't it?" He stayed unblinking, fixated on her eyes.

She returned a single nod, and he smiled in disbelief.

"I should've known better," he gasped, still struggling under Solomon's grip. "You've always been so persistent. And your eyes give you away."

Arianna felt a wave of pure joy wash over her as Liam finally recognized her, the real girl behind the mask; she had barely opened her mouth to respond before she saw the axe sticking out of his back. His head lolled to the side, and his bright hazel eyes clouded over forever.

Her entire body froze in that moment as she looked on in horror—Liam's limp body slid off the table, his hand slipping away from hers.

Solomon stepped over him like trash in the street.

A cry like Arianna had never felt before ripped from her throat… as she saw the life leave Liam's face, as the poison corroded her body, and as her most trusted master and friend died, for the *second* time, right before her eyes.

She didn't know where her Solomon Bell had gone. But this man, this *monster*, was certainly not him.

The cry went on and on until Arianna slumped to the floor next to Lessa, the red of her dress mixing with the crimson of Liam Black's blood.

She noticed Lessa didn't writhe anymore, and the cowardly crowds raced away from the chaotic scene.

Arianna was on her hands and knees now, hovering over the silver plate with Liam's blood splattered all around it on the floor. In her reflection, she only saw herself—the last face Liam would ever see. Then she held the plate up to Lessa and also saw her true face mirrored back.

In that moment, Arianna understood the poison had corroded their fake identities, ripping them away without mercy just as they had been stitched to their souls in the first place.

"What have you done?" shouted Kassime. "What's come over you, Solomon? You've been corrupted. Ophelia… she couldn't have created that concoction on her own. You both planned this all along!"

He glanced down at his four young guardians behind the table, completely out of sorts.

"But how did she know?" His voice reached over the screams of the crowds barreling out of the room. "We worked together to protect ourselves from her sight. Tell me how she knew!"

Solomon shook his head, clicking his tongue at him.

"Dear Ferlon, you know she's part of the Shadow Resistance and a *seer*. No amount of mind magic can stop her visions. You were so naïve! You always were." His eyes flicked to Arianna. "Ophelia saw this moment long ago and sent word to me in the districts. She's served the King for her entire life, and now she's paid him the ultimate honor by delivering the girl."

"That *girl* is your ward!" said Kassime. "Why send her to me at all if only to betray us in this way?" His eyes watered, but he blinked away any trace of tears. "Ophelia may have served the King for a lifetime, but have you? Were our years of friendship just a ruse? Don't go down this path after everything we've been through together!"

Solomon turned irate—Arianna had never seen him in such a state.

No, this isn't right. This isn't happening!

She tried to block out their words, but they were the only thing she could hear.

"You know nothing about what I've been through, *brother*. And you got sloppy," said Solomon. "So sloppy that a cripple and a clown were able to poison highlifes at your very own table. I'm so disappointed in you. You've become weak, careless, nothing like the man I knew before."

Keeper Kassime slammed his fist onto the table, shaking with anger. "You've betrayed the guardians, Solomon."

Kneeling down, he spoke quickly to Arianna.

"That's not poison. It's a potion, a counter-spell to reveal your true identities. I'm so sorry, child. You need to get out of here before anyone else recognizes you. It's not safe for you here anymore. Arianna, take your friends and go!" He pulled off his ring and forced it into her hands.

The crowd had completely scattered now, filing out of the palace as regulators and guards began to draw their weapons at Keeper Kassime's command—those who followed Solomon from the districts began to battle the ones from the city. Though they were all ruled by one King, in this moment he wasn't present to say who was in the right.

Chaos and confusion unfolded.

"This is treason," said Kassime, shouting to his men and women to fight. "Protect your palace, in the name of King Devlindor!"

"Your city keeper is the traitor!" retorted Solomon. "By order of the King, any aiding Arianna Belvedor shall pay with their lives. Fight in the name of honor!" His regulators didn't hesitate to attack the keeper's.

Solomon also pulled out his own swords, the bronze ones that Arianna had given him—he lunged for her.

People in the dispersing crowd began to scream, dodging out of the way of blades being thrown about, pushing and shoving to the doors.

"Where's Arianna Belvedor?" asked one woman as she squeezed through the exit. "I thought that was just a rumor! Did you see her here?"

"No, but if I do, I'll cut off her head myself and claim the prize," she heard a man reply.

Keeper Kassime was quick and pulled the axe from Liam's

back to guard Arianna from Solomon's attack. He whispered something in a magical tongue, and she faintly recognized it as a form of mind magic—though she couldn't place its effect in her current state.

He squeezed Arianna's arm for only a second, forcing her to look away from Liam and hear him. "Go!" he shouted again. "There's nothing left for you here."

And so began a battle like she'd never seen before.

Solomon and Keeper Kassime fought well, as if they'd practiced many times together in the past; Arianna assumed that they had. She watched them from the floor, still unable to find the will to move.

Each seemed to be able to anticipate the other's move without fail, spinning around the emptied room under the waning light of the chandeliers and the fireplaces.

Arianna was in such a tangled state that she almost thought for a moment nothing at all had changed—that the party still went on and that there were magnificent dancers upon the floor offering them a beautiful show to end the night; Solomon and Keeper Kassime took front and center, stealing everyone's attention. And the regulators and guards fought on the outsides around them, as if aiding in a dazzling routine.

"Nobody knew! They were safe. How could you do this to us, to the guardians?" screamed Kassime over the song of their blades.

They expertly maneuvered around the room.

"With the help of an *old* friend," said Solomon, smiling before taking a lunge forward—he missed.

He never misses…

"Ophelia, I'll kill her," spat Kassime. "This is the last time she tears my family apart. And you! You've gone dark."

"I've chosen the only way I can," he said, almost in a Solomon-like tenor. Then he turned fierce and unforgiving once more.

"You help her," came a familiar voice from behind Arianna. "I'll get Lessa."

"Come on, Arianna!" Suddenly, she was being lifted to her feet by Master Tayshin. He coddled her in his large, meaty arms as the potion worked its way through her body. She could feel it eradicating Aridyn from her forever, erasing everything she ever was or ever would be.

"Where did you come from?" she muttered, queasy from being lurched into the air.

"I'm always close by," he said—his face remained calm, but Arianna felt his hands shaking.

She heard Jeom groan with mighty effort as he and Demetrius got to their feet, leaning on each other for support. And Cyn was there, too, helping Lessa to stand; she was coming back to consciousness, the effects of the concoction starting to slowly wear off from all of them, it seemed.

"Cyn," said Arianna, her head drooping over Master Tayshin's arm. "But—"

"Dear, there's no time for this now. We've got to go."

"This way!" said Master Tayshin. "Follow me."

There was no way to make it through to the main entrance. They would get caught in a battle they most certainly couldn't win, so everyone followed him toward a back door—the same that Arianna had watched Godfrey use in his own escape.

"Wait, we have to help Kassime," said Arianna, trying to swivel around to see. "We can't just leave him."

"There's nothing we can do now," said Master Tayshin.

"No, you don't understand any of this!" she said, regaining some control of her strength. "We have to help him. It's our duty!"

"I know all about your duty," he said, still moving quickly out of danger's path—she was baffled at his speed while carrying her in his arms, the others hurrying ahead of them. "It was I who trained Solomon and Ferlon as guardians with Talis by my side!

And if I say there's nothing we can do, then there's *nothing* we can do. We have to protect what we can, and right now that means you, your friends, and the knowledge and faith the guardians have bestowed on you."

Arianna gaped back at him in utter shock.

"No, it isn't possible," she said. "You're lying. And the memory spell—"

Master Tayshin scoffed, frowning down at her.

"I taught Ferlon that damn spell. There's no way I was going to forget anything, so I blocked it. Why do you think I drink so damn much?"

He nodded to Cyn at their front.

"She was under, but Ferlon's lifted it now... in order to help save *your* life, so stop resisting! We need to go. Or this was all for nothing."

The others had already fled through the door.

"All right," she said, resigned, no longer fidgeting.

Taking one last look at the battle scene as Master Tayshin ran with her through the door, Arianna saw Solomon mouth something, his concentration much too intense; she'd know this magic anywhere by now because he'd taught it to her. "*Luzcora.*"

"Kassime, look out!" she managed to scream, her voice echoing loud over everything.

Everyone stopped mid-battle and watched as Solomon Bell took one last swing with his sword at Keeper Kassime.

It was almost invisible in its effort, but Arianna recognized the pattern. She saw his sword momentarily come ablaze with an electricity, inexplicable power exuding from his fingertips and into his weapon. His magic raced through it and broke the axe clean in half. Then his sword went straight through Keeper Kassime's center.

"Solomon... but why?" said Kassime with his last breath, blood sputtering from his lips as he clutched at the sword protruding from his body.

Solomon didn't even give him the honor of a reply as he yanked his sword back. And with the flick of his wrist, he sliced it through Kassime's neck, nothing left of him to save. The keeper fell to his knees, head rolling across the marble floor in an almost inconceivable display of blood.

"No!" Arianna felt all his pain in this moment, her scream alarming Master Tayshin so much that he stopped.

But before she could even comprehend this sudden loss, she watched the skin of Keeper Kassime's face morph from the smooth copper tones she knew so well to that of a pale, white stranger—the city keeper had vanished from sight, replaced with the real Ferlon Ragaric, a Guardian of Gold and a hero, his long-protected identity now revealed for all to see.

Solomon stepped over his body, not even looking down as he kicked the throwing star that had first won the keeper his freedom across the floor. Without even a pause in his step, he advanced toward Arianna, the keeper's blood leaving tracks behind him.

Arianna didn't feel afraid, only rage as she watched him get closer—the poison inside of her washed away in an intense rush of adrenaline, a tingle spreading all throughout her body. She knew that Aridyn Lareigh had now been completely expunged from her body, and there would be no way to bring her back from the dead.

LIES WILL DIE

LIKE A FOG HAD LIFTED, Arianna could finally see clearly again. All the anger, regret, pain, and sadness she had suppressed as Aridyn was felt doubly now as she stared back at Liam Black and Keeper Kassime in pools of their own blood—Solomon's swords were drenched in red.

"I trusted you!"

The voice that came out of her now shocked even her, making Solomon pause in his steps.

Her power burst out from her in that moment and exploded across the room

Everyone still in the gallery was blown off their feet, and Solomon fell to his hands and knees in the keeper's blood. And just as suddenly, the fires in the chandeliers, the candles, and fireplaces, all across the room, began to burn brighter—their flames wild and uncontrollable.

The regulators on both sides had no idea what had just

happened, fear in their eyes, and any citizens still left to witness it ran screaming. In all the commotion, the candles were knocked to the floor. And the chandeliers fell from the ceiling because of what seemed to be a sudden earthquake—the room went up in flames.

"Run!" cried Cyn, urging Lessa forward.

Master Tayshin still held Arianna in his arms, racing ahead and leaving the gallery behind.

"Sano…" said Lessa, just barely between breaths.

"We *can't* leave without the avatars," said Demetrius, speaking for her—he was holding on to the wall and Jeom for support.

They found themselves in the dreaded corridor of mirrors, and Arianna saw the reflection of the silver magic in her eyes fade.

Master Tayshin set her down on her feet; he and Cyn couldn't help but stay transfixed on the four as the contorting magic finished working its way over their bodies, fully revealing their true forms—Jeom shot up two feet taller, and Demetrius shrank down beside him, his pale skin tinting to a golden brown. Lessa's hair suddenly bleached back to blond, and finally the true warrior physique was present again in Arianna.

"I'm not leaving without Solza either," she said, collecting herself. She turned to Cyn. "Do you think you can get my friends to safety? I just need Master Tayshin for this."

She glanced to him and he nodded his support.

"Are you sure, Ara?" said Jeom. "I can come with you." He tried to push himself off the wall.

"I'm sure," she said. "Trust me. I just need to get to Solza." She was running on mere slivers of drive herself, but the promise of her energy-boosting avatar kept her upright.

"Just tell me where to go," said Cyn, her lips shaking—she was seconds away from falling apart. "And I'm so sorry. I should've been truthful to you about Solomon."

She touched her cheek, gently, gazing at her in awe.

"He's general of the Warrior's District now." She stifled a

sob. "I don't know how or why, but he's changed. Gone to us… truly *dead*."

"We can't think of that now," said Arianna, putting her emotions under lock and key as the keeper's real face flooded her mind. "We must think of the Guardians of Gold."

Cyn nodded, as serious as she'd ever been, and Arianna knew she had vowed to these same duties; she finally remembered the magic.

"I was late coming back this evening, so my carriage is probably still readied in the back of the palace," said Arianna. "Get there as fast as you can. I'll meet you soon."

Then she hiked up her dress and led Master Tayshin around the corner.

Smoke was beginning to spread throughout the halls, racing after them as they ran.

"It was really you who trained Solomon? You were his master?" called Arianna through heavy breaths—her rage was the only thing keeping her going.

"Yes," said Master Tayshin, matching her pace. "I kept a close watch on him during my time in the Warrior's District. I wasn't his trainer in those days, but I knew that he was special, even then."

Arianna saw a haunted expression sweep over his eyes in her peripheral vision.

"I requested him as apprentice for advanced training *after* he'd earned citizenship and proven himself in more ways than one. And I've been in South Luose ever since. I trained both boys in magic and sword."

"So you've known all along who I was, then?" Arianna couldn't help the accusation in her tone.

"I know everything," he said.

"If you know everything, then why didn't you stop this from happening?"

She picked up the pace, wishing to outrun her fury and grief.

They weren't far from her wing of the palace now.

"Solza," she called, coughing through the smoke. "Find me if you can!"

The deep roar of her avatar sounded from down the hall. Moments later, she burst through the smoke, her eyes alive and bright with magic.

"Ferlon trained you well," murmured Master Tayshin.

Solza leaped toward Arianna.

"We're all right," she said, instantly feeling strengthened at her presence. "Stay close."

They rounded the corner to their section of the palace, and Arianna kicked in the door to Lessa's room.

"Sano should be here somewhere," she said, before calling to him.

"Make it quick," said Master Tayshin, unsheathing his sword.

The bright, airy décor of Lessa's room almost made it seem as if the palace wasn't burning down around them.

"She kept a couple of rucksacks in here too, just in case something ever happened." Arianna searched around frantically for the packs and the avatar. "She insisted we add to them little by little for months. But it's been a long time since—" She threw open a cabinet door. "Aha!"

She tossed Master Tayshin one of the packs and slung the other over her shoulder, Lessa's potion bottles tinkling. Then she glanced around the room for anything else they might need.

"Sano!" she shrieked as he practically fell into her arms; he'd been hiding in the canopy of the bed. "Thank the gods." She gently set him down on Solza's back. "You two need to take care of each other now. Go and find Lessa."

Solza nudged Arianna with affection and then ran off into the smoke, more obedient than ever before.

"Come on, we need to get out of here," said Master Tayshin, tugging at her. "This place is going down."

"Take these," she said, handing him Lessa's treasured

longbow and the other rucksack. "Get to the carriage. Make sure the avatars and everyone are safe, and I'll meet you out back. I've got to do one more thing first. It's *important*."

"I'm not leaving you," he said. "You won't make it."

"And I'm not leaving without my swords," said Arianna, firmly. "Don't worry, I'll be fine. I won't be long."

The smoke was starting to seep in from every angle.

Master Tayshin nodded. "If you're not outside in ten minutes, we can't wait for you."

"I understand," she said, straightening her back.

With one last look at his apprentice, he left.

As soon as he had gone, Arianna covered her mouth and went back into the hall, ducking into her own room where she thought she'd left her swords.

"Damn!" She realized they were still in the attic after her last dueling session with Jeom—and in the moments she was deliberating whether or not to risk it, she spotted her attendant lying on the floor near the desk in her room.

Arianna ran to her to check her breathing, but she was gone, the beautiful emerald around her neck now stained crimson from her own blood.

"*Solomon,*" she said in disgust. There was no doubt in her mind that she'd died by his hand.

As Arianna closed her attendant's eyes, paying her a moment of respect, she noticed something sticking out of her closed fist. She plucked the paper from her grip and scanned the words.

To Miss Aridyn, Love Lily.

Arianna desperately fought away the tears that instantly welled; in an entire year, she'd never been privy to her attendant's name because of their segregating stations. She then saw on her desk, near to where Lily had fallen, a minuscule snowflower incased in a small, glass ball.

She pocketed the precious gift.

"Damn you, Solomon!" she growled, fists balled at her sides.

I need my swords.

Turning back toward the door, she caught a glimpse of herself in the mirror, still fully dressed in her Gathering Ball gown—she tore it off and ripped the jewels from her neck.

The beautiful fabric fell to the floor in a pile at her feet, gemstones sprinkling the ground; soon, everything in this room would burn to ash, forever forgotten as flames swallowed it whole. Material things had no weight in this world, only people did— and she learned that lesson fully with Solomon's harsh help.

They mean nothing!

Everything around her meant nothing, changed *nothing* about this cruel world and the terrible people in it.

In haste, she tied up her curls, pulled on leather pants and a plain shirt, and yanked Solomon's elder cloak from the wardrobe. She turned it inside out and threw it around her shoulders, the warrior red interior now proudly displayed. Then she slid on her old black boots, feeling like herself again.

After saying a final goodbye to that exquisite room and her noble life, and to her attendant, Lily, Arianna ran through the halls until she came upon the entrance to the dungeons; the guards stationed here had already fled, so she called to her magic.

"*Operium undrio!*" The heavy door flew open, and she stepped through.

Darkness engulfed her at first, but not for long with her powers now buzzing at the surface. "*Solza ven immito.*"

Candles flickered into life across the ceiling, lighting her way as if it were just any other day. And as the firelight began to blaze, she heard the eerie moans of those locked in their prison cells awaken along with it.

Everyone will burn alive down here, she thought before racing up toward the secret door to the attic.

The stars shone brilliantly tonight. But through the windows, Arianna spotted the west wing of the palace—Keeper Kassime's wing—already completely engulfed in flames, lighting up the night and sending smoke billowing into the air.

The remnants of the decorations from the Gathering Ball rose high into the sky, singeing to ash as they came to settle back on the earth; Arianna had only minutes before those flames would probably reach her as well.

Her stomach twisted in knots.

There was so much she had yet to learn, so much invaluable information here that would undoubtedly be destroyed. But she couldn't save it all now, so instead she raced to the library and gathered what she deemed the essentials—*Olleb-Yelfra the Fallen*, the scroll detailing dragons and avatars, and a small stack of spell scripts she and Lessa had been practicing with most recently.

She shoved everything unceremoniously into the pockets of her cloak, took one last look at the portrait of the young guardians, and then headed to the sparring room.

There, she strapped on her sheath and collected her twin swords along with Demetrius' staff.

"I think that's everything," she muttered to herself as she sheathed her swords. "Time to go."

"Not so fast." The voice made Arianna lose all sense.

Solomon slunk out of a corner shrouded in shadows, his black robes helping him blend in effortlessly.

"How did you find this place?"

Her instincts urged her to surrender and run to him for safety, and it was like living out one of her nightmares. Everything she had ever thought good about Solomon had been a dream—vanished in a rude, horrendous awakening.

Solomon scowled, circling her like the wolf he was.

"You've no idea, do you?" he growled. "I tried to teach you. I tried to *show* you, but you're so thickheaded, only ever thinking of yourself. This is so much greater than you!"

For every step he moved closer, she took a step back.

"I spent a lifetime here, girl." He opened his arms wide. "I've read nearly every scroll in the library and I helped build up this tower. It's protected by a spell that *I* cast years ago!"

He jabbed a finger at his chest, clearly maddened at the sight of her.

"You've no idea," he said. "You have absolutely *no* idea what I've sacrificed for you."

"I know that you just killed your best friend," said Arianna, stepping forward. "Kassime loved you like a brother! We came to him because of you, and this is how you repay him? You're not any master of mine."

The words seemed to make a minuscule dent in his hardened exterior, but it quickly vanished in a bellow of laughter.

His smile pained her, like a blade to the chest, and it was set in a scene so unnerving and unnatural—to have her beloved friend mock her so.

"I'll always be, now and forever, your master," said Solomon. "I made you who you are, and I protected that investment with my life. You're forever my creation."

With just the wave of his hand, Arianna was forced to her knees by his magic; she fought against it with everything she had, but she was weighted down, as if an invisible stone had suddenly been strapped to her back.

"No! You're a murderer," she screamed, kicking to try to free herself. "You killed Liam. You killed Kassime and Lily, and I'll make sure you repay them with your life!"

It wasn't until the words flew from her mouth that she realized how much she meant them. *Never forget!*

Her magic fell back into her control, and she got to her feet— a year of guardian training well spent.

"I wish you had stayed dead," she whispered.

A sob escaped her then, and she lunged for him with Demetrius' staff; Solomon sidestepped the attack, and his magic sent her skidding on her back toward the door.

She looked up at him one last time, tears flooding her eyes. Then she ran out of the sparring room and through the pentagon chamber to the attic exit. Taking the stairs two at a time, she fled as fast as she could, knowing very well that she couldn't win a fight against Solomon Bell…

Not today.

"Arianna!" His booming voice chased after her.

And in its echoes, she thought she heard him whispering another spell of attack; she quickly chanted one of her own.

"*Operium undrio!*" Eyes closed and hands outstretched, focusing as hard as she could, Arianna guided her magic out through the dungeons. She heard the clicks of the cells unlocking, ringing out through the tunnels.

"That should hold you off for now," she said, watching the hectic scene unfold; hundreds of prisoners—the ones still alive—burst from their cages and funneled out into the tunnels alongside her in search of a way out.

She kept running, though moving at a much slower pace for how much the magic had drained her.

The smoke from the fires had begun to fill the Luose Dungeon. She choked, eyes burning as she felt her way back toward the exit, the ceiling candles now dimmed in a heavy fog.

"Help me. I can't move," came a feeble voice as she nearly reached the way out—many people called for help just the same, but this voice sounded familiar.

"Who's there?" she said, pushing through the throngs of dungeon dwellers who didn't even seem to notice her as they crawled in all directions.

"Over here," the voice called again. "Please, help me."

There isn't time!

"Where are you?"

She struggled with leaving the prisoner to die, but her conscience got the best of her—she already had too many deaths weighing on her heart tonight.

She waved her hand across her face and her magic swept away the smoke before her eyes. And what she saw made her momentarily forget the fear of being caught by her vengeful master—to her horror and relief, a bloodied, beaten, deathly thin version of Elijah Neve appeared before her eyes, crumpled in a corner of one of the cells.

"Eli! That can't be you," she said with a gasp, her hand flying to cover her mouth. "We all thought you were dead."

He no longer answered, barely alive as it was.

"*Levantis bora*," she said without a thought, and she cried out from the energy it took to use yet another spell.

The levitation charm she'd long since mastered lifted Eli's body above the stampeding prisoners and up above her head. No one noticed anything amiss over all the smoke and commotion. And Demetrius' staff did its part in helping her push through to the exit.

Arianna climbed out through the dungeon door for the last time.

ON THE OTHER SIDE OF THE DOOR, Arianna realized that the dungeon vault had actually held out pretty well against the fires— it was so much worse above ground. She thought she might faint from breathing through the weight of the smoke, coupled with the strain of exerting what felt like life-sucking magic. She fell to her hands and knees to try to find breathable air and crawled toward what she hoped was freedom.

And just as she thought she might black out, blindly moving through the palace as it crumbled down around her, she reached the door to the outside. Master Tayshin was there, bending down to help her to her feet.

"I told you ten minutes!" he said, dragging her through.

She felt the burden of her magic suddenly ease as he surprised her with his own, helping to get Eli safely outside. With a nod of his head, the door to the palace slammed shut, the smoke trapped inside.

"The carriage is ready," he said. "We have to hurry. What were you thinking? I almost had to leave you!"

He slid his arm around her waist to help her walk.

"You have magic too?" she said, hardly able to think.

"Naturally," he snapped. "How else could I handle training you?" He sighed, flashing a faint smile.

Arianna didn't have the strength to reply as another surprise awaited her—Tobias was among her friends, preparing her horses as if it were any other day, ready to help her into the carriage.

"You too?" she gasped.

"No magic, miss," he said. "But I've been driving Master Tay-shin's students around for years, keeping them on the right track. He was hard-pressed not to induct me into the guardians long ago. I found him as soon as Ferlon's memory spell was lifted. I remember everything now… but I feel like I've missed so much." He tipped his hat, solemnly. "Ferlon died with honor today, protecting our cause."

Arianna just bowed her head, thinking that the way Solomon had slaughtered him was anything but honorable. The only thing of relief she felt in this moment was seeing Jeom and Lessa safe and sound in the carriage, the avatars and their rucksacks there too.

Everyone helped to pull Eli inside, laying him carefully across the spacious floor; Lessa began tending to his wounds, tears streaking her cheeks all the while as Cyn tried to impart some final words of advice to her, from one healer to the next.

Arianna also saw that Phantom was harnessed and waiting, leading the other horses as usual. But instead of Tobias, it was Demetrius sitting in the driver's seat, holding the reins tightly at the ready, prepared to leave at a moment's notice.

"I think it's time we're off," he said.

Arianna gave a curt nod, glancing back to the palace, afraid Solomon may have followed—instead, something else maybe just as awful caught her eye.

"You!" she yelled, ducking out of Master Tayshin's grasp.

"Pippa?" said Godfrey, stumbling backward as she grabbed him by the hood of his cloak; he had been slowly dragging a bag of what appeared to be jewels and gold from the palace, too much for him to carry alone and make a quick getaway.

"So good to see you're well…" His voice shook as he tried to wriggle out of her grasp.

"You poisoned us!" Arianna only saw red—the red of Kassime's blood, of Liam's blood, of Lily's blood. "This is all your fault. All of it!"

"I did *no* such thing," he said, shaking his head, utterly baffled as he considered her. "I haven't seen your face in the better part of a year."

Arianna let go, realizing he didn't recognize her as Aridyn anymore, didn't even understand that she *was*, in fact, Arianna Belvedor.

Her breath came heavy. "We trusted you."

"Well, you seemed to have fared well enough… your head is still on, isn't it? Poor Mya, though. I only wanted her help in bringing you to the keeper. You *do* look an awful lot like that Belvedor slave, you know? And I was just doing my civic duty by turning you in—"

He inched farther away, still holding tight to his bag of jewels. He was clearly trying to talk his way out of the situation, but every word he spoke only made her angrier.

"But then I heard it was a false claim." He shrugged. "Pity for my reputation, but I still got paid." He glanced over her shoulder, not sure what to make of all the other people standing there, watching. "Listen… if you give me a hand with all of this, I'll be sure to make it worth your while. I can pay you back for all that trouble. Bygones be bygones, eh?"

He grinned at her, showing off those broken teeth.

"Ara, *please*, just let it go," she heard Lessa call.

But she chose to ignore her.

"Sometimes I go by the name of Pippa," she said, coolly. "But I also go by the name of *Aridyn*."

"Aridyn is—"

"Dead," she said. "Thanks to you!"

"But… I don't understand," he said, his brow furrowed.

"And you never will."

She knew Godfrey wasn't worthy enough to have even an inkling of their enchanted world—not even Ophelia had let him in on the truth, just using him for her dirty work.

Arianna kicked him square in his chest so that he flew off his feet, slamming to the ground and spilling his blood money.

He cried out, rolling onto his side.

"My real name is Arianna Belvedor."

The silver glow of her glare gleamed back at her from the jewels and coin scattered on the grass as she straddled him. Then she jammed her dagger straight into his stomach.

She didn't even wait for the light to leave his eyes as she walked away, leaving Godfrey to pay for what he'd done. Alas, finally taking her revenge on him didn't relieve her in the way she'd always imagined it might—in fact, it felt quite the opposite, the knot in her stomach twisting even tighter.

"Thanks for your assistance," she mumbled, taking the sack of gold back to the carriage—they'd need all the help they could get wherever they ended up next.

Her friends peered down at her with sad eyes, but she couldn't find the words to say. Jeom extended a hand and pulled her up. Then, they all looked back to the elders.

"Aren't you all coming?" said Arianna, shifting to see how they could make room.

Cyn just shook her head, such worry in her eyes. "We wish we could, dear."

"But there's work to be done," said Tobias. "We've been without our memories for far too long. There are others to gather."

He pulled something from his robes, handing it to Demetrius. "Take good care of those horses, and they'll take care of you," he said. "And that's got a sprinkle of luck on it, too, so don't lose it!" He pointed to what Arianna now saw was an old compass. "Trust me. It'll *always* get you to where you need to go." He winked, stepping back.

Demetrius thanked him again, clasping the gift.

"You better get going now," said Master Tayshin, pulling off his gloves and outstretching his bare palm to Arianna. "Once those fires are under control the regulators will be combing these streets for the people to blame. We'll see you again soon."

Arianna sucked in her breath through her teeth as she recognized the golden dragon tattoo shimmering on his wrinkled skin; she grasped his hand, shaking it firmly.

"Soon," she said, unable to hold back the tears any longer. "Thank you, Master Tayshin. Good luck to you all."

Cyn and Tobias both gave her a quick hug, and then they waved goodbye—Arianna noticed their own dragon markings shining on their palms, too, only visible to those who held the truest bonds of trust, faithful Guardians of Gold.

Demetrius whipped the reins and they were off, fleeing yet again into the unknown.

Arianna peered out of the carriage window as flames consumed the Palace of South Luose in their wake, illuminating the night while the entire city watched in shock from a safe distance; nobody noticed them at all. As for the palace, there was only one tower not aflame and still standing tall.

The dazzling, stained-glass windows of their beloved attic sanctuary caught the moonlight. And Arianna was certain she saw a shadow move from inside, someone watching them ride away just as she'd seen Sir Vladamor do not so long ago.

Darkness swarmed their enchanted attic now with Solomon's presence, but she vowed in her heart to one day reclaim it. He'd sacrificed such rights to stand there in his fall from grace, and she would wholeheartedly fulfill the duties he'd forsaken. Just as she'd promised to Keeper Kassime, Arianna was prepared now to give her life, if she had to, in order to defend the truth as a Guardian of Gold.

28

NORTH LUOSE

THE SOUND OF HOOVES CLACKING against the ground, twigs snapping underfoot, reminded Arianna so much of bones breaking. The sounds of death were lodged in her mind forever now, repeating on a loop.

Liam is dead.

Her eyes stayed peeled to the silver trees of the forest, their dark red leaves hanging low overhead. For days, she and her friends sat in silence, only speaking out of necessity as the carriage rattled forward toward yet another unknown destiny.

Arianna wondered if her voice even still worked, but she didn't care to try.

Keeper Kassime is dead. And Solomon killed him.

The shock of it all penetrated her deeply, her eyes glued to the shining barks and blood-colored canopies all the while. Sometimes, when sleep eluded her, the monotonous forest background would morph into the final battle scene between Keeper Kassime and Master Bell. Her imagination recreated it in slow motion, as if she watched a well-practiced play.

When Solomon's bronzed blades took the final strike at Keeper Kassime, his dark blood had splattered the splendid metal in such a way that she would never forget.

Solomon lives… but he's not anyone that I know.

As the days wore on, the lines of time blurring, there was nothing to pull her mind from this abyss where her friends had died and the person that she'd always looked up to most had murdered them.

Instead of going back in the direction of the Blancoren Mountains, they had plowed through the wild forest terrain, headed in the opposite direction through an endless expanse of trees.

But Arianna found it hard to tell what course they were really on. She wouldn't have been surprised if they finally escaped the trees just to find the mountains again laughing down at them, the Jar beckoning them home.

Demetrius and Jeom kept to steering the horses, whispering between themselves for the entire journey through the Nicora Forest with only the compass to guide them. And Lessa managed to sleep for the majority of the time, a peaceful dreamland finding her at will. She was curled up with Sano by her side, and not even the consistent bumps or the loud forest hum could wake her from her slumber.

Arianna, on the other hand, lost herself to the scenery outside—unwilling to shut her eyes for fear of her own darkened dreams. Sometimes, the beauty of it all was captivating enough to give her mind a moment's peace from the terror of her memories. But only swift moments they were.

Solza laid at her feet, her calming effect barely noticeable now. And Arianna idly gathered that without her avatar's powers, she might've truly gone mad with rage.

At times, her attention would also flicker to their unlikely travel companion, Eli, who now sat across from her. He hadn't spoken a *single* word since Arianna had rescued him from the dungeons. And with nowhere else to look, their eyes would occasionally meet in the confines of the carriage.

In just one glance, Arianna was reminded that everything had changed for him as well. Long gone was the young lad from the tavern—confident and charismatic—who with one smile would have had Arianna blushing; she had no idea who this man was.

When Lessa wasn't sleeping, she consumed her time by tending to him. And Eli let her do so without hesitance, truly void of any emotion. Lessa believed him to be in some sort of disoriented shock, never even moving his lips to form a sentence; she gave him medicines to heal, to sleep, and for extra nourishment. But none of that could ever mend the damage done to his soul after a year spent in darkness and solitude.

"He just needs more time," said Lessa to no one in particular. "We all do."

She did the best she could as an apprentice healer, but the clever and composed Lessa had also yet to return, her hands shaking every time she worked over his wounds—South Luose had broken her, just as it had broken them all. And the damage was too extensive to heal as of yet.

Arianna said nothing, gazing back out of the window, letting her thoughts drift far, far away. *I don't want to heal.*

She could only focus on her losses, and it would take an army to rattle her back to normal now.

'*Every ending births a new beginning,*' Solomon used to say. But his words meant nothing.

What she'd gained in strength, in magic, and in wisdom seemed to have stayed behind in South Louse, burning down in flames because of him.

Though she was a stronger warrior and on her way to being a capable guardian, right now it didn't seem so. All the magic, all of the good in her, had been sucked away in full force when

Solomon had wielded his swords against her.

She couldn't wrap her head around the mess that had become her life. They had just barely begun to feel comfortable and safe under the keeper's watch, and now all they'd built together had gone up in the same smoke that had overcome the palace. And a list of betrayals and lost lives piled up behind them.

Eli flinched as the cracking sound of leather being whipped against the horses' hides struck the air, drawing Arianna out of yet another spiral. She tried—in vain—to put her focus on anything other than the past.

After a week of traveling, they still hadn't reached the end of the Nicora Forest. Talk of food, water, rest, and directions was all anyone could spare as far as communication went, their own personal thoughts controlling each one of them. And as the carriage bounced along the hilly land, Arianna continued to watch the trees pass her by in threads of silver, wondering where they might lead.

From the first day she'd set foot in the forest to this moment a year later, it seemed as if everything had stayed entirely the same—all except for her.

She felt like she'd been transported back through time to the day they'd first laid eyes on the Nicora Forest. She remembered the way it had barred their escape from Draminet.

Now, as if the clock had rewound, they found themselves right back where they had started.

Within the blink of an eye, the year spent in South Luose was wiped away without mercy, and their journey through the forest and across the Olleb had been instantly renewed. Before, the days had seemed to drag by blissfully. But looking back now, she felt as if in a shimmer those days were gone.

In the beginning, as Aridyn, Arianna used to muse at what lay beyond the city walls or where she and her friends might've ended up had they taken a different path that day they'd fled Draminet. And now, as the carriage pressed on through the woodlands, too soon they would find out.

They weaved through the colossal trees for days on end, fended off wild animals who might scare the horses, and stopped only to gather water or sustenance when they could—never looking back for fear the new Solomon Bell, General of the Warrior's District, would not be far behind.

The farther they got from South Luose, the colder the nights seemed to grow, despite them moving away from the forever-frozen Blancoren Mountains.

Nothing could ever be as cold as those nights.

Arianna had taken her warm bed in the palace for granted, and now she was right back to relying on a tattered district cloak for warmth.

Solomon's cloak…

Still, it gave her comfort.

On the fourteenth day, they reached what seemed to be an impasse. Arianna jolted forward with the sudden stop of the carriage, her eyes snapping open from an inevitable yet restless sleep.

"You have to see this!" yelled Demetrius from up front.

She heard his feet hit the ground as he jumped down from the driver's seat, and then the three of them hopped out of the carriage.

THE FOREST SUDDENLY DISSIPATED before their eyes; the trees became sparser, the silver bark now a pale, broken white. And their leaves littered the ground, sucked of any life. The lush vegetation and grassy hills had also quite drastically disappeared, opening up to a flat wasteland all at once.

The fresh forest air became stifled and rough, and the only sign of life was the birds flying clear overhead.

"Why would they lead us this way?" said Jeom. "That compass must not be working properly."

"I trust Tobias," said Demetrius, though he seemed a bit uncertain. "He said this would get us to where we're going, and I'm sure it's been imprinted with *magic.*"

He spoke the last word under his breath, for they had a nonbeliever in their midst. But, looking at where they'd ended up, Arianna wasn't sure she even believed it.

From here, as far as their eyes could see, the land was scorched to blackness. Scattered skeletons of trees and the bones of a fallen city stretched out before them, burned to nothingness by what Arianna thought could've only been the sun falling from the sky.

"What happened here?" She hadn't used her voice in a while, so it croaked out loudly, carrying across the wind.

She kicked at a rotting sign that appeared to be newer than the rest of the decay yet still barely legible. She bent closer to read the letters and deciphered the word 'Luose.'

"Welcome to North Luose," said Eli.

Everyone grew silent as he slowly got out of the carriage. He walked to the edge of the wasteland.

"It's said that a terrible storm happened here," he muttered, seemingly lost in thought, "drenching the area in fire. At some point in time, long ago, Luose leaders had occupied this part of the Nicora Forest too. But after those fires, nothing could ever grow here again."

The words hung in the dead air, the first he'd spoken at all since Arianna discovered him nearly departed.

"It's just like in the Agrarian's District," said Demetrius. "Just the same as the Dead Lands."

He pinched the ground and wrinkled his nose.

"There's no life here. Nothing but rotting earth."

He nudged a dried-up bush with his foot, black to the core, and its branches crumbled to the ground.

"I wonder..." said Lessa, inspecting the surroundings.

She began to walk farther out, the corroded foundations of a city looming over her.

"So this is really North Luose?"

Everyone looked to Eli, but he didn't elaborate, wandering off on his own in the opposite direction.

What before had been a maze of lush forest growth had just as suddenly gone completely barren; Arianna turned back, the healthy, shimmering trees beckoning her to return toward their haven. Not so long ago, she had feared that journey—distrusted something so foreign to her.

Now, as she stared at what lay ahead, at the nothingness her future offered, she wished for the naivety of her youth. But there was no going back now, so she tore her eyes away from the trees and planted them on the dark lands before her. *I'm still here. We're still alive.*

That was the only optimism she afforded herself as she started walking forward, the twigs breaking underfoot; it sounded just like the crack of brittle bones, echoing into the silent evening.

"What was in North Luose?" asked Demetrius as they all explored together.

"I read about it in the library," said Lessa. "In the world as we know it, there's always been a North and South Luose, the North being uninhabitable, as Eli mentioned."

She walked through what looked to be a former doorway, standing now as a lone structure.

"But in the Golden Age," she said, a strange gleam settling in her eyes, "this land was known as the City of Crissy."

"*Crissy?*" gasped Jeom, suddenly attentive. "You don't mean like the—"

"Three-Headed Dragon of Crissy," whispered Lessa, nodding. "That I do."

Jeom rubbed the concealed axe at his belt (thankfully he'd been in the habit of always carrying it around with him when they'd fled); the soul of the Crissy dragon flowed through it.

"You mean to say—" Arianna glanced over her shoulder to make sure Eli wasn't in earshot. "You think an actual *dragon* did this?"

"The very same one we learned about from the scrolls," said Lessa. "I'd stake my life on it."

Arianna was so glad she'd thought to save that parchment from the attic.

There was a moment of silence as everyone took in the scene with a new mindset, the value of knowledge again more than solidified; this city hadn't been torched by just *any* flame. The flames of a dragon did this—a warrior of the sky brandishing the weapon of fire.

Arianna twisted her palm up so that the shimmer of the dragon flashed before her eyes, her faint tribute to the guardians. Then she balled her hand into a fist.

"So what exactly happened after the Crissy Wars then?" said Jeom to Lessa. "Do you know?"

He appeared desperate to reconnect with his magical past, since their door to the Golden Age had been so abruptly shut.

"Crissy used to be a thriving city, much like South Luose," said Lessa, keeping her voice low. "Its foundation was built all across the edges of this forest."

She waved her arm out behind them.

"Like we learned from the scroll, the three-headed dragon was formerly a dweller of this very woodland, a creature that is an innate protector of the Olleb..." Lessa continued to wander around as she talked, the others following at her heels. "But I read further in the library of the wars," she said. "The queen of Crissy had sent armies to try and overtake the Nicora Elven Clan, who once inhabited the trees here in the Golden Age."

"Another human coveting magic outside of their reach," said Arianna. "How astonishing."

"But *far* before Devlindor's time and quite unsuccessful," said Lessa. "Wars broke out between the two, but the northern part of the forest was damaged in the process, aggravating the dragon. She set the entire city aflame in revenge. And for this, she was named after Crissy. South Luose, then just known as 'Luose,' claimed the scorched territory, dividing it up into the 'North' and the 'South.' But the land suffered irreversible damage, as you can see, and was quickly abandoned anyway."

A heavy silence returned as Eli's version of the story was overtaken by magic.

"I think I'll keep walking a bit," said Arianna, going to explore alone.

Demetrius jogged back to the carriage and began guiding the horses at a slower pace. Everyone else continued on foot.

Eli walked next to Phantom, separate from the group, never once taking his hand off the horse; he had quickly reunited with his beloved animal and glanced at Arianna only once to suggest his thanks for rescuing him.

She didn't mind his silence—he saved whispers only for Phantom as they walked across the deserted lands.

With each sinking step, Arianna wondered about the extinct dragon species. Creatures with the capability to literally wipe an entire city off the map had vanished from the earth. And although she would like nothing more than to have another reason to hate the King, her imagination wasn't wild enough to credit him for such a horror.

No one could be that powerful.

She wished she'd thought to ask Keeper Kassime more about dragons in all their moments together, but she had never imagined their time would end so soon…

Arianna pondered any other explanation for their disappearance as she looked around the wasteland; it just didn't seem possible that *anything* in this world could defeat such a mighty creature, let alone completely erase the species from existence.

No matter what had happened here in the Golden Age, deserved or not, the ashes of Crissy brought to mind the forgotten dwarf city, now just a vacant memory of what was once probably a beloved home. Arianna mourned the innocent people who had surely lost their lives in those wars because of another selfish ruler who had coveted too much power. Only here, there were no bones left to bury.

29

THE BLACK SAND SEA

SOON, THE SUN DISAPPEARED beneath the earth, and the ground suddenly blended with the night in a sea of blackness, sparkling and twinkling as far as the eye could see. A blanket of milky stars created a backdrop that started from the ground and rose up toward the sky, as if they leaned against a tapestry stitched with firebugs.

The barren land disappeared into nothingness as the universe opened up to them, welcoming them into its arms.

"The end of the earth," breathed Arianna, reaching her hand out as if to actually grasp a star.

"It's incredible," said Demetrius, scooping up some of the black earth in his hand, studying the grains. It flowed through his fingers in a soft, tinkling rain back to the ground.

Arianna touched it as well. "This dirt is strange."

"It's not dirt, it's sand," said Jeom. "We've found ourselves a desert here."

Demetrius nodded in affirmation. "Where did you learn about deserts?" he said with a soft smile.

"From Master Gansevurt. He focused much of my training on different terrains around the Olleb. Not all land is equal, and building, especially large structures, is all about the foundation."

He scooped some sand up too, and Arianna almost couldn't tell he was holding anything for how well it blended in with his skin; if not for the sparkles the sand gave off when the light hit it just right, she might not have recognized he held anything at all. It appeared as if for every ten grains, there was a minute diamond sprinkled within.

Lessa was fixated on the desert as well. Removing her orange boots, she let the grains squish beneath her toes and giggled at the sensation. As she did, Arianna noticed the small, silver scar on her ankle left by Sano from when he had healed her in the Vanishing Tunnels.

That time seems so far away now.

She gazed back and forth between the trees and the desert, wondering which option might return them to a new type of freedom.

"This is the Black Sand Desert," said Eli, his words barely audible as he got used to his voice again. "The Nicora Forest ends here, on the outskirts of North Luose."

Arianna looked him over, saddened every time she laid eyes on him. But how to console someone who had been tortured for so long?

She didn't have any reassurance left to give.

At least the color had finally returned to his skin, and his scars had all but healed to reveal again the remarkable tattoos that snaked up his arms and hid beneath his shirt; he didn't even realize the magic Lessa worked over his body. If not for the haunted look painted over his eyes, she might've thought him just a tired drifter, as he'd declared himself long ago.

It was easy to imagine Eli having been in another city for the entire year—a traveler off seeing the world, as was his dream. But no, he'd been trapped for countless days in the Luose Dungeon, and Arianna knew there could be nothing worse than drowning in such a darkness.

The only optimism she could draw from the situation was in that Lessa's healer touch had grown exponentially for him to make such a full recovery—Arianna tried to take solace that they'd saved at least one life on that horrible day.

His presence, though, was a constant reminder of Liam's absence. She had been *so* close to revealing their world to him; he'd just slipped right through her fingers.

Now they had Eli to worry about, to tiptoe around whenever they talked of a magical world or used their powers. He had been unconscious for days after they fled the palace, remembering nothing of their magic. It was a stressful addition at a time like this, and they tried their best to think of a good way to explain.

They knew by now that 'magic' wasn't a topic to just spring on someone without warning. And Eli was still adjusting to even being a part of the world again, while at the same time assimilating to their lifestyle as outlaws.

Arianna was sure he already must feel like the impossible had happened, but he was in for a rude awakening if he stuck with them for long.

"Well, let's get going, then," she said. "We need to get as far away as possible from this place."

"It's not the forest, Ara," said Demetrius. "If we get lost out there—"

"There's no way to survive," said Eli, no feeling in his voice.

"That's what they said about the Vanishing Tunnels," said Arianna, defiantly. "And look how well we fared then."

She noticed Eli perked up at her statement—he had yet to question them about their pasts.

Jeom cracked a smile, the first time he'd done so in days. "I'd say that was due to all kinds of luck."

"Well, what are our options?" she said with a sigh. "We need to get to another city so we can figure out a new cover or at least restock on supplies. We can't just pose as drifters and expect to keep that up empty-handed. Not with Solomon in pursuit. We hardly have enough food to last us as it is."

"If we cross the desert, it's a straight, uninterrupted shot to the City of Zambienth. We could restock there?" said Eli. "It's just a few days' journey. I was training for it before…"

He lowered his head, falling silent again.

"I think we'd have enough supplies for that," said Demetrius, giving Eli a reassuring squeeze on the shoulder.

"Only if we have a clear path," said Lessa. "We have enough to last us a week at best. That doesn't leave much room for a mistake."

She rested her hands on her hips, looking to the sky as she thought.

"Why don't we just go around?" suggested Jeom, looking back in the direction they'd come.

Lessa chewed on her lip, wrestling with the idea. "We might lose a few days, but it'd certainly be the safer option."

Eli took a deep breath, as if gathering up the will to address them.

"If we go back through the forest, we'll definitely be wasting time," he said, wrapping his arms across his body. "And in my experience, that's what the regulators are going to be expecting of you. They're trained trackers, and they can easily follow a three-horse carriage through a forest terrain."

He ran his fingers through his tangled hair, eyes nervously shifting back and forth.

"I wouldn't be surprised if they weren't far behind already. And I'm sure the King, or Solomon Bell, or *whoever* is after you now, will have regulators posted at all three of the cities on the edge of Nicora." He pointed ahead to what he claimed lay across the sand. "They won't expect you to go through the desert, though. And it's much less kind for leaving footprints to follow."

"Tobias told me to follow his lead," said Demetrius, holding up his compass. "He couldn't have been more clear, and I think we should trust him on this. He's one of *us*."

Arianna knew by 'us' he meant 'a guardian,' though Eli was none the wiser.

"And the arrow on this thing has gotten us this far, hasn't it? We're out of the forest," said Demetrius. "If it's an option, I think we ought to keep going straight."

They all considered the compass, the natural light from the stars enough to aid their sight; Arianna was sure that Demetrius was right—some kind of magic had to lace the remarkable device to make it glisten like that. And its arrow pointed dead ahead across the sandy sea.

"Looks like we're going through the desert, then," said Jeom with a huff.

"We have to try," agreed Arianna, the guardian in her taking control.

"But wait! I almost forgot," said Lessa, pulling out a scroll from her bag. "Will this help to guide us?"

Arianna stared down at the map Solomon had given her, his final gift to her before she'd left him behind in the Jar.

"I didn't know you kept it," she whispered, touching the leathery paper.

"Of course I did," said Lessa. "It's been packed all along for safekeeping. I know how much it means to you."

Arianna nodded, not daring to speak for fear tears might come instead.

Nevertheless, she was happily surprised at the large collection of items they'd managed to bring along in just two rucksacks; there had been enough clothes for everyone to ditch their attire from the Gathering and remedies that might last them months if they stayed healthy. She suspected magic played a part in Lessa's packing techniques and would have to question her on it later, when Eli wasn't around to overhear.

He glanced at the map too, letting his finger carefully slide across it. "That's odd," he mumbled.

"What is?" said Lessa, studying the map.

He leaned in for a closer look.

"This map seems… inaccurate," he said. "I've never heard of many of these places, and I've studied maps long enough to know the basics by now. For example, there's definitely no City of Undor near or *under* the mountains, and where is Draminet on here? Look, even the Four Corners is unmarked!"

He let out a chuckle but quickly sucked it back in.

"Whoever gave you this fooled you out of your money," he said. "That's for certain."

Lessa gasped, quickly shifting the map away from Eli.

"This is a map from the Golden Age," she whispered so that only Arianna could hear, a dumbstruck expression on her face. "I can't believe I never noticed! I haven't spent much time with this scroll since we left the tunnels. I never realized…"

Sure enough, as Arianna gave it a little more attention, words she had not understood at the time of receiving it from Solomon now held incredible meaning; it mapped out the entire Olleb, labels marking ancient, forgotten cities like Undor. Even North Luose was captioned 'Crissy' in small letters, and Arianna assumed the map was from a time period following those defining wars.

She even spotted the City of Kampaulo, the one she'd claimed as Aridyn. It was located far off to the southwest. King Devlindor had kept its name, like many major provinces in the Olleb. But she now saw it to be a true former kingdom laid out on this map, and one of many, it seemed.

Scanning the bottom of the scroll, she admired the illustration of Saindora drawn out in gold. The great kingdom bordered what appeared to be water sitting at the very edge of the earth. And though she also recognized several other places from her

Golden Age studies, this map was peppered with many cities and landmarks that Arianna had absolutely no reference for—they obviously still had a long way to go to live up to their duties as guardians of such knowledge.

"See what I mean?" said Eli, interrupting her train of thought. Arianna jumped.

"Yeah, I do," she stuttered, the girls still trying to block his view. "But I see the desert here anyway. You're right. If we head straight, we should run smack into Zambienth."

She looked up from the map, meeting his eyes.

"And you're *sure* it's just a few days on foot?" The thought of such a risky adventure at a time like this was anything but comforting.

Eli nodded. "With horses? Positive," he said, patting Phantom on the head. "My trainer could walk it in a week. We're going to want to keep south. And with that compass, we should fare fine."

He regarded it with admiration in his eyes.

"That's a real treasure, you know."

"I know," said Demetrius, squeezing it tightly.

At the top section of the map, 'Black Sand Desert' had been scribbled in bold letters next to a depiction of trees signifying the Nicora Forest. Stretching over a long, narrow space of wavy lines, it bridged North Luose and the City of Zambienth, just as Eli had said.

It was certainly intimidating on paper and seemed to border many other cities as well. But if they stayed their course, Arianna trusted Eli's expert judgment that they could make it through without, hopefully, too much trouble.

"Is this really the only way?" said Jeom, gazing with uncertainty out to the desert.

"It's risky, but what's the alternative?" said Arianna, gently, rolling up the map and handing it back to Lessa.

She turned back for one last glimpse of the forest, the trees in the distance still calling to her.

"Eli's right… Solomon probably won't be too far off."

"But what of this Zambienth?" said Lessa. "What can we expect there?"

Eli just shrugged.

"I've not yet made it that far, but my trainer calls it the *Great City of Sand*, with the desert as its setting. I've heard it's a place stacked with pyramids to the sky."

Jeom lit up at the description. "Now that's something I'd like to see."

"We should travel at night when it's cool, use the stars as our guide," said Eli, a faint glimmer of life returning to his face. "Most who cross this desert won't have such priceless artifacts as a compass, so that's already a huge advantage for us."

He pointed to the sky, and they all looked up.

"And see, that's the South Star, the brightest one of its kind. Keep eyes on it. The closer it seems, the closer we are. A desert-walker's most faithful guide."

Arianna marveled at the South Star, its brilliant light seeming to jump out at her. Unquestionably, it outshone all the rest as a golden halo grew around it.

"I *should* warn you though," he said, suddenly solemn again. "Not many take on the risk of the desert, not without proper training or an expert escort, which I confess, I am not. It doesn't have the best reputation as history goes. I've heard strange stories…"

"What are you talking about?" said Demetrius. "What kind of stories?"

Jeom shifted nervously on his feet.

"Men led astray in the night, going mad or worse," said Eli with a sigh. "Some people just lose it out there, I guess."

"Sounds like a story I heard once, in the tunnels," said Arianna, remembering the ghosts of her past. Her eyes flicked between her friends. "They're probably just born from travelers who went mad from lack of food or water. Anything more is surely rumors."

"*Maybe*," said Eli, not seeming convinced. "But in any case, that won't be us. I won't let it."

Arianna started to see some of the real Eli seep in again through the cracks of his hardened skin.

"I'm willing to take the risk if you think you're ready for this," he said. "I owe you all that much, at the very least."

Again, an awkwardness lingered in the air, all surely reminded of being hauled away to the dungeons; Eli wasn't the only one who had experienced such a fright.

"There's no better group of people who could handle something like this," said Arianna, breaking the silence and settling the decision. "Trust me." With her friends by her side, she was sure they could accomplish anything.

And as everyone stated their agreement, the first smile in days crossed her lips. *Another adventure awaits.*

Eli bowed to her, slightly. "Thank you… for rescuing me. I won't let you down."

Arianna went rigid, her smile fleeing, feeling as if the ghost of Aridyn had suddenly reclaimed her body.

"All right," she said, softly, careful not to spook him back into silence. "But, *please*, don't bow at me again."

THEY DECIDED TO LEAVE within the hour and walk until sunrise, so there was much to do. Splitting up one last time, they each did their parts to prepare for the journey.

Eli and Jeom watered and fed the horses while Lessa carried Sano to a nearby stream and refilled their water containers. Demetrius rationed the food they had left for the coming days, and

Arianna wandered to the outskirts of the scorched forest, with Solza by her side, looking for any extra morsels she could find to aid their journey.

Eventually, she came upon a massive, wilting tree, its former silver bark cracked to the color of dry, white ash.

Sitting on the trunk of the tree, she felt an overwhelming sense of hopelessness wash over her. Nothing in these barren and lifeless parts prompted any courage, something she would most certainly need if she had any hope of crossing a desert with all her wits about her.

With her head in her hands, she wept, her body shuddering from the effort as her dark emotions came back into focus. Arianna held so much in these days, trying to keep everything together in front of her friends.

She was alone now though, and so her stone wall came toppling down.

For Liam, for her happy attendant, and for Keeper Kassime, she cried out into the night. She even shed tears for Cyn, Tobias, and Master Tayshin, all left behind to clean up their colossal mess.

Master Bell… Arianna wept for him too—a great friend lost to the fire and an enemy born from the ashes.

As Arianna let her emotions run wild with no chance of containing them, Solza placed her paws upon her knees, vying for her attention; she seemed so sad, too, and Arianna knew her loyal companion could sense everything she felt.

"I'm sorry, Solza," she said, wiping her eyes on the back of her sleeve. "I can't help it. It hurts so much. What a mess I've made again."

She looked to the sky, the South Star still in perfect view.

"Is there any hope at all?"

Solza gazed at her with an odd expression. Then she set her paws back on the ground, letting her nose softly touch the earth—her eyes glowed bright with magic.

Arianna jumped to her feet in surprise as sprouts of green shot out from the spot where her avatar was standing; they headed in a beeline for the tree in a glittering display. Life was drawn back into it, as if Solza had breathed magic right through the soil.

Blossoms of exquisite white flowers and some sort of low-hanging fruit erased all of the worry from Arianna's mind, replacing it with wonderment. And as the magic continued to unfold, she even saw it began to stretch farther than just the now magnificent tree.

Mouth agape as she glanced around the vicinity, Arianna saw what could only be described as a paradise—flowers and plants glowing all abloom in the midst of the darkness.

She plucked one of the fruits from the tree and took a big bite, the sweet juice dripping down her face.

"Solza, this is extraordinary!" she said through a mouthful, hugging her close.

The former cub had almost fully grown into her adult body and looked strangely out of place in the barren backdrop of the desert. The little snow leopard she'd tried to rescue near the frozen lake was no more, replaced now by something even more stunning, if at all possible.

"This must be your power showing over the earth element…" she said, breathlessly. "You can somehow *literally* wield life on earth."

Arianna thought back to the scroll Jeom had found about the avatars and their shifts through the elements.

How will I ever be able to describe this to my friends?

There were just no words. And with Eli lurking around, it might be a while before she could tell anyone.

Arianna wasn't sure she'd be able to contain such exciting news as she picked more fruits to take back with her. And with one last look at the beautiful, bewildering scene, she set off toward her friends with a renewed spirit and Solza by her side. Squaring her shoulders, she felt uplifted through her avatar's faith and the confidence the guardians had bestowed on her.

Keeper Kassime had given his life to train them to be Guardians of Gold—and she would honor that sacrifice the best way she knew how. *Never forget.*

Alas, Arianna was too impatient, too motivated now to just sit back and wait for something to change, as Keeper Kassime had encouraged them to do and had done so himself for so long.

With just the touch of her paws, Solza had summoned life to the earth, and Arianna had seen Sano call back those on the brink of death—that kind of power wasn't something to be ignored, and Arianna wasn't about to waste the opportunity it presented.

They had the chance to truly breathe *life* back into Olleb-Yelfra, so she owed it to her fallen friends to try.

And though Keeper Kassime wouldn't get his wish to watch the fall of a tyrant, he'd laid out a foundation for Arianna and her friends to carry out that dream on his behalf.

Her thoughts sang out in a new mantra now, pushing everything else from her focus. With a fresh fire burning in her soul and a new challenge waiting ahead, Arianna led the way as she and her friends, her proven family, started the arduous journey across the boundless black sand sea.

Hail to the World! she thought. *Hail to Olleb-Yelfra. We're going to end the King!*

Dear Fugitive

Did you really think you could use magic to hide from the King? You escaped the palace by a hair, but you've left a trail of death and fire in your wake. Try to be a little bit more careful on the journey ahead.

It won't be easy, so keep your real friends close and trust in the magic you've gained. Help as many people as you can to believe in it, too, along the way!

If you could share one beautiful thing about magic and the Golden Age with a non-believer, what would it be?

Enlighten them on

amazon goodreads **BookBub**

At least you had a taste of freedom. May the gods of Olleb-Yelfra have mercy on you for what comes next.

Sincerely,
Ashleigh B.

ACKNOWLEDGMENTS

Belvedor and the King's Curse was first published in 2016, two years after *Belvedor and the Four Corners.* At the time of writing this story, I was new to New York City and utterly lost in the world, just like Arianna. Writing this book helped to anchor me down, and gave me an outlet to work through a pretty difficult time in my life. Thank you to everyone, family and friends, who supported me in my efforts to continue the *Belvedor Saga.*

Mom, Dad, Sis, and Lisa—I'm especially thankful for you! You talked me through the ups and downs every step of the way.

It's now January of 2021, and *King's Curse* has come a long way since its origins. To my witty editor, **Hannah McCall**—I'm so grateful for your efforts in sharpening my story. You caught details that I never noticed after years of working on this book, and I always have the most fun reviewing your edits; I'm fairly certain Arianna would appear to know absolutely nothing about horses without your corrections.

To the designers behind the scenes: **Mirella Santana**—the *King's Curse* cover is just as enchanting as the Nicora Forest. I can't wait to see what you unveil for the rest of the series. **Jessica Khoury**—the gorgeously illustrated map of Olleb-Yelfra continues to guide us on our journey away from the Four Corners, paving the way for future quests.

Lastly, to my readers, the ***Belvedor Bookworms***—I love you so much! Without you, Arianna's story would've ended a long time ago. Thanks for staying by my side.

Turn the page for

BELVEDOR
BONUS MATERIALS

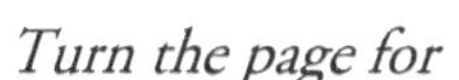

Behind the Scenes with the Author

Real World Magic

Invitation to the Belvedor Bookworms

Sneak Peek of Volume III
Belvedor and the Desert of Secrets

BEHIND THE SCENES

Ashleigh Bello answers questions from the Belvedor Bookworms!

Do you have a character you relate to best?

I'd have to say Arianna Belvedor (*shocking*, I know). While I don't have magic, have never lifted a sword, and sadly don't own a pet snow leopard, I did create her foundation in my image. Like me, she's a starry-eyed dreamer, too curious for her own good, and fiercely protective over her selected family. She has also been distracted by love, has trouble being content in the present, and tries to stick up for what's right—I can certainly relate to all that, the good and the bad.

But she's not the only one I identify with. Lessa, Jeom, and Demetrius all have a little of me in them too; their hopes, fears, strengths, and weaknesses combined were all conjured up from my own personal experiences.

Speaking of love, poor Liam! How will Arianna go on?

Many of my readers have asked me over the years about Liam Black. Some itched for more romance between Arianna and her crush, and others felt the relationship was forced. And some didn't care about Liam Black at all (poor guy)! My point of view? It wasn't a conscious decision not to focus on romance as a main theme in these books, but as it stands, the *Belvedor Saga* isn't a love story—it's a tale of friendship, faith, and a fight for freedom.

Now, I won't lie, I binge-read *Twilight* in college and don't regret a second of that love-triangle-filled chapter of my life (such a guilty pleasure). I love reading about love! But isn't it refreshing to follow strong female characters whose entire worlds don't revolve around the people they've decided to have romantic relationships with? Looking back, I know now that Arianna's character development was a way for me to reflect on the important lesson that a person's worth has nothing to do with someone else validating them romantically. *And* we ladies can certainly fend for ourselves.

Arianna loved Liam Black, sure, whether their friendship and potential romance had time to develop or not. And who's to say there won't be more love to come as the saga progresses? But at its core, this isn't a story. ♥

If you were a palace highlife and could have anything you desired, what would be one special request?

It would probably have something to do with cheesecake and wine on a very regular basis. That and a personal chef—cooking is just not my forte, but I do *love* to eat.

What can we expect from the rest of the series?

I won't spoil a thing! All I'll say is that Arianna's adventures are about to be chockful of more magic than she can even handle at times. This is what you've been waiting for, right? In the first two installments, we see snippets of the Golden Age and the hidden magical world starting to seep into Arianna's grasp. In the next books, we're treated with a deep dive into the enchanted universe she's uncovered.

I'm not sure if I can *really* say that I have a favorite book, but I'm inclined to give *Belvedor and the Desert of Secrets* the label by a hair—Volume III in the saga was so fun to write because I finally got to run wild with some of the world-building ideas I had cooked up since the inception of the series. I'm so excited for you to read it.

REAL WORLD MAGIC

The adventure of your dreams could be just outside your door.
Take the leap and go explore!

I don't think any place in our world directly correlates with a place in my fantasy one—that's what makes it fantasy. But I've definitely pulled from my travel experiences to help carve out the best of Olleb-Yelfra.

Take this for example: at the end of *King's Curse*, when Arianna and her friends reach the edge of the Black Sand Desert, there's a scene where she describes the night sky in great detail, stars blanketing the earth. This is one of my favorite descriptions in this book, because I witnessed a real sky exactly like that once on the way to a gorilla trek in Kisoro, Uganda.

Photo of Batwa Trail in Bwindi Impenetrable Forest.
Kisoro, Uganda (2014).

When you see the stars so fully, without any other light to dilute them, it's not something you soon forget. So I added it in my story as a reminder to myself, and now you, that we have magic in our world too.

*Photo of endangered mountain gorilla from hike—**this guy would crush little Sano**. I'm still awed by the memory.*

Now let's play a game. Remember 'Luose'? Unscramble that and see what you get. (Hint: it's a bustling city somewhere in Asia, in a country that I adore.) I didn't exactly base South Luose on this real place, but it did give me inspiration for the name.

AN EXCERPT

"ARIANNA WOKE TO SWEAT soaking her skin, the sun beating down with such a heaviness that she had trouble adjusting her eyes to see properly. Disoriented, she pulled her hood up around her face to block the harsh rays and find focus, peering out at the sea of sand stretching around her from every angle. Endless dunes carved across the desert, shifting with each gust of warm wind. The black grains sparkled beautifully in this light, like twinkling jewels sewn to the earth.

But she found it extremely hard to appreciate the scenery now with her friends nowhere in sight…

She reached for her swords, but they weren't there. And they would've done her little good here anyhow.

Stark white bones of those long gone protruded out from the ground, swelling atop the land as if in attempt to free themselves from their hasty burials and sandy prisons.

Arianna sat upon a grave—but the skeletons of the unnamed dead weren't her only company. Many colossal structures, possibly statues or headstones, stuck out from the sand. They took on the shape of crosses and were as white as the bones surrounding her. Stringy designs decorated each one; from the tops to the bottoms, a web of silver veins created intricate carvings across the stones.

This abandoned gravesite clearly marked the remnants of a great battle—a final resting place for the broken and battered, a maze of cracked stones and shattered bodies forgotten with time.

Probably another one of the many 'great' battles attributed to the King.

But Arianna couldn't recall a single desert combat from her studies in the Learning Center; she could only assume that if this history had disappeared from the books, she was going to have a heck of a time finding her friends—she must be well off course to have stumbled across such findings.

Everything about this environment unsettled her, and as she took it all in, she noticed that several of the skeletons seemed unusually large. The bones were scattered about so haphazardly that Arianna could hardly piece them together to make one whole. Not that she was any expert, but she'd seen her fair share of bones and bodies. And though it was hard to trust her disconcerted mind at the moment, these were definitely much larger than anything she'd ever known.

Some kind of animal… maybe?

She ran to the top of a high dune, clambering up the loose sand. Cupping her hands around her mouth, she called out for Lessa, Jeom, and Demetrius. She even yelled for Eli and Solza, hoping that her voice might be carried across the winds. But when she finally stopped her screaming, there was only silence in return—save for the hiss and rattle of an unfriendly snake slithering through the eye socket of a giant skull at her feet.

"Okay, don't panic," she whispered to herself as she tiptoed in the opposite direction to the maroon serpent, recalling the poisonous venom from their appearance at her Free Falls. "You can figure this out."

Heading back to the spot where she had awakened, Arianna looked all over for anything to help her out of this mess—a clue or a signal for the way back. The tip of what looked to be a buried parchment poking up from the sand, stuck underneath a large rock, caught her eye. She carefully dug it out. As she unfurled the paper, she found it to be blank but well-kept, thanks to a sturdy seal she didn't recognize.

A blank scroll could always come in handy, she mused.

Perhaps a goodbye letter?

She stuffed it inside her robes with a cynical laugh that quickly turned into a shriek as several brown, long-legged spiders, the size of her head, poured out of the hole she'd plucked the parchment from.

Bounding in the opposite direction and itching all over from just the sight of such horrid creatures, she glued her eyes to the ground, fearful of what other terrors might be lurking underneath the sand.

She spotted her own footprints, and to her relief, an idea surfaced—she could follow them out, literally retrace her steps, as she had once done to locate Lessa in the districts.

Alas, her hopes were soon dashed after trailing them for just a few minutes. Any trace of her tracks disappeared with the next breeze, wiped away as if they'd never even existed.

"Are you serious?" she shouted at the top of her lungs, turning in circles with her arms flung out wide.

She had no idea where to go next, though she knew she couldn't have gotten *too* far from their campsite on foot. Taking deep breaths, she gathered her wits to think of her next plan of action.

My friends should wake any minute now. That was her only comfort as the sun began lowering in the sky.

They had to realize she was gone soon, right? Maybe they already even did, because Arianna hadn't the slightest clue how long she'd been missing. And she didn't even let her mind wander over the 'how.' Trying to remain calm, she toyed with her options.

Either stay put and wait for someone to find me, or start walking…

There was no way she could just sit around in a desert and hope for someone to rescue her. The chances of no one finding her were incredibly high. She looked up and identified the South Star already in the sky, fighting the sun for its turn.

It was a natural compass and could hopefully lead her back to the same path as her friends if she didn't stray from its light. She'd follow the star, as Eli had taught them over the last few days, and pray that they might meet again before her body gave out from lack of food, water, or worse.

One foot in front of the other and eyes steady on the South Star, Arianna began the longest journey of her life; this was the first journey that simply had no end in sight, and the loneliness of it was even more suffocating than that thought.

The Black Sand Desert stretched onward with an incredible uncertainty about it. She could walk for hours—or just minutes—and still seem stuck in the same place.

Arianna never felt any closer to the end, but somehow she found the energy to keep going as the maze of monuments faded into the distance and the eerie display of bones disappeared. Occasionally, she'd spot a strange-looking cactus or a withering bush, and it would give her a tiny shimmer of hope that she at least wasn't walking in circles. As each step became more difficult with time, she shoved her fears to the side and focused on only one thing.

Just survive—a mantra that never seemed to lose its luster in this world.

THE BELVEDOR SAGA

By Ashleigh Bello

Find the completed series on Amazon.
Follow the Magic!

ASHLEIGH BELLO is the author of *A Myrmaid's Kiss* and the *Belvedor Saga*. She graduated from the University of Missouri-Columbia and currently lives in Brooklyn, New York. She also teaches and practices vinyasa yoga in her community and is the co-founder of Yoga Block Party, a female-owned yoga events and retreats business. She enjoys spending time with friends and family every chance she gets and is always daydreaming about her next novel. Her endless passion for travel and spontaneous adventure continues to be her inspiration for future works in the enchanting world of Olleb-Yelfra and beyond.

Connect with the Author
www.ashleighbello.com
@ashleighbello
#belvedorbooks

Follow Ashleigh Bello on TikTok!
Scan the QR code to see her main bookish social account